Published in the United States of America. ISBN: 978-1-962626-57-6

Then There Was You

To those girlies who live for the first kiss and then crave more after that. I got you covered!

FOLLOW ME

To keep up to date with her writing and more, visit S.L. Scott's website: **www.slscottauthor.com**

To receive the newsletter about all of her publishing adventures, free books, giveaways, steals and more:

https://geni.us/SLScottNL

Follow on IG: https://geni.us/IGSLS
Follow me on TikTok: https://geni.us/SLTikTok
Follow on Bookbub: https://geni.us/SLScottBB

ALSO BY S.L. SCOTT

Called **"The Most Romantic Book Ever,"** We Were Once, is available and FREE in Kindle Unlimited.

We Were Once

The international sensation, **Best I Ever Had**, has won readers over and is available in ebook, audio, and paperback, and Free in Kindle Unlimited.

Best I Ever Had

Audiobooks on Audible - CLICK HERE

Peachtree Pass Series (Stand-alones)

Long Time Coming /Lead Me Knot /Small Town Frenzy

The Westcott Series (Stand-alones)

Swear on My Life / Never Saw You Coming

Forgot to Say Goodbye / When I Had You

Never Have I Ever / Speak of the Devil - Faris Family

Hard to Resist Series (Stand-Alones)

The Resistance / The Reckoning

The Redemption / The Revolution / The Rebellion

The Crow Brothers (Stand-Alones)

Spark / Tulsa / Rivers / Ridge

The Crow Brothers Box Set

DARE - A Rock Star Hero (Stand-Alone)

New York Love Stories (Stand-Alones)

Never Got Over You / The One I Want / Crazy in Love

Head Over Feels / It Started with a Kiss

The Everest Brothers (Stand-Alones)

Everest / Bad Reputation / Force of Nature

The Everest Brothers Box Set

The Kingwood Series

SAVAGE / SAVIOR / SACRED / FINDING SOLACE

The Kingwood Series Box Set

Playboy in Paradise Series

Falling for the Playboy / Redeeming the Playboy

Loving the Playboy

Playboy in Paradise Box Set

Stand-Alone Books

Then There Was You

Best I Ever Had

We Were Once

Love and Warner

Along Came Charlie

Missing Grace

Finding Solace

Until I Met You

Lessons on Love

Lost in Translation

Sleeping with Mr. Sexy

Morning Glory

THEN THERE WAS YOU

S.L. SCOTT

slscott

PROLOGUE

KEATS MATTHEWS

The weather is as foul as my mood.

I should be home listening to the classics playing through a busted set of speakers, eating ravioli from a can, and wallowing in memories of better times, but Taylor insisted we meet tonight. Breaking my tradition should be a welcome reprieve. Instead, I'm left further annoyed.

It's hot in here and surprisingly crowded, considering the holiday. I expected to walk into a quiet place to talk, not a bar bustling with partiers. Unwinding the wool from around my neck, I look around to see if I can spot Taylor, hoping a table has already been scored. No such luck. None seems to be available either, so that leads me to wedge myself through the horde to order a beer.

One drink. Maybe two if things go well, and then I'll return to my apartment to pick up where I left off before I got the call. I take a long pull from the bottle, then lean against the wide wooden top to wait.

"Keats?"

I glance back toward the entrance when I hear my name, but I don't recognize anyone coming through the door.

"Keats?"

Looking toward the far side of the large room, I see Taylor waving an arm. I nod and start across the room, slipping through a large group taking over the walk space, so I duck around a table. Taylor throws her arms around my neck before I have time to right myself to my full height. "We did it," she says, holding me tight.

"Did wh—" My breath stops hard in my chest when my gaze lands on a pair of hazel eyes not five feet away from me.

Staring over Taylor's shoulder, words are lost to thundering heartbeats as blood zips through my veins, making me feel alive for the first time in years. The revelry muted, and Taylor is forgotten entirely, causing me to almost lose my grip on the beer. Every thought and cell in my body is solely focused on *her*.

Her expression turns from confused to familiar. In her eyes, the browns shift to a brighter green, making me wonder if the past is playing out in her memory, as it is in mine.

The feel of the inlet from the waist to her hip.

Her uncontainable giggle when I told a bad joke in bed.

The freckle on her left hip bone.

For the first time in years, life comes rushing back. Heat colors my cheeks, and my fingers itch to hold her again. I lick my lips, then take a breath as my gaze shifts to the hand covering her perfectly bowed lips. *And then I see it.*

Emerald cut. Four carats or more, if I'm guessing.

On her left fucking hand.

CHAPTER 1
SIX YEARS LATER

KEATS MATTHEWS

"Alright. Alright, Sierra," I reply, letting annoyance seep into my tone. I've been given a talk about that tone before, but damn, I've been hustling since I got here four hours ago. Ducking to the side, I avoid a tray of filet mignon heading out to the buffet table. "I'm getting a refill tray."

"You know the rules, Keats. Get in and get out." My manager points at the corner of the kitchen. "Grab the tray of micro-Wellingtons from the rack." The strain in her voice has me moving faster in the chaos of the kitchen.

I scoot around a server headed in the opposite direction and drop my tray onto the marble counter of a kitchen that puts Michelin-starred restaurants to shame.

My stomach rumbles at the scent of savory foods, and I pray there are extra steaks left over for the crew to take home at the end. I roll up my sleeves, focusing on the money I'll make. Sierra told us our tips might cover a month's rent. I'll trade Christmas Eve for getting that bill off my back.

I start chuckling when I retrieve the last tray of micro-Wellingtons. These were called pigs in a blanket when I was growing up. I'm not surprised by the name change. Rumor has it that an invite to this holiday party is the most coveted in Manhattan. The threat from management—not to fuck this up and keep our traps shut with the guests or we'd lose our jobs—gives the rumor weight. *Easy enough.* Money speaks louder than words.

With a tray in hand, I call, "Heading back out."

"Take your break after this round," Sierra says just before I exit the kitchen.

I hold the tray out for guests to take what they want, weaving through the black-tie affair. My tray tips, but I'm quick to save it before it falls as sausage-sized fingers grab two of the hors d'oeuvres. I steady it for the guest, then make eye contact by mistake. An older man with an alcoholic's red nose glares at me. I remember my dad sharing the same characteristic. Barely remember, considering he didn't stick around much past me turning six. The man says, "Seems like a simple enough job. Can you manage it?"

Now I know why I was told to keep my mouth shut.

My phone vibrates in my pocket, pulling my attention to more important matters—the email I've been waiting for all week. I walk away, heading straight for my break. I drop the empty tray off and grab my coat from a hook, dipping my arms in before exiting through the back of the house.

The cold strikes first, and the warmth from inside is replaced before the coat can compete. It could be below freezing out here, and I'd still be more focused on finding out the final grade on my essay. I steer along a stone path that trails toward the guesthouse with my eyes locked on the screen. I close the text from my mom, the first one all year, complaining that she never gets to see me, and open my email.

"Watch out."

I stop, looking up to see a girl leaning against the side of the guesthouse with her feet angled away for support. "For what?"

She glances at the light hung at the corner under the roof's awning. "It's a motion detector. You can come under it, though."

I step to the side, then stay near the wall as I move closer to where she's standing. Stopping with a few feet between us, I ask, "Are we good?"

"Just avoid the corner." She pushes off the wall and spins in the grass as if to prove a point. Her shirt is splattered in paint. *Paying homage to Jackson Pollock?* The moonlight's not enough to tell if it's her own design or if she bought it that way. "Are you hiding from the party?"

"I'm on a break."

"Me, too." She nods as if the world makes sense as she turns her attention to the main house. "So who are you?"

The girl is bold. I'll give her that. Dressed in baggy jeans rolled to the top of a pair of dark red Doc Martens and a tee she customized by roughly cutting the hem to reveal the slimmest view of her midriff, I grin, already entertained by the company. "Keats."

"Like the poet." Her smile is soft as it shapes her expression. "Heard melodies are sweet—"

"But those unheard are sweeter."

She's pretty, even more so when her smile grows. Her short blond hair ranges from sandy to the peak of summer highlights from the sun. Some strands are in disarray, exposing a gentle wave more obvious on her right than on the left side of her head. The street vibe she's going for seems in contrast to how sweet her face is. The Docs are scuffed, worn for real, not just fashion.

The light flicks on, causing both of us to glance over to find what set it off. Nothing new is seen. "Probably just the wind," she says with a shiver.

I take off my wool coat and hand it to her. She slides it on without question, letting it swallow her shoulders underneath the weight. She can't be more than five feet, judging by where the top of her head would reach on my lankier six-one frame. *Attractive.* Her nose tends toward straight, rather than the upward-sloped nose job that so many in this city are having done. I pull it closed at the front like I have a right to keep her warm. I don't, so I step back, leaning against the wall as if enough pressure from it can take my mind off her.

Cinching it together in her fist, she tilts her head while moving closer into the shadows with me again. "Saw you staring at your phone. Don't let me keep you if it's important."

Easily distracted by her presence, I'd already forgotten about the email. Instead, I find myself staring at her. She's cute, but I raise the phone to open it and give myself something to do other than being a creeper here in this backyard. When I look away, I'm still grinning like an idiot, as if I were busted doing something I shouldn't have been. "It's just a grade."

Her eyes go wide with hope, like a connection has been made. "You go to university?"

"I'm a senior. You?" She has a sweet face with innocence still rounding the edges. I catch myself looking her over again. The coat has come loose, giving me a sneak peek of how much it overwhelms her small frame underneath. I spy a dip at the waist that blooms to her hips. Her tits aren't overbearing on her body, but each would fit nicely in my palm.

"Junior, but I took this semester off."

"Why's that?" I shouldn't be so nosy, but my curiosity wins.

She doesn't appear bothered by the question, remaining casual with a total stranger. "I had an opportunity, but I'm starting back in January." Angling my way, she pops her eyebrows with curiosity. "What grade did you get?"

A section of hair falls in front of my right eye when I bend my head to read the subject line. *Final Grade – Memoir Paper.*

I drag my hand down the front of my pants, my nerves kicking in. Looking at her again, I say, "I spent a month working on this final project."

Holding her hand out, palm up, she asks, "Do you want me to read it to ease the blow?"

Annoyance clenches my jaw. "There's not going to be a blow. It's either an A or a B. If it's not an A, the professor is wrong." With her hand still open and waiting, she laughs. It's got a nice tone. "Fine." I hand her my phone. "I'm confident in the results."

"Cocky or confident?" She laughs a bit longer this time and gives the email her attention. She quietly scans the message from my professor, leaving me in suspense.

Running my finger through my hair, I ask, "Well?" She peeks up at me briefly as if she's gotten insight into my psyche. Dread fills my gut. "Shit, what does it say?" I'm already regretting not reading it myself.

"Here are the highlights." She reads, "Hides behind words, lacking authenticity . . ." Her eyes widen as she steals a glance at me before looking back at the phone again. “Masks behind ideas instead of truths.”

I should be shocked by the criticism, but Professor Johns is known as a hard-ass. “Not what I was hoping for. Did I fail—?”

“You got a B.” *Thank fuck.* Her expression softens into a matching smile, and she hands the phone back to me. “Can’t be all bad. I’d like to read it someday.”

Still in a bit of shock, I stare at the B listed at the bottom of the email and reply, “I’m thinking it needs some revision before anyone else sees it.” But that she’s shown interest piques my interest to look at her again. “But it’s passing and keeps me heading in the direction of graduation in the spring.” I drop the phone back in my pocket and start rolling down my sleeves for warmth. “What’s your name?”

Another light laugh befitting the cold night rings from her chest. “I’m Sosie. I should have introduced myself, but you know how hiding out goes. It’s not the most conducive environment to get to know somebody.”

“Seems we’ve done alright for ourselves.” I bend down to pull a cigarette from the pack tucked into my black polyester sock, and retrieve the lighter from the other one. I look into her eyes as I light up to see whether they're brown, green, or maybe hazel. It’s too dark to figure it out, so I take a long drag, then slowly exhale. “I like your name. It’s different.”

“Sometimes too different.”

“There’s no value in being the same,” I add, though I’m thinking she’s no stranger to standing out from a crowd. She’s too pretty to blend in. Taking another long inhale, I slowly release the smoke into the air, letting it billow into the slightest of December breezes.

"Tell that to all the dupes out there." She reaches over and asks, "Spare a drag?"

I hand the cigarette to her. "I have more if you want your own."

Instead of replying, she inhales the smoke, dropping her head back against the wall as if she's needed this all day. She's not the only one. With her eyes closed, she leisurely breathes the smoke out, letting her shoulders sink back against the stone like the side of her head. When she opens her eyes, she rolls her gaze my way. "I can't, but thanks."

I'm drawn to her lips when she speaks. Darker than pink but not unapproachable in deep red, it's like they're stained from eating too many cherries or she just finished a popsicle. Making her smile could become my favorite pastime. Tracing the bow at the top of her lips would be pure entertainment. But watching them wrapped around the cigarette stirs more than an urge for nicotine.

I turn my attention to the party happening on the other side of the large windows. The music is muffled along with the chatter, but it still manages to fill in the background noise. When I look at her, I say, "I've worked parties across the five boroughs, but this place—manicured backyard, a pool, a fucking guesthouse, and who knows how many bedrooms and baths are inside. A mansion parked at the edge of Central Park. This is peak wealth in Manhattan. What a life."

She inhales a quicker drag before she hands the cigarette back to me and takes a few steps into the grass. "I'm sure it's hollow for most."

"If I had that kind of money, I wouldn't waste it on parties."

"What would you waste it on?"

I'm not sure why her calling me out has me grinning,

but it does. Studying the red remaining from her lips, I tuck the butt between my lips, inhale, and look at her out of the sides of my eyes. "Living."

Shrugging the jacket from her shoulders, she catches it in her hands. "Who says they're not?" She twists her wrist to see the face of an analog watch. Other than the expensive brands, those are hard to come by. "I'm late." Coming up to me, she says, "One more drag?"

She opens her mouth and blinks twice with her eyes latched to mine. It's not an invitation, Keats, but she makes it damn tempting to kiss her. I give her what she wants and hold the cigarette to her mouth. Her lids dip closed as her chest rises. I shift my gaze to the orange glow to keep myself from staring so much. She makes me feel like a kid with a high school crush. She's carefree to my reserved, spontaneous to my scheduled. There's an air of excitement just being in her vicinity. I haven't felt like this about a girl in a while. I can't even remember the last girl I took an interest in.

What makes her different is the same things she'd argue are flaws, and that leaves me wanting to get her number.

She moves away too soon, tossing my coat to me, and says, "Thanks." Her smile knocks all twenty-three years from my chest as if life is just beginning.

My heart starts thumping, my breath shortens, and my thoughts spin wildly as I try to figure out what the fuck just happened. I'm not a frivolous guy. That luxury was never afforded to me, but being caught up in her makes me feel alive. It's exhilarating.

Sosie's too fast, running away before I have time to collect my thoughts. "Thanks for the cigarette." She hits me with that stunner of a smile when the light invades the moment we were sharing and resets time like it hadn't existed prior. "And the jacket."

While she rushes down the path toward the main house, I call, "Hey?"

She stops and looks back, the sides of her mouth gently curling upward. "Yeah?"

Slipping one arm back into the jacket, I ask, "What if I want to see you again?" My voice is deeper, heavier as time slips away from us.

Her smile spreads on one cheek, and she replies, "If it's meant to be, it will be, Poet."

"What crew are you with?"

Desperation grows into panic, my heart ticking like a time bomb about to set off, as she disappears through the back door like she's sneaking into the party. *Damn . . . What just happened?*

Why didn't I ask for her number?

Will I see her inside?

Fucking hell. *Was I struck by lightning?*

Feels like it.

She was more of a hurricane the way she whipped through my world, leaving nothing but questions in her wake.

Fuck me. I didn't expect to be blindsided by a girl tonight. My breathing evens as I finally catch my breath after the whirlwind of Sosie settles around me.

I take a drag of the remaining cigarette and put my coat back on before walking toward the house again. I don't even know where she came from, much less where she's working tonight. It's not catering since I know the entire crew. *Bartending? Singer? Cleaning?* She didn't have a uniform on and nothing visible to change into. Maybe she's a thief robbing the place.

I head back, knowing I'm a few minutes late. Just outside the bustle of the inside, I stab the butt on the stone wall, then drop it in the flower bed, kicking dirt over any evidence.

I don't know where she went, but I'm not leaving tonight without seeing her again. Next time, hopefully with her number.

CHAPTER 2

KEATS

Five minutes until midnight, I'm standing on the edge of the party with my hands clasped in front of me like a damn bouncer. The kitchen is clean with only the finale left before I get to go home.

I'll need to load the truck in a few minutes, so I use the time I do have and search the room, sifting through the guests in hopes of seeing Sosie again. I've done it more times than I can count. I searched the bathrooms, asked the piano player if he had seen her, talked to a kid hanging around the perimeter who said his parents dragged him there, and even found a valet to ask if he had seen her in front of the house. She's disappeared without a trace.

It's been frustrating. I thought I'd have that chance, but I didn't take it when we were outside. If I weren't already in a bad mood from being hungry and exhausted, this would tip the scales.

Sierra and Darren push the cake cart front and center. She lights a single tall candle on top of a champagne bottle-shaped dessert, then they join me in the shadows of the party. The hosts, Mr. and Mrs. Stansbury, take over, calling their daughter to come blow out the candle and rousing their guests to sing "Happy Birthday" to the star of the show.

Keeping my voice down, I ask, "I thought it was a holiday party?"

With her eyes locked on the display, Sierra replies, "They wanted to celebrate their daughter's birthday right at midnight."

I'm nudged on my other side. When I glance over at Darren, he waggles his eyebrows. "She's twenty-one. Hot. Have you seen her?"

I shake my head, not willing to admit I've been too distracted by another girl tonight, someone who has blown me off. I'm an idiot for believing there was a spark between us when she clearly didn't feel it.

The crowd sings off-key and parts like the Red Sea for the birthday girl as she comes through the opening. *Are you fucking kidding me?* Short blond hair, an electric-pink glittering dress that hits mid-thigh, and a pair of Converse that are the only thing remotely tying her back to the girl I met at the guesthouse.

Mystery solved. Right there in the center of attention I'm sure she lives for, Sosie blows at the candle. When it's still flaming, she licks her fingers and taps the hot wick, putting out the fire.

My cheek lifts in amusement, then drops to a scowl as irritation from being conned by her wins out. I excuse myself. "Going to load the truck."

I grab a stack of crates from the kitchen and head out to the street where the truck is parked. Too many questions and no real answers run rampant through my head.

Why would she trick me into believing we were one and the same? *Yeah, we're not.*

Was she testing me? I should have clued in that she was a mole when she was standing out in the freezing weather. I'm so easily distracted by a pretty face.

Is she going to report back to catering management to get me fired? Tell them I was smoking on private property even though she bummed most of it?

A little rich girl wanting to slum it on her birthday? *Boringly cliché.*

"Is that how she gets her kicks?" I roll my eyes as I send the door sliding up. I slip the crates into the cargo bay and jump up to stack them in the back.

I turn around to see Sosie standing behind the truck. It's a shock to the system when I believed we'd made a connection. And I thought I was safe out here, that I could finish this shift without having to face her again. No such luck. I eye her, barely recognizing the girl before me. "You're missing your party." My tone is flat, wishing she'd stayed inside and let me finish what I need to do.

"I should have told you."

"You think?" Sarcasm infiltrates the accusation. *Tread carefully, Keats.* I should probably heed management's warning and keep my mouth shut. After all, she's the client, and I'm just a mere server at her disposal. Yeah, that sarcasm isn't going away.

I start for the opening, ready to go inside for the second load and avoid this confrontation, which will be best for both of us. "I have a job to do. I'm sure you can't relate." *I tried . . .*

Bright headlights light up the back of the truck, exposing me to the gaze that doesn't hold any of the joy caught in her eyes earlier. She says, "I wasn't purposely keeping it from you. You assumed and I—"

"So now *I'm* to blame?" I laugh through my words. "That's rich." My gaze levels on her. "Like you."

Crossing her arms over her chest, she raises an eyebrow at me. "It's my parents' money, not mine." The contempt in her tone purses her lips. The confidence she wore so boldly earlier isn't lacking in her expression, with her eyes set on mine. Seems I've struck a nerve. Can't say I wasn't trying. I just wish I didn't find her so attractive, given that attitude that's sprung up in her stance.

"It will be, and that's what makes it a lie. Even now, you're acting like . . ." I look back at the mansion and throw my hand toward it. "Like you don't live here, as if you can relate to someone who struggles to make ends meet."

"Is that what it takes? A struggle for a struggle? My opinion holds no value because my life is different?" She shakes her head as she releases a heavy breath that fogs in a cloud in front of her. When she looks back up, regret slopes her shoulders forward. "I thought you were different, Poet. My mistake."

She steps onto the sidewalk and reaches the gate before I realize I'm triggered by something she has no control over. It was good earlier. The betrayal I feel now is manufactured. She's not a different person from the Sosie I met before. I'm just getting in my own way at this point. I liked the girl I met. "Hey," I call, rushing to the end of the bay and jumping down to the street.

Turning back, she stands in her pretty dress like she isn't freezing to death despite the goose bumps covering her skin. I don't have a coat to give, so I move closer to block the breeze from touching her and ask, "Why did you come out here?"

"I've realized I shouldn't have," she says as if it pains her to admit, and a shiver runs through her.

"No, please. For real. I'd like to know."

She remains quiet as if she doesn't want to rock the peace between us. "Because I liked our conversation." She swallows, still hesitant to respond. "And I liked the way you looked at me."

I search her face, her eyes, even staying longer than I should on her lips. A paler pink has replaced the red. I prefer the cherry stain, the dark eyeliner that ringed her eyelids, the cut T-shirt, and the combat boots, wilder hair, and confidence that didn't shrink under some guy's assumption and unapologetically smoked most of my cigarette. She's still so beautiful, but it's the change of seeing someone entirely new that's a shock to the system. "How did I look at you, Sosie?"

Raising her chin, she says, "Like I wasn't one of them." I've never felt more of an asshole than I do now. She didn't need my judgment. Who am I to put my issues on her anyway? When she glances back at the party, I dumbly look in the same direction as if I needed the confirmation of whom she's referring to. "I'm not." The spite in her tone matches the clenching of her fists at her sides.

Raising my hands in surrender, I reply, "I'm just a guy working your folks' event. That's all. I'm a nobody." I cock my head, still staring at her because it's so easy to do with a face like hers. But then I lower my eyes and shake my head, my hair falling forward again. *Don't do it, Keats.* Taking no accountability for the cold reception I've given her, I look her over again, already leaning into an urge I know I shouldn't. I can humor myself, though . . . "So why would someone like you care what I think?"

The question leaves her shifting her feet as she rubs her

arms again since we've been standing out here without coats or a better sense of self-preservation. I was too focused on leaving, and she rushed out after me. *Just to talk to me?* Futile efforts on both our parts because I have a feeling we're exactly where we're supposed to be. There's something more between us—a spark or inferno—and only one way to find out where it goes from here. Seems we're just two fools standing at the end of a cold December, making confessions and concessions as if we owe it to each other.

She takes a deep breath as if it will fight the cold by how she interrupts a shiver, and says, "Because you let me bum your cigarette when you could have just ignored me altogether."

I chuckle, though I don't hear the humor in it, so I know she doesn't. I run my hand over my head, not quite sure what to do with myself, much less her. "I have a feeling you don't get ignored much."

"More than you'd think." She comes forward, holding out a crumpled piece of paper in the palm of her hand. "You can leave tonight, forgetting any of this ever happened." I take the paper and open it up to see a number written on it. When my eyes meet hers again, she adds, "Or you can text me sometime. Doesn't have to be anything serious. It can be for a walk, or coffee, a concert if you have a spare ticket and no one to take, or just want to burn through a pack of cigarettes on a fire escape. I'm your girl."

It was then, the embers burning in her hazel eyes, that I knew I was a goner for this girl. *My girl.* I tuck the paper in the front pocket of my pants, still staring into her eyes as I drag my tongue over my lower lip. I can't seem to pin down words to match the thoughts spinning in my head. Maybe it's simple. I'm drawn to her, even if it isn't in my best interest.

"Keats?" I suck in a deep breath when I hear Sierra call my name from a distance and spy her silhouette up the long driveway.

"Yes?"

She says, "Come get the racks."

"Coming." I can see her eyeing the two of us, but her shoulders ease as she walks away, leaving us in peace. When I look at Sosie, the innocence in her rounder face and an expectation in her eyes causes my chest to clench. She carries a plea in her stance as if she's on edge unless given the word—the right word. *Yes.* "You should get back to your party."

"They'll never know I'm missing."

"Impossible." I grin, though it's more for show. I'm not sure what it is about her I find so damn captivating, but I'd be willing to bet that she wasn't entirely wrong when she said she was my girl. Seems to be leading in that direction if she has her way. And I selfishly have mine. "There's no ignoring the moon in a universe of darkness." And there I go safety-pinning my heart on my sleeve like I don't bleed easily. "But it's also too cold to be hanging around out here. You need to go inside and warm up, and I need to get back to work."

I may not have said the words she wanted to hear, but rejection doesn't reach her eyes. A small smile does. She rubs her arms once more, then takes a few steps toward the gate. Her eyes stay on mine when she stops and says, "It was nice meeting you, Poet."

"Same." I wish I had better words before she returns to her world, and I remain in mine. "Happy birthday, Sosie."

Her smile brightens my world more than any motion-detecting light ever could. “Thanks.” She rushes toward the house without hesitation this time, no lingering goodbyes or promises to keep in touch.

We don’t need it.

We both know this isn’t how we end.

But there is no middle ground when it comes to girls like her. She has the world at her feet while I’m trying to climb out from beneath them. We’ll get to know each other. There’s no harm in that. What’s the worst thing that could happen? She’s either going to be the best thing that ever happened to me or my downfall. But half the fun is finding out.

CHAPTER 3

SOSIE STANSBURY

The party wasn't really for me, but duty called, digging its claws into me as I watched the party from outside through the windows. With no other choice, I made an appearance as required, keeping my end of the bargain as my parents had for the past four months.

It's all for everyone else, just a dog and pony show I was expected to perform like I hadn't been threatened to be there. But I played my part to perfection, even garnering a "well done" and a kiss to the top of my head from my dad. My mom beamed like I was being crowned Miss Texas, like she once was.

Pursuing my dreams was exchanged for doing as they wished if I failed. I failed. I returned home to shame, *I told you so*, and an itinerary for the week, including this party. I agreed to parade around like the good girl they require to keep their reputation intact. I'll be admired and then forced back into a box I foolishly thought I had escaped, with no exits or other options.

I push my head above water before I drown in my own life. If I'm not careful, the riptide could pull me under at any moment. The wee hours are always the worst. My brain kicks into overdrive every night to put a better plan in place. I just need more time to figure that out before leaving for good next time.

At least I was rewarded with a necklace, even though they bought me the same one last year, and a credit card with a higher spending limit. I should be grateful, but if I were given the choice, I would have picked my parents over anything superficial. They can't say the same and prove it every year without fail.

I fasten the diamond tennis necklace around my neck, then toss the red velvet box on the bed when I pass it on my trek to the window. When I peek out, yesterday's snow is now slush, shoved off the curb to melt. No guests linger on the sidewalk waiting for their cars or for a ride. I breathe easier knowing the house is empty again, or will be soon enough, and I'll be able to get back to normal, which the holidays interrupt.

The crews hired to work the party continue to fill the space out front, and I find myself staying here a minute longer in hopes of catching a glimpse of a certain someone. Keats is cute with his natural good looks—strong jaw, straight nose, and sharper chin. I could get lost in his eyes, and I want to run my fingers through his hair even though I can tell he doesn't give a damn about it. And every time I look into his eyes, I just know he'll keep all my secrets. There's a reassurance built into the warmth of his browns, which tends lighter toward the caramel center rings. I shouldn't hype him too much, but I just got that vibe from him.

Tucking myself behind the heavy pink drapery, I peek

out, searching the small crowd gathered around the back of the truck and loading an SUV parked next to it. He might have already gone home. I haven't seen him in the past few hours. Of course, I wouldn't have since I got my piece of cake, a bottle of champagne, and came upstairs to celebrate with someone who actually cares. *Myself.*

"Oh shit." I tug the drape around me, hiding in the material like a serial killer. I laugh since he can't see me anyway. I peek again, having already memorized his body to recognize anywhere—his broad shoulders anchoring his athletic build—when he comes down the drive with a crate in his hands. He's too attractive to hide in a crowd, even if I can't see his face, and a coat covers half his body. The man could be a model. Wonder if he ever has, like every other guy in this city.

I should have turned my light off so I could stand here and ogle him in peace. But I'm not moving an inch until he's out of sight again. I don't want him to think I'm a creeper. I roll my eyes, still not daring to look down at him again.

The cargo door slamming closed drags my attention back to the truck, but the employees have already disappeared. I look down the street to see if I can find him, but they're all gone, loaded into the truck or the SUV.

Disappointment strikes fast, and more than it should, since I barely know him. I should let things take their natural course. My phone vibrates on my bed, and I dive for it. The number is unfamiliar, but I take a chance and answer it, "Hello?" My voice is breathy despite simply losing it by moving too fast for my own good.

"Are you coming or what?"

I pause, holding the phone out from my ear to look at

the number again. *Unknown caller.* "Listen, pervert, that's none of your business—"

"Sosie, it's Keats."

My head jerks back on my neck. "Keats?"

"The server you met tonight?"

I hate that he thinks I don't remember him, but I'm too busy grinning like an idiot because he called me. "Hi." I don't even mind that my response came out more as a purr. "What are you doing?"

"Freezing my ass off. You want to go do something together?"

Rolling across the bed, I land on my feet and scurry to the window. "I thought you just left?" When I look out the window, there he is. He waves, and even from here, I can see him smirking.

"I stayed."

I bite my lip. The possibility of spending time with him has my heart racing as I wave back. "Why did you do that?"

With a shrug, he replies, "Wishful thinking."

As much as I love this game, I cut to the chase. "What were you wishing for?"

"More time with you." He's good, very good, and already has me eating out of the palm of his hand with those sweet romantic words.

"I'll be right down."

CHAPTER 4

KEATS

Huddling under the lamppost in front of Sosie's house, I couldn't decide whether it was better to be seen so people wouldn't report me to the cops or to stay hidden so nosy neighbors wouldn't spot me. I went with remaining in the open.

The police car pulls to the curb, making me regret my decision. "What are you doing out here?"

"Waiting," I reply, thumbing over my shoulder. "My . . ." What is Sosie to me? A friend, boss, client, or new crush? I nod toward the house. "My friend is meeting me." I keep my feet moving and rub my knit-gloved hands together to stay warm.

The officer in the passenger seat looks beyond me and asks, "You sure about that? It's four in the morning."

"He's here for me," Sosie calls, trotting down the front steps as she runs for the gate. How am I the lucky guy she's running to? Seeing the exhilaration in her bright eyes could knock me on my ass if I'm not steady and release the tension that has been building in my shoulders. She might be saving my ass from the cops, but I'm the one on the receiving end of that incredible smile on her face. Have I entered another dimension, snuck in through a side door to an alternate reality? Like the way my chest tightens just looking at her, how is this real life? It sure wasn't mine. Until Sosie.

She latches the gate behind her and runs to me. I might be wrong, but I think she's about to launch . . . I catch her in my arms, her body landing hard against mine, legs wrapped around my middle and arms holding me tightly around the neck. But the kiss is what has me disappearing into her, my thoughts settling into the comfort of her in my arms, my soul feeling at peace, and her lips taking to mine like we do this all the time. The cushion of her lips and the way her fingers caress my neck have me hoping it's one of many more to come.

I never really considered myself a romantic, but I feel alive for the first time by the connection, my mind losing any cares outside of what our lips are doing, and I feel a shift in my core's axis. Holding her to me, I tilt my head to take this deeper, but she pulls her lips from mine too fast. Smiling at the police, she waves. "Thanks for keeping the neighborhood safe. Merry Christmas."

"Merry Christmas," they say, rolling up their window as the tires slide against a patch of ice before driving away.

Her boots drop to the ground as her arms loosen from my neck. Just like that, she's out of my arms too fast for my liking and pats me on the chest. Sosie's grin is much softer when she's looking at me. "What kind of trouble are we going to get in?" she asks, flipping my world upside down. If this is just the beginning, I'm in for a hell of a ride.

Although I ate dinner earlier after the party wrapped

up, I think the food will hit just right at this hour. But I'm not dragging her across the city to my rinky-dink apartment. How do I compete with a Gilded Age mansion situated in the park? *I don't.* My place will only be a letdown in comparison. Food and a warm restaurant to hide from the cold seem like a good place to spend time together. Since I know two solid options somewhat on the outskirts of this area that should be open tonight, I ask, "Pancakes or a burger?"

"Ramen." That grin is definitely trouble. "I know a great place five or so blocks from here. They stay open all night, even on the holidays."

I chuckle. She knows what she wants and isn't shy about letting me in on her cravings. "If you want ramen, ramen it is." She walks away, and a breeze blows in, leaving her scent in her wake and causing me to inhale. I can't pinpoint the notes as they drift away too quickly, but I catch something floral and something good. It's the kind of scent that I'd love to smell against her skin. This girl sure does make it easy to get ahead of myself.

When I catch her by the coat sleeve, she turns back, and I say, "You look cute."

Her smile blooms before my eyes from a simple compliment. "You think?" She glances down at her outfit and adds, "I didn't want to keep you waiting, so I just threw this on."

"I like it." Wearing a big cream-colored puffy coat that hangs past her ass and what looks like black sweatpants underneath, she's swallowed whole by the bagginess of it all. A violet scarf wraps around her neck with matching gloves, making her appear every bit the sweetest conundrum that Sosie is. Pulling her hood over her head, I tighten the toggle at her neck, so the strings keep it in place. And since I have her here and her complete attention, I say, "I'm glad you came out."

"Me, too."

The tips of her hair are sticking out the front, so I tuck them in, still holding her closer than I have a right to. "But do me a favor and keep your head covered in this kind of weather."

She laughs and tilts her head to the side to take me in with those gorgeous hazel eyes of hers. The light from the overhead lamp reflects the green and gold flecks, glittering like stardust in her eyes. And she smiles at me as if I had a hand in that magic and put them there. I wouldn't mind making a habit of seeing that look in her eyes more often.

What am I thinking? We just met, and I know so little about her. Somehow, at this hour, that feels like enough.

"Yes, sir." I shake my head at the little rebel and wrap my arm around her neck, holding her to my side as we start walking. "Careful, Poet, or I might mistake this for a date."

"Friends can care about each other." But I still shrug. "Figure we've kissed, though, so might as well make it official." I fight the urge to stare at her pretty face, but I catch her beaming up at me in my periphery like I'm something special. Man, she just has a way of making me feel like a million bucks that I'm the guy with his arm around her.

This is moving fast, quicker than anything in my past. I'm usually all for getting to know someone, who they are and what they dream of, with long, philosophical conversations about Descartes or Kant over coffee and a stack of homework. Maybe this is the change I need—to feel more than think, to follow my heart over listening to my head. Though, admittedly, my head is all in as well over this girl. I don't know why, considering we barely know each other, but this feels right, even if it is just a one-time thing.

Have fun, Matthews. This sure beats sitting home watching movies that only remind me of what I don't have. A family.

We turn the corner, and once we're another block down and away from her house, I ask, "What made you want to sneak out on Christmas with me?"

"You asked." The answer is so straightforward and maybe a little too honest. Pulling something from her pocket, she removes the cap and swipes what looks like balm over her lips. The pink of her lips deepens without hiding the natural color.

"I'm glad I did."

She wraps her arms around herself but remains pressed to my side as we cover another block, hurrying when we cross the streets, and the wind whips up against us. We find a reprieve when we keep walking, the building beside us keeping the wind at bay.

Reaching the next corner, she takes off running. "Come on." I run after her and catch up. She says, "It's way too cold tonight to be out here." I couldn't agree more.

Just up another half block, I open the door as she ducks under my arm and slips into the small restaurant. Each table has a small lamp in the center, collectively giving off enough light to look around but not much else. I'm surprised to see so many people eating here at this hour. Always a good sign.

"Sosie." A woman much older than her mom comes through a curtain hanging from a rod above the kitchen entrance. "You came to see us."

Taking her hood down and pulling her scarf from her neck, she replies, "It wouldn't be Christmas if I didn't." There's more to this story, it seems. "This is Keats. Keats . .

." She glances up at me. "This is Joy. Her family owns the restaurant."

"Nice to meet you, Joy."

"It's the best ramen in the city, handsome man." When she winks at Sosie, they giggle. "Follow me. I have a special table for the two of you."

"Oh no," Sosie utters under her breath, and I stiffen. Surveying the area, I don't see anything suspicious to cause her reaction, so I follow with a shrug, stripping off my coat. We approach a table for two on a platform in the middle of the restaurant, and suddenly, her concern makes sense. I press my lips together, catching Sosie's eyes as she struggles to hold in a laugh. The center of attention is not my idea of a good time, but she's more gracious than I am and thanks Joy as we step onto the platform.

"This should be fun," I whisper sarcastically as I tuck the chair under her.

Joy sets the menus down and whisks our coats away, leaving us on display.

As soon as I sit, Sosie leans forward and whispers, "I didn't have the heart to say no."

"It's okay." My gaze meets a couple who have stopped eating to stare at us. Maybe they think we're celebrities or some big deal. Nope. Sosie just knows the owner. "I'm sure we won't notice after a while."

We notice. We can barely talk without other patrons looking at us. It's like they're playing a game of guessing who the VIPs are who scored the platform table. "It's like swimming in a fishbowl, but we can't swim, so we just have to watch everyone as they stare at us."

"Or *Starry Night* by Van Gogh. There are plenty of paintings in that room of the MoMA, but everyone only stares at it like the other artwork doesn't exist."

Chuckling, I say, "Yeah. Just like that."

She pauses, does her own quick survey, and then cups her hand along the side of her mouth to whisper, "I'll tell you a secret."

I lean in, wanting all the secrets she'll share with me. "Stays between us."

With a conspiratorial grin growing on her face, she says, "I've always wanted to sit at this table." My shoulders ease under a breath. Her sweet confession reveals such innocence. "I always thought it would feel so fancy to sit on a platform made for two. I'm glad I get to eat here with you." I'm irritated that this is a highlight for her. Something so simple could mean so much, and she's never had anyone to share it with, which pisses me off. She should never have been eating here alone, much less on Christmas.

"Me, too." I realize that all the other eyes on us don't matter. Only the ones from across the table that are looking at me like I hung the moon do.

After ordering our food, she sips her hot tea, and I drink water. Setting my glass down, I say, "You took a sabbatical fall semester. Just time off or—?"

"I'm a photographer." Confidence shines in her eyes as sparks flicker to life. "I traveled and took photos to build my portfolio."

"Sounds incredible. I'd love to see your art."

She licks her lips and takes hold of her teacup again as the apples of her cheeks stain pink. I'm fascinated, so fucking intrigued by how she wavers between bold-faced confidence and a shyness that colors her cheeks. *Who is she?*

"I'd love to show you," she beams. I would be content to relish in her happiness all night, but Joy clears her throat as she steps onto the platform with steaming bowls in her hands.

"For you, Sosie. Your favorite." Joy smiles, setting it in front of her. And when she sets a bowl in front of me, she says, "Let me know if you need anything."

When she leaves, I catch Sosie's eyes shining like a thousand galaxies are trapped inside, and I can't help the involuntary smile that spreads across my face. I lean closer, hoping to steal an ounce of that warmth to savor later when I don't have her sunshine shining on me.

"Another time?" she asks.

"Definitely." *What were we talking about?*

"What about you? You're a writer?"

"I'm a finance major. Growing up with no money didn't inspire me to want to be a starving artist." I realize too late how that might sound. Attempting to remove the foot from my mouth, I reason, "It's okay to pursue passions. I just meant—"

"It's okay." Her smile is gentle, and no judgment resides in her eyes. "I don't take it personally. I'm fortunate to have the ability to take time off like that." Holding her spoon with broth filling the scoop, she says, "The email from earlier was a writing class."

Why am I holding back? If there's one person who would appreciate knowing my dream, it's her. "I'd like to be a writer."

Setting her spoon down, she tilts her head. "You would?"

"I know it's ridic—"

"It's not ridiculous." She moves forward, food forgotten, as if I'm the only important thing. "Not any more than wanting to be a photographer." She reaches her hand across the table. When I meet her just shy of halfway, our fingers fold together as if we've made a deal—not a business agreement but one of the heart. She asks, “May I read something you’ve written?”

I nod. “Another time, okay?” That has her smiling as she scoops another spoonful of her meal. “So what’s the deal with this place on Christmas? It sounded like it was tradition.”

“It is, for me. I don’t usually see my parents after the party.” She looks around, and when her eyes find mine, she says, “I found this place when I was fourteen, and I’ve come every year since.”

“What about presents under the tree and turkey or ham, you guys probably have prime rib? What about the celebration?”

She sits back, straightening her spine. “They always give me gifts. They’ll be there in the morning.”

Why am I getting the feeling that Sosie is the only one really living in that mansion? “But your parents won’t be?”

“I have no idea. I’m not usually given their itinerary until they’ve landed wherever they’re going. Listen,” she starts, “you don’t need to feel sorry for me. It’s fine. I’m used to it.”

Finished with my bowl, I set my napkin on the table beside it and lean forward to keep the conversation only between us. “I don’t feel sorry, Little Mouse.”

“Little Mouse?”

I smirk. “I’m trying nicknames on for size to see which one sticks.”

She sits back, tossing in the napkin as well. “I’m not sure I like Little Mouse. Try another.”

“I can’t force the process. That one just came to my head.” I chuckle, but we’ve gotten so far off track that I’m not sure there’s a smooth way to circle back. I try, though.

"Anyway, I feel bad for not wanting to take you to my apartment. I didn't think you'd like it."

"Because of my house?"

"Yeah, who would trade that for my studio apartment?"

She raises her hand just beside her face. "I would if it meant not being alone." It's odd to realize that no matter what side of the tracks you're from, problems aren't exclusive to one. "Want to spend Christmas together?"

Her brows pull together as concern reshapes her expression, dragging the corners of her mouth down. "Can I ask you something personal?"

"Go ahead." I don't brace myself, though I wonder if I should.

"Why won't you be spending the day with your family?"

I pause, inadvertently taking a deep breath. This is dumb. I don't think about this stuff anymore. It is what it is. So why am I feeling shame over something I can't control? I search her eyes and find the innocence in her question, which lowers my defenses. "It's not something I'd like to talk about, if that's okay."

The kindness reordering her delicate features reassures me. "That's okay. But you're not alone. We all have our own baggage to lug around."

Joy drops by again and compliments Sosie's hair color. Apparently, it was pink last month. I admire the way she lights up, turns the tables on Joy, and gushes over her decorative Christmas-themed sweater. It would be called ugly in a party setting. It's fun, and she seems quite proud of it. In the middle of their conversation, Joy drops off the folio with the bill slotted inside and goes to check on other guests. I reach for it first. Taking it in hand, I ask, "How do you feel about Stardust?"

"In a general sense?"

"For a nickname?" I open the bill to see it's been comped. I'm not going to argue when I'm paying out of tips that have been fronted from the party. But as a server, I'm still going to leave a solid tip for the service and generosity.

Her laughter brings the lightness back to our conversation. Scrunching her nose, she says, "I'm not sure about that one. Aren't you ready to give up?"

"When it comes to you? Never." I chuckle. I close the bill with the tip money tucked inside, then stand. I hold my hand out for her.

She slips her hand in mine and stands, coming face-to-face with me. "Well, you might just be stuck with Sosie."

I tilt her chin up with my finger, our eyes holding contact. "I can think of a million worse things than that." *Not lying one bit.* It would be easy to list.

With that smile doing a damn fine job of knocking the breath from my chest, she says, "Do you trust me, Poet?"

My heart may be in danger, but I reply, "With my life."

CHAPTER 5

KEATS

"Any regrets?" Sosie asks, skipping ahead on the sidewalk and spinning with her arms in the air like a ballerina on stage. She does another twirl before kicking out her leg and holding the pose two counts before lowering her leg back down and waiting for me.

I'm beginning to realize that she doesn't need a spotlight. She draws attention without even trying.

There was the man who couldn't stop staring at her when we passed the bodega a few blocks back. A couple of girls our age said she was stunning, then told me not to fuck this up. I said I'd do my best, which made Sosie giggle. And then there was the couple around our grandparents' age, holding hands as they passed us and said, "We make a handsome couple." I don't mind being dragged into her spotlight, but it makes me wonder if she always gets this much attention when she goes out. I don't. Not like this, and usually it's only from the opposite sex, not everyone I meet or pass on the street.

"Not so far." When I catch her peeking back like she might be testing me, I ask, "Should I?"

"No." The melody of her laughter travels farther in the dead of winter when there's no one else around. "You trust me with your life, so I don't want to let you down."

She couldn't. I don't need to assure her because I think she knows I'm open to her adventures, but I like that she cares what I think.

We've worked our way through the city on foot and caught a train. Two blocks from the station, which I think has landed us in SoHo, she stops and looks up at the tall building. When I arrive by her side, she says, "We're here."

"Where are we exactly?" I look up, unfamiliar with the building.

Leaving me in the mystery, she's already heading for the door. "Come on. I'll show you." She punches in a code that releases the lock. I tug the door open and follow her inside.

The lobby is nice, with enough elbow room for a conversation on the couch, inviting dark wood walls, and neutral-hued furniture. It's way nicer than my place, and it's the freaking lobby. The elevator is already waiting for us. Not a surprise at this hour.

As soon as the door closes and we're tucked inside, I lean against the wall opposite her. Her smile has mine appearing in natural reaction, and that glint in her eye tells me she's up to no good. "You know," I start. "I barely avoided getting arrested earlier for loitering. I'm not looking to go down for breaking and entering. Want to fill me in?"

She flies across the elevator. Her palms land hard against my chest, and she fists my coat in her hands. Her hair falls back when she looks up. She's not like any girl I've ever known. Oozing confidence like she has it to spare, Sosie takes no prisoners when she's excited about something. All seems to be her driving force. I don't mind going along for the ride. Someone has to keep us out of trouble. Who knew that would be me?

She laughs, letting the good times roll. "No one is getting arrested. My dad owns an apartment here."

People with money are so strange. "Do I want to know why your dad specifically owns the apartment and not your mom?" Why would anyone need an apartment when they live thirty-something blocks—*oh shit*. She's nodding as if she can tell it's dawned on me.

Raising her eyebrows, she nods. "Probably not." The door opens on the tenth floor, and we feed into the hallway. I only see three doors, and she's heading to the farthest from where we arrived. Punching in another code, she shoulders the door open and walks in like she personally owns the joint. I suppose she does in a sense.

Maybe that's where the confidence comes from. Who needs worries when money can solve all your problems?

The apartment is dark, which shouldn't surprise me since it's just gone 4 a.m., but she doesn't rush to turn on the lights. Instead, she pushes a button on the wall that begins drawing the wall of curtains open wide. "Wow . . . so this is what a few mil can buy in this city? That view is something."

We're not that high, and not in the tallest skyscraper in the vicinity, but the views of the surrounding area are remarkable. While I stand at the window, light filters into the apartment, enough to see her slip from the coat and drape it and the scarf over the back of a leather chair. Seems we're staying a while, so I'll remove mine, too.

"Drink?" she asks from the kitchen.

"Sure."

Hidden by the steel door, she hums and peeks around it at me. "Whiskey, beer, or wine? There might be scotch, but I'd need to check the cabinets."

I'm surprised to hear the offering and turn back. "Are we drinking? Not that I'm opposed." It's been a long day and a longer night, so a drink might hit just right.

"We should celebrate."

I haven't forgotten, but her birthday hasn't seemed like a topic she cared much about. "We should celebrate your big day."

"Oh God, no." Her hair swings above her shoulders from laughing. "How boring would that be if we spent our lives celebrating ourselves all the time?"

I chuckle. "Never thought of it that way." I come to rest my hands on the counter and study her profile.

Her eyes widen when she sees something she wants, and the long lashes that frame them when she pulls a bottle from the fridge. Pursing her lips with a tilt of her head, she says, "Don't read too much into it. I just don't think the world revolves around me."

I could argue she's wrong, but I know she won't believe me. "We hit the jackpot," she says, waggling a bottle of champagne in her hand. Twisting the wire cage off the top, she leaves it on the counter before taking hold of the cork and removing it like a professional.

Not her first rodeo. "Like a pro," I say. "You make it look easy."

"I've opened a few bottles of champagne in my life." Her tone is so matter-of-fact, like this is an everyday occurrence.

"To drink? It's Bollinger. It won't be missed?"

Setting the bottle of expensive champagne in front of

me, she says, “Yes, of course, to drink. What do you think, I bathe in the stuff?” She shrugs. “It’s not a bad idea, but not on the agenda for tonight.”

“Next time.” I smirk.

She laughs. “Yes, next time. And no, it won’t be missed. It will be restocked before my dad even notices.”

I’m no champagne expert, but I feel like this bottle would be missed right away. But if she doesn’t care, I’m not going to. Let’s drink the good stuff.

“We should drink from proper glasses.” She hops onto the far counter, propping herself up to grab two crystal flutes by the stem, then lunges to land on her feet again.

“I could have gotten those down.”

Waving the flutes in front of her, she replies, “So could I. See?”

“Maybe I should call you champ?”

The glasses are set before me, and she asks, “Would that be *shamp* or champ?”

I fill one glass and then the other. “I’m thinking champ.”

“I’ll give it a spin, though I don’t know if I feel like a champ.”

“You are in my eyes, *Champ.”* I set the bottle down, then chuckle. “Yeah, that doesn’t work at all.”

I lift the glass to hers before she takes a sip, the crystal producing a sharp note when they tap. “To . . .” I search for the words that fit the occasion. I’m pretty sure what I really want to say will only scare her away. What girl wants to hear about a guy catching feelings after only a few hours? I’m sure she prefers the bad-boy type.

I’ve pulled some outrageous stunts for kicks and done plenty of shit to survive, but I’ve also worked hard to leave that behind and make a better life for myself. Getting into university changed all that. My background—*deadbeat dad and absent mom*—paid off when it came to getting a free ride. A sinking feeling hits my gut. I would have chosen having parents in my life over that, but I had no say in the matter.

"To us," she fills in where I left off, like it's a foregone conclusion. Her eyes stay locked on mine as she takes a sip like this is something that happens all the time, like it's a given that there is an us in the fucked-up equation. I'm not even sure how I ended up in her life. Or did she end up in mine? Whatever the universe had in mind, I'm glad to be a part of the plan.

I take a gulp, then another. I've not drunk a ton of bubbles like this, but it doesn't taste any different from any prosecco I've had, which has been left over after parties. But what do I know? I'm most likely the first person in my family to drink champagne.

Dragging her hand along my abs when she passes, Sosie strides into the living room, sits in a chair, and spins to face the window. She props her feet up on the sill and sips her champagne, looking every bit the natural in this setting.

Effortlessly gorgeous with her hair tucked behind one ear. A shine that the champagne left behind on her lips. At ease in her own skin. The deep V of the fuzzy black sweater that covers her gives a peek at the top she's wearing beneath. It's the skin of her collarbone that I'm only given a glimpse of that tempts me to undress her.

Not liking the distance between us, I return to the window and sit on the wide ledge of the windowsill, more interested in the view of her than New York City. She's brighter and more vibrant to look at. Stretching out my legs, I take another sip, watching her over the lip of the glass. When I lower it, her eyes still stare ahead as if she doesn't mind me admiring her for so long. I say, "Nice place." I'm not sure if calling a place her dad owns as an escape from his family "nice" is appropriate, but the apartment didn't choose this life.

The smile she's been wearing most of the night has settled into a straight line as if unwanted thoughts are getting the better of her. Her eyes slide to mine. "It's where my dad brings his girlfriends." His preclusions might have been a battle she once fought, but judging by the resolve in her tone, she gave up on that fight. It's not her job to fix her dad's mess anyway. I learned that lesson the hard way.

We hold eye contact long enough for one of us to chicken out and look away, but neither of us does. I do blink first, though. "I'm sorry."

She takes another sip, not leaving much left in the glass, and asks, "Why would you be sorry?"

"Because at some point, you found out your dad is an asshole. Sucks when a kid has that realization dropped in their lap." I finish my drink, needing to drown the memories threatening to reach the surface of my present-day life.

Lowering her boots to the floor, she sits forward, bringing her closer to me. Not close enough for my liking. A half-hearted smile crosses her lips. "I can handle him cheating, but someone feeling sorry for me is the worst." It is the worst, and that's not how I want her to feel when she's with me.

"C'mere."

She stands, setting her glass down before easing between my legs and resting her arm over my shoulder. Her smile returns when she looks at me.

Never thought I'd be given the opportunity to stare at the sun without getting burned. But look at me now, basking in her sunshine. I rest my hand on her hip, sliding it higher under the hem of the sweater, but stop at her waist to give a little squeeze and evoke a softer laugh.

She sits on my thigh, perched like a prize I didn't earn. The sound of her swallowing is barely heard under my own harsh gulp. "Why'd you bring me here, Spark?"

She smiles, running the tips of her nails through the hair over my ears. She slides them to the back of my head, and whispers, "Are you settling on Spark?"

"Seems fitting since everything leads back to the spark we share. The cigarette out back, the sparkler on top of your cake, and let's be honest, the heat that's been building between us. It always comes back to fire with you."

"The fire between us." The exhilaration that brightened her eyes earlier is still there, but the energy has shifted. She has me craving more than her kiss. I want everything—to kiss, to fuck, to appreciate every inch of her. She runs a fingertip over my lips while desire clouds her eyes. As her chest rises with heavier breaths, it falls harder on release and readjusts on my leg. The relief she seeks, though, isn't going to be found with us sitting here. "You're not afraid of getting burned?"

I'm already shaking my head, accepting the dangers of playing with fire when she showed up in combat boots, looking fucking gorgeous, and bummed a cigarette. "No risk. No reward. It'll be worth the pain."

"If you're lucky."

"Luck has nothing to do with us." I smile in a failing attempt to lessen the need I have growing inside me. *Be a gentleman, Keats.* But with her situated right on my dick, she's making it damn hard. *Literally.* "We create our own destiny."

There's no space left between us when she shifts closer

and angles my head back for a better view. Not an ounce of doubt can be found in her features. "So it's settled then?"

It's weird how life works. I started the night worried about a grade on a damn paper, but six hours later, I'm staring at the face of someone I know will change my life forever. I'm suddenly nervous to kiss her. I've never been nervous with anyone, but Sosie's different. I'm not sure how she broke into my world, but I have a feeling her smile and carefree attitude played a part. Whatever it was, I'm glad she did. "It was settled the moment we met, Spark."

I thought I'd seen the stunner of her smiles several times over, but I hadn't been given the full privilege until now. With her arms linked around my neck, she says, "Tell me something, Poet."

With deeper feelings, urges, and cravings simmering between us, I try to distract from that. "Anything or something in particular?"

"Anything you want," she replies, but I knew she'd choose that option before she did. She doesn't look away. She doesn't even blink. It's as if she'll miss something important if she dares.

With my arms around her waist, I slide my hand to her hip. She takes a long inhale as if this is what she's been waiting for all day. I'm confident we're heading in the same direction with this relationship, but I don't kiss her lips. Not yet. I bend my head to kiss her neck instead. Just once, so she gets a taste of what's to come. I screwed up, though. It wasn't only a tease for her. Now I want more. *Fuck.*

Lifting my head, I look into those magnetizing eyes, already weak to this woman. "I think everyone can see your beauty, but only a lucky few get to experience who you are."

She runs her hand over my cheek, then holds it steady. I close my eyes and lean into her palm. She kisses my temple, daring to do what I wanted and didn't. When I look at her again, she whispers, "I knew you were a poet, Keats."

My name scratches at my ears, as if her nickname has already branded itself over my given one. I'd much rather hear her call me Poet.

Her fingers trail from my face when she moves to wrap her arm around me again. "But be careful. If you keep saying things like that, you might find yourself with a pesky girl wanting to steal all your time."

I chuckle, tightening my hold around her. "She wouldn't have to steal it. I'd give her every hour, minute, and second of the day if she wanted."

Leaning forward, she presses her lips to mine. Her lids flutter closed as she breathes me in and then kisses me. Soft and sweet, and over too soon. When she pulls back, I'm given a deeper view of those eyes that hold a myriad of colors.

A green so vibrant, softer than emerald and brighter than a forest of pine trees.

Golds that mirror coins found at the end of a rainbow.

And those lips I had the pleasure of kissing were raging in a deeper pink from our mouths connecting.

With her so close, that look in her eyes urging me to take another taste, I squeeze just enough to dig the tips of my fingers into the plush of her skin and pull her closer. "Fuck it, who wants to be careful?" I cup her face and kiss her again, deepening it before either of us can catch our breath or the world catches up to us.

CHAPTER 6

SOSIE

I'm engulfed in the heat of a thousand fires. I've never felt so consumed until my Poet's lips seal to mine.

His fingertips slide against my cheeks, cupping my jaw and holding me to him. I have no intention of being anywhere but right here and sinking into this kiss like quicksand. My lips part, and my tongue dips into the passion his mouth holds for me, welcoming, tangling together like this is how it should have always been. *Us together.* Everything feels so much, almost too much, to stand here with any strength when all I want to do is give in to him.

I want his hands on my body, squeezing my breasts. The craving to feel his fingers between my legs almost overrides all else, my thoughts blurring as I melt into him. But when the kiss deepens, I release the yearning I have in a moan. "I've waited my whole life for this. For you."

He stands to his full height, bringing me with him. I'm off balance, so relaxed that my body leans too far back, ripping our mouths apart from the distance between us. The heat of his palm slides to my neck and lower to rub my shoulders as he pulls me back. Words don't come, though I can see in his eyes that he's searching for them. I hold his sides as if I have something to lose. I do. *Him.* I don't want him to stop. I don't want this night to end. The past is the past. With him, this is new, our story unwritten until we pick up the pen.

I find the words for him. "It's okay."

With the slightest nod, he bends to kiss my forehead. "It's not too fast?" I'm pretty sure he knows he already has my permission. I haven't been subtle, but before I can reply, he kisses me with more intention and less frantic energy, slowing things down. Too respectful, *if I'm being honest.* I may be a virgin, but I'm not naive. I know what I want. Keats. But I never took him for anything less than a gentleman.

I'm the one who pulls back this time, taking his hands in mine. His smile is sweet, and a timidness in the corners has me squeezing my grip on him even more. "It's not too fast. I want this." I wield honesty like a weapon to my advantage, desperately needing to satisfy an ache he's awakened deep inside me.

I pull him with me, but he stops, bringing me to a halt with him. "Is this where we really want to be?" Glancing over my head, he grimaces. "It's where your dad—"

"I don't mind." As quick as I am with a plea tingeing my tone, one extra second gives me time to realize he's right. I come here to remind myself of what power does to people. I take food and drinks and leave a mess in silent protest to get back at my dad. This isn't where I should bring the good in my life. As much as I feel ready to be with my Poet, beholden by every word he speaks, this place is tainted when he's what's good in the world to me.

He's love and beauty that I wasn't sure existed before meeting him. God, am I already falling in love? Ready to throw myself at him to accomplish a self-inflicted goal of ridding myself of something that feels more like a burden than an attribute? *Yes.* Keats is a writer and speaks in poetry, calls me Spark, and knows how to romance me. He grins, watching me exist in the universe without expectation or demands. Just accepts me as I am. What's not to love?

That's so attractive.

Geez, he won't even let me seduce him in this apartment because he knows deep down how it makes me feel. The great view can't counter that. And although I know he can, it shouldn't be here. Not the first time or ever. We're better than this.

"Hey." His finger rakes below my chin, and he lifts until I see the understanding in his eyes. "Don't think I don't want you. I do. Admittedly, I would be with you here if I didn't think it had repercussions attached to it. This place isn't the best for you."

"What's best for me, then?"

"Being somewhere that doesn't remind you of betrayal. That's not something I want to be associated with when you think of me." He leans down and kisses my cheek, lingering there long enough for me to close my eyes and inhale the musky scent of his chest. When his lips leave my skin begging for more, his arms wrap around me, holding me against him.

I wrap my arms around him, wanting him as close as can be. *Why?* Because he makes me feel special, like I'm the only one in his personal viewfinder. I like that he can't take his eyes off me and feels comfortable enough to tell me the truth. He makes me feel protected, and that's not something I've ever felt before.

He says, "You deserve better than that, Spark."

There's no trying it on for size anymore. That's the name, and I'll grow into it, though hearing his dulcet tones claim it like a possession has me wholeheartedly embracing it.

As for what I deserve . . . I'm not sure, but I don't feel worthy of him right now. What did I do other than smoke his cigarette and take up most of his time on his short break? I slide my chin over the cotton of his button-up shirt, which he's still wearing from work, looking as handsome as ever, and offer, "We can go to my room back at the house."

His eyes widen before his face settles again from the shock. "Um. I'm not looking for that kind of trouble." He waffles his head on his neck and says, "Look, it's not the Ritz-Carlton or anything, but I live alone in a small studio—"

"That sounds perfect."

He chuckles. "You might want to hear the rest before you agree to come over."

"I don't care unless rats are running around."

Lowering his hands to my hips, he rocks me back and forth. "No rats. Not in the past six months anyway."

"Oh great." I shudder from the thought.

His laughter grows louder. "I'm kidding. It's been at least eight," he deadpans. I'm hoping he's joking, though I'm not sure anymore.

Waggling my finger in front of him, I warn, "I'm trusting you."

He grabs it, then kisses the tip. "I'll protect you, I promise."

I grin with pride, already aware that I'm in safe hands when it comes to us. If only he could protect me from the life I'm avoiding. "I'm holding you to it." Hope blooms as if it had been on standby waiting for him, hope that had been long buried years prior is renewed, and comfort flows through me as I stare into the warmth of his eyes. If only I'd met him before instead of when I'd run out of time.

I move out of his arms, though that's the last thing I want to do, and start gathering the glasses. It will get us out of here sooner, before momentum is lost in the wee hours we're operating under. And I return to being a dutiful daughter tomorrow.

Keats crosses his arms over his chest and peers out the window. With his gaze lengthening, he says, "I don't know how we're even standing at this point. Do you know what time it is?"

"I don't want to know because I'll get tired." Walking into the kitchen, I say, "I think at this stage, we're powered by ramen and adrenaline."

"Attraction helps." His words are as light as his tone, stating facts. The physical attraction is undeniable, but the chemistry with him, the comfort in my own skin, has me realizing he doesn't make me feel small in his presence despite the size difference. I cling to that tidbit that means more to me than he'll ever know.

I wash one glass and set it on the counter. When I reach for the other, it slips from my soapy hand and shatters in the sink. "Shit."

Rushing over, he takes me by the wrist to investigate the wound as if it's life-threatening. Turning on the water, he dips my hand under it and says, "You're bleeding."

"Is that the official diagnosis, Doctor?"

He chuckles. "I think you'll live, but we might have to

amputate if you keep bleeding like this." The water runs clear, bringing a smile to his face. "Saved in the nick of time." Bringing the wound that I can't even see to his mouth, he kisses it.

Playing along, I wiggle my finger. "It feels better already."

His gaze shifts to mine. "Glad I could save the digit."

I laugh. "Oh geez, I think I've created a monster."

He grabs a towel and gently dries my hand before wrapping it around it tightly. "Hold it up, like this." When his eyes return to mine, he's still holding my wrist and asks, "Do you trust me, Spark?" The question mirrors one I asked him earlier.

"With my life." My response comes just as swiftly as his did.

Caressing my cheek, he runs his thumb over the apple of it several times, then kisses my temple. "Good." Shifting me by the waist to the side of the sink, he adds, "You take care of your hand. I'll clean the glass up."

My heart clenches between each heavy thump in my chest. The secrets I thought I could never confess out loud rush through my veins, ready to escape. As trust builds between us, I don't want to dance around my feelings or hide them from him. Keats makes me want to be who I am and inspires me to have the courage to do so. I lean against the counter, gripping it with my free hand behind me. "Do you want to know what I fear most?"

"Snakes? God, I hate snakes." He glances at me with a boyish grin. Why does he have to make it so hard to look away from him? "I was joking. Well, not about the snakes but—*ugh*, I'm fucking up here. Save me, Spark."

"You're not fucking up at all." My voice is so quiet that he looks at me. "Quite the opposite."

With a handful of glass, he briefly glances at me. "I want to know everything about you." And there's that charm again, dragging me into his light.

His honesty is a habit I could get used to. I open the cabinet for the trash, swallowing hard as I struggle to find his flaws. Taking a deep breath, I say it before I can stop myself. "I fear living my life like a trinket on display in someone's old French vitrine. I don't want to be tucked away like a trophy and forgotten. The loneliness would be too much."

He dusts his hands and then stands up in front of me. His towering frame isn't intimidating, but I don't like that the line between his brows has deepened. His mouth is harder with his lips pressed together. He glances down at the trash can between us, and that's when I notice the tic of his jaw. Did I screw up by saying too much? Too soon? Should I have kept my mouth shut?

He brings me into the fold of his arms. With his head bent to rest on the top of mine, he says, "I'll never let that happen." I close my eyes, resting my cheek against his chest as I slide my arms around him, and soak up the kiss he presses to the top of my head. "Never. Okay?"

My soul clings to his words, but there's no desperation in it. I believe him. Breathing is easier, and I grin, though he can't see it. "I hate snakes, too."

He chuckles and leans back to look me in my eyes. Cupping my face, he says, "I knew I liked you." Simple words, but they hold so much meaning.

I playfully push off and ask, "How far are we from your place?"

"Too far to walk in this weather." He looks toward the window and notes, "It's snowing."

"We should get going before we get stuck here." I walk

to the chair and grab my phone from the pocket of my coat. "I'll call a car." Even if it was nice out, the man worked a long shift earlier. I'm surprised he's still upright. "What's the address?"

I enter it into the app when he says it, and I return to the fridge to grab the packaged charcuterie board sitting inside and the bottle of open champagne in the other. Keats watches me, and though I can see the questions written in his expression, I don't make him ask. I say, "He was planning for the company."

"Will he be mad if it's gone?" The concern is sweet, but I'm past worrying about the consequences.

"I don't care anymore."

"Alright, then." He brings my coat and helps put it on. I'm even zipped up nice and snug before we leave this apartment behind. I look back once, feeling this might be the last time I ever come here.

The car waits at the curb when we push through the door and onto the street. I have the tray, and he carries the bottle, though once we're tucked inside the back seat, I take a sip, apparently not caring about much anymore. Maybe I've finally reached some limit I didn't know I had. Or maybe it's being with him that has me seeing a new side of life—one where I can be happy even if guardrails keep me in line. If destiny exists, our future is already determined.

With the tray in my lap, he takes my hand and holds it on top of his leg. His smile is wider than I've seen it, encouraging me to ask, "Why are you so happy?"

"I get to spend time with you." His grip is firm and caring, leaving no doubt that this is right between us. Bringing my hand to his mouth, he kisses it before settling it back on his lap. I can't stop staring even when he looks away.

Charming.

Smart.

Makes me laugh. My cheeks have ached from smiling so much around him.

I didn't expect to meet someone tonight. I never could have dreamed that my very own romantic was under the same moon, much less in my backyard like kismet itself put him there. Maybe it's silly, but I'm starting to believe that Keats Matthews was put in my path on purpose. And once I believe in fate, love follows shortly after.

Could I love this man?

I don't conjure a response, leaving my heart to figure it out when ready.

The car saves me from falling too deep into that notion when it pulls to the curb. Keats takes the bottle from me, and I carry the tray. "Happy holidays," the driver says as I pop the door open and get out.

"Happy holidays," I reply as I look up at the building before me.

The street is nice, especially with snow falling. Trees grow in front of some of the buildings, but none in front of his. The red brick shows its age with peeling black paint around the trim, a stoop that doesn't have more than three steps, and only a matchbox-sized landing, but it's the way Keats is already backing toward the building with his free hand up in explanation that bothers me. He doesn't owe me anything. "Prepare yourself," he says. "I know it doesn't look like much on the outside, but the inside looks even worse." He cracks a smile.

"I know I'll love it." I grab his hand and lead him up the steps. Just inside the entrance, I catch the names on the mailboxes, landing on his. "Four B?"

"There's no elevator," he warns, staring at me like he expects a certain reaction.

Eyeing him, I wink. "No wonder you're in such great shape."

I start on the stairs, but I'm caught by the back of my coat. When I turn to look, his hand slides to the nape of my neck. The air grows thick when the tension from earlier returns, stirring an unsatiated hunger in my belly. His heated stare tells me he feels the same as his eyes travel from mine and lower to my mouth. We were playful, even eager to arrive, but now that we're here, my heart feels exposed despite the layers covering my body. I want him. I want him to be my first, but I also care about him. Maybe I'm a fool for falling so fast and easily for someone I just met, but I'll be the fool for him without hesitation.

There's no reason to ruin this. I don't want careful or gentle. I want what feels right, not him worrying about whether he's hurting me. I've been holding this secret, and tonight, I want it behind me. We both know what's happening is special. This time is for us. We will either lasso the stars or scorch the earth.

Standing two steps higher, I find our eyes are at the same height, our lips even with each other. My gaze travels from the soulful intensity of his browns to the lips he licks, drawing me to him. "We've lived in the same city for all these years." Closing my eyes, I press my mouth to his and whisper, "And I finally found you."

CHAPTER 7

SOSIE

A heavy-handed confession like that doesn't stall the momentum building between us. It's only a matter of my back hitting his door under the pressure of our passion that has us taking a breath from kissing.

"You okay?" Keats asks, swiping a hand behind me to cushion me from the hardwood. He leans his head against mine as he catches his breath. But then he trails kisses down my neck, pressing his erection against me as his knee anchors itself between my legs.

Tilting my head to the side, I reply, "More than okay." I'm breathless, trying so hard to keep from panting like a cat in heat in his hallway. I reach for the zipper of the coat, needing cool air to penetrate before I burn up. "I'm too hot."

"So hot, Spark."

I paw at him. "No, no," I say under giggles that escape. "I need this coat off before I have a stroke." Juggling the bottle in one hand, he grabs my zipper and starts pulling it down. "We should get you out of it, then."

I burst out laughing, my head hitting the wood again, but this time, I don't care. This man is stripping me, so who am I to stand in his way? "We should, but inside."

He suddenly stops and looks up as if it just dawned on him. "Right." He glances down to the other end. "Yeah." Pulling a key dangling on a long string from his pocket, he unlocks the door so fast that I tumble backward inside. Balancing the tray on my palm, I reach out to be saved with the other. Keats catches me by the front of my coat before I land on my ass.

"Oh thank God. Nice save." I'd heap more praise, but I'd rather get back to the kissing.

He flicks the light on as I steady myself, still holding the tray with a death grip, and look around the room. The entire studio apartment is smaller than my bedroom. I slowly turn to take in everything from his personal items to the colors he's chosen for his furniture and decor. Do guys care about that stuff? I find it endearing how nothing matches, but it somehow feels like him—warm and inviting.

I would choose this place over the pink palace of a cage back at my house any day.

Taking the charcuterie from me, he zips into the shoebox of a kitchen with it. I can finally free myself from the confines of this puffer and the down filling the insides that felt like they were threatening my very existence. Just as I unwind the scarf, Keats swipes both from me and hangs them on a hook by the door next to his.

"I like your place. It's nice. Warm."

"We're lucky the heat is working. That's not always the

case." He kicks off his shoes and pulls off his socks. "I'm going to change."

"Changing sounds like we aren't picking up where we left off."

My heart skips a beat when he smirks with a look in his eyes that tells me we're on the same page. He comes to me. Gliding the tip of his finger under my jaw, he steals a kiss. "Are we going to let that champagne go to waste?"

"No way. We dragged it across the city." I slip away to grab it from the counter and hand it to him. He takes a long pull straight from the bottle. When he hands it to me, I swallow a gulp. His champagne lips cover mine, and we kiss like it's the first time again.

Still holding the bottle, I wrap my arms around his neck, pulling him to me until the bubbles go to my head, and I feel woozy under his kiss. His arms tighten around me as he laughs. "We're going to fall if we're not careful."

"Careful is the last thing I want to be tonight." I laugh as my tongue twists itself in knots. "I should clarify since we're in a compromising position. I don't want to stop what we're doing."

"I don't want to either. The beauty is that we don't have to stop." He lifts me into his arms and carries me to the kitchen. "Leave the bottle."

As soon as I set it down, I twirl over his shoulder in a fit of giggles I can't contain. Standing back in the living room of this one-room apartment, he says, "I knew I shouldn't have put up the bed. Wait here while I remedy it."

I'm set on my feet to watch him unfold the green loveseat to reveal the foldaway bed hidden inside. Cushions are tossed, and the blanket and sheets are straightened as soon as it's flat and steady on the metal rod it has for feet.

Glancing at me, he asks, "Do you mind grabbing the pillows from the closet?"

"I don't mind." Finding the closet is a harder task than I expected.

He chuckles as he shoves the cushions into the space at the top of the bed. "Outside the bathroom, right over there."

"Ah." I get a glimpse of the tiny bathroom when I pass it in a tiny hall that leads nowhere but to the closet. I don't even know how he manages in that small space. Looks like I could barely fit. When I open the closet, I grab the pillows on the top shelf, though I have to jump to reach them. But I don't rush off when I see stacks of books lining the floor next to a few pairs of shoes. One shelf holds a couple of folded towels and a plastic bin of toiletries, including cologne, which is tempting to smell. Though I know it will never smell as good as he does.

Two battered shoeboxes are stacked next to towels and tucked against the wall. One is labeled photos. The other is miscellaneous. Both intriguing and more so, because the boxes have aged, with yellowing around the ripped edges, and appear to have housed women's shoes.

"Hey, Spark? Get distracted?"

I blink several times, snapping out of where my head wanted to travel before turning to him. I smile in reaction to the grin he's wearing for me. "Yeah." I close the closet and return to the bed to toss the pillows on it. "Is it good to go?"

"Yep."

I sit to take off my boots while he crosses the room to turn out the lights. I expect to be thrown into darkness. We are except for the little Christmas tree that I hadn't previously noticed perched on a small bookcase in the corner.

I'm not surprised since I was big-time distracted by my Poet. It's shining bright with little lights, giving the apartment a glow.

My eyes don't have to adjust. I can see him as he starts unbuttoning his shirt. I get both boots off while he's pulling a City Events Catering Company T-shirt over his head. He unhooks his belt buckle, his eyes on me as I pull the sweater off over my head, then carry the boots to the door to park them next to his. "I like that necklace on you."

I clutch the diamond tennis necklace wrapped around my neck. "I'd forgotten I was wearing it. This and the earrings." I take my pants down and step out of them.

"They're nicc."

"Thanks." Reaching around to the back, I unclasp the necklace and reach to my ears to remove the dangling earrings, so they don't catch on anything. I set them on the coffee table that he shifted to the side of the couch.

He catches me by the wrist and pulls me to him. I grab onto his sides as we lock eyes. I run my nails over the incredible hills and valleys of his abs and watch as his breathing picks up from the lightest touch. My lips part as my body demands more air.

He runs the back of his fingers along my arm. "Sometimes I have to convince myself you're real and not a figment of my imagination."

Goose bumps spring to life wherever his hand is, but it's his gaze traversing my body that has me feeling his touch all over. I lean forward and kiss his bare chest as I unbutton his pants. He starts at the hem of my shirt and lifts it, leaving me heaving with anticipation of being with him. I unzip his pants, letting them fall to the floor. He steps out, taking his boxer briefs with them before aiming for the hem of my tank. The built-in bra's elastic catches under my breasts as he pulls it off over my head and tosses it behind him.

Now I'm bare like he is. My instinct is to cover myself, but I hold his eyes instead, letting his gaze drink me in without shame. I look to the side when it becomes too much. But he's quick to pinch my chin and angle me back to him. "You're so incredibly beautiful, babe."

He slides his hand over my shoulder and along the column of my neck until he's caressing my cheek. I lean against it as he kisses me—slow and steady—but the tease is too much, so I deepen it. The tips of his fingers slip under the strings at my hips and start to descend.

When he's kneeling before me, his eyes track my middle and land on my hip bone. He rubs the pad of his thumb on the spot, then glances up at me with a wry grin. "I like this freckle." He kisses it, making me smile in response.

Keats stands, lifting me with him. Our bodies are naked and pressed together as he moves us to the bed and lays me down. I don't scramble, forcing myself to stay out of my comfort zone for the payoff, but I do dip my legs under the covers on the far side from him. When he climbs in next to me, there's very little room to spare. We're close, so close we don't take up the entire mattress.

As if we're being chased, we kiss like time is of the essence. Our lips caressing leads to hands wandering. The heat of his palms on my cheeks, and my shoulders, and in my hair. His legs rub against mine as I arch into him. The need builds as seconds become minutes, and minutes slip away in the incredible feeling of our bodies being turned on.

A moan escapes as I shamelessly rub myself against him, craving more than kisses and sweet touching. "I want you," I whisper, so ready for more of him.

But when he shifts, a bout of insecurity strikes when I realize that this is it. This is the moment I've been waiting for. I didn't ogle him, not to be rude, but feeling his erection against my leg has me wishing I did, so I know what I'm getting into. Or what's getting into me, technically. I smirk. This doesn't have to be serious, I convince myself. We can have fun after all.

His fingers dig into my hair and dip to massage the back of my neck as we roll to our sides with him hovering over me. He kisses my chest and swirls his tongue around one nipple and the other before looking up. "I need to get protect—"

"I'm on birth control." I wrap my arms around him to hold him right where he is so he can't escape.

Lowering to kiss just under my ear, he whispers, "Are you sure?"

"I'm sure." It doesn't take but half a breath to feel him between my legs. With his hands planted on either side of me, he dips down to kiss me, and again, while the tip of his dick nudges forward. He pushes against my entrance, causing me to suck in a harsh breath.

"You okay there?" I nod, but I've lost my voice. Focusing on his eyes, I start to count down with each breath I take. He drops his head just slightly as a line between his brows forms. "Why are you counting?"

Oh no. "Um . . . I thought that was in my head."

"Are you nervous?"

Do I lie? My instincts tell me yes, but that's not who I am with him. "Yes, a little."

Concern wrinkles his forehead. "How can I make it better?"

His sweet tone has me relaxing. I nod in reassurance. "I already am."

His expression shows relief as he gives me a gentle smile. "When I ask if you're all right, I really want to know. Okay?"

"Okay," I whisper while the ache in my belly for him spreads to my limbs. "I'm okay. I really am. I just want to be with you."

His gaze stays on mine as if he expects to find another answer hiding in my eyes. Leaning in again, he drags his tongue over my bottom lip, punctuating it with a kiss to the corner of my mouth. A rogue smile redirects his expression before he whispers, "I'm going to make you feel so good, Spark."

I touch his face, tapping across his jawline and admiring how handsome he is. My pulse quickens, knowing I'm the lucky one who gets to be with him. It's my heart I worry about when he says things like me being a dream he can't believe. At the rate I'm falling, I can only hope it doesn't get broken.

He presses his body to mine where I'd been missing his heat. I steal a kiss before he nudges my head to access my neck, making me smile as I close my eyes and savor his mouth against my skin. Not like I'd deny him or anything else he asked, but I wrap my arms around him just to relish the feeling, which has been jumbled since we shared a cigarette.

He places one softer kiss on my lips as his hand travels down my body to a lower destination. He shifts, and the pressure of his erection returns between my legs. With his eyes on mine, he pushes into me. My mouth falls open as a gasp takes hold. It's all so quick, him taking possession of my lips and breath, my thoughts, and my entire being as he slides all the way in and back out again. With another slow thrust forward, he exhales a satisfying moan. I grab on to him, needing a reprieve to acclimate. "Wait."

He stills inside me, but his hands still roam freely. His kisses are dispersed like candy, and he murmurs, "So beautiful," and, "Tastes of heaven," against my skin. But what I needed wasn't for him to stop. Now that I've had him, I need so much more than before. "Okay."

He withdraws so fast that I don't anticipate the power of the next thrust until I'm jerked on the bed. Anchoring his elbows against the top of my shoulders, he uses them as leverage to pull back to push in again and again. My mouth hangs open, but my throat is dry. The pain is there, but the pleasure overrides it.

I take a breath and move, bucking against him and apart, wanting more of this connection. And deeper. Wrapping my legs around him, I'm lifted off the bed every time he drives forward. My eyes are closed as I take him thrust by thrust, deeper until he's all I feel on the inside.

The pauses are too quick to get my bearings on what's happening and where. The scent of that musk, and soap, even a hint of cigarettes, fills my nostrils. The change in positions happening so fast. His hands are on my waist and squeezing my hips, kneading my breasts, and pinching my nipples.

My back arches as I finally release the moan I'd been holding in. "Oh God. Oh God. Oh God," I chant on the verge of losing myself in the pain and pleasure, the stretch, and the emptiness when he leaves me.

The heat of his breath covers the wetness his mouth left, and if I regulate my breathing, I'd be able to hear the jaggedness of his breath as well. Running my fingers through his thick brown hair, I grab hold as if they offend me, biting my lip before needing to plead, "Please, don't stop."

But his body feels so good against mine—the hard abs, the muscular legs, the shoulders that feel protective as they consume me beneath him, and the erection that I'm finally getting used to. Releasing my breasts, he moves higher while his knee bumps up against the side of my legs, situated with his eyes on me, and I can't hide my desire. I've been waiting for the one to come along, and he has shown up for overtime duty.

Squeezing him between my thighs like a captive, I loop a foot over his calf, creating my own leverage. He kisses me, this time with his body hovering just enough to control the pressure. He invades my mouth and body like he's conquering new territory, giving me little reason to deny him the victory. "I never knew it could be so good," I say with my mind caught up, analyzing how incredible he feels inside me.

"So good," he says, breathing through each thrust. Reaching between us, he slides his fingers between my legs. My hips jolt when he touches my clit. Circling it, he teases, and I start to lose control. The slick sounds of our bonding . . .

Our bodies fit together so well. The all-consuming feel of him filling every part of me comes to a head when my body shivers and quakes beneath him. I pant, wrapping my arms around his neck and holding on like my life depends on it. "My Poet. My Poet, my Poet," I utter on repeat, slipping off my tongue as if he owns me. He does. It's only a thrust or two more before I'm sent spiraling into darkness and emerge where the brightest lights exist.

Clamping my eyes closed, I feel the tremors surge through my veins, and I come for him. And when I'm slick and floating, he comes right after me. "Oh fuck, babe." He bites his lip as his erratic push and pull, thrust and release, steadies in pace and then ceases.

Keats drops on top of me. Although he's too heavy for me to bear his weight for long, I devour every second I do have just like this in the aftermath.

The room is quiet, leaving only the melody of our strong breathing to be heard. I rub his back, bringing a smile to his face. When I turn to get a better look, it's languid under heavier lids that appear to want to be closed over open. Scruffy hair and a messier expression are caught somewhere between heaven and hell. I feel the same but wouldn't have it any other way.

He finally rolls to my side, but keeps his arm draped over my center. "You weren't breathing," he whispers.

"I didn't notice."

Leaning over, he kisses me sweetly and brushes hair away from my face. "Tell me something, Spark."

He makes me smile because we've been here before. "Anything?"

"Anything you want, but something not many people know."

I don't know why my heart starts racing. Am I saying something I shouldn't? No, but it feels forbidden to tell anyone. I swallow down my trepidation, and whisper, "My birthday is New Year's Eve, not on Christmas Eve or Christmas."

Keats stares at me, blinking once and then again before pressing his lips to mine and kissing me again. With his hands still holding my face, he whispers, "Why was it celebrated on Christmas Eve, then?"

"Convenience. My parents aren't usually in the city on New Year's Eve."

"Hmm," he hums as he glances away. When his eyes return to mine, he kisses my cheek. "Not many people know this? So your birthday is being celebrated by others who have no idea that's not the day?" When he drops his head next to mine, his chin resting on my shoulder, I hold him to me. "Jesus," he spews with irritation.

"Don't feel bad for me, okay? That only makes me feel worse." I feel him nod before he trails an Orion's Belt of kisses along my neck. I should tell him I'm no longer a virgin because it feels like something to celebrate, and it would be a surefire way to distract him from my birthday situation. But he deserves some rest even more.

"Can I tell you something?"

I smile just from the sound of his voice. "Yes."

"I'm glad you bummed that cigarette." A smile plays on his lips, but his eyelids are growing heavy as the long night finally catches up to him at five in the morning.

"Me, too." I stretch to place a kiss on his head before sleep drags him under, and whisper, "I'm so glad we met."

CHAPTER 8

SOSIE

It's surprising how bright an overcast sky is when you're trying to hide from the light. I blink several times to block it out, but I'm too awake to fight against the invasion of our space through the window. It's not the only thing waking me this fine morning. Keats's erection is pressed against my lower back.

"We had sex."

I clamp my hand over my mouth but can't stop the giggle that follows. He stirs, so I freeze in place.

But I *finally* had sex. I sigh happily.

I want to squeal and celebrate, but I grin, unable to stop myself because we had sex, and it can never be taken back —*oh* . . . Okay, so even minor movements have me feeling every muscle in my body and a few I didn't even know existed. Keats really did consume me, making me feel sexier than I've ever felt in my life.

The tiny lights on the miniature tree still shine in the corner, catching my attention while I lie here tucked in his arms. Somehow, his apartment brings me more comfort than my own home. I'm safe here, protected from my family's demands of me. I snuggle closer to my Poet. He shifts, but the consistent breathing of his sleep remains a peaceful lullaby.

It's tempting to fall back asleep, to ignore the world, and remain here in this perfect little universe, but I need to go home and take a shower, brush my teeth, and clean the makeup that I'm sure looks like a dreadful mess off my face. So I fight the urge to stay in bed with him all day, slip out from under his arm, which suddenly feels like a ton of bricks, and roll off the side of the mattress.

Lying on the blue rug and hardwoods, I look back at the man I just gave my virginity to, and smile. "How are you so handsome even when sleeping?" I whisper, not expecting an answer. It's not just his looks that have drawn me in. It's him, the whole man—the poetry, and the way I danced on the street and he wasn't embarrassed. When he kisses me, it's like we've done it a million times in a different lifetime.

My heart races as I touch my lips and smile again. If smiles were measured in decibels, mine would be louder than a foghorn. And it's not going away anytime soon.

I push up to my feet and wrap my arms around my naked body as I scamper to the bathroom. I wash my hands, then rest my palms on the sink's edge, scanning for any changes. I lean closer to the mirror. "Dang, I look tired." I swipe at the mascara under my eyes, but it will take some scrubbing when I get home. I lean back, still smiling like a goofball, and touch my swollen lips once more. "That man is better than injections . . . wait, that's funny." I was injected alright. I crack up but cover my mouth again to keep the noise contained in this tiny room.

When I collect myself the best I can, which isn't great

because I'm way too happy to filter this joy, I tiptoe back out to my coat and pull my phone from the pocket.

A harsh breath chokes in my throat when my gaze trails lower to the message at the bottom of the screen:

Get home. Now.

My dad's text twists my stomach into knots, and the bubble of bliss I was happily living in instantly bursts. I slide my gaze to Keats to see him rearranging his body around my absence. Legs tangled in the sheets, the blanket barely covers his backside. He doesn't wake, but I kind of wish he would. I could use some advice.

Although I already know what I'm going to do. I may not like my dad's impatient approach, but I know I'll still go as demanded. Do I have a choice? He controls my entire life in the palm of his hand.

I start searching for my thong because the sooner I deal with him, the sooner I can return to Keats. My search-and-rescue ends empty-handed, so I pull on my sweatpants and then my socks. I spin once to locate my shirt, snatching it from behind the table where it landed. I don't bother with my sweater. I can find it later.

Scooping the necklace and earrings up from the table, I quietly pad over to the other side of the room. I hook each earring to a branch, making the perfect ornaments for the bare tree, then tap to watch them dangle and catch the light.

I drape the necklace at the top and wind it around until I run out of length. Admiring my work, I grin with pride at such a simple act. It looks so much better on this tree than it ever could on me. That tree is also now holding thousands of dollars' worth of jewelry, so I'm not surprised it's so eye-catching.

But decorating the tree is a momentary reprieve from the impending doom I'm about to face. Putting off these "meetings" has never served me well, so I might as well get it over with.

I don't see a pen or paper, so I text Keats that I'll see him later. Setting my phone down on the console, I slip my feet into my boots, grab my coat from the hook, and quietly exit the apartment. As soon as I close the door, I bend down to tie my laces, but realize I just left my phone inside. *Dammit.* I gently turn the knob only to be blocked by an automatic lock. "No." *Ugh.* "For real with this?"

I can't knock without waking Keats, so I abandon the idea and leave without it. The stairs aren't so bad when going down. It's the up that about killed me last night. Fortunately, I had Keats's lips to resuscitate me.

Keats. It feels like I'm living in a dream with him.

I shouldn't need an ally against my own parents, but I have no doubt he'd be here with me if I asked. It's ridiculous that I trust a man I've only known for one night more than my own family.

I push out the door and luck into a cab passing by. Hopping in, I sit back with my father's text plaguing me. I thought they'd be long gone on their vacation, so it leaves me worrying about why they stayed and what they want to talk about.

When I'm dropped off, I hurry to the gate to punch in the code, hoping to sneak in a shower before they realize I'm home. I shoulder the gate out of habit, only to realize it never unlocked. *Huh* . . . I punch the pound sign several times to clear the other code and reenter it. Again, the gate doesn't budge. "*Okaaaay*. Odd." I purse my lips to the side, confused. My stomach drops as my mind finally catches up and fills in the blanks. I press the voice communication button and wait for someone to answer.

"How may I help you?" I don't recognize the male voice, but it is a holiday, so maybe he's temporarily filling in.

"Hi, it's Sosie. Sosie Stansbury. Do you mind buzzing me in?"

"Right away, Ms. Stansbury." The lock unlatches so easily that I'm starting to think it's no coincidence that my code didn't work.

I've had knock-down, drag-out fights with my parents before, but my gut tells me that is not what's about to happen. *It's worse.*

CHAPTER 9

SOSIE

It's quite an accomplishment to rip me from the high I was riding after the best night of my life to making me feel small and nothing more than a burden. But as I stand here waiting to be let into my own house, my father has managed to do just that with three simple words. *Get home. Now.*

It leaves me wondering at what age will I finally be treated like someone he cares about or, at the bare minimum, a human?

The door opens to an unfamiliar face staring back at me. Dressed in a suit, he holds his chin in the air with a stiff, straight back and says, "Your father is waiting for you in his office." *That's not good.*

No shower.

No brushed teeth.

No clean clothes.

This won't go over well. I wipe my cashmere-gloved

hand under my eyes in hopes of getting any of the remaining makeup cleared before entering. My pace is slow, the distance growing between this stranger working here and me. I swipe on lip balm and start taking off my coat, only to realize I forgot my sweater. A black tank, sweatpants, and combat boots aren't going to go over well for a Stansbury. I stop just before entering the hall that leads to the office and the library wing of the house and take off my boots. Tucking my gloves in my pockets, I take a breath as I double-step to catch up. Just before the door opens, I attempt to smooth down my hair so it's less disorderly.

I'm not going to fool him. It's not about how I look, though he doesn't appreciate it when I look like a "city kid," as he calls it. This will be another lecture on behavior and expectations. *Keep your mouth shut and listen, Sosie.* Easy, and the best way to get through this unscathed.

The man opens the door and stands with his back to it. "Ms. Stansbury, Mr. Stansbury."

I plaster a smile on my face and whisk myself forward. "Merry Christmas, Dad."

He glances from the monitor on his desk to me before shifting his gaze to the new guy working the doors in this place and shooing him away with a flick of his hand. "Sit down."

An acknowledgment of my existence would have been nice, but apparently, we don't see eye to eye on the issue. I sit in a chair on the other side of the large, ornately carved desk and clasp my hands together in my lap, like a good daughter, and wait for the first round of attack.

I'm kept in suspense as seconds drag into a minute that feels like ten. But if my dad taught me anything, it's that the one who holds out the longest wins. You'd think he'd be impressed that I was paying attention. He's not.

Dressed in a freshly steamed light gray suit, his tie is straight, and not a hair is out of place. He doesn't look rested despite his appearance and finally makes eye contact with me. His eyes mirror mine but hold a starkness I don't recognize, and I hope I never inherit. He's been mad at me before, but I'm sensing something else is happening. Why is he acting so weird?

"Where have you been?" He finally speaks. The blunt question is asked in a harsh tone. He's a yeller, always has been, but that's not what this is. This is simmering anger about to explode. *I tread carefully.*

"With friends. It was late, so—"

His hand flies up to stop me from talking. "Let me tell you about my night." *Okaaaay.* "I hosted our annual holiday party for the company, our friends, and family. It's usually a great event."

"It was. I was there as requested."

"I'd like to finish." It's not a question, so I keep my mouth shut. "Unfortunately, I had to listen to your mother and the Lafoons asking about you all night. Is she coming? When will she be here? Is she upstairs?" His voice teeters on mocking, and his eyes hold no love or patience like they used to. "You finally make an appearance but blow off Gregory all night, so what was the point?"

I'm not sure if I'm supposed to answer or if the question is rhetorical. With him staring at me, I figure it's time to step into the ring. I reply, "I didn't know my sole job was to entertain Gregory Lafoon."

"It was one of many of your duties last night."

"You do realize I don't want to date Gregory, right? I'm not attracted to him like that, so why are we being forced together?"

His hand slams onto the desk, and he stands, causing

me to jump. "Forced? You should be begging him to date you. Instead, you're treating the Lafoons like they're nobodies when you don't realize who you're messing with."

"That's not true. I like Gregory *as a friend*. Why does it need to be more? Why me, Dad?"

"Why you?" A deep-seated and humorless laugh escapes before he cuts off its air. "I'm tired of this, Sosie. You're acting like a stupid girl and making a fool of your mother and me." The insult sends shock waves through my system. He's known for getting angry, but I always figured it was part of becoming a titan of industry. I'm unable to process that he just called me stupid for not wanting to hook up with a guy. "You've had your fun."

He sits down, the sudden drop forcing an exasperated breath from his chest. "You don't appreciate anything we've done for you. You've had the world given to you on a silver platter and reject it like it's beneath you. Listen to me, Sosie, the Lafoons are billionaires."

I'm left speechless as disgust coats my mouth. It's always about money and the bottom line, whether it's personal or in business.

He calms before my eyes as if reason has reentered the picture. "They only have one son." *I knew I was giving him too much credit.* "Gregory is set to inherit everything." *And there it is . . .* "But you chose to run around with a server instead." *Wait . . . what?* How does he . . . my chest tightens and my breath labors from the inference to Keats. Did the police bring it to his attention? The cameras on the property? "I'm not going to tell them, but you're twenty-one. It's time—"

"Actually, I'm not," I snap in full defense. "I know my birthday has never been convenient for you, but it's on the thirty-first, New Year's Eve, not Christmas. You seem to have forgotten." The lines already embedded in his brow deepen, becoming more dominant. His mood shifts as he does, sitting forward despite the light streaming through the large windows, trying to keep things light. A view of the garden out back doesn't stand a chance under these circumstances. His hair is more salt than pepper these days, and patience seems to be something he no longer possesses by the disdain he holds so dearly in his expression.

"That's irrelevant to the conversation we're having now. You've been chasing dreams instead of living in reality. That time will come to an end today, so the ammunition you provided me last night won't be necessary."

My jaw practically hits the desktop as too many emotions to pinpoint just one run through me. I land in shock, but it's more disbelief, if I'm honest. I thought there was a floor to his cruelty. I was wrong. "Is that what you needed to get me to conform to your wishes? You need ammunition against your own daughter?"

"Nothing else was working. I knew letting out the lead just enough would benefit me. You did not let me down, dear daughter." The dog reference makes my blood boil, but somehow that just doesn't feel like the worst of it.

The temperature between us is rising so fast that if we're not careful with our words, we'll never be able to turn back. I guess this is the moment I realize I'm already there. But I can't give up just yet. "I'm in school." I slide to the edge of my seat, pleading my case. "I start back in a few weeks. I'm not doing anything that wasn't previously agreed to, Dad." My voice rises in pitch as my heart rate increases. "I've done everything you've wanted—"

Rocking forward, he steeples his fingers like we're in a

negotiation. I guess I was too naive to realize it before now. "Except what I needed you to do, and you refuse me at every turn." I've seen him close deals before. This is when he goes in for the kill unless I stop him.

"Date Gregory? Is that what you need from me, Dad? I'm supposed to give myself to some guy so you can close a deal to secure your fortune."

"My fortune? You've never had a job. You've never had to think about a damn thing in your life. It was all taken care of before you rolled out of bed in the morning . . ." He checks his watch. "Afternoon, in this case." He's not wrong. I've been fortunate in many ways, but that doesn't make what he's asking acceptable in any world.

"You have millions, Dad. When will it be enough because it's about to cost you your daughter!"

He's too composed as he stares at me like I'm a stranger. I'm losing the battle. My hands start to shake, so I tuck them under my legs on the chair so he can't see how he affects me. "You've always had a flair for the dramatic. That's why your mother enrolled you in acting."

"I'm not actually dramatic, but yes, I have emotions. I'm real and the only kid you've got despite wanting a son all along." There. It's out in the open. I always said I'd never let them know I overheard them when I was younger, but it's been so hard to live with their disappointment. "I will never be enough for you, will I?"

"Take a breath and calm down." I'll take the breath, but calming down seems to be out of reach. Resting his hands flat on the desk, he says, "You have options."

"Which are?"

He sits back in his leather chair with tension seeming to escape his posture. He knows he's winning. On the flip side, I've never been more on edge of losing in my life. I don't know where he's driving this discussion, but I'm certain it won't end favorably for me. He says, "A server isn't going to provide the life I've set you up for."

That he has the nerve to even mention Keats triggers a tornado of rage inside me. "He's a student."

"In fine arts. He's a nothing, Sosie."

"And I'm just a photographer."

"They are similar that way."

Slipping my hands free, I feel more confident than ever. Tapping the desk, I say, "Be careful, Dad, before you say something you can't take back."

He laughs. Not with me. At me. I see it in his eyes. To him, I'm a pampered princess with nothing to offer anyone except apparently my body. Like, is that what he's really asking me to do, or am I being dramatic like he claims? What world am I living in that I need to question my own father's motives?

"I have work to do before your mother and I catch our flight." They never tell me when they're leaving or where they're going. I'm informed on a need-to-know basis like an employee. Though I think his employees outrank me. "The Lafoons are good people. You'd be lucky to snag Gregory, especially considering how poorly you've treated him all these years."

"It hasn't been poorly. We're friends. It just never developed into more."

"For you. But he's in love, and we should capitalize on that." He drags an envelope from the side of the desk to place it in front of me. Still in shock from the mere suggestion of using someone like that, I glance at the recipient to see my name written in calligraphy. "You'll either be accepting his invitation for New Year's Eve—"

"My birthday," I say just to take the dig.

"Or you can spread your wings and live exactly how you please. Elsewhere."

"What?" I've been threatened before, but not with intent. Judging by the consternation of his tone, this isn't a threat. *It's real.* "Where would I go? I start school soon. Do you want me living in a dorm?" How did he manage to turn this discussion into a transaction? And what will I have to sacrifice to please him?

"That will not be our concern any longer. We think you're a bright girl and can figure it out."

Why does the part about figuring it out sound like it means more than I initially thought? "Will you still pay—"

"No." He shakes his head like I'm a bother to him. "We won't be paying for anything. No school. No food. No place to rent. Your lifestyle or the subway card."

"Credit cards?" I stand, crossing my arms over my chest. "I don't understand. Nothing?"

"Nothing. You'll be on your own. I'm sure you'll make it work." He returns his eyes to the monitor like I'm nothing more than an interruption in his day.

I pace the room, stopping when I see the spot where Keats and I met, smoked, and laughed. That's where the switch flipped on, showing me there's another way to go in life. The irony that meeting him has sent my life into a tailspin, and now my dad is pulling the rug out from under me, isn't lost on me.

Returning to stand in front of his desk, I ask, "The options are: go on a date with Gregory for New Year's, or I'm completely on my own?"

He glances at me with a self-satisfied grin. "Yes."

"And Mom's okay with this?"

"She's in complete agreement."

There's no good option. The easiest and most obvious

choice would be to go on one date to secure my life as I know it. But the insult of being told to date someone I have no interest in has me wanting to walk away from everything. How will I survive? Other than a trust fund from my grandfather that kicks in when I'm thirty, I have no money of my own. I have no job. I won't have a place to live. No food. No school. No nothing.

Tough love has always been my parents' style, the hands-off method a close second. But to cut me off is a new tactic to make me bend to their will. My indignation has me raising my chin as fear of the unknown tidal waves over me. Before I burn the last of this bridge down, I reply, "I'll think about it." The attitude voiced in my tone probably won't go over well, but too bad.

"Don't take too long." When he looks at me again, he hands me a piece of paper and the invitation. "The rules have been laid out." When I take the paper and envelope, he adds, "Merry Christmas."

My mouth falls open, too stunned to say anything more to him. I've been gutted by the betrayal of their actions before, but . . . there's no coming back from this. Not in my book. Unfortunately, I still must consider all options and consequences.

Before I reach the door, my dad says, "And just in case I wasn't clear, if you choose the second option, your new friend won't have a job any longer or any other in this city, NYU might find that he was cheating and expel him, and stealing champagne that cost over a thousand dollars is a felony in this state. We have him on video carrying it out of the building." I stare at him, this unrecognizable man who claims to love me. "Choose wisely, honey."

And there it is . . . the price I'm expected to pay. *Keats.*

I'm not going to argue with him. He's said his piece and

thrown me into an impossible situation. I feel sick. If I choose Keats, then both of our lives will be destroyed. And choosing Gregory means I lose the man I've already fallen in love with. Either way, my heart gets broken, and my Poet gets hurt.

CHAPTER 10

KEATS

Merry Christmas, Keats.

The text from my mom invades my space, breaking the concentration I had buried in my laptop for hours. I look up, blinking a few times and finally noticing the room has darkened. Though the little Christmas tree on my bookcase is doing its damnedest to brighten up the place. I'd forgotten it was Christmas.

And I'm alone. *Again.*

It's nothing new, considering how I grew up—my dad absent most days, then gone altogether, and my mom at her jobs most days and then drinking down the block at the bar where she worked on weekends and holidays. I remember the one time I dared to walk down there to deliver her present since it was the only way I was going to see her that day.

I was twelve when I realized I was truly on my own. It wasn't just because she was drunk, which she was to the point of being sloppy. It was because it finally dawned on me that she preferred to be in that condition, surrounded by regulars at the bar, rather than at home raising her kid.

Do I make the trek over to her apartment to see her like I do each year? I had pushed the guilt down deep enough to pretend I didn't need to. Would she miss the visit? Do I still owe it to her?

She's not knocking on my door either. Is it time to leave that relationship where it is—caught in a purgatory of responsibility versus forcing it because we're related? If asked, I'm not sure I'd say I had any family. But even thinking that makes me feel like shit.

Placing blame ended years ago. She clearly never asked to be a mom. Not everyone is cut out for the job. That she was the closest I had to a parent and the only one technically keeping a roof over my head made me respect her, as she was still trying her best. She was just failing. So is it fair to abandon her like she did to me so many times?

Fuck.

I hate the holidays. I foolishly convinced myself that spending the night with Sosie would override the past and we'd make new memories this year. The text she sent left that impression as well. The chance to change what this day was to me was tangible, and then I lost it.

I've lost count of how many times my gaze has bounced to the door, hoping to see her bound through like she's done it a thousand times. She was comfort and beauty, familiar in ways that I can't make sense of, but mine at the same time. Sosie was all mine for a short time. And I want more. Worry embeds itself, leaving me bereft that she might not return.

She's a grown woman who can handle herself. And

surely, she would text if her plans had changed. *Wouldn't she?*

She's probably caught up opening presents or doing her duty as a Stansbury for a few hours. Except it's been more than a few hours. It's been over six. Okay, I'm being ridiculous. It's *only* been six hours on Christmas Day, for fuck's sake. I'm damn lucky she even came over last night. Images of her naked beneath me, watching her tits bounce with each thrust, her lips swollen from kissing, and the taste of her skin taunt me.

I shift, the cravings for seconds hit hard, making me more irritable that she's not here. Completely un-fucking-reasonable, Keats. I'm acting like a fucking creep. In true creep fashion, I tap the screen. The phone on the cushion next to me lights up once more for me to check messages. It would have been impossible to miss any texts since I've been here all day. I check anyway. Though I've tried to work on my capstone paper in finance for hours, I've mostly been staring at this damn phone, waiting to hear from Sosie.

Merry Christmas. I need to run home, but
I'll be back. Keep the bed warm for me. ♥
Sosie

The text she sent earlier still sits without a follow-up, not even to my reply. But maybe I've interpreted the words to mean something they don't. I read it again, not able to see it as anything but a quick popover to the house and return for us to get some food to stuff ourselves with until we digest and have sex again. Did I read too much into it? I might have, especially that ending.

I feel stupid even seeing my naive reply, much less reading it. *Can't wait to see you. I'll be waiting.* Not because it's untrue. Waiting is all I've fucking done today. Setting my laptop on the coffee table, I rest my arms on my legs and look out the window at the darkness of night invading not only my apartment but also my thoughts. I feel like an idiot. Maybe it's not the texts that I misinterpreted. *Maybe it's her.*

Maybe she realized she doesn't want to slum it over here.

Maybe she's gotten caught up in the fanfare of whatever rich people do on the holidays.

Maybe I was nothing but a fun time, and now that that's been had, she's gone.

Fuck!

With my hands scraping through my hair, I get up and start pacing. But five steps in any direction, four if I stretch my legs, isn't satisfying enough to take the edge off my frustration. To the bathroom and back again. From the kitchen to the living room. My feet stop. My eyes fixed on what's in front of me, what's been right there the entire fucking day. Sosie's phone.

Shit. No wonder I haven't heard from her.

I grab it from the TV stand and read my text displayed on the screen when it lights up. With little battery left, I plug it into my charger on the bookcase where I charge mine. That's when the sparkle of her jewelry catches my eye. The earrings hang like ornaments, evoking the first smile since I discovered she left. I touch one earring and then tap the other to watch it swing. But it's the necklace wrapped around the top that has me realizing I was overreacting. She wouldn't have gone to so much effort if she wasn't planning on returning. Sure, she probably bought it off the street corner, but she seemed to like it enough to wear.

Besides the jewelry, she wouldn't leave her phone here if she weren't planning on returning. *Right?* I don't care how much money someone has. Everyone is attached to their phone.

I drop back on the couch in another attempt to focus on this project. It's not due for another two months, but it's not something I'll be able to accomplish overnight. The expectation that I'll convert the internship I had last summer into a career in finance now, and how I'll contribute to growth in that sector, keeps me up at night. I want to be writing, but writing papers wasn't the goal. Graduating is, though, so I pull my computer back to my lap and focus on where I left off.

But my mind isn't on Wall Street. It's on a girl dancing in the snow at the corner of Greene Street and Grand. *Okay, Keats, focus.* For real.

I work on finishing the paragraph where I had left off earlier, once I get words on the page. I get into the flow, notating my observations and contributions that lead to a 3 percent improvement in how the software recommends services to new clients.

My heart's not in it.

Stopping again, I pinch the bridge of my nose, trying to figure out what the actual distraction is for me. Sure, I can place the blame at Sosie's feet, but that's not fair. She doesn't owe me anything. No one else ever has.

I grab my phone and shoot off a text to my professor:

> The studies I cited are from my own research. I can back up my findings and support my—

My phone rings.

My head jerks on my neck, and I answer, "Hello?"

"I don't know if you celebrate the holidays, Mr. Matthews, but I do," Professor Johns starts. "With my family. So, as much as I appreciate the time you're taking to work on your project, this isn't something I'll work on today. Three texts in two hours tells me you might need to take a break as well."

"I'd rather not." I shouldn't be curt with him when he has every right to call me out.

He sighs. "Seems you're not going to give up, so would you like to join my family for dinner? It's not elaborate, but we have plenty to set another plate, and we can discuss your paper afterward."

I realize what I've just done. Dragging this man away from his family to deal with my incessant questions makes me a real asshole. "No, I can't, but I appreciate it."

There's a pause, and then he asks, "Do you have family to spend the holiday with, Keats?"

Now I'm the one hesitating. Not wanting to make a big deal out of it, I reply, "Yeah, I'm supposed to see my mom tonight."

"Good. I need to get back, but cite your studies, and as long as the information is supported in the attached papers, you're good. Enjoy your holiday, Mr. Matthews."

"Thanks. You, too." I'm not sure whether I was lying or being honest about spending time with my family, but I can turn that lie into the truth by deciding to visit my mom. With other issues more pressing, I glance at Sosie's phone on the bookcase, then at the tree she decorated with a part of herself. This is stupid. She's a girl. Why the fuck am I pining like I fell in love? This paper matters more than a good time that obviously won't turn into anything more. My full attention should be on my capstone project. I'm just surprised I allowed my brain to detour so badly. Last night was fun, great even, but why am I risking my goals on a one-night stand?

I haven't eaten more than a few cheese cubes and some salami from the board she left behind, which means I'm not thinking clearly. Since my assumption of waiting until her return for us to eat together was way off base, I need to get food in my stomach and Sosie off my mind, or I'll never get this section of the paper done as I planned today.

Grabbing my winter boots from the closet, I stick my feet in and wrap up for trekking outside.

I tuck my phone in one pocket. Sosie probably needs her phone like I need mine. I'm not convinced that she would leave it on purpose, especially since she texted me. I should return it, even if she intends to come over later. *Wishful thinking again . . .*

Crossing the room to retrieve her phone, I swipe it up, noticing the empty space under the tree where presents should be. I should have bought my own damn self a present. But bills are more important than unwrapping something I'd be buying to convince myself that someone cared.

When there's no one left, it falls on my shoulders like it always has. I can be bitter about life or accept that this is how it is. No matter what happened in my childhood, I'm only who I am because of the life I've lived. So, be better than what's expected. Focus on the person I want to be. That's why I'm doing this—the jobs, the school, the life I'm struggling through. The outcome will outweigh the pain along the way.

And yeah, I need to see my mom. It doesn't have to be a big deal. Pop by to say hi and do a quick check-in. It will mean a lot to her, but it seems my soul is empty and needs filling. Maybe she can help with that.

Looking around the room, I don't find anything I can take from here that would fill in for a gift. Is a visit enough if I show up empty-handed? It will have to do unless I can find a shop open on the way to her place.

I hit the streets, surprised to see anyone out today, though there aren't many. I like the solace of the darkness and winter. The holiday keeps the hordes off the streets, giving me plenty of room in my mind to wander without bumping into reality.

Dipping into a corner shop, I pull a small bouquet of pink flowers, my mom's favorite color, from a bucket at the entry. I then wander down the two aisles to see if there's anything else I can take her. I don't see anything until I approach the counter where a box of holiday chocolates is waiting to be purchased as a last-minute gift. They found their sucker to buy it.

"The flowers and the candy?" the man behind the counter asks.

I glance behind him at the acrylic boxes on display, and reply, "Two tickets, and . . ." I didn't crave nicotine when I was with Sosie last night. Trading one bad habit for another? Probably. I chuckle under my breath as I reach for my wallet, knowing I came out ahead in that deal. Maybe not today since waiting around was a bunch of bullshit, but last night was fucking fantastic. I'd do it again if I had the opportunity. "A pack of the smokes on sale and this lighter."

Lighting up as soon as I step onto the sidewalk, I stop to appreciate the instant calm the first inhale brings. I exhale slowly with a dip of my lids closing to extend the pleasure before heading toward the nearest station and catching the subway.

There are plenty of seats tonight, so I lean up against the corner of the train. Nobody makes eye contact, but after a sweep of my surroundings, I stare at the flowers. I don't know what I'm going to say to my mom and don't want to rehearse anything. It's my mom. Even if she didn't always know how to tell me or show me, I know she loves me. This doesn't need to be a big deal. I'll go, give her a hug, and then head on out to Sosie's.

But is visiting my mom killing time before going to Sosie's, or is it genuine? I want to see my mom again, and an inkling of hope that this time will be different still exists deep inside me.

And since trepidation has been squeezing my chest, volleying me between fear that last night is all I'll get and the agitation that I want more and that might not happen, this will give me time to work through it. So yeah, I give myself a break as I walk into the unknown of two different situations, relying on hope in both cases.

A few blocks from where I exit, I pull on the door that opens because the maintenance man still hasn't fixed it since my last visit six months ago on my mom's birthday. The entrance is dark, and when standing here, I can hear fighting on the other side of apartment one's front door. I walk down the hall to the back of the building and stand just behind the stairs to take a breath before knocking on the door that's hidden there.

I hear a man's voice before the door opens. A boyfriend that I didn't even know would still be around peers through the crack over the rusted chain. The door closes before muffled words are exchanged. I hear my name, and then the chain is released. When the door opens again, it swings open like no one was ever on the other side. The invitation rings hollow as I'm left to decide whether to go inside or stay where I'm at.

Stepping forward, a football game is on loudly in the small living room off to the left, but John's hearing wasn't good, from what I remember. The scent of something cooking hits my nostrils, stirring my hunger, and has me wondering why I wasn't invited over. Does my mom not realize that I'm sitting alone on the holidays because I didn't feel I had a home outside the one I had to create on my own?

Do I give her the benefit of the doubt that she isn't aware that I'm working sixty hours plus on school breaks to make ends meet? Christmas dinner was the last thing I had time to plan, much less go shopping for, with the schedule I've been working. Hoping for scraps left over from rich people's parties was a fucking highlight of a shift. So to stand outside my mom's apartment knowing she's cooking dinner for a guy she's dating over her own fucking son leaves me feeling as empty as Sosie has all day.

I set the flowers and the candy on the pilling red rug in front of her door and walk away. I was stupid for coming here in the first place. If she really wanted to see me, she would have made the effort or invited me to dinner. Instead, she sent me a guilt text earlier in the week saying she never gets to see me and a lame Merry Christmas today.

That's fucking it.

I push through the main door, landing back with my boots in the slush that's gathered at the stoop. Shoving my hands in my pockets, I start walking. I knew this was a mistake. My gut told me not to come. Not alone anyway.

What was I thinking?

I was thinking I might have an ally at my side if Sosie had stayed. But would I have really wanted to expose someone like her to the life I'm trying to escape? No.

She was wise not to return. Otherwise, taking her would have been the second major mistake I would have made. I just round the corner when I hear my mom call, "Keats?" And then I hear nothing on the quiet street I've turned onto and take a deep breath.

"I'm so stupid," I utter, the air fogging in front of my face as I lower my head, trying to reckon with my bad mood. My reality is that some old wounds just aren't meant to heal. I don't know why I keep thinking they will.

I should take my bad mood home, but I came out for a reason. Visiting my mom was the detour I shouldn't have taken. There's no turning back. I've always been too determined for my own good. Despite my gut telling me this might not be a good idea, it's all-or-nothing. I'll put my heart on the line in hopes she wants to see her Poet because the only thing that feels right is seeing my Spark again.

CHAPTER 11

KEATS

My pace is steady until I'm close to the Stansbury mansion. One block up, the lamppost where I almost got arrested comes into view. I laugh and walk faster. Hope isn't something that I've felt much lately, but it's ballooning in my chest like it lives there. I'm already envisioning my Spark bounding out of the house, wrapping her arms around me and kissing me like we were always meant to be.

It's not been a great day, but she'll be the highlight. I charge ahead, not able to wait any longer to hold her in my arms again. I stop just shy of the light from the lamp hitting my feet. "Breathe, Keats." I laugh. I'm acting like a fifteen-year-old going on his first date. But when I give myself more than a second to think clearly, I'm not surprised. Not only did I not see this girl coming, barging into my life like it's hers for the taking, but she already has me wrapped around her finger.

I was never impressed by wealth or the people who

hoard it before, but she was right last night. She's nothing like them. I suck in a breath and close my eyes, seeing the way Sosie's eyes crinkle in the corner when she smiles. She showed me who she was from the minute we met. From her lips to those eyes, the way she moves within her body, her wit, and her smile . . . damn, she's spectacular.

What am I doing wasting time out here when I can be with her again? I square my shoulders and walk past the lamppost, ignoring my breath fogging in front of my face and charge forth.

The large gate in front of me doesn't feel as imposing when I realize my heart rests on the other side of it. I glance up at her window in the upper left corner and grin. I'd climb that trellis like a fool in a romance novel if she asked me to, especially if the reward was a kiss. I'm not a greedy man, but I can't wait to taste her lips again.

I push the buzzer, too anxious to hear her voice. It's also as cold as the North Pole out here. Warming up in each other sounds like paradise right now.

There's no response, which is strange. I would have imagined an entire team of employees on standby at the Stansburys' every beck and call. It's not late, just past eight, but I find myself checking the time on my phone again to confirm it. I'm good. I hold down the buzzer longer this time. When I release it, I shove my hand back in my coat pocket, a case of nerves sneaking in to ruin the reunion as I run my fingers over her phone.

"How can I help you?" The man's monotonous tone has me thinking he'd rather be doing anything other than answering my call. But I'm too determined to see my girl to let it sidetrack my mission.

"Hi," I reply, staring at the intercom like a video of Sosie will suddenly pop up. Although there are no screens for me to see her pretty face, I'm confident there are cameras on me. As soon as I spot one on the corner of the house, I straighten my posture and raise my chin to look the part of someone worthy enough to date the Stansburys' daughter. "I'm here to see Sosie." I clear my throat. "Sosie Stansbury."

"She's not available."

The response is so quick, I wasn't prepared for it. "Oh. Um . . ." I glance at her window again. The light is on in her bedroom. This time, I study it more intently. Light escapes the edges of the curtains as if someone is in there. Am I imagining things, or was that on before? I return my glare to the intercom, wondering if this guy is lying to me to cover for Sosie. No, she'd tell me to my face if she didn't want to see me. I grin, liking how straightforward she is with her wants and needs. *So fucking sexy.*

But does that mean this guy is taking it on himself to keep me from seeing her? Not going to happen. "When will she be available?"

"No comment."

I laugh, taken aback by the change in his tone from indifferent to brusque. "No comment? I'm not the paparazzi. I went on a date with her, for fuck's sake." Fuck. I shouldn't have sworn. That's not going to get me anywhere with a family like hers. "Listen, I just want to talk to her—"

"If she wants to contact you, she will."

The intercom goes silent—no further exchange, no feedback. Only silence exists between me and this damn house. I push the button and lean in closer. "Can I leave a message for her?"

"I think it's best if you return another time *after* you've received an invitation to be on the property." And here I was stupidly thinking the intercom might not be working properly. It's working, and this guy seems to be doing overtime by standing between my Spark and me.

I glance down at my feet, and reply, "I'm not on the property. I'm on a public sidewalk." Don't play into this farce. They know I'm not trespassing. But why is this becoming a bigger thing than it should be? This blockade feels personal when I'm just here to see Sosie. If she knew I was here, I know she'd come running out, even pirouetting down the steps until she was in my arms again. The connection we share is too deep for her to sacrifice her phone and jewelry. If a commonplace schmuck like myself feels it, I know someone who expresses every emotion that captures her heart feels it, too.

"It's best if you leave, so I don't need to call security."

What the fuck is going on? I take a step back and study the gate as if I'm going to somehow get through it to reach Sosie and explain what's happening outside her house. But I'm not going to climb it and break in, so I'm not left with many options. I lean in again, and reply, "I think there's been a misunderstanding. I have her phone." Guess I should have led with this information. "She left it with me, but I'm sure she'd like it back."

I expect to hear the lock unlatching, but as I stand there, music from a passing car is all that is heard. The intercom's feedback startles me, and I smile. Finally. I prepare to push the gate open, but instead, the man says, "Please stay there." See? He's doing his job. He can't let just anyone in off the street.

I lick my lips and stare at the front door with a ridiculous smile on my face. I clamp my lips together and twist my grin to the side. Games are the last thing I want to play with her, but looking like an idiot in love might scare her away.

A few minutes pass, so I start shuffling my feet to stay warm. I notice nerves creeping in again, this time leaning toward the negative, compared to how excited I was earlier. It's a big mansion. I'm sure it takes time to traverse it to find her and then for her to come down to meet me.

When I glance up at her window, I see a shadow moving across the cracks of the curtains as if the person inside is pacing. It's her room. Logically, that should be her, but why would she still be in her room when she knows I'm out here?

I don't sweat much, assured in the choices I make, going after what I want, and determined to make things work in my favor. I'm not feeling that same confidence right now. Did I read her cues all wrong? A few more minutes have passed, so I press the intercom button again. "Excuse me?"

This time, no one answers. The front door opens instead, and her father fills the framework. *Shit.* He stands on the top step, glaring at me as if I've interrupted his good mood. Watching him pull on each of his leather gloves in an excruciatingly measured gesture suggests that intimidation might be his MO in this situation. Unoriginal, but not entirely unexpected. What kind of father would let just anyone take his daughter out? But once he gets to know me, I'm sure it'll all work out.

He grabs the lapels of his suit jacket, tugging them together to keep the cold out, as he descends the steps. "How may I help you, Mr. Matthews?"

Mr. Matthews? Of course, he knows my name. Rubbing a gloved hand against the back of my neck, I stand taller, and figure if we can share niceties, it will make seeing Sosie more regularly a lot easier. I hold the phone in the air in surrender. No need to go to war with the father of the woman I can't stop thinking about. "I came to return Sosie's phone."

"You stole her phone?" he accuses, stopping on the other side of the towering wrought-iron gate.

The allegation stings, and I lower my arm to my side again. "No." I steady my breath and even my tone even though the anger has managed to slice through my calmer demeanor. "She left it with me, so I'm delivering it to her."

"Why would she leave it with you?" His eyes narrow, examining mine as if he'll find lies hidden in there.

"She left it behind," I reply, telling the truth. Do I want to go into the details of where and why? Not really. And I'm certain her dad doesn't want to hear about the night his daughter and I shared. "I'm sure it was an accident."

He's tall, almost matching my height. Distrust filters through his expression. I'm sure it's a trait that's helped him get to where he is in business today. He must be shrewd and have some talent for getting his way since he's on one side of this fence, and I'm on the other. His hair is graying, but he still has a full head of lighter brown fighting to hold on. The lines in his face aren't deep. I'm sure he could pass for younger if he wanted to. Apparently, it works quite well on other women, according to Sosie's understanding.

"Give me the phone, Mr. Matthews." He holds his hand out as if I'm supposed to give away my only lifeline to his daughter.

I refuse to cower to his attempt at strong-arming me with demands. I'm not scared of this guy. He's got nothing on me, but I worry about Sosie and how an encounter gone sour could fuck things up for the two of us. I tuck her phone back into my pocket, and ask, "Is Sosie here? I'd like to personally give it to her."

"That's not a good idea," he says with his hand still held out. "I'll take it."

I stare at him through the opening between two large iron bars. Something's off and raising red flags too fast for me to grab my armor. "We've never met, so how do you know my name?"

"I make sure to know who's invading my peace and threatening my family." What the hell? What does that mean? I shake my head as confusion rattles my game plan. His words don't just smack of arrogance; they're meant as a warning. *A warning to me or for me?*

"Sir . . ." I take a breath to compose myself from glaring at him. His antagonism is winning, and I can't let him. "I'm not a threat to your family, Mr. Stansbury." I catch a shift of light in the upper left window in my periphery, and it pulls my attention in that direction. The curtains sway like someone was watching, and now they're hiding from sight.

Dread sets in. Have I been fooled? Played by Sosie? No. She wouldn't do that. I may not know her well, but I know her well enough to know she didn't only reveal her body to me last night. She revealed her soul. That look in her eyes when I was inside her showed me we were something more than one night.

The pounding of my heart reaches my ears as it begins to feel like the opportunity to see her is slipping through my fingers. I take a step closer and lower my voice. "I come with good intentions." I keep the desperation out of my tone, but it's racing in my veins, trying to hold on to anything that keeps me connected to the best night of my life. This can't be all there is for us. *No.*

His silence is unsettling, the empty palm still waiting to be filled. I shift, my gaze volleying twice between the window and the man standing in front of me. "If she's home," I say, my words staggering. "I'd, um, like to speak with her."

Shoving his hand through an opening in the gate, he demands, "Give. Me. The phone." The words are as cold as the weather, leaving no room for misunderstanding. Warming up to the guy isn't an option. He's closed off that opportunity.

My hands fist, but I keep them at my sides. "Please, Mr. Stansbury—"

"I'm going to call the police if you don't give me the phone." Silence burrows between us as we stare at each other.

One. Two. Three. Four. Five. He doesn't blink, but I do in hopes of appealing to his humanity, if there is any. "Your daughter means a lot to me—"

"Don't talk about my daughter. Don't contact her. Don't come to my home. Do you understand, Mr. Matthews? If you so much as look in her direction, I'll destroy you. NYU will be a failed memory. Your scholarships will be wiped from your accounts. That mother of yours—"

"I'm not a threat to you or your family, Mr. Stansbury. With all due respect, I care about your daughter—"

"You don't *know* my daughter. You might think you care, but Sosie is careless. You're just another guy she spent time with to piss me off." The sharp blade of his words pierces my heart. "She loves to play these games, and you fell for it. I feel sorry for you, Mr. Matthews . . ." Sorry for me? He feels bad for me, looking down from the marble pedestal that he's built on the backs of others like me?

Fuck that. I slam my hand against the gate, rattling it. "Fuck you."

"Temper. Temper, Mr. Matthews," he says, under a stilted chuckle. "We're filming you."

"Film me all you want. I'm not doing anything wrong. I'm here because—"

"You came here to return her phone. So return it and go."

Hope bleeds from my chest as I finally realize who I'm dealing with—the rich, the powerful, the elite of this city. I have no weapons left to fight this battle. Maybe he's right, and I did foolishly fall for his daughter. Maybe I'm just another guy who fell for Sosie, though that connection still feels damn real to me. With nothing to say that will change the trajectory of this conversation, I reason through why it's wise to turn the phone over to him. But my heart just can't seem to get on board with that decision.

"What do you want?" he asks. "Money?" He digs into the interior pocket of his jacket and pulls out his wallet. Too stunned by the insult, I scoff. "I'll give you a reward for returning it."

I stare at the hundred-dollar bill he's holding through the slats and then drag my gaze back to his. Disappointment, even shame, and a lot of frustration still flurries in my veins, but I keep my voice calm. "I don't want your money. I want—"

"I don't care what you want, you little bastard!" he shouts. "You think I'd let my daughter date someone like you? You are sorely mistaken, so give me the damn phone. Now."

I grab the gate with my full strength, pulling myself mere inches from his face. "Don't you ever fucking demean me," I warn through gritted teeth. "I've worked too fucking hard to get where I am."

"You haven't paid for a thing," he says as if he has me all figured out. He doesn't know jack shit about me. I'm still paying for the turbulent choices of my parents.

Tugging it like I can loosen the hinges, toss it aside, and rush the door to find Sosie crowd my thoughts. "You think you're better than me. You're not. This fortress gives you a false sense of security. These bars might keep me and my kind out, but your daughter will find her way back to me despite what you want."

His head jerks on his neck before he growls, "Watch yourself, son."

"Don't threaten me." I tighten my grip to keep myself from barging my way through this gate. "Sosie—"

"Sosie," he yells before taking a breath. The sides of his mouth pull upward as he nods like the final nail was hammered into my coffin. He did win this round. He fucking got what he wanted—a reaction to use as ammunition against me. "You overestimate my daughter. Sosie will do as she's told like she's doing right now by staying in her room."

My gaze flicks to the window again, and I swear I catch a flash of her before the curtain falls back in place. I stop, struggling to keep my heart from dropping to the pit of my stomach. I look back at him, releasing my fists from around the iron as defeat sinks in.

My gut told me she was near. I could feel her presence stretching the lengths between us. I can't look at him. Seeing the victory in his eyes will reveal a side of myself I don't want to let loose. I drop my head as truth conquers the last shred of hope I held for us and hand him the phone.

"I suggest you move on with your life," he says, his voice too calm, too the opposite of the tornado I'm feeling inside. "Find someone else to entertain you because it's not going to be a Stansbury." He turns, giving me a cold shoulder as he walks away, but when he reaches the first step, he glances back. "Good night, Mr. Matthews." Such a simple pleasantry after dealing the final blow to protect what he claims is his.

She's not.

She was mine last night, and I have no doubt she will be again.

My heart thumps against my rib cage as panic rises. "No." No good night. No goodbye. Hours aren't enough. I need days, months, and years. I need to see her. There's no good without a Spark in it.

If she wants me gone, she needs to tell me herself. I need her to look me in the eyes and tell me last night meant nothing. She won't be able to, just like I can't.

No love is lost when I shout to his back. "That's it?" With my hands thrown out from my sides. "Fucking coward." The door slams shut behind him. I grumble, "Had to threaten me to get me out of her life. Asshole."

Stepping back feels like stumbling into an abyss. I don't know when I fell for this girl, but I'm drowning in the deep end. I walk down the block, my feet as numb as that fucking organ in my chest where only echoes of heartbeats are heard. Grabbing hold of the fence in front of her window, I yell, "Sosie?"

It's a bad movie gesture, a last desperate attempt at making a difference. For her? For me? No, for us. I know it. Does she?

When the curtains don't move, I silently wish to see her sneaking a peek again, but she doesn't. There's only a shadow that drifts from one side to the other. It makes me sick to give up, but she's there and not coming to save me.

"Hey?" Anger takes over as it rages in that hollow cavern of mine, needing her to acknowledge I exist. I exist in her world as much as mine. "It's me. Sosie? Come on. We're not just one night. You know that." Can she hear me?

The anger starts to resolve as I try to appeal to what we have, what we share—that connection that keeps me standing here in the freezing cold. "We're bigger than this, babe. We're meant for more." Throwing my hands on the top of my head, I step back but keep my eyes locked on that upstairs window. "Don't let the world decide who you are. Not your dad. Not anyone. Sosie, please."

I stand in one place, hoping for anything she'll give me. "Hey, Spark?" I laugh without an ounce of humor. "One sign. That's all I need, and I'll keep fighting for you. I'll fight for another night and do it all over again tomorrow." The shadow disappears, and hope fills my chest at the same time as the cold of our unfinished business seeps in. Lowering my head, I close my eyes and whisper, "One sign. Please." I look up, letting my shoulders fall and my guard down, open for what comes next. I'm not the praying type, but I pray her heart hears mine. "That's all I'm asking for. One more chance."

Four months later . . .

"Keats Matthews. Bachelor of Science with a focus in finance."

I walk across the stage, shaking hands with the dean of the department. I also shake Professor Johns's hand since he'd suffered through all my texts over the past year. He's stayed firmly in my corner since day one. I hope I've made him proud. He grins, and when we shake hands, he pats my arm. "Well-earned, Keats."

"Thanks." I take my diploma to the other side of the stage and stop for the university photographer. This is the only photo I'll have from my graduation since no one showed up to take one. Who else is there anyway? My mom? I never expected her to show even though I had hand-delivered an invitation.

When I return to walk down the long aisle to my seat, I look up at the theater filled with family and friends of the graduates. I glance to the right, and my eyes lock with the one person who doesn't feel real all these months later. It was only one night, and I'll never forget it. Neither will my heart because she took it with her.

I stop dead in my tracks but mistakenly blink, and the dream is over.

CHAPTER 12
TWO YEARS LATER

SOSIE

The air is on the warmer side this cloud-free March day. I tilt my face toward the sun to soak in the rays before I check the time. "Shoot."

I should catch a cab or call a rideshare, but after being cooped up all day in class and then trapped at the internship I need for graduation in two months, I want to stretch my legs and enjoy the fresh air. Kids run by, causing me to jump out of the way to avoid a game of tag that's taking up most of the sidewalk. Resettling the strap of my schoolbag, I roll my eyes when an older woman yells at them for causing an unnecessary ruckus in her life.

Seems kids having a good time is just the sort of uproar she needs to shake that cranky mood of hers.

I reach for my phone to capture the lines of her face, her mouth open and shouting, and the kids, with the opposite reaction, still laughing. People's expressions as they react to life were always my favorite subjects to photograph, though I'm still partial to landscapes as well. The lonelier moments that make everyday places feel more desolate. I stop myself, pulling my hand from the pocket of my bag, and grab the bag's strap to keep temptation at bay. I was supposed to get photography out of my system during my sabbatical, but some habits die harder than others.

Tucking my hair behind my ear, I aim my gaze at the ground and start walking. The ends of my hair drift over my shoulder. I'm still not used to it even though I've been growing it out for so long. I miss the ease of my shorter hair, and the lightness that it made me feel inside as well. Exhaling a long breath, I know it doesn't matter what I want when it always comes down to appearances.

I'd almost forgotten the time again. I rush over a block and gallop down the steps to the station. The echoes of people talking, even the faint sound of a guitar being played, greet me when I'm underground. I hold my phone over the sensor and then push through the stall. Looking left, I spot the train. *My train!* I run just as the doors start to close, hoping someone else just ahead of me blocks the doors from closing.

No luck, but I'm not giving up. I run so fast that I slam my hands against the windows to stop myself from crashing into the closed doors entirely. "No. Ugh." I step back. But then slam my hands against the windows again when I see the man sitting on the other side with his eyes glued to the open book in his hands. "Keats?" I yell, banging again. "Keats?"

The train shifts forward, forcing me to back up. "Keats?" My voice is drowned out as the train speeds off, sending my hair into a flurry around my face.

My heart pounds in my chest.

Breathing becomes harder.

Tears flood the corners of my eyes.

And a friggin' guitarist strolls behind me singing Mazzy Star like he's auditioning for *American Idol.* I push my hair from my face and wipe under my eyes before raising my chin into the air. I shuffle to the tiled wall to lean against it, trying to catch my breath and talk myself out of whatever I think I saw. I didn't, *did I?*

How do you run into someone randomly like that in a city that has a billion people always roaming around? Where am I that this could even happen? I tilt my head to glance down one direction, then the other, and see Fulton Station listed. I'm never at this station. Is he?

My heart regulates, and my breathing evens as I lean my head against the wall, wondering if I'll ever see him again. I look down the tracks where the train disappeared, regret flooding my system. There's not just remorse but also pain. One night with him wasn't enough.

It was only a glimpse, but seeing him again reminds me of the sacrifices I've made to please people who never deserved my obedience. I used to think it was about the money I'd need to survive, but that doesn't seem to be much of a factor anymore. What did it bring? Not happiness.

Even I know that gave me something to fall back on. But at what cost? Glancing once more down the tunnel where the train disappeared, I know the cost. *Keats.* The best night of my life has become a painful memory. That is when I allow myself to think about it, which isn't often and usually forced by something that triggers it, like passing through a cloud of smoke before it dissipates or the cork of a champagne bottle being popped.

I don't eat ramen or visit Joy's restaurant anymore.

My dad's apartment has been a no-go zone since Keats and I last went there.

But it's the time that I walked in on a poetry reading that had me turning around and leaving. I never even got to read my Poet's work. I bet he was an amazing writer. Hopefully, he still is. Though he stuck to his plan and got his finance degree. I had to clamp my hand over my mouth to keep from screaming in excitement when he crossed that graduation stage. I've never felt prouder, as if that was my right even though I only had less than twenty-four hours with him.

My feelings for that man developed fast and furious. I should have known I was doomed to fall for him the minute I saw him sweep his hair out of his eyes when he was focused on his phone. That playboy hair with the soft wave that ran through it so casually that I know he didn't style it. He just knew how to wear it like that attitude of his—a little feral and equally calming. I'd never met anyone like him before. *He was who he was.*

No pretenses.

No forced expressions.

No small talk that didn't feel like it was meant for more.

The arrival of the next train pulls me out of memory lane. I press a fingertip to the inside corner of my eye to keep the tear from falling. "Don't be silly, Sosie."

The doors open, and I sit in the same seat I saw him in on the other train. Instead of distracting myself with my phone, I stare out the window and exhale, unable to organize the messy state that meeting him has left me in. I shouldn't still care about him, but I can't help myself.

He looked good and is probably happy. I'd be shocked if he hasn't had some other girl fall madly in love with him.

Lucky girl.

I don't have any claim to jealousy regarding him, though I feel it, but I do still have a hole in my chest that he temporarily filled. I once read it's better to have loved and lost than to never have loved at all. I'm not so sure I agree with Lord Tennyson anymore.

More than two years later, the pain of losing Keats hasn't dampened. It's only morphed into something else—loneliness, discontentment . . . I don't even know. I still struggle to find one word that encapsulates the emotion of having the universe open its arms, only to have a door slammed in your face the next day. The high of the hope and the low of the loss.

"Sorry I'm late." I drop my leather messenger bag onto the wooden bench and slide into the booth across from my friend.

"It's okay," Marcy says, looping her fingers around the stem of her martini glass. "Hope you don't mind. I already ordered a cosmo."

I smile as my friend, who's become a bigger part of my life over the past year, sips the pink drink. We hit it off in our Classical English Literature 3 class last spring and now have a standing date every Wednesday at a different restaurant. She's been the addition to my life that I needed. She's not in my family's social circle or looking for a bad boy, which used to be my tendency to spite my parents. She's started making me see people in a new way, steering my views away from the extremes. It's not one or the other anymore. It just is. I've found comfort lolling through the middle of the two. Maybe I'm a little numb as well, but that beats the heartbreak I barely survived two years prior.

"How very *Sex and the City* of you." My phone buzzes, and I reach down to see who's texting. "Gregory." I don't mean to say it with such disdain, but he's just always around—my house with his parents, at large dinners out, even the events we attend. It's annoying, though he's not. He's sweet. I wish I could summon an attraction to him, but it's just not meant to be. I read the text without swiping on it:

> My parents are hosting a party in the Hamptons next weekend for my birthday. I'm hoping I'll see you there. What do you say?

What I'd like to say is "I have no choice," but since I can't, I reply:

> I'll be there.

"I don't know how you resist that man," she says. Again. This happens anytime he's mentioned. "He's tall, gorgeous . . ." I drop the phone back into my bag, hoping to get away from life for a little bit. "Okay. Okay. I won't go on. Though if you don't want him, you could at least introduce me." She laughs, but I don't, as it finally dawns on me.

"That's actually a great idea. What are you doing next weekend?"

She smirks. "Whatever it is, I'm in."

"I'll send you the details when I have them." Taking a deep breath, I do something I never do. Gossip about my dating life since we're circling the topic. I whisper, "You won't believe what just happened."

I'm not one to open up about certain things—Keats being someone off-limits to even mention although I still keep him burrowed deep in my heart. Am I protecting something so precious that speaking of it will make me realize we were only an illusion? Holding back hasn't helped me recover. Maybe talking about it will.

Her dark brown hair is pulled back in a high ponytail, her eyes looking wider than usual and full of mischief. "What is it? Tell me." She grins like I'm about to hand her the secret code to a happy marriage. I swear she's on the hunt for a man and would major in getting her MRS if she could. She's the perfect audience for this story.

"I saw a guy I . . ." I *what*? Used to like? Hooked up with once? Fell in love with over the course of twelve hours? My brain can't seem to wrap around what Keats *was* or what he *is* to me. What were we together?

"You saw a guy?" She looks around, taking another sip of her cocktail, and then says, "We're in a room full of them. I see lots of guys. Did you notice the cute one in the beige three-quarter zip spinning at the counter stool?"

There's so much wrong with that sentence, from beige to spinning at the counter stool, that I don't even know where to begin. I shake my head. "No, I didn't notice him." I don't bother to look now because I don't want to sidetrack this conversation. I need to get this off my chest so I can start healing from a one-night stand that I can't seem to forget. "I saw a guy on the train that I once dated." I unwrap my silverware and slide the napkin to my lap, keeping my gaze on my fidgeting hands. The admission feels so heavy on my chest that I wonder if I should take a walk outside for fresh air.

I finally look up. Sympathy has dragged the corners of her eyes down along with her mouth. "Did you talk to him?"

"No. I wasn't on the train. The doors closed." I can still feel the pressure of my palms slamming against the glass, the exasperation of being one second too late that washed through me, and then a soothing balm just from being in his vicinity. "He didn't see me. He was reading—"

"He was reading? A book?" I nod, finding it odd that's the only part that stands out to her. "God, that's sexy." Her shoulders fall as she exhales loudly in a swoony sigh. "Sounds like the perfect guy for you, Sos." She smiles without commiseration but with genuine curiosity. "So what happened?"

"The train left the station." I laugh to myself, finally able to breathe as if the confession was keeping me from doing so all along. I also catch the irony in the phrase and laugh again. Resting my elbow on the table, I drop my chin on my fist, finally finding humor in this heartbreak. "That is so fitting for what became of us."

"Going in two different directions?"

"Yeah." I rest back, smiling for some odd reason. "I suppose we were."

The server taps his fingers on the table's edge, and asks, "What can I get you to drink?"

Feeling out of sorts in this new realization, yet comforted by seeing Keats again, I reply, "I'll have what she's having." Glancing at the menu before he rushes away, which is what he seems to be on the verge of doing by how antsy he looks, I add, "And the burrata to start, please."

"Gotcha." He dashes off as I knew he would.

"And another for me," Marcy calls behind him.

He waves like he's got it under control.

Marcy leans back with a gleam in her eyes. Crossing her arms over her chest, she says, "You never order cosmos. What gives?"

I lean back too, mimicking her. "I'm not sure. Maybe it's time to move on and try new things." I hate to admit that it might include letting my Poet go. He didn't look miserable.

He looked good, like life is treating him well. I hope it is. He deserves it.

"Why are we here again, Marcy?"

She laughs, the sound echoing around us on the street. "Shhh." Her finger is pressed to her lips, but then she startles like I had done it. Pointing at me, she sways. "You dragged me here."

"I'm drunk," I state, defiantly poking my chest as if being wasted wasn't obvious. "I'm in no state to be leading anyone anywhere." A finger wag catches my attention until I realize it's mine I've been watching. "Why would you trust me?"

I turn in a circle to find Marcy not looking her best. Her head swivels on her neck, and with her hands planted on her hips, she replies, "Of course, I trusted you. You think I have my shit together? I'm drunk." She looks at the building, then back at me again. "Is it safe here?"

"How would I know? The only time I was here was with a guy who was way bigger than I am." It fascinates me how I can remember hugging myself to his chest, the scent of his cologne coming back, but was he six-two, six-seven, or . . .? He could have been seven feet for all I know. I just remember not worrying about my safety with him. I was protected and felt it.

I look down the street one way and then the other, not feeling so secure in this idea of coming here at night with another girl who's just as drunk as I am.

"Well, we're here." Throwing her hand in the direction of the building, she says, "You came to see if he was here, so you need to follow through, or the eighty-three dollars for the ride over was for nothing."

I'm still surprised I even found the place. We circled three blocks in the area before I recognized the building. "Okay." I reach into my bag and pull out my lip gloss to put on as I study the entrance. I look at Marcy, hoping she'll save me.

She doesn't, and says, "Good luck."

"Yeah, thanks." I head toward the steps, clearly leaving my better judgment at the restaurant where this plan got concocted over a fourth round of cosmos and not enough food in our stomachs. I pause on the bottom step because this doesn't feel like a great idea anymore. What will I do if I see him? What will I say? Oh hey, I saw you on the train today and was wondering if you have any good books to recommend?

God, this is the worst idea ever.

I take a step up, then the next three, before jiggling the handle to see if it's open. It's not. Staring at the locked door, I say, "Now what?"

"Buzz him to let you in to confess your undying love for him."

I swore that tonight was a fresh start, and Keats would no longer be a part of my daily thoughts. I'd kick him out of my chest, where the memory of us thrives, and try to find someone else to fill his spot in my heart. Impossible.

We are still unfinished business. Until it's resolved, there's no moving on.

I tug on the door. It releases and sends me back a step. My gaze whips back to Marcy, who jumps up and down in a silent cheer. She stops to sweep me inside with the back of her hands. I can't believe I'm doing this, but I enter the small lobby and am confronted by the stairs that will lead me back to him.

The door slams behind me, causing me not to just jump but to start the trek up the four flights to his door. I don't know what I'll say. There's just this urgency I feel building from a need inside me.

I reach the landing and notice a doormat with a black cat design that reads wipe your paws. Keats never came off as a cat kind of person, but is that something I'd have known in the short time we were together? No . . . maybe? I don't know. How would I know this information? He didn't have one back then.

I knock before I lose my nerve. Straightening my back, I raise my chin, hoping I don't look drunk. The sound of feet coming is heard just before the locks are unlatched and the door is opened.

I blink. And then again.

The woman is shorter than I am by just a little. Her hair is longer, and her eyes are a darker brown. She's pretty. Very pretty. I feel sick . . .

"Can I help you?" She glances over my shoulder toward the stairs like she expects someone else. "Do you have the food?"

"Food?"

She tilts her head, and her brows pinch together. "Do you have my order, or are you some psychopath knocking on my door?"

"Oh, um . . ." I catch a glimpse of the couch that Keats once folded out and the bookcase in the corner. The Christmas tree is gone, the books are more organized, and the rug is pink, but it's mostly the same otherwise. I back away, my butt hitting the stair railing. "I have the wrong apartment." Tears flood my eyes as I realize that could have been me. Cozy and cuddling in his arms every night could have been my life.

I never needed the life I have, but I wanted a life with him.

"Who are you looking for?" she asks as concern crinkles the corners of her eyes. Unsurprisingly, this makes her even more beautiful. *Figures.*

"No one. I'm sorry. Wrong apartment."

"Babe?" A man's voice sends me running down the staircase as soon as she turns away. My feet are moving so fast that my body struggles to keep up. My thoughts are spinning, and as soon as I push through the door, I stumble onto the sidewalk where my heart shatters all over again.

"Sosie?" Marcy runs to me.

Bent over, resting my hands on my legs, I can't breathe. My tears fall from my eyes like traitors hell-bent on revealing my weakness. Him. It will always be him.

Wrapping her arms around me, she pulls me to her. "Oh Sos, I'm so sorry."

It takes a minute for my eyes and mind to clear, and when it does, I take a deep breath. "We should get out of here," she says, hooking her arm with mine and pulling me away. "This was not my best idea."

Just out of the spotlight of the building, I stop in the shadows and look back. "It's okay. This was the closure I needed."

CHAPTER 13
TWO YEARS LATER

KEATS

It's been a long time since I've been to a black-tie affair, and this is the first one I've agreed to attend where I wasn't serving others. "No, thank you," I say to a server as she passes hors d'oeuvres through the crowd on a silver platter.

Admittedly, I would be more comfortable carrying a tray than mingling with strangers I've been sent to charm my way into connecting with, also known as networking. I've found success on a more personal level with my clients. I've made more money than I ever thought I could, and I was a big fucking dreamer. In four years, I've had a handful of promotions, earning me a title that sits under the president of the finance department. I didn't have to fuck anyone over. I didn't have to step on coworkers to get to the top. I kept my head down and focused on the clients, meeting them where they are in their businesses. From Kickstarters to established firms, I shook hands in their office, at coffee shops, and at small dinner parties.

Standing in the middle of this crowd, I adjust my silk bow tie and wish I had stuck with the black tie I originally chose to wear with this tuxedo. I don't feel like myself.

Taking a drink of champagne even feels pretentious. I work my way to the bar. It's tempting to order a beer or even a whiskey neat, but I'm supposed to be blending in, so I go with a bourbon, as if that makes a difference.

As soon as I take a sip, my shoulder is squeezed, and from behind me, someone says, "Here's the star I was talking about." I instantly recognized my boss's voice. I hadn't seen Mr. Young even though he insisted I come to this event at the Plaza when I could have been at home wrapping up edits on the manuscript I just finished. With the goal of sending it off to agents on Monday, I would rather be working on it than making appearances at over-the-top parties.

Wealth is seen in every detail, from the crystal chandeliers to the scale of this event and the guest list. *Money. Money. Money.*

I turn to look behind me, already grinning. Mr. Young has treated me well at the company. It's good to have one-on-one time with him out of the office. Though I have a feeling this conversation will no doubt end in business. "Nice party," I say, shaking his hand.

"It's been fruitful so far. How are you hanging in there?" He tugs at his bow tie like I had just done to mine. Leaning closer, he keeps his eyes forward like he's about to reveal a secret he doesn't want others to hear. "I don't love these events, but they're a necessary evil."

"I believe that."

He chuckles although I wasn't. "David?" He angles away from me, between two people, to shake hands with someone he sees. "David?" Signaling back with a nod toward me, he says, "Come over. I want you to meet the guy who's killing it in Manhattan financing right now."

The other man says, "The one you were speaking so highly about?" Our gazes hit like a head-on collision.

Although I'll never forget Sosie's father and his threats, I'm surprised he would remember me at all by how he tried to make me feel so small and meaningless. I was nothing more than an ant he tried to stomp out. Look at me now, fucking up his world on the recommendation of one of the most respected businessmen in Manhattan.

Still glaring at me, Mr. Stansbury clears his throat, plasters on a grin that holds no love, and shoves his hand forward. "David Stansbury."

I take his hand, not moving toward him an inch. "We've met, Mr. Stansbury, at a holiday party you hosted at your house."

The back of Mr. Young's hand lands against my chest. "That's the hottest ticket in town, Matthews. How'd you score an invitation?"

Mr. Stansbury laughs too loud, and it's too forced to sound natural. Watching him squirm is a long-overdue reward. He keeps his attention on my boss. Guess he's not comfortable with me seeing him for who he is. "I'll make sure you and your lovely wife are on the guest list this year, Jeffrey."

Refusing to deviate one millimeter from his discomfort, I reply, "I worked it. I was a server for the catering company they hired."

"You always have been a hard worker," Mr. Young says. "Did you know he graduated at the top of his class from NYU?"

"I didn't." David Stansbury looks me over as if he misjudged me the first time. "That's quite an achievement.

Berry & Young are lucky to have you." His shoulders ease, which is his first mistake. The smile comes naturally, which is his second. "Seems everything worked out for the best then. Wouldn't you say, Mr. Matthews?"

My boss redirects his attention to me as his confusion grows in the jagged lines of his expression. I don't mind exposing this asshole for who he is, even if he's friendly with Mr. Young. What I can't tolerate is that smugness sitting on his face like he has a right to it.

Fuck him.

I reply, "Manipulating a situation with threats and—"

"Ah!" His eyes go over my shoulder, and he waves as if I wasn't speaking at all. "My lovely wife and daughter managed to find me talking business." My heart plummets to the pit of my stomach as the words I was going to say choke in my throat. I slowly look over my shoulder, not sure what to expect, only to be greeted by a goddess in a peach-colored dress. Sparkling beads only highlight the sparkle in Sosie's eyes as she smiles at someone in another direction. As much as I wish that smile was for me, an ache tugs in my chest, remembering how leaving me came so easy for her. Her father whispers to Mr. Young, "I promised I'd take the night off."

"I hear you," he replies with a laugh. "I'm already in the doghouse myself for sneaking away from my wife's side to talk to acquaintances I recently made. They were more interesting than hearing about the ladies who lunch together but gossip behind each other's backs at the club." He pats Mr. Stansbury on the shoulder. "You go on, and we'll keep this meeting a secret. And the three of us should do lunch soon."

"We should. I'd like to hear more about Mr. Matthews here."

Never fucking going to happen. I can't even summon a fake smile for him to make a good impression on my boss. So I glance back once more at Sosie, clocking how many seconds I have left before my world tilts on its axis like it did the first time with Sosie. Considering how fast my heart was beating, I knew she was near before I saw her. Now that I catch sight of her again, it's hard to turn away. She's stunning with her shoulders bared and her makeup light. Her hair is pinned up on one side, giving the large diamond earrings the spotlight. But it's those pink lips that have me craving just one more taste of heaven again.

Despite the fucker her father is, the truth hurts. She didn't want me and made that clear by never returning. I still have the necklace and earrings. They stayed wrapped around the tree in that studio until the day I moved out. Now they're buried in a box in my closet that I've never unpacked.

"Excuse me," I tell my boss and slip through the crowd and away from anything to do with a Stansbury. I finish my drink on the way out and push through the ballroom doors to the large corridor. The trek to escape in a timely manner is hindered by the maze of this hotel. I'm practically running by the time I reach the lobby.

As soon as the May air hits my face, I breathe easier, as if I were losing the capacity to do so as I was getting away. I haven't smoked in a couple of years, mainly because it fucked up my chances to run farther than a mile without feeling a tightening in my chest, but I could sure use one now. "Hey?" I ask a nearby valet, "You got a spare cigarette?"

"Sorry, I only vape."

"No worries." I start to walk down the block when I

spot a man in a suit stamping out a cigarette on the sidewalk. "Can you spare a cigarette?"

"Hope you're not the groom." He laughs as he pulls a cigarette from a soft pack.

I look at the tux and chuckle. "Nah. It's a charity event."

"Good." He hands me the stick and lights it for me. "Don't get married, kid. They'll take you for everything you got and leave you with a daily headache."

"Thanks for the cigarette, and don't worry," I say as he walks away. "I don't plan on ever getting married."

His laughter trails him as he returns to the hotel. I lean against the building, closing my eyes, and take a long overdue drag that begins to soothe the anxiety and heartbreak away.

"Never?" I open my eyes to her voice, the musical notes of her tone bringing me back to life.

When my eyes lock on those hazels that haunt my nights, I pretend Sosie didn't just kill me a second time. "Never what?"

"You're never getting married?" *Oh.*

"Um." I painstakingly pull my gaze away from her and watch the traffic dance being performed on 5th Avenue. Taking another long pull, I glance at her through the corners of my eyes, then hand her the cigarette. Sosie takes it, holding it between her lips, and inhales. Her lids dip closed like she finds sweet relief in the act. Maybe it's been a while for her as well. I exhale, the cloud clamoring in front of my mouth until a breeze sweeps it away. "It's not something in the cards for me. There's no track record of success on either side of my family. So I'd rather be single than end up at a party doing anything I can to avoid my wife."

It's only the minutest of nods as she watches people at the curb pour out of a cab, but there's understanding in her gesture. With the cigarette between her fingers, she lowers it to her side, taking full ownership like she did the night we met. It shouldn't make me smile like it does. When her gaze shifts to the street, I steal seconds that aren't mine to drink her in—the gold flecks in her eyes that still glitter like stardust, the rosy cheeks that seem to darken just for me, and the pink streak running through her hair as her last rebellion before transforming into who she never wanted to be.

She exhales, and says, "I used to feel the same."

"What changed your mind?"

When she looks back at me, she can't seem to stop the small smile that appears. "I'm not sure my mind is changed, but I can't say never with any kind of authority. What if I'm the one to break my family's curse? What if you're the one meant to be the first in your family's lineage to make marriage work?"

"That feels like a burden."

"I look at it as more of a challenge." That doesn't surprise me about her.

Something I've learned about working with people who have money is that sometimes it doesn't matter if they win or lose. They just want to beat the other guy in the game. "I don't want my marriage to be a 'fuck you' to the universe." I push off the wall, realizing I'm not getting another smoke with her around. "I don't mind a fight, but that fight needs to be us against the world, not between us." Damn, it's so good to see her again that I'd be a fool to walk away before fully appreciating the woman she's become. I'd be an idiot to stay. "It was good to see you, Sosie." I walk toward the hotel entrance, knowing full well that I have no intention of returning to the event.

"You look good, Poet."

My feet stop without my permission, and as tempting as it is, I don't look back. I can't. She's not the direction my life is heading. Not anymore. She made sure I knew that four years earlier.

Despite not having a say in the matter last time, I leave this time. It's still not easier to walk away, even if it is on my terms. But it does remind me that there's no healing old wounds when she exists on this earth. The pain is as fresh as it was back then.

It doesn't matter that I have a view from a bigger apartment, a stocked fridge, and a closet full of tailored suits. I'm still returning to a place where I'll be alone again, left to think about the one who got away.

CHAPTER 14
PRESENT DAY

SOSIE

The cold is not a welcome companion tonight, but here it is smacking me in the face as soon as the doorman opens the door for me and I step outside. I stop in repulse and pull my coat's belt tighter, even knowing it will wrinkle my dress at the waist. It's dinner and then a company holiday party. If someone's going to judge me for having wrinkles in the fabric, then that's their issue to deal with, not mine.

"It's cold out," Gregory says, standing beside the car, rubbing his leather-clad hands together. When he smiles, it's not as roguish as Keats and doesn't make me weak in the knees. I resigned myself to my fate six months ago when we made an agreement to get our parents off our backs, giving us time to get our lives sorted and figure out what we want. But I'm not feeling it anymore.

My body itches for a life that I haven't experienced, to travel again and not look back this time, to disappear from under the Stansbury microscope for once in my life. Why does everything feel so out of sorts today? I'm struggling to keep up appearances. Maybe it's the day—Christmas Eve again—coming around like clockwork to haunt me, or maybe I'm becoming too intolerant to play this game anymore. Like the cold, here I am doing it anyway.

How did we even get here?

We've taken it too far. At almost twenty-seven, I've been so hindered by fear of striking out on my own that I ended up locking myself in the gilded cage I was always afraid of. The next time the door swings open, I need to fly away and try, instead of living this lie any longer.

Bundled up in a long light gray wool coat and plaid scarf, I swear if he tells me that's his family's tartan pattern, I'll lose it. I don't hate him. I hate what I've become as his fake girlfriend.

"It is cold," I reply, making polite small talk like we're strangers. For two people who have known each other most of our lives, we are in the ways that matter. We're friends who are good at pretending, but acquaintances when it comes to our personal lives. I was once foolish enough to believe in happily ever afters. That ending is only reserved for the lucky ones. *Not me.*

Sliding my hand over my hair on the sides, I'm hoping no strands have escaped my French twist. I start down the stairs again, trying to adjust the mood that rolled in like an afternoon storm, hitting me before I could run for cover. It settled into my day and hung around like a fog, refusing to lift no matter how I tried to turn things around after that.

People wanting to celebrate my birthday should be fun, even if it is celebrated on the wrong day for their convenience and not mine. *Right, Sosie?* I should appreciate the gesture, but along with my birthday comes the memory of the one who got away. That's what Keats Matthews became when he left me at the Plaza.

Most people wouldn't see being left as a good thing, but I like that his principles remained intact. Sure, I would have liked it to turn out differently between us, and I've imagined what our lives might have been many times if we had stayed together. But how can I be mad at him when I left him with nothing but memories the first time? I know he didn't leave because he was seeking revenge. He left because I gave him no reason to stay.

My regrets have troubled me ever since.

But I can't turn back time. I chose a path. Made a choice and then another that led to where I am now. Is it too late to detour?

When I walk into Gregory's hands, he grabs my arms, and we exchange cheek kisses. "You look pretty, Sosie." He lingers against my cheek like he always does and then shifts as if I've changed my mind for our lips to meet instead.

"Thank you and for the ride," I say, slipping out of his hold and into the back of the black Cadillac.

"Of course." The door is closed before I can reach for it. And if the way it was slammed is any indicator, he's not too happy with me.

Gregory slides into the car next to me and tells the driver. "We can go." When he sits back, he looks at me. "Happy birthday."

"Thanks." There's no zip of excitement or thrill of celebration. I almost feel numb to it all at this point. What am I doing? Is this because I watched a stupid movie? *Stop comparing*. Most people don't get a wrapped-up package with a perfectly tied bow as an ending. Why am I trying so hard to convince myself that I have options? My options are to walk away from everything I know or stay and do as I'm told.

"So . . ." Gregory pulls my attention from outside the window back to him. "I've been thinking about us."

"What about us?" I don't mean for my voice to pitch, so I take a breath despite my walls rising sky high like a fortress around me.

"Well, it's been a few months of being seen as a couple." He hesitates when our eyes connect. I'm just hoping I'm not looking horrified. "Um, people have come to easily accept our relationship." I remain silent, unable to contribute to the conversation or to what he's trying to get at. "I was thinking maybe we can make it real?"

"Real?" I rapid-blink a few times, then look away from him. My thoughts don't align with his, and my heart hangs out in left field, hoping to fall in love again one day. Again. The word strains my heart like a pinched nerve. I felt love for the first time and let it slip away after one night. That's not what I feel for Gregory. Not at all.

"Yeah," he says. "We can try for real instead of being just friends, though I hear friends make great lovers—"

"Lovers?"

"Well, lovers as in people in love, not sex, though of course sex would be a part of it—making love or if you're into something—"

"Stop." I lower my hands that have flown up between us. Hearing him talk about us as lovers has me cringing inside. But more so, I'm worried. "Why are you saying this? We made a deal to go to events, to hang out on occasion if something required a plus-one, and attend dinners with our parents to get them to stop pressuring us."

"What if they weren't pressuring me?"

And there it is . . . I release a heavy breath long and slow to calm my heart that had begun racing when he said the word real. "Listen, Gregory." I start softly to temper any disappointment he might feel. "I know you care about me. I care about you, too, but it's diff—"

"I don't mind different. We can grow together, and over time, you might fall in—"

"Please. Don't do this."

He glances through the windshield and then back at me. "Sosie, I need this to be crystal clear for you. We are what other couples dream of being. We're both extremely attractive . . ." My eyes go wide just as the car pulls to the curb. "We were born into enviable families of wealth and means. We like each other—"

"Not like that."

His lips press together so hard that they lose color. He takes a breath. "You will come to love me."

The valet opens the door before I can get another word in edgewise. I'm not sure what to even say to that anyway. If I'm not careful, I'll take it as a threat, and I know he wouldn't threaten me. As soon as I land on the sidewalk, I look back at him as he climbs out of the car. Would he?

No. Surely not.

He's not like my father. It's one of the things I've always appreciated about Gregory. He's a nice guy. And I still have free will, even if I lose access to my family's money. Trying to give him the benefit of the doubt as we walk to the door of the restaurant, I reply, "Love can't be forced."

Just inside the warmth of the busy restaurant, I loosen the belt of my coat. He slides it from my shoulders and hands it to the coat check before we start through the maze of tables to where our parents are already waiting. He stops me by the arm just before we reach them, and I turn back.

He says, "It doesn't need to be forced. I promise to love you enough for us both." His chin raises, and a huge smile appears. "Hello," he greets our parents as if he didn't just tell me that he doesn't care if I love him if he gets to be with me.

What in the world is happening?

Cold fingers wrap around my bare arm, and I whip my head to see my mom. "What are you doing? Come to the table." *Heaven forbid, I embarrass her . . .*

I go to the empty seat and sit down between Gregory and his father like I'm a Lafoon now. *Am I being difficult? Making something from nothing?* I exhale a breath, hoping my bad mood leaves with it. Until I'm situated into my better-suited self, I put on a fake smile and pull the cloth napkin across my lap while pleasantries are exchanged. "You look so pretty tonight, Sosie," his mother says, leaning into her husband as if it's a secret no one else can hear. "Your dress reminds me that I need an outfit for New Year's Eve. It's so festive."

"Thank you, Mrs. Lafoon." I glance down at my dress as if I'd forgotten what I was wearing. I loved it the moment I tried it on—metallic threads running through it make it shine, the neckline and spaghetti straps highlight the span across my collarbone where a tennis necklace would have become the star, if I had one. I adore the ease of the A-line that isn't going to show that I ate more than a few morsels today. I feel pretty, making my confidence bloom.

It's been so long since I felt good about myself that it's nice to sit inside this state of mind for a while.

Clasping her hands together, she adds, "Your new hair color really suits you. Gregory always did have a weakness for blondes." She winks at him as if they've discussed this before. *Yuck.*

"Thank you," I reply again, not really wanting to be the center of our parents' attention. Dropping my gaze to the menu in front of me, I tap the seafood section. "I'm thinking, the shrimp risotto."

My father clears his throat and shifts in his seat. "We'll start with wine or . . ." He glances at Gregory. "Or should we order champagne?"

As if I don't even exist in the space beside him, his eyes stay forward on my father. "That's a good idea."

"That's settled," my father replies as he signals for the server.

Out-of-body experiences usually happen because of something life-threatening, but my hypervigilance has kicked in at one of the nicest restaurants in Manhattan, where I'm being offered champagne like I'm about to be gutted. It's safe to assume I'm not in physical danger, but I'm not so convinced that I won't be harmed in other ways.

While my dad orders, I overhear my mom say, "I was telling her how darling that shade of blond would look on her."

Mrs. Lafoon raves quietly, "It does. It's her color."

My mom's smile is genuine and filled with pride as if she constructed her own Bride of Frankenstein by piecing me together just for Gregory. The pieces come together like a puzzle as I stare at the two of them. As disbelief scrapes at my stomach, I remember how my mom had the stylist change the color when they stepped away. When my hair was dry, it was at least three shades lighter than what I had chosen.

Fisting my napkin, I slowly turn my head to the side to look at Gregory. I know he doesn't care about my hair. Why would he? If he did, he would have made it known long before now. I've had all colors, including streaks running through it, and he never said anything. So before I jump to conclusions that he's colluding with my mother, I take a beat.

He looks at me, and his smile reaches his eyes. "I really do like your hair. It's the perfect color on you."

"Because that's your type?" My stomach churns. I feel sicker by the second. "What I want doesn't matter because I'm *your* type. How was I this blind?" I push back in the chair, tossing my napkin on the table, and stand.

"What are you doing, Sosie?" he asks, standing as well.

I cup the base of my neck as I stagger to inhale another breath. "I can't breathe in here. With you or them. God, I need to leave."

"For air?"

"Yes. And you." I slide my hand lower, flattening my palm, feeling my heart thunder in my chest. "I can't perform this charade of a relationship anymore or live like this."

He's shaking his head. "What are you talking about, Sosie?" I see the way he glances nervously at others as if I'm revealing some great secret. Maybe I am. Do they really not see how miserable I am? Can they not tell this isn't real between Gregory and me? Is everybody that blind to reality, or are we just too good of actors for them to see the truth? "You can't leave."

My head jerks back. "What do you mean I can't?" I slip out from the chair that had trapped my legs and wedge around the back into an opening to escape. "I can't do this anymore."

"Sosie." The deep voice is dark in the undertones of my name and demanding that I stop.

Tears fill my eyes as I realize how many years I've lost playing the role of somebody else—first a girl and then the woman they always wanted me to be. I lost everything that mattered to me. Photography. A career of my choosing. *Keats.*

I lower my head in shame that I dragged other people into my nightmare. Is this what having money and power means? I traded my soul in exchange for the privilege of access, and where did that lead me? *Purgatory.*

I suck in a jagged breath and turn back to look at my father once more. It's been a long time since we had a fight. I remember the day and time, and the subject matter. Keats Matthews. We don't generally speak unless there's business to discuss, or we chat over dinner sometimes. He doesn't know me. Neither does my mom. Though they would tell anyone that we're close.

When our eyes connect, a wave of fear rolls through me like I'm that little girl still scared of monsters. The only difference now is that my monster wears a three-piece suit.

He remains seated across the table from me, and asks, "Would you like to talk outside?"

No, but I can't seem to voice the response. I know that look in his eyes, the unforgiving tone, the control he has not only over me but also anything and anyone I care about. Or did. Keats couldn't save me, even if he wanted to back then, but he saved himself. I've always found peace in that knowledge. He looked good last time I saw him, healthy, and I can only hope he's living the life he always dreamed. I never want to be responsible for ruining his life or my father taking that away from him.

It's only me left. I must save myself, and leaving is my only way out. I'll go silently in the night, sneaking out like I used to in high school, but this time, come dawn, I'll be long gone. He'll never have another say in my life if I can get the resources together to get out first.

I breathe easier with a plan. It's something I should have done years ago, but fear has kept me paralyzed. No longer. I'll play along tonight and escape by morning. "No," I reply, finding my voice again, and I sit down, which is expected of me.

CHAPTER 15

SOSIE

"Wow," I say, glancing up at Gregory, "this is quite the turnout for a company party on Christmas Eve." The pub is packed, but I guess when the boss of the shipping division is picking up the tab, a party with your coworkers is enticing for some.

Am I being too harsh? For all I know, Lafoon Industries could be an amazing place to work. That would say something about the family itself. Mentally, though, I'm already miles away from this place and them. It doesn't matter if he's nice or they treat everyone like gold. I was born into the wrong family, so there's no way in hell I'm marrying into the copy-paste version.

Two suitcases.

One for clothes.

One for shoes and bags.

"We're announcing bonuses tonight," he says, leaning toward my ear while rubbing between my shoulder blades.

Dinner was exactly what they preferred. Polite small

talk among the women while the men talked business. Nothing controversial was introduced, especially not me being unhappy or wishing I were anywhere other than there with them. They didn't even notice I stopped participating, choosing to spend my time mentally packing my bags. "That's exciting," I reply half-heartedly.

Grab my jewelry from the safe behind the dresser.

"I have a few other announcements I think you'll enjoy as well." He winks at me with a tilt of his head. He's an attractive man, and sometimes when he looks at me, like he is now, I can see him planning our future together. A white picket fence . . . if that was a thing in Manhattan, two to four kids, and me waiting for him at home when he returns in the evenings. The whole picture is laid out so clearly that I could almost mistake it for a photograph.

Would it be that horrible to be caged by a man who loves me?

I blink, the image clearing, and the loneliness of that life setting in. I'd have the wife title, but never truly his heart after giving him what he wants. I've seen how that kind of life plays out, with my mom and Mrs. Lafoon as prime examples.

I can't forget Winifred the wallaby at the top of my closet.

Gregory stops in front of me and takes my coat from my hands. "The ride over and then dinner got off to a rough start, but I'm glad you seem happier now." I don't bother telling him I'm an Oscar-worthy actress at this stage in my life. He asks, "What would you like to drink?"

Happiness by the gallon, a pool full of the freedom to live life on my terms, and to love by the oceans full. Instead, I reply, "Espresso martini, please."

Sometimes I'm not sure if it's fair to take my predicament out on him. He's stuck in this like I am. The difference is that he's made his intentions for me clear and been more than patient with my swinging-from-the-chandelier emotions. He's not forcing me to do anything. My parents are. Extortion via my own family wasn't something I expected, but I'm not willing to risk further damage to a life I deserve to live. A shiver runs down my spine from the darker feeling that's been troubling me for some time. My father's threats have started to sound like they're more than verbal in the tone he uses with me. Leaving is the only choice I have left. They'll never see me again if I have my wish.

The stack of cards I've collected over the years are tucked into the top drawer of my dresser. I can't forget those.

I watch Gregory make his way through the crowd toward the hallway to check our coats, remaining where I am and smiling as if I belong here. I don't. I get out of the flow of traffic and head to the back, though there are no real openings where I can wait without being in the way. "Sosie?" a woman calls my name, and I look around until I'm met with a smiling face.

My shoulders ease as I walk toward her. "Jerilyn, it's so good to see you again." We met a few months ago at a party the Lafoons hosted. She was the only one who seemed genuine. She reminds me a lot of Marcy.

She throws her arms around me like we're old friends. "It's so good to see you, too." I find comfort in the stranger, something I don't find much around other people currently in my life. "I thought about texting you to see if you wanted to grab coffee or a cocktail, but I didn't know if you'd remember who I was."

"Of course, I do. You made that night tolerable, the only bright spot from what I remember."

She quirks her head, her high ponytail falling to one

side. "Wasn't that the party where the Lafoons announced they were expanding their overseas offices?"

To her, it's a good thing to be close to their power. They used it for something beneficial for the company, so I understand her excitement.

For me, I just want out of their world, no matter the circumstance. "That *was* good news," I say, needing to guard my true feelings, especially at his company party.

Her smile reappears as if she didn't clock the negative blip in my reaction. "How are you so gorgeous? Gregory is a very lucky man."

I'm the worst at taking compliments, but I kind of hope my looks are the least interesting thing about me. "I should hang around you more often," I reply with a laugh. Swinging it back to her, I say, "Look at you. I love this dress. It was made for you."

"Thank you." She peers down at the dress, and her smile is more contagious than ever. I hate the jealousy that swarms under my skin. I used to be like that. Living life like there were endless possibilities. I'd love to know her secrets to finding this kind of happiness, but I have a feeling that not being threatened by her parents might be adding to her glow.

Gregory appears from the revelers with our drinks in hand. He hands me the martini glass, then says, "I'll be right back. I need to make announcements." He gives me another wink, which seems like overkill at this point. Is that a new habit he picked up from the office, or is the alcohol from dinner kicking in?

Jerilyn nudges me, whispering, "No offense, but I thought you two were just friends the first time I saw you together." The "no offense" already raised my hackles, but maybe I'm not such a great actress after all. "Were you friends before you got together, or was it love at first sight?" The question lingers with the lilt at the end, begging me to confess to the truth that neither applies to him. But that's not something I can do.

I should hate how often Keats comes to mind, but I always welcome the memories and the warmth that wraps around me like he once did. If love at first sight exists, that is what we were.

Despite how she makes me feel like a close confidant, she works for him, and I need to remember that. A thrill runs through her expression just before she adds, "I'm so happy for you. You make a beautiful couple."

I'm starting to believe that's all we are. *Attractive*. Everything seems to come back to that. There's no mention of our chemistry. We look good together on paper and in real life. But that's where it begins and ends for Gregory and me. "Thank—"

"Hello! Hello," Gregory says with a microphone in his hands. "Thank you for coming tonight when you could be heavily drinking with your families instead." That earns him a round of laughter from the drinking crowd.

A few glasses are raised in the air, and someone shouts, "Thanks for the drinks, boss."

I keep wanting to brush Gregory with the same stroke as my father, but he's not him. He never has been, so it's not fair to hold him to that standard of evil. It hadn't even occurred to me how he'll react when he finds out I've left. His feelings were never a concern of mine. Should they have been? Did I lead him on in some way that he would think that I would fall in love with him?

When his eyes connect with mine, I smile and lift my glass enough for him to see the praise, but I'm conflicted. Sparing myself from further pain means inflicting it on him.

Pain seems heavy-handed. Will he really be that heartbroken when I'm gone?

Jerilyn's eyes are fixed on him, along with the smile on her face. She'd be a great match for him.

His laughter through the speakers pulls my gaze back to him, and my mind from matchmaking. He says, "Thank you for being here tonight."

A bartender leans over and says, "Keep the path clear for the upstairs party."

"Yes, it seems a publisher is upstairs celebrating, but down here everything is on the house for Lafoonery to begin." I hold my expression, but inside, I'm cringing from that bad joke. Seems this is his audience, though, because they laugh. "Anyway," he says, "I have some big announcements. The first is what I know most of you are here about. The bonuses."

I sip my martini while tuning him out to tick through a few more items I need to remember—money. I'll need money and fast before my father cuts my cards off and freezes my accounts. My passport. I could go to Paris, or somewhere exotic, and disappear for a while. London isn't exotic, but it's always a good time, and it's a bonus that I speak the language. Other than the basics, what else do I take with me if I never have the chance to reclaim anything ever again?

My photo album and my laptop. I lose all my work if I forget to take those with me.

The roar of applause wakes me from my thoughts, landing me smack dab in the middle of a celebration. Jerilyn leans over and says, "Incredible, right?"

I glance at Gregory, hoping to find a clue to how much the bonuses were so I don't get busted for letting my mind drift away. "It was a good year."

"Sure was." She's still clapping when Gregory clears his throat.

"I know the bonuses are the stars tonight, but for me" —he places his hand over his heart—"I want to share something personal that would make my year." His blue eyes land on me, and he grins like the cat's out of the bag. Though I'm lost to what cat and what was in the bag to get it in there in the first place. "I'd like to invite my girlfriend to join me. Everyone, welcome Sosie Stansbury."

Mortification sets in as every pair of eyes in the room is redirected at me. Jerilyn gives me a little shove from behind and encourages, "Go on, Sosie."

My feet don't take the command willingly, so I force the first step and then the next until people are parting ways like the Red Sea for me to reach him. "What are you doing?" I whisper. "You know I hate attention."

His smile should be reassuring, but the embarrassment is too much for it to compensate. My face feels hot, and I'm beginning to sweat.

Running his hand over my shoulder, he's still holding the microphone in the other when he says, "We've been friends since we were kids. I crushed so hard on you when we were in high school." I start to blink, my breath coming too fast, my heart ready to escape and take cover somewhere else. I shake my head just enough for him to see and hoping no one else does. But he keeps going. "During the past few years, I've fallen in love with you, honey." *Honey?* Oh my God, what is he—"I want to marry you, Sosie. Will you be my wife?"

Somewhere between honey and marry, my mind went blank, and I felt faint. Grabbing him to stay upright, I'm righted as he bends down to look me in the eyes. "I love you," he says with the biggest smile on his face.

When the world comes rushing back, I look at all the people closing in to congratulate us while the thunderous applause almost hurts my ears. Gregory kisses my cheek, then whispers in my ear, "Smile."

And that's when I realize they're all one and the same. Him. My father. And I have no doubt his father as well.

I pull myself away, feeling him hot on my heels as I hurry to the hallway to find my coat. It's time. I'm leaving and never looking back. Yanked as soon as I hit the shadows under the stairs, I'm turned around so fast that I wobble on my heels. Pressing against my arm, Gregory holds me by the arm so tight that I find myself lifting on my tiptoes. To the side of my head, he asks, "What do you think you're doing?"

"You're hurting me."

His breath is labored, each exhale a huff against my shoulder. "Are you going to calm down?"

I'm not calm in the least, but I'm in no position to fight my way out of this without causing a scene that I don't want to be a part of. "I am calm." He releases me, and I sidestep to catch my balance. "What are you doing? Marriage wasn't a part of the agreement." I throw my arms out to the sides of my body. "We're not even really dating."

"You aren't. But I've been so fucking committed to you, Sosie, and you treat me like dirt."

"I don't treat you like dirt. I was treating you like a friend, but that's not enough, is it?"

"No. It's not. Not anymore."

When I lower my arms, the giant diamond on my ring finger catches what little light there is back here. Shock brings me to a standstill—my thoughts, my body, my entire soul leaves my body from the sight of it.

I blacked out. When I came to, I was engaged? I reach

to take it off, but Gregory grabs my hands. "Please. I'm sorry." Holding my hands tighter in his, he says, "If you just keep it on tonight, I'll figure out a plan to announce the engagement is off next week. Please, Sosie. Do me this favor."

"Do you this favor?" I pull my hands free and waggle my fingers in front of his face. "Pretend we're engaged when we're not?" I puff out a deep breath and look at his coworkers celebrating. Some people come toward us but detour up the stairs to the other event being hosted here. When we're alone again, I ask, "Why would you do that, Gregory? Why would you ask me to marry you when you know I don't feel the same about you?"

"Because I truly believe we aren't so far apart in our feelings. We just need to give the time for yours to grow some more."

"More?" I drop my head, wondering when I entered the upside-down-backward dimension of my life. "You hurt me. You grabbed my arm." I look at him. "That was intentional, and now you want me to do you a favor? I don't even feel safe with you anymore."

"I'm so sorry. Please. I got upset—"

"I'm the only one who has a right to be upset between the two of us." The gall. The arrogance. The utter insult. "I've been pretending my entire life. I won't pretend for you."

I push past him, needing air to help clear my head and cool the anger storming inside me. As soon as I walk back out, my hand is grabbed by Jerilyn. "There you are." She hugs me so tight, I feel trapped in her bony arms. "Congratulations." Releasing me, she says, "Let me see that ring." She holds my hand up. "Oh my Lord. That is . . . wow." She takes me by the hand again and pulls me like a rag doll.

"We must show Jennifer from marketing. She'll never get over this."

Glancing back over my shoulder, Gregory comes from the hallway looking like a kid who just had his favorite toy stolen. I won't feel bad for him. I can't. I'm suddenly engaged to a man I would have never said yes to if he'd asked privately. That's what this is about. A public spectacle to guilt me into it.

He's so easily distracted by a group of guys shoving a drink in his hand that I'm quickly forgotten. Is this what it was about? Being a big man in their eyes when the bonuses would have sufficed.

With the gaggle of women around me *oohing* and *aahing* over a ring I had nothing to do with, I look up to find the only man I ever cared about embracing another woman.

My heart stops.

My hand covers my mouth to keep the gasp inside.

My eyes lock on his as he stares back at me.

I've had dreams of this happening, another casual run-in at the subway, quippy conversation that led to confessions of the one who got away, midnight kisses, and getting a second chance with Keats to start again.

But as the other woman holds him like she's his, his eyes dip to my hand and the damn ring wrapped around my finger. *And my world falls apart again.*

CHAPTER 16

KEATS

Stepping out of the tight embrace, I lower my head to pinch the bridge of my nose. I know she's not real, but this happens sometimes.

Sosie's become a figment of my imagination. I once sat across from her at the ramen restaurant we visited. That was real. The other time I went, I swear I could see her smile and hear her laughter like we were together that time, too. The illusion was ruined when the bill was set in front of me, with only a meal for one listed.

I used to feel her presence haunting my old apartment. I could see her in my bed and feel her beneath me. I held on to her so tightly when I'd fall asleep, but when I woke up, my arms were empty.

She's become a dream I can't wake up from, even imagining her running to catch up to me on the subway. The hallucinations used to be bad, but I thought I'd shaken them. It never made sense that a woman I knew for one night would have such an everlasting effect on the rest of my life.

I gave up making sense of my fascination with Sosie Stansbury years prior, so I'm not getting sucked back in again. She's not real, Keats. She's nothing more than my mind playing tricks on me.

Taylor grabs my wrist like we're on personal terms. We're not. We haven't been before she hugged me like she might want to cross that line. I look at her. There's no denying any guy would find her attractive with her classical features, but there's no pull between us. Not for me anyhow. She says, "We got the deal."

"What deal?"

"The book deal. You know, the one we've had out on submission for more than a year now?"

I say the words, but the shock is there. "We got the book deal . . ."

"Yes. Now, come on upstairs." She grabs my hand like this is something we do and drags me toward the stairs in the hallway. "They're waiting at the party for you so they can make the announcement."

Releasing me, she's three steps ahead when I stop at the bottom. My soul is unsettled by the sudden appearance of my past staring back at me. "I think I need a few minutes."

Taylor stops and looks back at me. "What do you mean?"

I thumb over my shoulder, and reply, "Fresh air. It's warm in here. I'm going to get some fresh air, and then I'll be there."

"I can go with you." She takes a step before I raise my hand.

"I need a minute to process that this is happening."

She laughs, but it dies off into sympathy, which levels

her smile. "It's a lot. I get it. You've worked for years for this book deal." She tucks her hair behind her ear, and says, "Take a few minutes, then come join us, okay?" She doesn't wait for an answer. I'm not sure what I would say anyway. I'd sound like I'm losing my grip on reality if I explained the real reason I need a moment to recuperate.

I cut through the crowd and push through the exit to land in the dead of winter on the sidewalk. The bite of cold air shocks my system, instantly cooling my heated skin. My scrambling thoughts start to slow, and I regain some perspective. *See?* She's all in my head.

In my veins.

Living carelessly in my heart like she belongs.

Will I never be free from that night?

No. Not as long as the torch I carry inside remains lit. And there's no snuffing that out anytime soon. She's got a vise grip on my affections that I can't seem to shake loose.

"Keats?"

I squeeze my eyes closed, refusing to allow myself to start hearing things as well. When I reopen them, cars are still lining the curb, the light is now red instead of green, and the number of people out this late on a holiday still amazes me.

"Hi," she says, her voice barely above the shiver in her tone.

My shoulders drop, knowing I can no longer pretend. I turn back to see Sosie standing there in her shimmering dress, her eyes still holding an ember of hope. I don't know what to say, so I stare at her, wondering if she can fill in the blanks.

She takes a tentative step forward. The smile I remember is absent from her face. Instead, I look into eyes that hold concern. Concern for what? That I'll escape?

There's no escaping her. I've tried for years, and we still end up rotating in each other's orbit as if our magnetic paths were always meant to cross. Again. "I'm sorry."

"For what?"

With a shrug, she shakes her head. "I don't know. Just felt like I needed to apologize to you."

She was always too beautiful for her own good, almost oblivious to how breathtaking she was. Still is. If she's the same as she used to be, I bet she'd find that annoying. Sosie's heart always ran deeper than the superficial stuff. She was twenty when we met. It doesn't seem as long as the years claim, but looking at her now is like seeing who she was for a brief second of my life and then blinking. Her features are more refined, her hair perfectly in place, wearing expensive everything. The woman she claimed she never wanted to be now stands before me.

Why does she have to be so damn stunning?

Will I never learn?

I reply, "You don't." Although New York is alive with the sounds of horns and chatter, the wind that blows down the avenue, and life happening around us, silence fills the space between us. "Your hair is a lot lighter."

She's quick to touch it like she'd forgotten it was there. Pulling the clip holding her hair together in the back, the long lengths tumble down over her shoulders. "It's . . ." She toys with the ends on her left side as if some nerves have kicked in, and says, "Yes, it is."

Her skin is paler, not like she's seen a ghost, but more as if she hasn't seen the sun in too long. It's December. What do I expect? I just remember a natural flush that covered her so six years ago. Goose bumps cover her this time. "Why do you never have a coat?"

She laughs, rubbing her hands over her arms. "I don't

know." Glancing back through the windows of the pub, she says, "I didn't want to miss you."

"Anymore?" I still can't manage a smile, my insides feeling too raw with the emotions she drags from the graveyard every time I see her. I slip my coat off and move closer to her. I don't know what to expect—her to move from my reach or to allow me into her personal space again. I move behind her. When I slide her hair to one side of her neck, my fingers graze her skin, leaving more goose bumps to react to my touch. I could stand there all day tracing the graceful line of her neck with my gaze and counting the freckles that dot across her skin. I don't because she's another man's wife.

I set the coat over her shoulder, and when she's quicker than I am at lifting her hair, I wrap it around that side of her body as well. Coming around to the front, I remain closer this time as if the pull is too strong for me to fight. She slips her arms into the sleeves and then pulls it closed in the front. "Is this the same coat you had back then?"

It swallows her whole, but she looks so damn good in it. "It still has a lot of life left to it."

"Keats?" she asks, looking straight into my eyes. "I . . ." The bravery that had her edging toward slips when the words disappear from her tongue.

"I hate that this is fucking awkward."

"Me, too," she whispers.

Running my hand through my hair, I say, "I told my agent I wouldn't be long."

"Your agent?"

I'm not sure if it makes me feel better to clarify what she saw inside, if it's more for her benefit, or maybe both, but I rub the knit hanging around my neck. "Yeah, she was sharing news we'd been waiting for."

"Is it good news?" The expectancy in her eyes has a hint of delight, as if she could stand out here shooting the shit with me all night.

That's just not who we are anymore. I'm not sure we ever were since we were cut short. "Why did you come out here, Sosie?"

Any joy that dared to gleam in her eyes vanishes, and her gaze drops to the sidewalk between us. "I, um." When she looks up, she says, "I needed to see you again, Keats."

"Why? What are you looking for that you don't have in there?" My gaze tracks with my hand toward the pub. When I look at her again, I say, "You're married—"

"I'm not."

"Okay," I say, shaking my head at this game of semantics. "Engaged? Does that work?" Sarcasm drips from the question, leaving her with raised eyebrows.

"It doesn't work. No."

"That big fucking rock on your finger says otherwise, sweetheart." Yeah, there's no keeping the annoyance from my tone. Why am I fighting it anyway? We're nothing to each other. The lie tastes bitter on my tongue, though the words scrape like a razor blade down my throat, refusing to let them survive long enough to be voiced because I know the truth. She's everything. Absolutely every fucking thing in my godforsaken universe. The stars and the moon, the night winds bringing in the chill, and sunnier days that allow me to forget, for just a minute, that I once experienced something special and lost it. "Can't you see?" Defeat mixes with the anger that's been building for years.

"See what? What can't I see, Keats?" I can appreciate the edge of impatience in her question. She was strong, could stand on her own, and do what she wanted. That's how I remember her. She was a muse, a fairy that only appeared for one night, a siren who put a spell on me that hasn't broken yet. She was amazing.

When I dare to look at her again, admittedly, she is still incredible in my eyes. But is she still that strong, enough to fend off the life she deemed her fate? Not if that ring on her finger is any indication. "You gave them what they wanted."

I turn to the side to face anything other than her. She clouds my judgment, making me feel irrational for getting angry. She owes me nothing, but for some reason, I still expect her to say or do something that will change our past and give me something to believe in again.

She comes to me, running her hand down my arm with her fingertips lingering on the back of my hand where my skin is exposed. "Please. Please talk to me."

The heat of her touch almost has me forgetting that we're standing outside at the end of December. "You didn't fight for me, but . . ." I look at her through the corners of my eyes, unable to give her more despite the desperation I feel to do just that. "But I thought you'd fight for yourself."

Her body jolts as if the words themselves were knives I used to stab her. Tears fill her eyes, reflecting the light from the sign hanging above the door. She steps away from me and angles her body toward the street. Gnawing her bottom lip, she focuses her eyes on the traffic, though there's also an emptiness inside them. "I did, too." She looks at me with more distance—ice, a cold night, and life—coming between us.

Holding her hand out just enough to look at the ring on her finger, she laughs, the action causing the first tears to fall down her face. "I hadn't even looked at it." Her shoulders fall with a heavy exhale before she looks back at me again. "I'm not."

"Sosie."

The severe tone causes both of us to look toward the entrance of the pub to see what I can only assume is the fiancé. I'm met with eyes that hold no kindness. Not a surprise since I'm not sure I would react any differently if the roles were reversed. But it's when he looks at Sosie that boils my blood. The hard lines of his expression, the shortness of his tone, and the finger pointing at the ground beside him have me closing the gap that had invaded.

He says, "It's time for you to come inside. We celebrated your birthday, and then Jerilyn tells me you're out here with some guy."

She looks at me, but I can't read her thoughts in the brief exchange. And damn do I want to. When she doesn't say anything, he glares at me again, then comes at me with a handshake. "Gregory Lafoon."

I don't take the bait, not needing to explain jack shit to this guy, much less give him the courtesy of shaking his hand. Call me petty, I guess.

"Gregory," she says, her hands going up as if to halt his progression. "I'll be in soon. I need a few more minutes."

His gaze flickers to me before he sets his sights on her again. "People are talking. It's inappropriate for you to be out here alone with him."

"Don't talk to me like that. You have no say in what I do."

"As your fiancé—"

She balks, drawing my attention back to her, and when she tugs the ring from her finger, she snaps, "We're not engaged." Moving forward, she's not tentative in her steps toward him like she was with me. She has nothing to lose with him . . .

She holds out her hand until he opens his palm to her. "I don't want your ring or anything else with you, Gregory."

His eyes slide to mine over her shoulder before he takes hold of her upper arm and leans in. Is he looking to die? Because he's about to. If not by me, then by Sosie. Gritting his teeth, he lowers his voice as if there's privacy on the streets of New York. "We've already talked about this. You said—"

"The only agreement we ever made is the one you broke." She pulls away from him, and although she's not standing at my side, she's standing on her own. That's the Spark I remember.

He takes a step forward, but this time, I hum, "Uh-uh," as a warning. He stops. His expression shuffles from offense to disbelief to irritation.

"What are you doing?" he asks her, his voice tipping into anger.

After she takes what appears to be a sobering breath, nerves don't rattle her stance. "I'm getting my life back." She crosses her arms over her chest and stares at him like it's settled. I'm fairly certain the can has only just been opened, and there will be more to come, but I'm proud of her. I don't know where this will lead, but I'm hoping I get to witness her reclaiming herself.

I exhale, causing both to look my way. "It's not her birthday," I say, his earlier comment still grating on my nerves.

The slightest of smiles tickles the corners of her mouth as she unfolds the defensiveness of her arms.

Pivoting his body toward mine, he tilts his head back as if I'd be intimidated by this soft-handed asshole. Starting shit with me is one thing, but treating Sosie with anything less than respect will be his biggest regret. "What do you know about *my* fiancée's birthday?" he asks, raising his voice.

What's he so fucking threatened by? Me? *Good.* He should be. This is the kind of guy who would take it out on her behind closed doors. He has such a punchable fucking face . . . but I should tread more carefully for her sake. "I know that Christmas Eve isn't her birthday. It's interesting you don't know that."

His eyes flare into a full blaze of fury when he lands on Sosie again. "I expect you inside in five minutes before I handle this situation differently." He storms back into the pub, taking out his little man's anger on the door by yanking it open.

She stares at the back of him as if she can comprehend the warning. She glances at me, and there's no lingering confusion in her eyes. She seems set on whatever she's decided with that mischievous glint in her eyes. That's the spirit—a bit wild, a little rebellious, and not taking anyone's shit—I remember from years ago.

When it's just the two of us again, feeling a lot like it's us against the world, I ask, "What happens now?"

The light I remember, which made her eyes shine like gold, returns, and she shrugs. "I could eat. Are you hungry?"

That's my Spark alright. "I am, but I need to do something first. You game?"

With a smile blooming across her beautiful face, she replies, "For anything."

CHAPTER 17

SOSIE

Keats stops at the top of the stairs, pulling me up with him as if there was no way he'd leave me behind. Maybe my huffing and puffing behind him from dashing through the kitchen to avoid the other party, then racing up the stairs in heels, tipped him off that I might need assistance. Either way, I'll take his hand, even if only offered as a sweet gesture.

Caught between two events that neither of us wants to be a part of, the dark hallway is quiet, isolated from the world, leaving us alone together, even if only for a few seconds. I lean against the wall with our hands still holding tight to each other. My breath comes fast, so I loosen the coat I'd snuggled around me to get more air into my lungs. My breathing doesn't even with the gap between us tightening.

"We didn't even say hello," he whispers.

"No." I can only manage a half-hearted smile under the circumstances because a hello isn't what I missed about him. This closeness is. The heat from our proximity starts to consume me, and his musk brings back a trail of memories with it, reminding me of kissing him until my lips swelled. A hope I don't deserve rises like the sun, illuminating the horizon like a new beginning. "We didn't." The words are breathy, wanton for him in ways I shouldn't feel, but I can't pretend he doesn't affect me. It's not only my body that betrays me, but my soul longs for this man I'm not sure I'm allowed to have. With so much of our past controlled by others, what happens to us when we're given back the power to decide?

Do we fall together or apart?

Is this our time to figure it out?

I can't help but hope it is.

Resting one hand high above my shoulder, he tilts his head to the side for his eyes to latch onto mine. The tip of his tongue slips out to drag along his bottom lip while his gaze lowers to my mouth. When a heaviness in his lids causes them to dip closed, he scrapes his teeth across his lip.

The internal anguish he seems to be fighting is painted across his features. Brows pulled tight over narrowed eyes. One heavy exhale that tickles across my skin. Even my swallow is too hard. My heart racing, but I dare to reach forward, resting my palms on his chest. His eyes open, and his expression eases when he sees me again. "You're real," he whispers no louder than a taken breath, and when he leans in even closer, my eyelids flutter closed as the butterflies in my stomach awaken. I want his lips on mine again so badly, to feel the passion we once shared again, even if only for the briefest of kisses.

I can feel the heat of his breath on my forehead, my own catching in my throat in anticipation. But when I expect to feel him press to my skin, I don't. Opening my eyes, I can see his lips were so close to landing before he stopped himself. His eyes are still closed as if he's debating, but when he takes a sharp breath, he pulls back, and says, "I'll give you a proper hello later. I promise." It's a promise of more to come, but I can't stop missing the kiss that almost was. "And hey, we won't stay here long."

"We can stay as long as you want."

A smirk plays at the left corner of his mouth when he pulls back, looking at me with something wild in his eyes. I feel the same inside. Looking up at the ceiling, he chuckles in disbelief. "Trust me, this party isn't what I want right now."

It's not where I want to be either, but celebrating his achievement is worth the pause in whatever is building between us.

He suddenly pushes off the wall, stealing my breath with the quick motion. Walking toward the door, he glances back, reaching for me. "Let's get this over with so we can go."

He treats me like I belong here with him . . .

As if we were always meant to be together . . .

I take his hand, looking up when I'm practically tucked under his arm, and say, "Thank you for trusting me."

"Trusting you with what?"

I glance at the door, not sure what to expect on the other side. "With this part of your life."

The back of his fingers graze my cheek, his eyes taking me in one last time before he turns and opens the door. I stay behind him, letting him take the lead. It's his event, and I don't want the spotlight. Or scrutiny. I'm not sure what to expect.

He shuts the door behind us and asks, "You alright?"

"Don't worry about me. What kind of Stansbury would I be if I didn't know how to entertain others?"

The party is smaller than the one downstairs. It's quainter and more social; people can talk and mingle. In fact, there aren't enough people to avoid detection, but there are plenty who allowed us the moment of privacy at the entrance. He gives my hand a gentle squeeze. "You don't have to entertain anybody, Sosie." The edge to his tone pulls my gaze to his. "You're not on display here. You're my guest. I can stay with you."

"I didn't mean it to sound—"

"Keats," calls the woman he was with downstairs. With a toothy smile and her hair slicked back, she rushes from one side of the room to where we're standing. "Everybody is so excited about securing your book to publish." Her eyes fall on me, and she smiles. "Taylor Murchison. I'm this brilliant writer's agent."

He releases my hand subtly, but the cold drifts across my palm that had been warmed by his. We probably shouldn't have walked in like we were something we're not, so I try not to let it turn what's been so good into a negative. Keats runs his hand through his hair and grins. "She's paid the big bucks to say that."

She says, "My fees are standard for the industry. The compliments are free."

We laugh together, but then he says, "This is Sosie Stansbury."

"It's nice to meet you," I say, shaking her hand. With his coat still swallowing me, I feel the heat of her attention, though it's not because of anything she's done. Do I explain who I am and why I'm suddenly here at his side? That there's an invisible drawstring that pulls Keats and me back together every couple of years? Yeah, that won't make sense to anyone who has not experienced it. It's best to keep my mouth shut and let Keats take this one. Especially because that also makes me sound like a one-night stand.

Oh my God.

Am I a one-night stand?

That's not *all* we are, at least not to me. It's not like we've had the opportunity to define what simmers between us. Although he doesn't seem to see me that way, that is what we are at the bare minimum. Though I'll never be convinced we aren't more even if we don't have the chance to prove it.

"You too, Sosie." Glancing at Keats, she says, "I need to steal you away for a few minutes." Looking at me, she grins. "The CEO of the publishing house is anxious to meet him."

Keats looks at me as if I determine the outcome. "Go," I say, giving him a playful shove. "I'll be fine."

He searches my eyes. Finding what he was looking for, he grants me a smile. "I'll be right back."

They maneuver through the room chatting like old friends. It makes me wonder how long that friendship extends. I look around, feeling much like a fly on the wall left to observe before slipping his coat from my shoulders. I drape it over my arms in front of me as Keats is surrounded like a celebrity.

While he shakes hands and makes small talk, Taylor brings him a drink. It's not the act. It's that she knows what he likes when I don't. He drank champagne with me because that's what would piss off my father. What does he drink when he has a choice?

What's his favorite food?

Flavor of ice cream?

Book he's ever read?

Movie?

His middle name and where he grew up?

I know so little about the man, though my heart is so attached to him.

It's been six years since we first met, and Keats has lived an entire life that I wasn't a part of or know anything about. I don't even know if he has a girlfriend. My stomach sinks from the thought. *Please don't let him be dating anyone.*

From this vantage point, I'm given a new view of the man he's become, both the insight into who he is and the way his body has changed. Keats is tall, always was, but his frame is broader than it used to be, his jaw harder and more defined. More handsome, which is hard to imagine is possible. I remember those strong arms wrapped around me, like his coat was, and how, feeling small tucked against his body, it was only a size difference and had nothing to do with condescension like the other men in my life.

Only seconds separate our glances from connecting, not a minute passing without a smile exchanged or an entire silent conversation spoken through our gazes. He's so easy to read that I start to think he's a book that was written just for me.

With him, I feel like that girl I once was, basking in his presence—carefree and determined to make my life my own at the consequence of not giving a damn. But I gave a damn with him. He was once a dreamer with a rebellious streak like I was. That night was fun for him, but it was everything to me. No other man has come close, not close enough to share what Keats and I have. *Had.*

His pedestal is too high, a standard that nobody else can measure up to or reach. Has that been fair? *No.* But I've tasted something real, so deep, and authentic that less than that just won't suffice.

But this time, when I'm hit with the intensity of those

incredible brown eyes of his, I feel every inch of the woman I've become—sexier, stronger in mind, and more beautiful than I've ever felt before.

He's the only person I'm willing to break my own heart to see succeed. I did that once, and watching him now, I know I'd do it again, if needed.

Where does that leave me? Moving forward with my plan or seeing if there's another chance for us? Either way, they are complications that he doesn't need, not when his hard work is finally paying off. And what I do know of Keats Matthews is that he hates a fuss being made over him as much as I hate being the center of attention. He still stands with confidence, listening and nodding. When his eyes find mine, he smirks like he might need saving. I laugh in response, ready to step in to throw him a life preserver when Taylor announces, "May I have your attention?"

She steps out of the spotlight, encouraging an older man to take over. He starts with a speech about profits and this year's successes before introducing Keats as next year's superstar author.

I clap along with everyone else, but my emotions overshadow the moment. My heart squeezes, and tears fill the corners of my eyes in pride of seeing him get the accolades he deserves. The flood of emotions I have for him stands in stark contrast to the numbness I feel otherwise. How is it possible to feel so much for a man I barely know and so little for myself?

I've been an expert at putting on the mask society expects of me, but navigating the pride I have in Keats comes naturally. Taking a deep breath, I'm steadfast in my resolve to leave the shame behind. There's no more living in that house or working for my father, celebrating birthdays that don't exist, or allowing the friendship I had with

Gregory to get out of hand again. There's no life at all for me there.

He's done this all on his own. I can do that. I must prove to myself that I can.

Keats says a quick thank you to the others. I spy a hint of color on his cheeks, reminding me of the boyish charm he showed when he accepted his diploma years earlier. I hold his coat to my chest, dropping my head to inhale his scent, and smile that nothing has stopped him from going after what he wants. Not even me, so I can't regret giving him up. That choice paid off. He wouldn't be here signing a deal if I had gone against my father and followed my heart.

Another round of applause drags my eyes up from the coat I'd been clinging to. Being near him again is overwhelming, my emotions spinning with pride over his accomplishments. But mostly, I feel like such a girl when my knees weaken just looking at him coming toward me. Without missing a beat, he slides his hand along my neck and then slips the pad of his thumb over my cheek. "Why are you teary-eyed, Sosie?"

I hate that he uses my name when I feel so desperate to be the person he once knew, to hear him call me Spark again. I know it's too soon for my Poet to do such things, frivolous even, at this stage. The desire still stands, though.

Bending my head down, I tap the back of my hand under one eye, then the other. "It's silly," I reply, looking up at him again.

"Seeing tears in your eyes is never silly to me."

Nudging his shoe with the toe of my heel, I pull my grin to the side of my mouth to restrain it from filling the room from his sweet words. "They're happy tears. *I'm* happy for you. Congratulations. Sounds like it's quite the deal."

A self-deprecating smile zips across his lips. He glances

between us, then slowly looks up at me, and says, "My book went to auction." He leans down and whispers in my ear, "The winning bid was a seven-figure deal."

I lean to the side to catch his eyes. "Are you serious?"

"I am." This is the first time I've seen him shine with his own pride. Naturally, it's not even a brag, but something that sounded like he just needed to share with someone. How lucky am I to be that person for him? *The luckiest.*

I throw an arm around him, shamelessly holding myself against him. "You deserve this and so much more."

There's a space where time clicks by before his arms come around me and his head dips to the top of mine to rest his cheek for the briefest of seconds. It reminds me of how much damage has been done, and sharing a few minutes doesn't resolve any of it between us. Conversations need to be had. Confessions need to be aired. But maybe it doesn't have to be tonight.

When we part, his smile speaks of freedom, as if our days and minutes aren't numbered, and when he laughs, it sounds like we got away with a crime. Maybe we did this time. Perhaps the third time's a charm.

CHAPTER 18

KEATS

Sosie tilts her head back to take in the full scope of the building. Peeking over at me, she grins as if she's caught me in a lie I never told. Raising her eyebrow, she grins. "You've done well for yourself, Poet."

The name strikes chords in my heart that haven't been played in years. They might be out of tune, but the familiarity ignites blurry memories. I shrug, trying to act like I'm unaffected. I am. I missed hearing it, but I yearned to hear her voice even more—the tone that dances between the girl who had the world in the palm of her hand and the woman who's fought battles to be where she is. "I've done okay," I reply casually as if spending time with her is nothing more than lunch on a Thursday.

It's so much fucking more. *To me, anyhow.* And I've done more than okay, but since I blabbed about the book deal, it feels strange to be vocal about money when it's always been a silent enemy between us. Our worlds used to be divided by miles, Central Park, and society. I was just a kid from a part of a borough where it wasn't safe to walk at night.

I've been beaten to the point I couldn't see out of either of my eyes, had more concussions than doctor's visits, and raised myself on pasta and slices of white bread. I walked to school with the stench of alcohol under my feet and played basketball with randoms who showed up at the courts and were rich enough to own a ball. In this part of the city, I'm a borough and a train ride away from my past. It's also a long way from the mansion where Sosie grew up. But what it isn't is anyone else's. This apartment is the payoff for the work I've put in, the late nights, the early mornings, making the right decisions in the stock market, and keeping pasta stocked in my cabinet when I start getting too full of myself. Nothing like plain pasta to remind you of a time when salt and pepper and butter were too expensive.

Something Sosie and I have in common is that we don't need fancy food. Pizza will do.

Holding up the box, I spin it on my fingers. "The pizza is getting cold."

As much as people love to brag about having a doorman, I didn't need one to feel important. I enter the code and pull the door open for her, watching her slip under my arm into the warm lobby. "How long have you lived here?"

I can't stop noting how comfortable I feel with her as we walk to the elevator. We've picked up like there wasn't a sea of change and past pain between us. It still needs to be addressed, but is it wrong to just want to eat some pizza first? "Around four years. I rented near here after graduation. When I got recruited, I took advantage of the bonus to get out of that shitty studio where I was living."

Stepping onto the elevator, she moves to the back corner, resting her hands on the rails and watching as I punch the button for the twentieth floor. When I lean against the opposite wall, she says, "I remember that apartment."

"What do you remember about it?" I remember our night together and her the next day. I remember seeing her ghost around the place like her spirit couldn't let go. It was all in my head, a byproduct of burning through late nights working to wrap up my final project and classes filling my days. I got no rest, and the ghost of her loved to taunt me. I couldn't fucking wait to move out of that place.

"It felt . . ." Her eyes go to the ceiling as if the answer will be found there. When her eyes lower to me again, she replies, "Warm—"

There's still heat between us, flowing too freely like there's a chance to pick up where we left off. I glance up at the lit number for the floor we're passing to tamp down the thought. "I don't think it was working well that night?"

"I meant you, as in who you are as a person. It felt warm like you."

Staring at her, I'm not sure what to say, my thoughts conflicting with her recollection. I was warm but apparently not worthy of her returning to me. I try to get out of my head. It's pizza and hanging out, not an interrogation. At this rate, I'm not sure we'll make it past a few slices before I say what I need to get off my chest. What am I supposed to do? Sit across from her, this woman who broke my heart in two, and pretend we don't have a mountain's worth of baggage between us? *Impossible.*

The elevator stops, and when the doors open, I follow her. She only walks a few feet before looking back at me. "Which apartment?"

"Last door on the left."

I study the back of her while we walk down the corridor. The change in her hair is obvious, which was the first thing I noticed outside the pub. I like it, but I'm not sure it fits her. The coat is cinched at the waist, highlighting her slimmer body and reaching her face. Her features are more refined, and even though it's Manhattan, I think it's all natural.

Trailing my gaze to the heels that give her some solid height, I'm reminded of the combat boots she once wore. I wonder if she still chooses her footwear to please herself, or if she buys it to please everyone else. I really hope it's because she loves them and they're not for that asshole Gregory.

Fuck him.

I wish I had said more, done more. Though almost kissing Sosie in that hallway wasn't because of Gregory. Should I have gotten close to his fiancée, *ex-fiancée*? *Probably not.* But if I know one thing about myself, it's that Sosie Stansbury is my Achilles' heel. And apparently always will be. The hurt I felt hasn't been washed away, but I sure as shit forget how she made me feel at one time, which isn't helpful.

I would have thought things had changed. They haven't, not in the way I would have predicted. The chemistry between us hasn't tempered. It's only magnified. So I'm positive that if the pain I endured before didn't fuck up the attraction, I'm stuck dealing with it for life. It's incredible how one unplanned night has led to . . . *Oh shit.* Are we repeating history?

I open the door and walk into the dark apartment first so she doesn't run into anything. I flip on the hall light and glance back as I hang my coat on a hook. "Old habits die hard." When she doesn't react, I add, "Keeps the bills down." I flick on another light in the living room, nothing bright or harsh, giving our eyes time to adjust. This one is positioned to spotlight a painting I bought last year.

After closing the door, her eyes flick to me and beyond. "It's not what I expected."

"No?" I set the pizza box on the kitchen counter.

She hangs her coat on a hook next to mine and makes her way into the living room, looking around. "I was still imagining you in the old place with a blue rug and green loveseat." Dragging her fingers along the back of the leather couch, she walks to the windows anchoring the other side of the apartment.

I try not to stare, but it's hard to take my eyes off her, my emotions suspended in disbelief and feeling raw. I'm not even sure how we ended up this way, here in my apartment, like this is normal. Nothing about this is typical for me. I can only imagine she feels the same since she's caught in this whirlwind with me. I busy myself by getting plates and paper towels and stacking them on the box.

Sosie looks out one window, then strolls to the other as if the view will be different. With her back to me, she says, "I went to your other apartment."

"Why?" I carry the box into the living room and set it on the coffee table. Sitting down, I try to remember a time when she might have stopped by. My neighbors were nosy as fuck and would have told me. "I had probably already moved unless it was—"

"A woman answered. Pretty, around our age." She turns around, and it might be the first time I've seen hurt shape her expression. Her smile can't fight the internal dialogue playing out in her eyes. "I thought she was your . . ." Her posture stiffens like an offense was taken before she exhales a heavy breath that drags down her shoulders. "I thought she had moved in with you."

"Would it have mattered?"

She scoffs but tries to hide behind humor by smiling. It's fake, like the one she's honed her skills on for others. I don't appreciate it being used on me. Raising her chin, she says, "It sure did at the time." Her jealousy or whatever else she's confessing is familiar. I felt it tonight, though I kept it in check.

Maybe I shouldn't be so hard on her that she can't. I'd rather see the real her through a myriad of emotions than have her true thoughts be shielded from me. So I give her grace for the instant reaction that she couldn't hide.

"What about now?"

"Doesn't matter." She sits next to me on the couch, only quickly glancing at me before fixating on the pizza box. "The timelines don't match. She wasn't your—" She bites her bottom lip, struggling to say the word that would usually follow that line of thinking. She's done it twice now. Sitting back, she tucks one foot under her other leg, taking up space not only on my couch but in my life again. I should probably mind it more than I do.

"She wasn't my girlfriend." I help her out since I'm sensing she needs it. "You must have visited after I had moved."

With the gentlest of nods, she seems to breathe easier. "Must have been." Sliding off the couch onto her knees, she rips the paper towels off the roll and doles them out before opening the box and handing me a plate with a large slice. She resettles on the floor and takes a bite of her own piece.

We eat in silence, making me think I should turn on the TV for background noise. I resist that urge, wanting to talk instead. With the crust remaining, I say, "You gave the ring back, but are you still engaged?"

She laughs, covering her mouth with the back of her

hand. When she swallows, she angles to face me from the floor. "Am I engaged?" She's already shaking her head. "No. I never was."

"That's not what that ring on your finger suggested, and since I was there, I don't think the asshole knows you're not."

"The truth?"

"We're nothing without it."

The outer corners of her eyes soften as she picks at a piece of pepperoni. "I was ambushed in front of a hundred or more people shortly before I saw you." Placing the meat in her mouth, she looks at me again.

I was purposely putting off going to the party. My gut tightens when I realize I could have saved the embarrassment if I had only shown up on time. If I had been there—*fuck*. Timing? That's what fucked with us? Just like the last time. It's always at play. Maybe one day it will work in our favor.

"Why were you wearing the ring if it wasn't real?"

"Do you have a girlfriend, Keats?"

My head jerks back from the question she's lobbed my way. It's a soft ball since the answer isn't something I wouldn't share. "No."

Resting her arm on the cushion beside me, she says, "I don't have a fiancé. I don't have a boyfriend. I don't have a significant other or a partner. I was wearing the ring because I'm not someone who wants to humiliate anyone. I had an agreement with Gregory to attend events together —nothing more and nothing less than it seems. I've never kissed him. I've never been with him in any way that would have given him the impression of wanting to date him, much less marry him." She fidgets where the seams come together and then looks me straight in the eyes like she has nothing left to hide. "It's just me, like it's always been."

Sosie has never made me nervous even though I felt she was out of my league. She made me feel bigger than myself, like I mattered to someone in this world. She gave me what I needed to hear. I'll do the same in return. "I've not had a girlfriend, not since I met you."

"Why is that?" she whispers.

"I didn't make time. I didn't prioritize my personal life. Anyone I met wasn't you."

I don't know how I expect her to react, but it's not with the smile tugging the left side of her mouth up. When she slips her hand onto my leg, the electricity still exists like a live wire between us. "Is it wrong to be glad I wasn't suffering alone?"

Chuckling, I reply, "Probably, but I know what you mean, so I won't hold it against you."

"Thank God." She pushes up off the floor with a laugh and pads into the kitchen. "Water?"

"Sure." I set my plate on the table. "There are glasses in the cabinet and a pitcher in the fridge."

"No bottles?" she calls.

"Nope."

She chuckles as she opens cabinets in her search. "Why does that seem so fitting?"

"Because I'm cheap?"

"That's not what I meant. Holy macaroni. Why do you have so much pasta in this cabinet?"

"Another habit I'll never get over." The cabinet door closes, and the fridge opens. "Hey, Sosie?"

"Yeah?" The sound of water filling the glasses is heard before I look back.

I ask, "What happened to us?"

She pauses with the pitcher in hand, looking at me from across the room. Without more than two seconds passing, she says, "We were running on a timer neither of us knew existed."

"Timing is everything." I frown, wanting to ask more, but I'm hesitant to ruin the ease that has trickled between us. I can ask more later, but I hate that I don't seem to have a say when it comes to my relationship with her. Neither does she. We're just victims of karma, fate, and the universe toying with our lives.

Looking like she belongs here, she returns to sit next to me and hands me a glass of water. "I don't know if you believe me or not, but I feel the need to tell you that I never said yes to him." Her eyes always tell the truth, and there isn't a lie in sight. "I didn't say anything at all."

I stare at her, finally admitting to myself that I've loved her without reason for so long that it was hard to separate fantasy from reality sometimes. But now I see. Now I know. I've always known the reason. It just wasn't clear before.

We're not meant for anyone else.

CHAPTER 19

SOSIE

"Ten thirty," Keats says, lowering his wrist back to his lap. That damn invisible timer is still counting down. I hate the undue pressure it puts on every minute we spend together.

I turn my body, putting my head back on the armrest of the couch. Instead of keeping my knees crimped, I stretch my legs out and rest my feet on Keats's lap. "Not quite Christmas," I reply. Looking around, I notice a lack of decor—clean surfaces and empty countertops. There's a lack of knickknacks and none of the warmth his other apartment had. My Poet's personality isn't seen anywhere in here. "No decorations this year?"

"Some."

I sit up and take a look at the other side of the room. It's barren of decor but not in style. I love his choices in palette and calming neutrals, but it's missing the pieces of him that make an apartment a home. Flopping back down, I ask, "Where?"

"I'll show you later." Slipping one of my heels off and then the other, he bends to set them on the floor before sitting back again like it's just a regular ole night of us hanging out. I feel every breath I take and my heart beating in my chest. But sure, this is normal . . . *not one bit.*

"Those shoes were killing me." Grinning from relief and too curious to let this go, I prod for more. "Are they secret decorations?"

He chuckles, resting his hands on my ankles. The heat expands through my entire body. "Not a secret. I just like sitting here with you." Wrapping his hand around one foot, he begins rubbing as if it's his job to do.

I'm not going to interrupt the man from giving me a foot rub, but my mind spins with possibilities of where he's hidden some holiday decorations, and honestly, where a foot rub leads to next. "That feels really good." I win another smile out of him. They've been coming more frequently since we arrived at his apartment. His guard is down, and the tension that had been holding his shoulders up earlier has dissipated. It's impossible not to find this man incredibly handsome, but when he gives me a smile that feels like it was created just for me, I'm reminded of how easy it was to fall for him the first time.

He has me appreciating these quieter moments we're sharing. There's no hurrying through the streets to one part of town or the other like our first night together, and no mystery to who the other person is, though there's still so much to learn about each other. There's an ease to being with him that could become addictive if I'm not careful. Since I don't even know where I'll be living tomorrow—London, Paris, or Los Angeles, somewhere tropical, or even exploring the Amazon jungle—I should be more cautious getting too close. There's just something magnetic about Keats Matthews that draws me to him every time.

He was forbidden for so long that I thought I'd trained myself to keep my distance. I never stopped by his apartment again. No texts. No calls. Still blocked as I had to that night despite what my heart was trying to convince me to do otherwise. I fell victim to the circumstance, but I can't pretend I'm not the one who directly hurt him. No matter what the real reason is behind my actions.

And this is where we were led to. Two magnets are drawn together and become stronger for it. But he's not mine, just like I'm not his, so I need to enjoy the time we're given instead of wondering what comes next. *Stay in the present, Sosie.*

Changing feet, he rubs the other and looks at me. "Can I ask you something personal?"

"Sure. Anything." I wouldn't give most people that option, but I trust him.

His hands are still, and I brace myself, fisting the sides of my dress. "What happens when you see Gregory next time? He said he expected you back inside, and you left." The question isn't what I expected. I hadn't even thought of Gregory since we left. Hell, I barely acknowledged his tantrum when I was there.

"I'm not worried about Gregory. Pfft." Shooing my hand with half a laugh, I say, "He's not tough like he was trying to sound."

He stops rubbing and readjusts under my feet. "It's not about him sounding tough, which is a whole other thing, considering he was talking to a woman. It's the bruising his ego took." I already miss the foot massage. "Some men—"

"Little men—"

"It's not funny, Sosie." His tone is firm, the words curt,

and so unlike what I've ever heard him say. "I've met guys like him." Concern lassos his brows together in the center, the determination reaching his eyes. "He's not going to just let this lie, so I need to know if you're in danger."

Sitting up, I cross my legs in front of me, letting the gold fabric of my dress drape over them. "You don't have to worry about me. I can handle him."

"You shouldn't have to handle him." He leans forward, resting his arms on his legs. "And I shouldn't be fucking worried that he's going to do something to hurt you."

I had narrowed my eyes, not understanding the concern before, but hearing the anger in his voice put it in a new perspective. He's worried about me. I exhale a calming breath and reach over to wrap my hand over his. I can't muster a fake smile, and I wouldn't want to even for his benefit. He needs to hear me. "I'm not in danger."

Our eyes stay locked, and until he blinks and the line between his brows eases, we remain in a standoff. I finally add, "He's never been a threat." I sit back and shrug. "It was nothing more than an agreement between friends. It was easy—"

"It was settling."

I sigh, the spell we were under now broken. "Why are you upset, Keats? Do you think I can't handle Gregory?" Too unsettled to sit still, I stand. "I'm twenty-seven. I've dealt with this my whole—"

"You're twenty-six."

Throwing my hands out from my sides as impatience sets in, I snap, "What?"

He stands, letting the disappointment that's writing a soliloquy across his face pull him away from me. "Your birthday isn't for another week." Walking to the back of the couch, he stops and asks, "Or did you forget?"

My arms fall back to my sides as my mouth does the same. My mouth goes dry, so I swallow twice as hard as if that can save me from the error I, myself, made. My pride is too fragile to take the blame, though. "I know when my birthday is, Keats."

"At least someone other than me fucking remembers." He walks into the kitchen, leaving the light off, but opens the fridge, providing plenty of light to see him.

"You don't get to do that."

He shuts the fridge empty-handed as if that was something to occupy him rather than to retrieve anything from it. Pushing his palms to the counter, he glares at me. "Do what?"

"You don't get to be mad about things that only affect me." I come around the couch and walk to the other side of the counter. "Why are you so upset when it was me living that life?"

He stands straight, crossing his arms over his chest, but his gaze never leaves mine. "Because I remember your birthday like it's my own, but it was that asshole who got to put a ring on your finger." The intrusive thought escapes him, verbalized and set free into the universe.

Keats isn't one to talk only to hear his own voice. When he speaks, it's because he has something to say, but those words are thoughtful and come with a purpose. What he just said didn't come from his head. It came from the heart.

Now the sarcastic retort that was on the tip of my tongue tastes wrong. I catch the remorse in his eyes, the confession that came out without a second thought. He knows as well as I do that we're still just two people who have stuff to work through. The pizza and foot rubs, the comfort between us is nice, but they're only a distraction from our real issues. I whisper, "It's probably too soon to be declaring our undying love." The grin I'm wearing feels too faint to make an impact. I move into the kitchen, but when he doesn't shift, I slip between his arms and lean against the counter, facing him. We're so much closer with him leaning forward as if he welcomed the invasion. I playfully poke him in the chest and say, "I was only teasing about love."

His gaze dips to my mouth before licking his lips and sliding back to my eyes. Taking hold of my hand, he brings it higher against his chest and holds it to his heart. "I don't think you're so off base." He stole my breath the moment he spoke, but the admission is what makes my heart thunder in my chest. His arm wraps around me and pulls me close. Dropping his head to mine, he whispers in my ear, "The feelings I have for you never died, Spark."

I want to crumple to the ground, to wallow in the swoons of hearing my nickname again. I don't. Instead, I try my best to hold my composure despite the tears wanting to blur my vision by clinging to him in return. Tucked in his arms, I've never felt so safe in life. As no time has passed, every emotion I felt for him six years ago comes rushing back. "I'm starting to think we're cursed."

"Why do you say that?"

"Our timing is always off."

"Don't worry about timing and some made-up construct of the value." He kisses the side of my head and whispers, "Tonight, everything has changed, but I still owe you something."

I lean back and look up at him. With his arms wrapped around me like I'm his entire world, I ask, "What is it?"

"Hello." One of his hands slides up into the back of my hair, loosening the strands from the comb and hairpin I used to secure it. Plucking one, he tosses it to the kitchen counter before retrieving the other and doing the same. My hair comes down in waves of light blond sections, hitting my shoulders and then falling over them.

I smile and whisper, “Hello.” It might not have been a proper hello with a dramatic kiss like I thought about—in the hallway outside the party, on the street when we left the pub, earlier when we confessed feelings that probably should have stayed locked up a while longer. It’s worthy of propriety and what we need to start over.

And then he kisses me.

CHAPTER 20

KEATS

I didn't expect to kiss her, but she welcomed it by gripping her fingers into my shirt and pulling me to her. Her lips mold to mine, and a moan escapes her as she kisses me back. I move in, my body pressed to hers against the counter, and caress her cheeks while my fingers dip into the sides of her silky hair.

I pull back, leaving my forehead against hers. My breathing is as erratic as I feel inside. She drives me wild. Always has. With my eyes closed, I kiss her temple and lean back to look into those hazel eyes again. "I want you so badly."

Her hands slide up to my wrists as if she needs something stable to hold on to. Gripping them, she whispers through jagged breaths, "I do, too, but—"

"It's not the right time. I know. I just—"

"I know." She nods, her lids dipping closed as if she aches for me as I do for her. "I feel the same."

I hate doing it, but I take a step back, shoving my hands

in my pockets, and give her space. It's torture being this close to her again without taking it a step further. I'm just not sure what tomorrow brings with so much unresolved still hanging over our heads, taunting us.

She brushes her hair out of her face, the length so much longer than I've seen it. Strands puff in front of her face when she blows out in annoyance. "Do you have a hair tie or rubber band, or something that I can tie my hair back with?"

"Um . . ." I glance around, but nothing triggers an idea in the kitchen. I open a few drawers to look before I say, "I have a paperclip?"

"Can I ruin it?"

I drop the paperclip when another idea comes to mind. "How about a shoelace?"

She smiles so damn prettily that I might have to restart my heart. "A shoelace works."

Rushing toward my bedroom, I say, "I'll be right back." In my closet, I look for the cleanest pair of shoes I own. No way am I giving her a dirty shoelace to put in her hair. I pull my nicest Italian shoes from the shelf. It's a pair I only wear on special occasions and undo the lace.

When I walk out of the closet, I stop when I see Sosie standing in the doorway. Her eyes travel from the small tree on my nightstand to me in the opposite corner. "So this is where you keep your secret stash of holiday decor." Her smirk holds hints like she knew I was a closeted Christmas lover, to signs that she loves being let in on the secret of where I hide my decorations. "Hiding them in the bedroom so only you get to enjoy it." She crosses the room but glances at me. "Unless you have it in here for when you have company." Her grin falters before she sets it right.

"I don't have company."

Reaching the end of the bed, she stops and looks back. "Like ever?"

"Never."

The smirk defining her earlier expression fades into sincerity. "Neither do I."

Although she seems to be satisfied with the tidbit of information, I can't help but wonder if she'll be upset once she sees that tree up close. She moves in, and I follow, keeping some distance in case . . . I don't know what in case of. I just give her some space.

She bends down and taps one earring and then the other before running her finger along the strand of gemstones. Looking back over her shoulder, she's still smiling, and it's grown. That's a good sign. "You still have the tree."

"It never came down. Though I must admit, I reworked the electrical system two years ago."

Turning around, she comes to me, taking the shoelace from my fingers and slipping it under her hair. "I missed those earrings. They're quirky."

"They're yours. If you want them."

"I think they look better on the tree." Gathering the laces together, she ties a bow in her hair, leaving it to hang down behind her back. "I honestly forgot about the diamonds." She laughs. "My parents gave me the same necklace two years in a row. Guess they forgot to tell their shopper to update the list."

I'm not surprised her parents sent a stranger to shop for her Christmas gift. It's the "diamonds" that stand out. "When you say diamonds, you just mean because they look like it, right?"

"No." With a heartier laugh, she touches my cheek. "That's not what I mean." She peeks back once more at the necklace draped around the top of the plastic tree, and then says, "That necklace is worth a good amount of money. It's real, alright."

Not sure why my stomach drops from the thought. Maybe because there were nights I couldn't afford more than a cup of soup or that damn pasta with no butter or sauce. To learn that I could have bought a car for what that necklace is worth makes me kind of sick. Not that I need a car in New York, but damn. "It never crossed my mind." I look at it shimmering against the little lights, feeling a bit stupid. "I guess I should have known."

Taking my hand between hers, she draws on my palm with her fingertip. "Would you still have it if you had known?"

"Not if I were smart." I crack a smile and then nod when she looks up. "Probably. I mean, I needed something to make my tree sparkle. And since you weren't here . . ."

"I wish I had been." Lowering my hand, I sit on the edge of the mattress, still holding it. "You don't know how much I've wished things could have been different."

Standing there, I'm tempted to pull my hand away, get defensive, and scrape my fingers through my hair. I don't. I have to face the pain, especially if she's willing to address it. "You didn't need to make wishes, Sosie. I was there, begging you like an idiot in front of your house and neighbors to come out, to fight for me. I would have burned the world down protecting you from your parents. I wasn't given the chance."

"Me either, Keats." She stands in front of me, staring up like I'm the judge and jury. "You must believe me. Our night together was everything to me."

I can't hold on or back any longer. I walk backward in this bedroom that has more space than I'll ever need for just me. "I was never enough my whole life, but for one night, I felt like somebody because I was with Sosie Stansbury. Not because I gave a fuck about your last name or gave a shit about Manhattan society. I didn't even know that was a thing until I worked catering."

She stands next to the bed, barefoot and in a pretty dress that shines when it catches the light, staring at me like she knew this was always going to happen. "I don't want to fight with you, Keats."

"I don't want to fight with you either, but I need to know why you didn't fight for me."

I tug at my hair, trying so hard not to attack her for the pain I've lived with for so long. Too long. But I can't. "This has been years in the making. It's now or never."

"We could say the same for us." Her voice is a mere whisp of its normal volume, but the words hit hard. "Are we willing to take that risk?"

It is a risk. I don't want to lose her, but I don't want to feel so empty inside anymore, either. "I guess I've kept this bottled up for too long to shove it back down and cork the top again."

"Fine, let's get it all out in the open. I can take it."

"You're not going to fucking take it. You're going to fight back, Sosie. You're going to tell me whatever it is that you need to say, so when we walk back out that door, the slate is clean."

"Is it?" She takes a few steps, but there's hesitancy built into them. "Can it ever be?"

"Yes, because I need it to be. I need to know that this wasn't all in my fucking head."

Her silence has my mind filling in the blanks of what she's thinking when all I want to hear is her saying it. She finally raises her chin and looks me in the eyes. "It wasn't in your head. It was in our hearts. We both felt it."

"Then what happened?" If we don't get everything off our chests, I'm afraid we'll live with too many regrets to fix. She sits on the edge of the bed, looking so small in the center of that huge mattress. With her gaze on mine, I say, "Please tell me because I've run through a million scenarios of why you walked away after the night we had. None of them were kind to me, and I've had to live with that for six years. Please put me out of my misery and tell me what I did wrong."

"It wasn't you." I catch the chin wobble and the glassiness of her eyes when she replies, "I can handle Gregory or ignore my parents' rules without a second thought. Those don't affect me, Keats." I lose her gaze to the floor. "I don't want to cry."

My heart is held in the palm of her hands. I just don't think she realizes how she affects me yet. Her pain is mine. I feel it when she's with me and removes the mask she wears too often for everyone else. "It's okay." I go to her and kneel in front of her. "You have to be strong with them. You don't have to be with me. You can cry if you need to."

"I'm sorry for hurting you. Just know that I had no choice because I would never willingly cause you pain."

"But you did. You ghosted me. You were nowhere to be found as I stood at that gate, then under your window, realizing I had just lost the best thing in my life. A goodbye would have been the minimum, but an explanation is long overdue."

She reaches out to caress my cheek. "I don't know what to say."

"Tell me why you're giving back rings and wearing my

coat. You're crying over my deal being announced and looking at me right now like you're afraid to lose me."

"I am, because this time I know the devastation that accompanies the loss."

I get up when it becomes too hard on me to hold her gaze and hide the accusations I've been dancing around to spare her feelings. I move to the chair by the window, sitting forward with the energy to straighten my back. "That night meant everything to me. You claim it was a loss, but I've been stuck in the purgatory where you abandoned me ever since. Why? Please tell me."

She grips her hands together as she seems to be hoping for the best by the way the plea infiltrates her expression, shaping it by anchoring her brows at the ends. "It was the best night of my life. That's why I'm here to see if it can be recaptured."

Pinching the bridge of my nose, I exhale. Everything she says is right, and I agree. Deep down, I know I dragged her here for a reason. Selfishly like her, I hoped for the best. That doesn't fix what she did to me. "You left me, Sosie." The words don't sound right, but still manage to drag shame and defeat to the surface.

"Not by choice. I swear to you."

"Does it matter what you would have done? I would have taken the risk of losing everything I had worked for if you wanted me to. I would have done it because I was invincible for the first time in my life with you." I stand, unable to remain in one place and pace the room. "You made me see myself as a new person, as someone who mattered . . . and then treated me like none of it did, like I didn't matter to you."

"You mattered, Keats. You mattered to me so much—"

"I bought this apartment to prove to the world that I

was worthy." I hate that I lost control of my voice by raising it. "I wasn't enough for you to stay, to lower yourself to date the poor guy, a fucking server surviving off tips and scholarships."

Rushing to me, she grabs my arm until I'm looking her in the eyes. "I never saw you like that. Everything we had together was genuine." Tears slide slowly down her cheeks. "Please believe me." Her shoulders wrack with the emotion she can't hold back any longer. "He knew the only way he could hurt me was by threatening you."

"Who?"

"My father."

I turn to face her, peeling her fingers from my forearm to hold her hands. My mind is reeling as I process what she claimed. The breakthrough lands, calming my tumultuous insides. "What did he say to you?" It's the first time I've seen fear in her eyes. I cup her cheeks and bend down to eye level. "It's okay." Her breathing jags as if she might be having a panic attack. I bring her into the fold of my arms, holding her against my chest. Stroking the back of her head, I whisper, "You're safe with me. Always."

There's so much left to say, but maybe it doesn't need to be all at once. Her body rattles with the emotions she's probably kept pent-up as much as I have. "Keats?"

"Yeah?"

"Can I stay the night?"

CHAPTER 21

SOSIE

I've never known home quite like the warmth of Keats's embrace. It was selfish to ask to stay, but I couldn't quite bring myself to stray from a place I've always wished to return to so badly. Why would I choose a palace where no one truly cares about me when his arms give me the escape I need from my life for one night? It's just one night when I don't return to deal with the consequences of what I've always gone along with. I'm culpable. Sure. I've been an accomplice to what I created and what was damaged in the process.

Should he allow me to stay? *Absolutely not.*

Keats owes me nothing. But he's already given me everything I didn't deserve. He stood by my side this evening while I dealt with my so-called fiancé and treating me like I'm not the enemy when he has every right to. So I don't know if he'll give me more, a night to escape my life. *I can only hope.*

The shame and sorrow that overcame me earlier have

subsided. I finally take a whole breath without wheezing. I asked him without thinking of how he might feel, so I pull back just enough to see the truth in his eyes when he answers.

He says, "You can stay as long as you need."

"I don't need much, just tonight. It's been a lot and . . ." I crimp my eyes closed, wanting to forget anything that doesn't exist in his arms. "I've made a mess of things. I can't say sorry enough, but I am. I'm so very sorry, Keats."

"So am I for not realizing how much it affected you." He holds me close again, this time not letting me worm my way out of this, though his grip is too light to keep me against my will. I wouldn't fight him, or this. It's like a vacation from everything that drags me down, a reprieve that allows me to breathe without worrying I'm stepping out of line again.

"I don't know what happened." As embarrassment begins creeping up my chest, I turn away from him, still in his arms. "God, I must look a mess."

I start for the bathroom, but my wrist is caught. I turn back, our eyes latching onto each other's. He says, "Don't put on a mask for me. Please, Sosie. You don't have to hide, not from me."

One truth I've always known about him is his integrity. He won't sacrifice his truth for anyone. I wish I had learned that same lesson. That would have saved me so much heartache. "I guess it all caught up with me."

"Holding on to that kind of pain, pretending to be what everyone else wants instead of yourself, is exhausting. No one expects you to be perfect—"

"My parents do."

He takes both my hands in his and says, "Listen, I know you grew up with a lot of bullshit expectations. I grew up with none, so I'm not exactly a voice of reason on this, but I'm going to give you my opinion anyway." His grip tightens around my hands as if the importance of what he says is more evident. "You don't owe anybody jack shit, Sosie."

I almost expect something different, longer, more rah-rah, go get 'em, tiger. I grin because he didn't say what I wanted. He said what I needed to hear. I nod because how can I not? He's right. I've had them controlling my life for so long. They can only do it if I continue to allow it. What did I sacrifice my autonomy for anyway? Money. A roof over my head. Clothes. Spending what I want. "I don't. And I've already given so much of myself that I have nothing left. Keats?" I purse my lips and, feeling stronger, reaffirm my earlier decision to leave. "I'm going to prove I can stand on my own."

"I have no doubt you'll make that happen."

I move closer just because I want to. "Hey." I fidget with the material on the front of his shirt. "I wanted to say something. What you've accomplished can't be taken away from you. My father can't hurt you now. You've made a name and a life he can't compromise."

Rubbing his hand over the side of my head, he digs his fingers into my hair. "I graduated, so unless he knows how to have my diploma revoked, he can't touch me."

I blink and hold my eyes closed a moment longer as my father's threat comes floating back to me. When I reopen them, I'm met with his eyes set so intensely on mine that his concern radiates in that gaze. "I knew you would graduate one way or the other. I was worried about the threat of a felony, though." Waffling my head back and forth, I add, "I don't know if he's truly that evil, but I also wouldn't put anything past him anymore. If he'll treat me—"

"Wait, what are you talking about?" One of my hands is released, but I grip onto his other. "What felony?"

"The champagne. He told you that, right? When did you return my phone? He told me he had you on video stealing the champagne." Looking down, I shake my head. "We both know you weren't stealing it." I look up at him only to be met with anger tingeing his eyes and pressing his lips together. "Keats?"

He turns away from me and walks to the window to look out. His head is dipped forward, his hand sliding slowly through his hair. I want to go to him and wrap my arms around his middle to comfort him. I move closer but pause, careful not to touch as if he'll break if I do. I whisper, "He told me he would report it as a crime to have you arrested if I saw you again. But you two argued as well? What did he say to you?"

He looks over his shoulder but doesn't give me the full view of his eyes, only the corners. "I thought your father was just another asshole." He rips his gaze away, letting it drift through the window. When he crosses his arms over his chest, I can see the rise and fall of his chest from his heavy breaths. "Even categorizing him as overprotective of his only daughter."

Turning around, he just looks at me as if he finally sees my father for who he is. I know that look. Disappointment. Anger. Resolve. Revenge. Acceptance. I've felt all these emotions and more, separately and all at the same time. Nothing ever changes.

He says, "He doesn't care about you."

"No, he doesn't." I drop my head in the shame my father cultivated to keep the upper hand.

There's a sudden desperation in the way he cups my face. "He uses you to get his way. He'll hurt you to get what he wants. Fuck, Sosie. Your father is an asshole, but really, he's a monster." He hugs me to him and whispers, "I don't know how you stayed so strong for so long. You're really incredible, you know that?"

I smile against him even though he can't see it. It's not for him, though. It's for me. To have someone validate my feelings wasn't something I knew I needed.

In the years we've known each other, I've watched him turn from a guy with boyish charm to a man who owns every inch of his body and every decision he makes and stands by them with conviction. Fear doesn't seem to be something he carries even when under threat. Though this is so much emotional exertion, I breathe a sigh of relief because I know we're on the same side of this scenario. "What did he say to you?"

He sits on the chair, falling back as if he's feeling the same weight lifted. "He threatened to end my scholarships and get me kicked out of school." He scoffs, a laugh seemingly too far from finding humor in the situation. I sit across from him on the edge of the bed again. This time, no hard feelings are getting in the way, no nerves to tiptoe over so we don't hurt one another. The truth is finally coming out, and the lights shining down reveal that we were both played as much as the other. "He told me he felt sorry for me and that you were only using me to get back at him."

"That's not true, Keats. I promise you. If . . ." I take a breath to collect my thoughts. Anger keeps tugging at my rationale to drag me into a fight with him, which I'd regret. I won't let my father win. Not again. "If he hadn't threatened you the way he did, I would have left that night."

A smirk starts creeping up the right side of his face. "Where would you have gone?"

"Straight into your arms." I can only imagine how

different things could have been all these years if I hadn't lost that battle with my father.

"His worst nightmare." He pats his leg. "Come here."

I go because anytime I'm close to him feels like I've won the war. As soon as I settle onto his lap, his hands take hold of my hips, and he rubs gently. The thin material of the dress with not much underneath means the heat from his hand warms my skin. I lost track of time and let my body ease against his to rest my head on his shoulder. Touching his chin, I wait for him to look at me before I say, "I would have chosen you, Poet."

"I know. I know that now." He kisses my forehead and lingers against the surface. I don't know what he's thinking. Maybe he's wondering, like I am, whether this is the beginning or just another one-time thing. Maybe how much time we've lost, or was the time apart always needed? I'm not sure they're questions we can answer, but they linger as his lips did.

Dropping his head back like it weighs a ton, he says, "What a night, huh? I go from the highest of highs with my deal being announced to—"

"The lowest of lows being stuck with me?" I burst out laughing, knowing he'd never think that. But the laughter feels good, that we can laugh together with our past no longer unresolved between us, lightens my entire being.

He rests his hand on the hem that's slipped up my thigh. The mere touch of his finger on my skin creates enough heat to make me long to be with him. The feel of our bodies connecting again isn't just a faint memory. My body awakens, the desire to kiss him tingles on my lips, to make love, and to feel the connection we almost lost again. Resting my head back next to his, I remember feeling that ache between my legs for days. The pain in my heart never went away. Not until tonight. Leaning over, he kisses the exposed length of my neck, the tip of his tongue dipping out to taste me there.

A plume of desire inflates my chest, causing me to gasp quietly for air. "It's been so long," I whisper, knowing sex is not something we should jump back into this quickly. But my body is apparently in disagreement, a traitor when it comes to Keats.

He slides a hand up my side and over my ribs. The tips of his fingers add pressure, evoking a moan from me. I should be worried about how he perceives me, but I can't seem to care. The one thing my Poet has always done is accept me for who I am.

Strangers would argue we've known each other for mere hours, but our relationship extends years, our hearts tied together across this city. I hated our time apart, cursed it through tears and anguish, but I could survive knowing he still existed in this world.

Angling on his lap, I hold his face while I run my lips across his neck. The scruff is sharp but turns me on, making me alive again. He moves his hand higher until he's cupping my breast, squeezing and kneading, causing my nipples to harden. My hips sink and rise, the need between my legs already deciding what comes next. Turning to me, he meets my eyes as he readjusts under me. His hand leaves my body as he takes hold of my chin. "What are we doing, Spark?"

"I don't know, but should it feel this good?"

He chuckles. "It's you and me. It's always going to be this good."

I gobble up his confidence like an aphrodisiac. But before I get lost in kisses and hopefully more, I say, "I need you to know something."

"What is it?"

In a short span of this reunion, I've already discovered that this man is better than a memory could have been, but when I felt alone, he's my biggest ally. "I'm leaving." I'm quick to make the correction. "My house, my parents' house. I had already decided during dinner that I was leaving. The pub was only one last favor before I would be gone forever."

I've not accomplished much of anything worthy of pride in my life, but it still shines in his eyes when he looks at me. Brushing his fingers over my bare shoulder, he says, "You should have kept the ring." His smile quirks to one side with the late-hour exhaustion hanging on the lower end.

I burst out laughing. "Now, why would a girl like me need a four-carat diamond ring?"

Chuckling, he replies, "The money gone from his bank account would be a good reminder of your absence."

I sweep my loose ponytail forward over my shoulder and twirl my finger around the end of the lace. "I don't need a ring or his money." I kiss him, but before our lips part, I whisper, "I have a shoelace that means way more to me."

CHAPTER 22

SOSIE

The cold stone in the bathroom seeps through my dress where I sit propped up in front of the mirror. The lights aren't Hollywood-style, but they might be bright enough for the space station to receive a signal in Morse code.

I continue to brush my teeth as I blink a few times and angle toward Keats instead of being blinded. Keats is much more entertaining to watch anyway. It's fascinating how he performs a perfect circular motion on each tooth before moving to the next, as if he learned how to clean his teeth from a dentist in a YouTube video.

Catching me staring, he nudges my knee and rolls his eyes. "What?" comes out muffled through the mouth full of foamy paste. I shrug, enjoying the performance that would have made a great afternoon special for kids after they got home from school. Am I being too hard? Nah. I'm just amazed that he's still perfect in my eyes even when he does mundane things.

He scrunches his face and sticks his tongue out of the corner of his mouth, causing white foam to dribble down his chin. Bending over the sink, he spits, then rinses with water from his hand, washing away the paste on his skin. Experiencing him being goofy feels like we've reached a new level of trust. His guard is down, and our night is finally carefree from our other troubles. At least until tomorrow, that is. But those can be handled in the daylight. I'll take these tonight and spin them into the waking hours.

With my toothbrush still shoved in my mouth, I can only imagine I'm looking as attractive as ever. Cleaning isn't something I typically do with witnesses around, but I love how fun and just normal this feels with him. Coming to the side of me, he leans over me and kisses the top of my head as if he is feeling the same, and asks, "You just going to stare at me all night?"

Giggling, I move my hand over my mouth just in case I end up spewing, too. I lean forward and spit out the paste. "What can I say?" I give a little shrug. "It's a nice view." I scoop water into my hand and sip to rinse. When I sit back up, he hands me a hand towel to wipe my mouth. It's not lost on me that he wipes his right after like we're a couple who share towels and everything else. Or maybe he doesn't want to create more laundry than necessary. I prefer the former to the latter, though.

He lifts me from the counter and kisses my lips before he sets me on my feet again. The toll had to be paid, and I'm happy to pay it. "So," I say, walking back into the bedroom like I own the place. This is what happens when I don't have any walls to hold up around me. I become invincible. Twirling to watch my skirt float in the air around my legs, I stop and ask, "Do you have anything for me to sleep in? Or do you want me naked?"

"I, um, naked . . ." He scrapes his teeth across his bottom lip under widened eyes that tell me everything I need to know regarding his wishes.

It was a cruel setup of a question, but his reaction was worth the risk of asking. I lift his jaw off the floor while laughing. "I'm teasing. I don't need anything to wear." I burst out laughing again. "Kidding. Kidding. A T-shirt works if you have something for me."

"I'm starting to question how many drinks you had tonight." He crosses the room with a big smirk on his face. "Not that I don't appreciate the humor, but the teasing only embedded images of you naked that I can't seem to erase." I watch him shift his legs right before he disappears into the closet. "I don't have anything that's not going to swallow you whole."

"Whatever will work."

He returns, but I can't say he managed the prominent situation in his pajama pants, which he's changed into. "I have this, though." He tosses me the shirt.

It hits me in the face since I've been caught off guard. Why would I care about a tee when he's walking around half naked now? Those shoulders of his aren't just broad, they're muscular with divots between the muscles. His arms are defined, with good bicep strength. But it's those abs of his—*good Lord*—carved like a Romanesque statue that have me ogling his build as I've never seen a man before. It's definitely been too long since I've seen him.

The shirt is plucked away. Analyzing my face for damage, he asks, "Are you okay? Sorry. I didn't mean to . . . I thought you'd catch it."

I can't exactly tell him why I was so distracted, so I stammer and shift on my feet. "It's fine. I'm okay. You said you have something. What?"

"Yeah." He hands me the shirt. "I wouldn't mind seeing you in this one."

Unfolding it, I hold it up in front of me and grin. I head back to the bathroom, briefly glancing over my shoulder. "I'll be right back." I don't bother to shut the door. I know he's not going to peek, and closing off our connection is the last thing I want to do. I slip my dress off and unclasp my strapless bra, so happy to finally be free of the contraption. I hang both items on a towel hook, then pull the shirt he gave me over my head.

I never turned on the bright lights, but there's some sneaking in from the bedroom to see enough of myself in the mirror. I move closer to it and pull my ponytail free from the collar. With the shoelace barely hanging on, I take a moment to tighten it before returning to Keats.

He stands at the end of the bed, struggling to restrain the smile that wants to crease his lips. I don't bother holding back the giggle that erupts and spin for him. "Do you like?"

"I love. You look amazing."

I can't say I'd call this look amazing, but that I am in his eyes is all I need. As I look down at the City Events Catering Co. logo, who knew seeing me in an old, stained catering tee would bring him so much pleasure? "Was this shirt chosen for any particular reason?" I could guess, but I'd rather hear him explain.

"It's one of the smallest tees I own, and it reminds me of meeting you."

Tapping one faded stain on the cotton under the logo pressed to my chest, I ask, "Is it the food stains? I admit I'm a messy eater." I crack a smirk.

He chuckles. "No, I was wearing that tee under my dress

shirt the night I met you." His own grin takes over his handsome face. "It had fewer stains back then."

Never missing an opportunity to make me feel like the star of his very own show, I ask, "Do you always say the right thing?"

"Is that the right thing to say?" He laughs. "And no. But you always give me more credit than I deserve."

"It's deserved." I scan the mattress between us, then work my gaze back to him. "Which side are you taking?"

"I was waiting to ask you the same."

"I'm good with either." Since I'm already on one side, I claim it by folding down the sheet and blanket. I wasn't cold standing in a thin dress, but now that I'm so close to lying in his arms again, I'm freezing and speed up the process by slipping my legs under the covers and pulling them up to my neck. "I liked your old apartment, but I must admit, this place is quite the upgrade. I'm proud of you."

He strips down to his boxer briefs, then climbs in on the other side and moves to the center. With his eyes set on mine, I see the boyish charm return to his expression—a gentler grin and eyes that ease at the corners. Even his hair has flopped forward over his forehead. "I learned not to concern myself with how others see me. It only got in the way of progress." Leaning forward, he kisses me before falling back on the bed. "But that means a lot to hear somebody say that to me." Glancing back at me, he adds, "Thank you."

I hadn't realized until he said it that I could relate. I've seen pride in my dad's eyes, but only when things are going according to plan—never for anything I accomplished on my own, of my own choosing. Keeping the invasive thoughts of negativity at bay has been easy with Keats. I've been living like I'm not a Stansbury. The change has been welcomed, so I won't let my thoughts ruin it now.

The motion is quick—his arm swooping me against him—before I can let out a squeal. A trail of kisses is peppered across my shoulder, the hardness of his chest pressed to my back. Strong arms wrap around me like I'm something precious to protect, leaving only heat between us. *That and his erection.*

He's not making any moves on me to remedy the situation, but he sure knows how to tempt me. I can't disagree. We should be taking it slow. A lot has happened, and there's even more to process. We'll have time to reconnect physically, maybe more organically than on a night when I asked to stay.

Anyway, we need sleep. I do for sure. Tomorrow is a big day. Leaving everything you've known in life behind is going to take a lot of energy. Releasing a big yawn, I snuggle back into him even more and sigh in utter contentment. He kisses the back of my neck, and although things were heating up earlier, I'm enjoying the slower pace. *I'm enjoying him.*

I turn my head to catch his gaze. "Good night."

He kisses me gently and replies, "Good night."

When I turn back, my eyes are wide open. I lie there staring at the bathroom and listening to the quiet, which is notably different from the silence in my room. Here, comfort is found not only in his arms but also in the air. It's not thick with tension permeating every inch of the house by people who don't seem to care about me, only what I can do for them. Here, I'm free from the regret I so often feel when I lay my head on my pillow at night. With Keats, I'm me, and that's good enough.

"Sweet dreams, Poet."

"Sweet dreams, Spark." I hear the smile in his voice, loving that he feels the same way.

I fell asleep without warning.

The bed is so comfortable, like a pillow in heaven, floating on a cloud, and hearing the breathing of the man behind me has me feeling peaceful inside. But I need to pee, so I slip out of bed and use the bathroom. After washing my hands, I catch my reflection in the mirror. There's only enough light from the little tree in the other room stretching in here, but my eyes adjust quickly.

I had washed my face, but the usual dark circles aren't as noticeable. We've only gotten a few hours of rest, but I almost look refreshed. The makeshift ribbon wrapped around my hair has slipped to the ends. As I refasten it, I drag my hands over the blond hair. I don't even recognize myself anymore. Not because I'm wearing a ponytail, which is something I rarely do. It's because this color isn't for me. It was for Gregory, just like growing my hair long was for my mother. I was told I looked prettier with long hair, a lighter color, and less makeup, but apparently, more makeup was needed to appear more natural. It doesn't matter what I do or how I contort into the box they want me to dive into. I will never win their approval.

Releasing the exasperation that had clustered in my throat, I stare at myself, realizing they only think I'm pretty when I don't resemble myself. It's such a mind-twister to live for everyone else and still always come up short.

"Short . . ." I look at the ponytail hanging over my shoulder, knowing what needs to happen next. Can it wait until morning? Sure. But why wait when I've never felt surer about something I want? I pad back into the bedroom and crawl into bed to hover over Keats, who is still soundly sleeping and still gorgeous as ever, even sleeping. "Keats?" I whisper and kiss his cheek. When he doesn't move, I touch his shoulder, prodding him not as gently as I should. "Keats, wake up."

My hand is caught like he's a ninja with incredible reflexes, and his eyes lock on me. His grip instantly eases, folding his fingers with mine, and the easiest smile relaxes on his face. I grin. "Guess I'm safe with you around."

"I might be a little out of sorts. As I said, I don't have guests over. Until you." He scrubs his hand over his face, then props up on his elbow. "You okay?"

"I'm fine," I say, keeping my voice low out of respect for the hour. Just after three in the morning. "But I need you to do something for me."

A yawn takes hold of him briefly before he nods. "Okay. What is it?"

I sweep my ponytail to the front in a presentation. "Will you cut my hair?"

"What? Why?" He sits and leans over to check the clock on the nightstand behind me. "What's going on, Sosie?"

"I don't want to be a Stansbury anymore."

The sigh isn't loud, but I recognize the reaction. He understands me. Reaching up to massage my shoulder, he says, "You don't have to cut your hair or erase your name. You can just take ownership of it."

"This *is* taking ownership. I want my hair the way I like it, not how they want it. Please, Keats. For me?"

It's not like I'm leaving him any room to react differently, but it means everything to me that he doesn't hesitate. "If that will make you happy—"

"It will."

He rolls over to get out of bed. "Then I'll get the scissors."

Not five minutes later, Keats is behind me, our gazes connecting in the reflection of the mirror under unforgiving bright lights, blinding us. When he sees me blinking, he moves to the switch and dims the light. I laugh out loud. "I thought you were some bathroom psycho killer with lights so bright."

He chuckles. "Glad I put your mind at ease." He tries to hand me the handle end of the scissors, but I don't accept.

"I want you to do it." Our eyes stay fixed. The glint in his eye is one of understanding and curiosity. I don't know why I'm asking this of him. It's not that big of a deal. I can just cut it off myself. But I don't want to. I want him to cut my hair so I can transition back to myself. "I trust you."

The confusion disappears, and only empathy colors his eyes. Stroking the length of my hair, he wraps his fingers around the ponytail. "Where do you want me to cut?"

I could let him decide, but this isn't about him. It's about me, and what I want, so I reply, "Right above the shoelace."

"That's short."

"Like when we met."

He smiles, and without any apprehension, he starts cutting. My breath lodges in my throat until the last strands are freed from the thick string. Holding the pony, he looks back at me in the mirror and asks, "What do you think?" His voice holds the same confidence as if he just made a brilliant stock market trade.

As I stare at my hair in the mirror, not one strand comes close to grazing my shoulders, and none falls beneath them. Shaking my head back and forth, I watch as the hair taps my neck, no longer than chin length, and then reach back to rattle my fingers through it. My smile is swift, and the giggle that follows is effervescent as it tickles my throat. "It's been so long since I had it like this." I dart my eyes to his, and say, "I love it."

He slides his arms around my waist and dips his smiling face to my shoulder, planting a kiss on my neck just below the freshly cut hair. "Good. That's all that matters."

Reaching my arms around his neck, I hold him there. "Not to me. What do you think?"

"I love it, too. It suits you."

I turn in his arms and reestablish mine around his neck. "I should have done it years ago. Sometime in the past six years, I lost myself. It feels good to be back."

"Have I mentioned how good it is to see you again?"

"Must have slipped your mind," I tease in a whisper.

His hands lower to my hips, then slide to my ass. "I've been distracted." Lifting me, he sets me on the counter with my back against the mirror. "I've also been wondering—"

"What have you been wondering?" The sly smile that's taking up space on his face has me asking.

The width of his palms covers the tops of my thighs, and when one starts sliding the hem of my shirt up, the other moves between my legs. He wedges them apart and takes possession of the available space. "What's under this T-shirt?" Coming in closer, he kisses me gently and then like he means it.

Spreading my legs, I want to feel him against me, his hands all over my body, and his breath panting against my skin. Our lips part and our tongues meet in a sensuous kiss that is both needy and raw, like our emotions have been. His groan vibrates in my throat, and I cling to him even more, wanting to taste his hunger for me. "There's only one way to find out." My breathing is already off kilter, my yearning for him growing at a rapid pace.

He slides me to the edge of the counter against his hardness. I wrap my legs around him just as our bodies weigh backward until my head hits the mirror. He feels so good between my legs, but this strip of fabric and his cotton boxer briefs are going to be the death of me.

Grinding against me, his forehead rests against the mirror. His eyes are closed and his breathing ragged, fogging the glass with each exhale. "Why do you feel so fucking good?" he growls against my neck. He moves to nibble the edge of my jaw, then kisses the corner of my mouth.

I'm pretty sure the question is rhetorical, but since I feel the same about him, I manage to utter, "We're so good together." The words were released like a dove from the cage where it had been trapped, free to fly and exist in the universe. We were never meant to be a one-night stand. We were meant to be forever.

"Keats," I say, unable to hold my desire in any longer. "Touch me."

He slips a hand under the shirt, his warm hand grazing over my thigh and then between my legs again. This time, a finger slides under the strip of fabric, igniting goose bumps across my skin. The tip of his finger glides through my slit and presses right where I need him. My hips buck in response, as if I don't control them, he does. Small circles tease before he goes lower to my entrance. Kissing my neck and then my lips, he steals my breath when he pushes in as I exhale. "*Mmm,*" I hum with our mouths still connected.

He dips inside me and pulls back to watch my reaction. His chocolatey eyes are glazed with goodness, as if the view has drawn his emotions to the surface. Anchored to the counter, I sink lower on his finger, letting my head drop back, and my lips fall apart from each other.

One of his hands tugs the collar to the side to seek more exposure while the other adds another finger and thrusts in again. "It feels so good, too good. Don't stop." He doesn't, giving me what I ache for over again until my body moves of its own accord while pushing toward the precipice of relief.

His own moans mingle with mine as my body, slick with need, is heard. He pumps harder, a grit to his breath in my ear. I beg, "Please. So close. God, Keats. So—*ahhh*." I fall to pieces beneath him. His lips heated against my skin, the pad of his palm pressed to my clit, and the feel of him inside me is all-consuming, leaving my body tremoring to completion. And when I'm left drifting among the stars, my body goes limp under him.

I release a long breath and slowly regain myself in this realm. His eyes are set on mine, but you would have thought he'd come by how the corners are lackadaisical, like the corners of my eyes feel. I caress his cheek and sigh with all the swoons of being utterly satisfied in the tone of it. "Hi," I whisper, grinning.

He drops his head to my shoulder and says, "I fucking came."

Laughter is the best medicine as it ripples through me. I wrap my arms around him and stroke the back of his head. "I'll take the compliment."

Looking up at me, he's now grinning, too. "You should." Kissing me gently, he confesses, "I was always weak to you, Spark."

CHAPTER 23

SOSIE

Weakness is something to overcome.

I can't count how many times I heard my father say that if I dared to cry in front of him. I like Keats's version better, and he's not wrong. I'm weak to him, and nothing is wrong with that. I'm starting to believe we were built for each other. It's a nice thought anyway.

The day broke hours ago, the sun sneaking in through the smallest cracks of the shades hanging down. I glance over at the clock on the nightstand and regret it the moment I do. 10:23 a.m. Less than six hours ago, I was recovering from the pleasure Keats brought me on the bathroom counter while he showered. When he peered out to invite me in, I wasn't turning him down for anything. We finished cleaning up and fell into bed right after.

The sheets are soft against the newly exposed skin of my neck, reminding me of my haircut. The lightness pulls a smile into place as giddiness zips up my spine. I grip the covers over my mouth to keep my joy from waking him.

Peeking over at him once more, I untangle my legs from his and slip out of bed backward. I go into the bathroom and start to close the door until it squeaks. I freeze, but then check to see if Keats reacts before deciding it's safer to leave it open.

I take a long look in the mirror, oscillating my head just to feel the brush of my hair tickle my neck. Turning around, I try to get a glimpse of the back, but I can't really see it. I know it's uneven, considering how it was cut, but for some odd reason, I'm not bothered by it. This hair feels more me than any other style I've had in the past six years.

"Sosie?" The urgency in his voice has me running to the doorway.

"What?"

Keats fell back on the bed in relief, his hand over his heart like it was about to leave him. When he drapes his arm across his forehead, he closes his eyes and says, "I thought you had left." The hint of panic and the tinge of frustration are heard through his words, but it's his body that gives him away. "Last time, you were gone before I woke up."

My heart sinks at how that must have made him feel. "I was only using the bathroom." I climb back in bed with him and cuddle up to his side. After placing a kiss on his chest, I draw figure eights over his incredible abs. They're as hard as steel, like they don't know how to relax and take a day off.

When his arm comes around me, he leans over to kiss my head. "You never returned."

"I did. I just took a few detours to get here." I caress his face, running the tips of my fingers over the dusting of scruff that appeared overnight. "I'm here now, Poet."

He lifts me, leaving me straddling him with my legs. My

need to kiss him is so strong that I don't restrain myself. My lips crash against his as I slide my hands down to the mass of muscles in his shoulders. I shift my hips, needing the pressure. But when a moan escapes, his hands wrap around my ribs, and I'm held, unable to move above him. "I'm trying to be so good, Spark, but you're going to be the death of me."

Grinning like I just won a best in show contest, I push against his hands until he lowers them to my hips and kiss him. With another kiss placed on the tip of his nose, I sit back up. "There's no fun in being good, Poet. Trust me on that, so we might as well be bad and make it worth the while."

I'm flipped onto my back, and my hair covers my eyes when I land. Keats takes up most of the bed, it seems like, and all my heart, but his erection between my legs is about to make me beg for more.

He pulls back and is on his feet before I can talk him into having sex. Talking isn't the preferred method, but damn, I whine, "It feels too good to stop." Laughter trails him as he goes into the bathroom. I prop up on my elbows, glaring at the darkened doorway I'm left with to discuss this important issue. "It's not funny, Keats. Kisses and being left in this giant bed all alone while turned on are all I get?"

The laughter gets louder when he comes closer. He pulls his toothbrush from his mouth and says, "You're going to survive this. I promise."

"So you say." When he disappears again, I flop my arms out wide on the mattress.

I hear the water running, then silence before he reappears and crawls over me. He teases me by hovering over me, our faces mere inches away from one another. "I do say.

And it's all you get *for now*. 'For now' being the operative part of that sentence." He taps my nose before jumping off the bed again. "It's game on later."

I sit up quickly, wanting to see this man in motion as he strides into the walk-in closet. How is it possible to be so attracted to another human that the thought of him leaving to even go into another room causes me to miss him? "Promise?"

"That's a promise I'll keep. If not for you, for me." He chuckles, stretching a blue tee over his head. "It's Christmas. We should go do something, like eat ramen."

Resting my weight back on the palms of my hands, I say, "I haven't been back since I went with you."

"Seems like a good time to return then."

"Um." I start, not sure how to say this. I don't want to upset him, but I must stick to my plan before it goes sideways on me again. "I, uh, I have some things I need to do today. Remember, I mentioned moving out?"

He comes to sit on the bed next to me. No anger or conflict is resting in his expression when he says, "Of course. How can I help you?"

"You can't. I mean . . ." I waffle my head back and forth but settle it again when my eyes are fixed on him. "You can, but not by doing anything other than wishing me luck."

"Do you need luck?" His tone turns serious, and his eyebrows knit together.

"No." I smile to reassure him, but I can't do the same for myself. Even knowing my parents have flown out to wherever they're spending the next week and won't be there, I'm nervous, even scared, if I'm being honest with myself. They'll be alerted before I have a chance to catch a cab on the street. I need to plan everything in advance and not waste a minute thinking about what's next. "I'll go, collect my stuff, and then I'll be gone. It's that simple."

"Is it that simple, though? I'm thinking your parents won't take this lightly, so I don't think you should go alone."

I rest my hand on his and hold my chin up. "Don't worry. I'll be alright."

"You sure?" He drops his gaze to the bed between us and says, "That sounds an awful lot like famous last words."

Famous last words.

I've been haunted by those words the entire ride back to the house. I should be using it to my advantage. I need my armor in place before I arrive and be ready for anything. My parents may be gone, but Gregory isn't, and I didn't exactly leave him on good terms.

The car parks at the curb, the engine rattling as smoke from the cold meets the exhaust clouds outside my window. "We're here," the driver says as a subtle nudge for me to get out.

Staring at the house, I take a breath, then smile at the driver. "Thanks." I pop the door open and step out. Leaning back down, I say, "I'll only be ten minutes. Fifteen at the most."

I turn around to face the large structure before me. The house is suddenly bigger than I remember, grander and more intimidating. The wrought iron of the gate appears more Gothic, something I never noticed before, while the house sustains remnants of the Gilded Age. I punch in the code, releasing the gate, and jog up the steps to enter the second code to open the front door.

The inside is quiet, as I expected, and some lights are on, but for the most part, it's shut down when my parents are out of town. I find peace in the solitude and kindness in the few staff who check in on me. No one is here to greet me, so I run up the stairs with all the things on my packing list spinning in my head.

I shut my door and lock it before leaning against it to catch my breath. While my gaze darts from one piece of furniture to the next, to the bathroom, and then the closet, the idea of where to go next still goes unanswered. I've pushed off the thought each time it pops into my brain because I didn't have the answer. I'm not sure I do now, but I'm thinking I can't go to my Poet's apartment. Not that he wouldn't have me. He would, which is a whole other issue of feeling worthy of his generosity, compassion, and endless support. It's that going from here to there doesn't feel like I'm standing on my own. It feels like I'm falling back on someone else despite wanting to be with him so much.

Is he going to hate me if I don't go to his place?

Ugh. I suck in a breath with the lack of certainty messing with my head and rush to the dresser first. I grab a bunch of panties and set them on the bed. Reaching into the back, I find the stack of credit cards that I know are still active with available balances I can use in the short term before they get cut off. I retrieve my suitcase and matching carry-on from the shelf in the back of my closet, tossing both open on the floor at the base of my bed.

Safe. *Check.*

I keep my jewelry in the velvet bags and boxes, stacking them neatly in the smaller case with the credit cards.

Credit cards. *Check.*

Purses. *Check.*

Only wanting a few handbags that I use regularly, two that I specifically chose myself and have been well-loved, I pack them, then start raiding racks of shoes. I don't have much room, so I only choose five pairs before pulling clothes at random. The things I seek out most are the sweater and sweats I wore that night with Keats. They're two pieces that mean the world to me because of the comfort they provide when I need it. I stuff all of it into the two cases, then make one more trip to the safe to grab a stack of cash I keep in there.

Once I get my makeup and a bottle of perfume, I toss them in the smaller case and take inventory. I don't know what I'm missing. I don't know what I need. I just know time is running out. I glance at my bed and run to grab Winifred, my stuffed wallaby, and tuck her neatly in before I shut the cases and lock them.

I pull the suitcases to the door and take one last look at the pink palace of a cage I've spent my life locked in. It's only a few seconds, but that's all I need. I open the door and rush to the stairs. Carrying the suitcases down the stairs, I don't stop at the bottom or wait to hear if anyone is around to catch me. I leave and head to the car. After pushing through the gate, the trunk has been popped for me to load my suitcases myself. Heaving them into the back, I shut the trunk and hop into the car again.

"Where to?"

"The Maribelle Hotel in Midtown."

When the car pulls away from the house, I lean forward

to look back out the window as it disappears from view. As soon as we turn down another street, I rest back on the leather seat and smile. "I did it."

CHAPTER 24

KEATS

Sosie happened so fast. *Just like the first time.*

Her presence fills a space I'd been ignoring in my life. It was easier to focus on work, writing, and anything that didn't involve my heart in the process. I lost contact with the organ so long ago that I wasn't even sure I still had one. In her absence, heartbeats became echoes and then faded off as if they'd never existed at all.

I'd forgotten what it felt like to be alive. To be touched by hands that care. To be loved. To be breathing the same air as Sosie again has changed everything. Our connection lies in the distraction when I should be focused. In the empty spot between my arms where she should be. She's the proof that soulmates exist.

The background noise of the TV is only a mere distraction as I sit on the couch and scroll to her name in my phone's contact list. I never blocked her, but she blocked me. I only found out when I slipped up once and texted her.

Too much whiskey and a bad night at work left me something I'd worked hard not to be. *Penetrable.* The stab to my chest wasn't real, but the pain it caused was still pulsing from the fallout six months earlier. It was not the best time in my life.

"Get your mind back on your own life, Keats." I look up. Tiny snowflakes flurry past the window. The sweater and pajama pants have kept me warm, along with the apartment's solid heating. Having unreliable heat in my old apartment left me wearing layers upon layers to stay warm or walking around in my underwear when it was blazing in August. I chuckle, remembering how it had a mind of its own.

Now the snow only reminds me of Sosie. She was bundled in her coat when she left, but she wasn't wearing much else to protect herself otherwise. Chain mail couldn't protect her from her parents. They always manage to find her Achilles' heel to hurt her.

What if they didn't leave the city? Or got wind of how last night turned out for jackass from the pub? She hasn't checked in, and worry twists in my gut as dread sets in. Is she okay? Did she get out? Was she threatened again? *Fuck.*

To calm the tides of concern rippling through my veins, I pace the apartment. Should I go over to make sure she's alright? That's the worst thing I could do. It undermines what she's trying to accomplish. It would defeat her independence to do this on her own. She's capable. She's stronger than she realizes, considering the shit she's been through. Hell, she's stronger than all of us. Most people would have crumpled under the weight of the pressurized threats.

But what did she have to give up in exchange for maintaining her survival? Her freedom to choose her own fate. Is she doing that now? Will she choose me to go along for the ride?

My phone buzzes on the coffee table. I hit my knee on the couch diving for it. It falls to the floor as I go tumbling after it with an achy shin, and I'm pretty sure I have a newly acquired concussion from catching myself on the hardwoods with my head. "Fuck."

Reaching under the table, I grab the phone and hold it up to read the message: *New deals on phones this holiday season.* "Fuck. Fuck. Fuck. Come on, Spark, call me."

My phone rings as if the heavens actually listened. And when I see her name on the screen, I sit up and answer, "Hello?" Too fast. Too high-pitched to sound like I wasn't waiting around for this call. I clear my throat and lower my voice. "Hello?"

Laughter trills through the speaker like music to my ears. "Are you okay, Poet?"

Despite myself, I smile. "I'm good, fine, never better." The foot I shove in my mouth clams me up, but getting out of sounding like a raging idiot is a different story. Pushing up to my feet, I sink into the couch. Dropping my head into my hand, I ask, "How are you?"

My pulse quickens in the silence.

She says, "I got my stuff without issue, and now I'm in a hotel room lying on top of the bed and savoring every second of being free."

We didn't discuss the plan for when she left. It wasn't mine to have a vote or decide what happens next in her life. I'm not owed an explanation, and I have no right to demand a say, but hearing that she checked into a hotel still comes as a surprise. And stings, though logic tells me I don't have a right to that reaction either.

What do I have with her?

Where do I stand in her eyes?

After one night of reuniting, where do we go from here?

"Do you have a nice view?" What the fuck am I saying? I'm not banned from broaching important topics, but what issues cross the line?

"Umm. It's okay. I wasn't thinking about the request when I checked in. I was just happy I got away with it."

"I am, too." I finally feel the relief that she exhibits in her tone. "I'm proud of you." It was the simplest phrase, four words that hit deeper than she could have realized when she said them. Saying them to her comes easily when I decenter my own concerns. I am proud of her. It's interesting to root for a person I haven't known as long as some people in my life, but the connection runs so deeply that I've been fully invested in her success since the moment we met. She deserves it. She needs this. *And I need her.*

"Really?" The tone strikes a note of surprise. "You mean that?"

"Really, Spark." I stand at the window, watching the city blanketed in fresh snow, and smile at her voice. "I mean it. What you've done wasn't easy, but you did it."

I can hear a soft breath exhaled, reaching the receiver. "Thanks."

"Now that you're free to do as you please"—I walk into the kitchen to find a snack—"what happens next?"

"Are you still hungry for ramen?"

Victory runs through me like she called my final bingo number, and I rub my stomach. "Starving. Want to meet at the restaurant?"

"Five minutes tops." The slide of her legs across the sheets of the hotel bed scratches through the phone before she adds, "It will take about twenty to get there, though. Meet you out front?"

"No, wait inside where it's warm. I'll see you soon."

I rush to get dressed. I'm not sure where in the city she's staying, but I know I'm not close to the restaurant. Grabbing my wallet and coat, I stuff my phone into my pocket and head out, adding the extra layer during the elevator ride down. The lobby is empty, but the street seems more so. I shove my hands in my pockets, keeping my chin down as the snow I marveled at minutes prior pelts my face now that I'm outside.

When I reach the top step of the underground station, I can hear that familiar rattling on the tracks. "Shit." I dash down, jumping over the remaining three steps to catch the end of the train as it disappears down the tunnel. Worse, it's not running its regular schedule today because of the holiday. "I should have caught a cab," I grumble as I walk down to lean against the wall and wait for the next train.

Not much scares me. Not after my childhood or the rougher teen years. It wasn't until I was sixteen that I realized this is it for me unless I make a change. No one was going to help me except me. A professor who showed interest in a kid standing in front of the Winnie the Pooh exhibit at The New York Public Library, writing stories on a pad in pencil. If a guy could write about stuffed animals coming to life, I could write fiction inspired by my own life.

That young professor became my mentor, wrangled a tuition scholarship, and shook my hand at graduation. He was the first and only person I texted when I got my book deal because I knew he not only cared about my writing and career but also about me. That's not who comes to mind when a group of guys, maybe kids, dressed in large puffer jackets and headphones over their heads, but only covering one ear, start causing a ruckus—banging on the bars with a metal pipe, getting in the face of a guy down the way, and not leaving when they reach the exit. *Sosie does.*

I'm a big guy, but there's only one me and three of them heading my way. I start walking, but isolating myself further from the entrance turnstiles isn't a good idea either. *Fuck me.* I turn back, coming face-to-face with the jokers who think they own the place. The few feet in the bottleneck of this part of the station don't allow either them or me enough room to shuffle out of the way. So I head down and keep my eyes on the ground between them and keep walking.

"Watch where you're going, punk-ass." He checks my shoulder before I can angle to avoid it, the impact forcing me to look back as the aggression sinks in, and the muscle twinges.

The one shouting earlier, his voice echoing down the empty tracks, eyes me with ill intent and a snarl twisted on his upper lip. Dropping his head to the side, he glares as if I offended him personally. Wagering forward, he pulls at his coat like I've fucked it up. "What'd you say?" There's no room for error. The matches in his eyes are begging to be struck. I say the wrong thing, and no good comes of this.

I shrug, an attempt to keep things casual. "I didn't say anything. Just keeping to myself and waiting for the subway." I turn my back and start walking again, keeping my pace steady and not showing fear to avoid being their prey. If not me, someone's going to fall victim since they're obviously looking for a fight.

"I swear I heard you say something to my friend here." His voice grows distant, so I keep walking, ignoring the situation instead of feeding it.

Despite the adrenaline pumping through my veins and

muscles stiffening, I hold myself together. Sosie is waiting for me. That alone is worth letting this bullshit roll off my back and keep moving.

The heavy soles of their shoes should be fading as I head in the opposite direction. With my guard up and my body on full alert, their footsteps are gaining ground instead, steady at first before they burst into a sprint. Their taunts to come back close the distance. My head jerks back on my neck as my body flies, stumbling forward. I catch my balance and turn around, standing my ground. *Fucking assholes.* But I know guys like these, same as in the old neighborhood where I grew up. They want victims. Not someone who will fight back. Is it naive to believe we can talk through this to come to an understanding? "I didn't say anything. I'm not looking for trouble, friend. It's Chris—"

"We're not your friends."

Raising my hands, I sway my head, keeping calm. "I didn't mean anything by it."

Fighting used to come second nature. It's been a long time since I had to defend myself, and I don't stand a chance against the three of them and a metal pipe. But when one guy swings, I angle out of the way only to be struck by another fist landing squarely across my jaw. A metallic taste coats my mouth before my brain, and the pain catches up to what's happening. I swing, taking the middle guy out, splattering his coat with blood. Skidding along the concrete, he sics his buddies to attack.

My body bounces when I'm thrown against the wall, but I duck when he punches, hitting the tile behind me. The crack of his bones doesn't sound good. I kick him toward the track, then throw an uppercut to a guy charging me. I never saw the other one coming . . . my ribs ache as I tumble sideways to the ground, my shoulder breaking the fall before my head hits it.

The pain radiates, making it hard to know where I'm injured. Kicks rain down on me from the first one, then two others take their turn. Shielding myself, I burrow into my arms to protect my head. "Let's go," someone shouts before they take off running. I peek my eyes open to catch them jumping the turnstiles to escape.

"Aghh," I groan, rolling onto my back, unable to take a deep breath without fire consuming my body. Not a bone, muscle, or limb remains untouched from pain. I close my eyes, hoping to isolate where it hurts most because it's a struggle to move parts of my body.

I grew up miles from where I now lie bleeding, stupidly believing that by changing locations I could change my outcome. With my dad's voice echoing "little shit" around me, did I actually believe I could outrun my upbringing?

I fooled myself into believing I was more because Professor Johns said I could be whoever I wanted to be. I convinced myself I was worthy of someone spectacular and full of light like Sosie. And she fell for me, doubling down on that notion. But I fell for her the first time I heard her voice . . .

"Are you hiding from the party?"

"I'm on a break."

"Me, too." I felt empty when her gaze left me and whole when it was bonded with mine. She slowly sways, tapping the toe of her boot to the ground. "So who are you?"

"Keats."

"Like the poet." God, that smile was everything to a guy like me. "Heard melodies are sweet—"

"Poet," she whispers in my ear. "Stay with me." I reach to embrace her, to hug her to my chest so I can feel my heart beat again. But there is no her, or heart, or beats. Only the sound of the horn forewarns of the oncoming train.

“Hey!” an unfamiliar voice asks just as I close my eyes. “You okay?”

“Yeah, I’m—”

CHAPTER 25

SOSIE

"I'm sorry, Joy." I glance up at people crowding the door, waiting to be seated, as guilt washes through me for taking up valuable table space. "Do you mind bringing the bill?"

"It's on me, Sosie." She never changes or ages. I should be jealous, but she's too good a person not to be inspired by instead. "It's been too long and good to see you again."

"You, too, and thank you." My gaze drifts out the window for the thousandth time, hoping to see Keats running toward the restaurant. I can see his smiling face and a wave before coming in to kiss me like we've missed each other for years, not just a few hours. But my lips are bereft of his, my arms still empty, and my imagination fills in the rest.

When Joy disappears into the kitchen, I set money on the table that will more than cover the hot tea and edamame I ordered. Getting up, I pull my coat back on as I walk toward the door. I squeeze through the crowd, and the cold air hits my cheeks when I exit.

Looking down the street in one direction, then the other, I see no sign of him. I pull my phone from my pocket and check for a missed text or call, only to find a blank screen. It's been two and a half hours, when it was supposed to be only twenty minutes. I've been worried, but something else causes my chest to clench. It's not dread, but something heavier, darker, more concerning. I just can't pinpoint what it is.

I pull my knit hat on and slip on my gloves before trekking through the snow to the corner. Since my seven calls have gone unanswered, I hail a cab that's one block down, leaving me no choice but to go to his apartment.

As soon as the car arrives, I pay and rush through the door just as someone is walking out with their dog. I'm not sure I can catch the elevator, but I run as fast as I can, stopping it with my hand. It opens. My breath leaves me in a heavy sigh when I realize it needs a card key to move.

"Hold the elevator!"

I perk up when I see a woman running toward me. She walks on and taps her card as the doors close. I punch the floor for his apartment. She says, "Thanks. I'm so ready to be home."

I work a smile into place, but it doesn't reach my heart because my home has become unreachable for hours. "Me too." When she gets off on her floor, I say, "Have a great night." It's easy to forget it's Christmas when so much more important stuff is going on.

"You also," she replies as the doors shut.

On his floor, I would have thought I'd be running, but that feeling from earlier has returned and makes my feet feel like concrete. I knock. And then again. There's no bell or button to push. I text him that I'm here, suddenly hopeful that maybe he fell asleep or got caught up writing and lost track of time. Wanted to shower or clean the house from top to bottom. Make a four-course meal to surprise me, or go out shopping for a present and get stuck in a long line. Shoot. I pat down my pockets like I might find a gift even though I know I don't have anything for him.

Hope fades as seconds pass and minutes vanish with me still standing like an imbecile outside his door. "Get a clue, Sosie."

I can't seem to grasp that Keats would purposely hurt me like this. He wouldn't. I know he would never lead me on just to get revenge. That's not in his nature. So my mind wanders to the only other possibility . . .

"Hi," I greet the nurse behind the glass by bending down to speak through the opening, feeling rude for interrupting her. "I'm looking for somebody, and I was wondering if you could . . ."

"Name?" Her eyes never meet mine, but her fingers are poised on the keyboard in anticipation.

"Keats Matthews." I stand, rolling my shoulders back and thinking she can probably hear me without pushing my mouth to the small opening. "He's around six."

"Hold please." Her fingers dash over the keys as she glares at the screen. Finally, looking up at me, she says, "There's no one at this hospital by that name. Do they go by another name?"

Poet, but only to me. "No." The clock on the wall catches my eye. More than four hours have passed since we agreed to meet, and I'm already at the hospital thinking the worst when the answer might be more obvious. And harder to accept. Betting on the long shot, I ask, "Have you had anyone brought in without ID?"

Her eyes stay on me for an uncomfortably long time as if I'm someone to be wary of, and then she says, "We had one gentleman brought in—"

"Brown hair with this slight wave in the front, great eyes, brown with the secrets of the universe hidden inside."

She narrows her eyes at me. "Giant. Like six-eight—"

"That's not him."

"Fine, he's a giant to me. Probably six-three, if I had to guess like one of those carnival—"

"Do you have a photo of him?" Her blank stare has me wondering when she lost the ability to show compassion.

Resting my arms on the counter, I lean down toward the opening again. "There's this timer that keeps running out on us. So I would have a photo, probably hundreds by now, but—"

The screech of her chair grinding against the linoleum has my spine straightening. "Stay here." She just leaves me with my worries for Keats, wondering if he's safe. My mind flashes through memories of Keats and me together, when the light hit just right and at the perfect angle. I would reach for the camera that wasn't there, and the stark realization that I can't remember when I last took a real photo. I left my camera hidden at the top of my closet, favoring the simplicity and convenience of my phone.

There's no commitment through the basic lenses. There's no expectation to take an award-winning photo, or one I can sell to make a living or build a career. I take photos of things that make me think or bring me pleasure. In that case, I should have albums full of Keats. But I don't even have one.

Pictures don't matter. *He does.*

I'm afraid they'll require proof that I can't produce to see him, so I wait and fret for her to return and hand me my fate.

I pull the hat from my head and scrape my hair back from my forehead. Twirling the hat around at my hip doesn't help time tick any quicker. I scan the area and the nurses in scrubs behind the counter, the docs chatting quietly just around the corner. The waiting room is full, and the old TV hung in the corner has a static line running through it. My back stiffens as soon as I see her. "Anything?"

She stops and waves me down the hall. I hurry to catch up, both excited that I might have found him and terrified that I've found him in the hospital, which means he's injured. Or worse. I'm holding my breath when she says, "It might be him. Are you open to seeing if—?"

"Yes," I blurt, my hands already shaking from the prospect that it's Keats.

She turns on her soft-soled shoes and leads me four doors down from where we were standing. The door is already cracked open, so she turns and whispers, "Please don't speak to the patient. He needs his rest. If you recognize him, we'll get his information, and then you wait for him to wake up in the waiting room near the entrance."

I'm already nodding, anxious to see if it's him. "Okay."

Pushing the door open, she stands against it with the handle tucked in her hands behind her back. It's dark in the room, but even with the little available light, I'd know my Poet anywhere. "That's him," I whisper as if I need her approval. I hurry to his side without it and grip the railing of the bed. One eye is angry red, and his cheek on that side is swollen from a hard impact. With a bandage and an ice pack tucked under it, it's distressing to see him in this shape. The loose neckline of the hospital gown shows bruising on his shoulder. Tears spring to my eyes as I imagine the pain he must be in. Looking back, I ask, "What happened?"

The nurse signals me outside the room. I don't want to leave him, though. What if he wakes up when I'm gone? He'll be all by himself. The thought makes me feel sick. It would be awful. "Miss?" A hard nod toward the door is all I need to know I'm on borrowed time. I reach down and gently touch Keats's hand, and whisper, "I'll be right back. I promise."

When I turn, his fingers grapple for mine. "Spark?"

I rush to caress a part of him not swollen or in pain, but I don't know where it's safe to land. I wrap my fingers around the railing and lean over it. "I'm here, Poet. Right by your side."

The squeak of the nurses' shoes alerts me to look back and catch the eye roll as she shuts the door. "I'll be back with the paperwork," she says, knowing it's futile to argue with me. I'm not leaving him. Not ever.

"Hey there, you had me worried."

Wincing, he groans in response. "Sorry I didn't show."

"No. It's okay." I skate my hands over his arm, still unsure where I can touch him without adding to his pain. "I'm just glad I found you. But what happened?"

"Three guys walk into the station." When he stops to chuckle but then groans again, I'm not sure if he's telling the story or trying to land a joke.

"Keats?" I slip my hand under his, leaving it to him if he feels he can hold it without hurting himself. We're touching, so that's all that matters to me. "Is that what really happened?"

He opens his mouth, then closes it with the one eye that still has the capability. After taking several shallow breaths, he opens his eyes and says, “I was jumped in the subway. Pretty sure I was robbed as well, but I’d have to ask the nurses.” My own breath has shallowed as a sob rattles my chest. I try hard to keep the tears at bay, but my vision is going blurry faster than I can erase the image of him being attacked. A tear slips down my cheek, landing on the back of his hand. When his fingers curl around mine, he says, “I’m going to be alright. You know how I know?”

“No,” I whisper, losing my voice to alarm bells ringing in my head from how bad his injuries are. “How do you know that?”

He grins this time, still accompanied by a twinge of pain rippling through his expression, and a quieter groan. “Because you were with me after it happened.” He brings my hand to his mouth. It’s good to see he has the strength, but it also tells me he has some healing to do. “You’re my own personal guardian angel. You stayed with me until I was rescued.” He kisses my hand before holding it to his chest above his heart.

I’m not sure what he’s talking about, but he sounds confident that I helped him somehow. I don’t need to know the details just yet. What’s most important is that he’s now safe and can recover completely. That means breaking him out of this place and setting him up at his apartment, where it’s more comfortable. “I’m glad you were rescued. I can’t lose you again.”

“You won’t. Not ever, Spark.” With a look that I’d liken more to lust than being injured by how his pupils widen when he catches my eyes, he says, “You know what I want?”

Should my body react to him on demand like this? Probably not, but I'm not stopping it. "What do you want, Poet?"

"I'd kill for some ramen."

The laugh hits me quickly and escapes too loudly for being in a hospital room. I lean over and kiss the side of his head as he does mine so often. When I right myself, I reply, "I can make that happen."

CHAPTER 26

KEATS

"A guy could get used to this," I say, tucking my arms under my head on the pillows piled behind me in bed. A smirk lifts my cheek like a damn creeper, but the view is fantastic.

Short T-shirt showing off her midriff.

Fitted workout pants give me a good look at her incredible ass.

And I'm certain she's not wearing a bra by how her nipples peak against the cotton.

The vixen.

She knows what she's doing. *And it's working.*

How can my entire body be sore or worse, hurting, and my dick manages to sport an erection like I didn't just get out of the hospital two days ago? I know the why and how. My Spark. I'm a lucky fucking guy.

"You seem to be already used to it," she smarts with those pink lips I wouldn't mind seeing wrapped around—"I have an apartment to see in an hour." She glances at me, casually dropping the bomb as she walks into the bathroom while tucking her hair behind one ear.

I'm all for her having her independence and finally breaking free from the shackles of her family. But as a couple who haven't made any declarations but are filling the leading roles, I'm starting to wonder what we're doing. Or is it all just make-believe? It's not for me.

She's been here to see me every day since we reunited and spends the nights taking care of me like she lives here. No complaints from me. But is it fair to her?

I'm used to living alone. I've done it since I was a teen, but she hasn't. So it's a big ask to see if she wants to make this situation more permanent since she's between places to live, and I'm enjoying her company. Selfishly, I hate it when she leaves, even when it's only for a few hours to go to the hotel to change clothes or run errands before she returns.

I don't think I can broach the topic without it coming off as possessive. Is that what it is? I don't want to share her with anyone else. *Fuck yes, I'm possessive of her.* The smile shining just for me and a laugh ringing like church bells, summoning me to congregate at her altar, are big drivers of the emotion. I lick my lips, remembering just how sweet her altar tasted this morning.

I grin, unashamed. My tongue is working great.

Yeah, it's probably too soon to talk about moving in, but it doesn't stop me from thinking about it. Logically, it's reckless to jump in like we've been together for years. But my heart could argue why this makes sense in front of the Supreme Court and win.

Propping myself up, I lean against the wooden headboard and ask, "Where's the apartment?"

She comes galloping out of the bathroom with a huge

smile on her face and climbs onto the bed next to me. "You're going to love this. It's only eight blocks from here."

"Then what's the point?" Shit. *Why'd I say that?* Her head tilts on the jolt back from her neck. The smile washed away under the tide of the insult. "I didn't mean—"

"The point is I need a place to live." With her arm flying in the opposite direction of her parents' house, she says, "I can't just go from their house to yours."

I've already fucked this up, *sooooo* . . . "Why not?"

"You know why, Keats." When her shoulders soften, the corners of her eyes drag down with them. "How would that be standing on my own two feet?" She turns, anchoring a foot to the floor to push off the bed, but I catch her by the arm. "Please don't leave because this conversation is uncomfortable."

Relaxing her back, she says, "I'm not leaving because I can't have this conversation. I was only going to get your medication."

I glance at the time. Yep, three minutes until the alarm goes off. "I'm an ass. Sorry."

"Are you sorry you're an ass or because you assumed the worst?"

Shrugging, I try for lighthearted, hoping I didn't just majorly screw this up. I want her to trust me, not think I'm one of the others demanding something from her. "Both."

Half of one of her smiles is still worth millions to me. She stands and says, "It's okay. I'll be right back."

Left to my own devices, my thoughts wander to the emails I have piling up in my inbox, the missed miles I haven't run, or the weights I'll have to build up to lifting again once I'm healed. Instead of worry, a wash of gratitude overwhelms me in quieter moments like these. I rest my head back, staring out the window as a grin pops into place. I did it. I got a book deal. Although it's not new news, I don't think I've had a genuine moment to celebrate. I reach for my phone on the nightstand and text Professor Johns:

Assaulted and mugged in the subway, but recovering, and I got a book deal.

Figure it's worth getting everything out upfront so we can talk about the other, more important stuff like the deal.

My phone pings:

What the hell, Keats? Are you okay?

I reply:

Can't say I haven't been better, but I've probably been worse off as well. I'll live. And I have money from the advance to use as bandages. So yeah, I'm good.

The daze of devastation I wandered in for months after Sosie ghosted me was far worse. At least with bruises, there's an expectation of healing to follow. With her—no word, no explanation, no nothing left me feeling hollow for years.

He texts:

This is a lot for text. I have some free time in a few hours. How about I stop by?

He's always been more of a conversationalist than I am. I prefer text, but it's him, so I reply:

Sure thing. Just buzz when you're here, and I'll let you in.

I set the phone down just before Sosie walks in with a tray I didn't know I had. When she sets it on the bed next to me, I study the clockwork of items placed on it. Orange juice at one. Water at two. An English muffin at four and butter and jelly at six. My stomach growls so loud when I spot the Andes Mint sitting at nine o'clock that Sosie asks, "I have a whole box if you want them?"

I take the green-packaged chocolate, grinning like a kid who just got candy . . . I laugh because it feels like I just scored a touchdown, if my school had a team and I had played football. "I used to think these were candies that rich people ate."

"We do." She laughs, sitting on the edge of the bed.

"When I was ten, I'd bought chocolate bars at the bodega with a bulk discount I'd wrangled out of the owner. I went around selling them near Park Avenue to raise money for new sneakers. Figured I'd hit the wealthier neighbors since they had money to spare. They didn't in my neighborhood." She settles in next to me against the headboard as she has nowhere else to be, more important than here with me. The warmth of her presence isn't only felt in the proximity. It's found in the touch of her nails, gently scraping through the hair above my ear. "What kind of sneakers?"

"The white, black, and red low-top Jordans. I probably would have gotten my ass kicked and had them stolen, but I just wanted them."

Her eyes travel across the room to stare into her own memories. "Those were always so cool. I had pink and white ones."

I sink into the gulf of peace she brings me and then take her other hand in mine to bring to my lips and kiss. Still holding it, I continue, "I walked by some five-star restaurant where the opera crowd was gathering to have dinner. They were dressed in tuxes and long dresses. The women were wearing lots of jewelry. Anyway, I talked a few of the ladies into buying, who then told their husbands to chip in to buy me out. I'd hit the jackpot. I walked away sold out, a hundred and fifty dollars in my pocket, and one of the women had given me her after-dinner mint." I hold it up. "Just like this."

Her smile brightens the room more than the sun filtering in through the windows. "Did you buy the shoes?"

"No. I was about to. I had planned to take the train out to Jersey to the mall, but my mom's shoes were parked by the door next to mine. She needed new soles more than I needed sneakers that fit."

"You bought your mom shoes?"

I release her to drop my head and rub the bridge of my nose to break up the water forming in the corners of my eyes. Damn, the heaviness of the long-forgotten memory hits me harder than I could have expected. "She did the best she could." My canned response comes quickly. The excuse to defend her has always been ready on the tip of my tongue, but I realize I don't genuinely say it to defend her when she's not paying much attention to me. I've been saying it, so no one thinks less of me for having parents who couldn't be there for me, which cost them nothing and would have meant more than shoes ever could have.

Tilting my head back, I tap it to the headboard before resting it there. "She needed them more than I did."

She scooches closer, her body just kissing mine without the pressure to cause any pain. "You're a good man, Poet. You always have been."

"I don't know about that, but things work out how they're supposed to."

"Even with us?"

Her gaze slides to our hands held between us. "I was fucking miserable after that night. Knowing what I had and lost was worse than never having it at all. But—" I look at her. When her eyes greet mine, and a smile appears, I add, "I'm starting to believe this is how it was meant to work out. Time and perspective allow me to see things in a new light I couldn't back then."

"I would have preferred we'd had those years together."

My cheeks split in reaction. How did I deserve this incredible woman? I lean over. "Ow." And kiss her despite the pain because deep down, I gave her the answer I tell myself, but I wish we had had those years together as well.

"Time for meds."

She hands them to me with a glass of water. As soon as I swallow them, I say, "You know what would make me feel so much better, Nurse Sosie?"

"What?" She appears ready to serve, which only makes me hard again.

"You naked."

The bubble of trying to be all serious bursts with her laughter. Taking the chocolate from my hand, she unwraps it and says, "Open wide." I do as I'm told and eat the mint chocolate. As soon as it's melting in my mouth, she cocks a brow as a smirk comes over her. "That will have to do for now." Walking toward the door, she grips onto the frame and, with her weight hanging from her fingertips, she adds, "Until I get back. I have an apartment to go see."

We've managed to loop back to where this all started—her leaving when all I want is for her to stay. But I set my selfish wants aside and butter my English muffin like a good patient. "Will I see you later?"

"You're not getting rid of me that easily, Poet." Righting

herself, she moves to the hall and looks back. "I may not be trained, but I have every intention of nursing you back to good health." She dashes back and gives me a kiss. "I'll be back before you miss me."

As soon as she takes a step, I say, "I miss you."

Her laughter trickles out as she walks to the door. One glance over her shoulder, and she says, "I already miss you, too."

CHAPTER 27

SOSIE

Chatter from the other room is dulled when Marcy asks, "What do you think, Sos?" The clack of two sets of heels echoes off the hardwood floors right after, the sound disappearing when my friend enters the bedroom with the agent.

Turning away from the view of the solid brick wall less than ten feet outside the window, I find Marcy standing next to the real estate broker, and my excitement bubbles over. "I'll take it."

"Really? It's the size of a shoebox. You can't get more than a queen in this bedroom, and there'd be no room to walk on the sides," the broker says with perplexion, creating lines despite the heavy Botox to keep them at bay. "The price is unbeatable, but that view—"

"I love it." Not one thing on the list sounds negative despite her tone and the disapproval she's struggling to keep from her expression.

"You qualify for so much more. I'm waiting for an off-market apartment on the Upper East Side to get back to me. Seventeen hundred square feet. Three bedrooms. A terrace—"

"I don't need to see it. This is the one." I may not be in a skirt, but I twirl with my arms out anyway. "See, it's big enough," I say, coming to a stop in my sneakers.

Marcy crosses the room in five steps and peeks out the window, looking in both directions before nodding. "This is quintessential New York, baby."

Always on my side, my friend is so good to me. "When can I move in?"

The agent is already walking into the room. Grabbing her Birkin handbag from the counter, she says, "One month. It's empty, but the current renters refuse to give it up even a day early unless you want to pay an extra five K."

One month? I hum, thinking about how much I'm spending per night at the hotel. "I might want to do that. I'd spend more than that for a week at a hotel."

"Well," the agent says, finally able to smile even if it is forced. "Let me know, and I'll draw up the paperwork."

"Draw it up."

"I'm late to my next appointment, so I'll work on it when I get back to the office." She walks out, leaving Marcy and me grinning at each other in silence until the sound of her heels is no longer heard on the stairwell outside the open door.

Throwing her arms around me, she says, "You did it, Sosie."

Jumping up and down only causes us to tip a bit since she's in heels. I steady her and release our embrace with a sigh of relief the size of the Grand Canyon. The pull to call Keats is so strong that my hand is already wrapped around my phone in my pocket. But I don't. Not yet. This feels like the kind of news that should be shared in person, especially when our relationship remains so undefined but feels solid and certain, inevitable in ways that I'm also excited about.

Marcy leads us out of the bedroom, where I can already see Keats and me lounging around on Sunday mornings. He could be reading the paper because he seems like the type who likes the ink on his fingers and something tangible in his hands. And I could be scrolling through social media, sending him an endless stream of memes and cat videos, or flipping through fashion magazines. Bagels in bed, the everything kind that makes us laugh when the crumbs are all over the sheets, and coffee as we lazily begin our day.

I stop in the doorway and look back. I don't even know what he likes to do on the weekends. What if he's a morning person who likes to go running in Central Park while the sun is barely awake? Well, I guess I could try to shift my routine and do yoga at sunrise, or maybe take up running? I've never loved it, but I've never refused a buddy or a boyfriend to exercise with.

My cheeks hurt from smiling so much, and I turn to join Marcy for a coffee before heading back to my sexy patient. "Is it wrong to fantasize about him rescuing me? He looks so sexy with a black eye."

The belt of laughter startles me, but I laugh in response. Opening the door to this perfect, darling of an apartment, Marcy's brown hair swings over her shoulder, and she says, "It's apparently super common."

"I can see why."

I shut the door behind us, and we start down the five flights of stairs. The memory huffing and puffing as I hoofed it up his four-story walkup causes a giggle to bubble up. I'll have a great ass at least.

She stops and looks back. "What made you cut your hair?"

When I catch up, she starts trotting down with me following her again. "I needed a change. This is more me than the long hair."

"I like it. So you just cut it?"

"I had Keats cut it." We land on the bottom floor and push through the door. Both of us bundle our arms around ourselves when a harsh wind hits. Strands of blond hair block my vision until I flick my neck to send it back on one side. "It's totally uneven but . . ." I shrug, tightening the wool belt around my waist. "I kind of like it. I've been thinking about getting some pink strands like I used to have as well."

We reach the corner and take a right. "What about work? Is that allowed?"

"I have no idea. I'm not returning."

"What do you mean you're not returning?" She stops and stares at me. "Sosie, you just qualified for an apartment because of your salary. You could lose it."

Oh. I hadn't thought of that. "But I have the money?"

"Do you have enough to cover the first and last month's rent?"

Marcy has always been sensitive to my spending without thinking. Now I understand why. She had to be since she pays her own bills.

I scan the surrounding area. The graffiti on the steel garage door and kids kicking a soccer ball in the direction we're heading. Standing in front of what would be my drugstore, I try to peek in and decide it's nice enough. We head toward a local coffee shop ahead. A mom and her young son leave the corner store, and a neon sign next to it catches my eye, advertising a nail salon. The trash bags piled ahead on the driveway don't bother me, and the bustling of some guys outside the vape store isn't my concern. *Money is.* I can already see myself living in this vibrant community. It's noisy and a little chaotic, if I'm being honest, but it's full of life, and it's busy. It's the opposite of where my parents live.

And though it's eight blocks from Keats's apartment, the distance on the map was deceptive. They're longer blocks than expected. I'm altogether in a different world in this area of the city. Which feels like an adventure, but am I in over my head? Especially if I don't have a job any longer? "I'm sorry, Marcy, can I get a rain check?"

"Why?"

I run my freezing fingers through my hair and then rub them together for warmth. "I don't think I've thought through everything I need to. I want to get my laptop and figure things out."

Sympathy runs through her expression, and when she tilts her head to the side, she nods. "I get it. But you're buying the next round of coffee."

"If I have money for it, it will be my treat." I give her a hug and say, "Thanks for helping me check out the apartment."

"Eh." She flips her hand. "It was kismet that I was in the area, and we could connect. It's been a while."

She starts walking backward, but before she's out of earshot, I say, "Too long. I want to fully catch up soon."

Pointing at me, she laughs. "And you owe me a meet and greet with the infamous Keats." Her feet come to a sudden standstill. "You were supposed to introduce me to Gregory, and that never happened. What gives?"

"Oh my God, long story, but not only did I dodge a bullet, but you did. Trust me."

"I'm trusting you, but I'm twenty-eight. It's my turn to meet Prince Charming." She turns and runs smack into a tall man in a dark wool coat, and he's handsome.

One shot, friend. I quietly cheer her on. "You got this."

After watching two strangers fall in love at first sight, a girl can dream for her friend on the street. I rush to the corner to catch a cab back to the hotel to shower and get to Keats's place. I throw my arm in the air and step off the curb to get in the taxi that slammed on its brakes to pick me up.

The job hadn't really crossed my mind once I left. We've been closed for the holidays, so I haven't had to face or deal with it. Nobody knows I'm not going to show up next week. Do I give them the courtesy of submitting a resignation or just walk away from my father's company like I am him?

Between the cards and cash I have on hand, I have enough money to cover the rent for a year. That doesn't concern me. It's the other stuff. The living stuff—food, bills, my phone, taxi rides, clothes, travel, and more than I can list off the top of my head. Am I naive for thinking I could pull this off? Dumb for even trying?

I can get another job. I have a degree and a résumé I've built, even if it's not particularly impressive, since it was a job my father created to keep me occupied. But it counts, and I did a damn good job at it.

I hate that my hands are shaking, and my stomach is twisting in turmoil. This shouldn't be happening. It was a new beginning for me, but now my past is catching up with me and ruining my present. *Take a breath, Sosie. Breathe in. Hold it. And slowly exhale. It's going to be fine. Everything is working in my favor.* I manifest several times before the car pulls up to the hotel. I dash up the short flight of stairs, and though I'm not running inside the small lobby, my pace is still quickened.

"Ms. Stansbury?"

I hear my name just as I punch the button for the elevator. I look back. A woman waves her arm like she's trying to flag down the Coast Guard from a dinghy. Our eyes connect when she leans over the desk. "Yes?"

The elevator dings, making me want to hop on. The sooner I get changed, the sooner I get to Keats. He'll give the pep talk I need, and he's a finance guy. Surely, he can help me put something together, so I understand my options and how long I have before I need to have a paycheck coming in again. I walk to the desk since the hotel attendant calls my name again. "Hi," I say, standing in front of her with a big smile like I'm seeing my personal shopper at Chanel and she's the key to scoring the exclusive bag I want.

"Sorry to interrupt your day, but there's been a matter of payment declination."

My brain riddles through the last word like it's foreign to me, which isn't entirely untrue. "I don't understand."

"Your card has been declined," she snaps. "We'll need another to add to our file. Unfortunately, due to this mishappenstance . . ." Is she screwing with me? I'm absolutely positive that is not a real word. "We'll need to charge the full stay this time."

Glancing around, I see a couple having cocktails on the couch, but otherwise, *thank God,* I don't have an audience for this humiliation. "That's not a problem," I whisper, keeping my voice down like my head as I dig through the purse tucked between my hip and the heavy coat I'm wearing. She peeks up at me every few seconds as if I can magically produce another credit card. Fortunately, I can since I grabbed the stack from my dresser.

She's typing on a keyboard. I'm sure she's making a note that I'm a delinquent guest. *Ugh.* I tap the counter with another card, then hand it to her. "There's no credit limit on this one."

Her fake smile vanishes quickly as she snatches the card and slides it down the card reader. We both wait in painful silence while our eyes volley between each other's and to the machine for the card to clear. "*I'mmm* sorry. This one has also been declined."

"What?" I rapidly blink a few times. "But there's no limit. It's limitless." I hate the way I sound like a fool who can't shut her mouth. The woman knows without me having to explain. "Do you mind trying it again?"

"Of course, Ms. Stansbury."

Was that loud or just my embarrassment kicking in? Does the entire city need to know I'm being rejected repeatedly?

A throb in my head matches the heavy beats in my chest when I pretend to scratch an itch on my shoulder using my chin. I peer around the place for any eyewitnesses to my utter humiliation. Fortunately, it's not busy at this hour. Sure, the couple drinking glance at me, but I don't think they can hear what's happening across the lobby. I exhale to relieve the pressure, but embarrassment is already strangling my neck.

"Ms. Stansbury—"

"Oh God." I startle, protectively covering my heart with my hand. "Yes?"

"Are you alright?" There's no concern in her eyes, but there is impatience.

"Depends on if that card goes through or not," I joke,

but I'm unable to laugh. "I appreciate you trying these for me." My voice isn't louder than a mouse as I press against the counter, hoping no one else can hear me.

She sets the card down beside the keyboard on top of the other, and I swear I see a devious glint in her eyes when she looks back at me. "Declined."

It's then that I realize, this is by design with my father as the architect. He knows I'm gone . . . fear rattles through me as I pull out another card for her to try. There's no hope, but a lot of mortification tied up in me asking for one more chance.

"Declined as well."

I can't hold my chin up anymore. My cheeks are flaming hot, and I'm close to tearing up when I offer one more card to run through the machine. "I'm so sorry for wasting your time." I have more cards, but the outcome is obvious, so there's no point in making either of us continue this suffering.

"You will need to pay for the nights you've stayed."

Ironically, I haven't stayed. It's only been a landing place for my belongings until I figure out the next steps. I hand her my debit card, which swipes just fine, but my cash is limited, unlike what that card was supposed to be. I sign the receipt and set the pen down. Knowing I don't have the cash on hand to stay here and cover months of rent and living expenses, I say, "I'll need to check out, please."

As if she were waiting for me to admit defeat, she replies, "Already done. Have a nice day, Ms. Stansbury."

My face begins to cool despite the shame that overwhelms me as I walk to the elevator. I keep thinking I have things under control, but then something new hits me sideways. Should I have expected this to happen? Yes. But how did they find out I was gone for good?

Gregory. The betrayer.

The elevator opens, and a bellman enters with me. It's still tempting to cry and get it out of my system, but tears won't wash away the shame that's settling inside. What am I supposed to do? Where am I supposed to go? How do I tell Keats that it's only day three and I failed? I take a deep breath, but a stifled sob catches in my throat.

The man tugs a tissue from a new pack and hands it to me. "It will be okay. You're young, and you'll recover, and whatever happened back there will just be a story you tell or not, and nobody has to know but yourself."

"I can only hope."

"Well," he says just as the elevator comes to a stop. I step off and turn back. "You're lucky. They usually cut the cards in half."

"Oh no." I gasp just as the doors shut.

CHAPTER 28

SOSIE

I was buzzed into his apartment building like a pizza delivery person.

Like a stranger.

Not at all like someone about to have to ask her boyfriend—*oh my goodness,* I have a boyfriend. My cheeks crease because even when distracted with a million other problems, I can't restrain my smile. The nerves return from the momentary reprieve of what I'm about to have to tell him. Am I telling or asking? *Ask him?* Can I ask him for a place to stay until the apartment is ready? My thoughts are all over the place as I drag my suitcases down the hallway in shame. And I thought the scene at the hotel was bad, humiliation in real time with each swipe of the card. This is worse. I feel like a failure.

The door opens, and an unfamiliar face stands there expectantly. I bend backward to catch the number beside it to make sure I knocked on the right door. The bronze number matches Keats's. *M'kay.* It's the right apartment.

"Hello?" I say, debating whether I need to barge in and save Keats, or if this is some sort of ruse?

"You must be Sosie." The man's smile is welcoming, highlighted by his brighter green eyes and receding hairline. He opens the door wider, then waves me in like he lives here.

I stay right where I am with my suitcases parked at my side, a pair of black stilettos anchored onto the front of my coat by the heels, and multiple bags wrapped around me because I was packing my crap as fast as I could on borrowed time. "Um."

"I'm Michael. Professor Johns," he says, nodding behind him. "An old mentor of Keats's." He's not that old. Not as old as I imagined when Keats mentioned him in the past. "Let me help you with that." He reaches for the handles.

"They roll," I say as if he doesn't know how suitcases work. As if I didn't feel enough shame, I continue piling it on for a second, third, and fourth helping. The man will think I'm an idiot if I keep this up. The last thing I want to do is embarrass Keats as well. "Is Keats here?"

"Sosie?" Keats calls ahead in the living room. His being out of bed is a surprise, but I'm glad he's not being attacked in his apartment.

"Hey, it's me." I follow Michael as he pulls my cases and parks them just inside by the door. I add the shoes and handbags in a pile on top before taking my coat off and hanging it on a hook I've already claimed as mine. Glancing to the side, I see Keats propped up on the couch. Coming from the shadows of the hallway, I hurry to his side, bending down to kiss him before sitting on the coffee table beside him. Selfishly, I prefer him in bed where I can cuddle in, but it's good to see him in a new environment. There's an effortless comfort that comes over me just from the proximity to him again that I gulp down, wishing I could bathe in it. In his eyes, I'm seen in a better light than how others see me. I don't feel like such a failure, though that myth is about to be dispelled when he hears what happened. There's time for that, and that time doesn't involve blurting it all out when his favorite professor is visiting. "How are you feeling?" I ask, reaching to cover his hand with mine. "Any pain?"

"I'm good. Meds kicked in shortly after you left. They're still working. This is Professor Johns—"

"The one you called an asshole back at NYU?"

The professor laughs as he sits in a chair beside the couch. "I wouldn't be surprised."

Keats chuckles. "I didn't say that."

I nod and silently mouth, "He totally did." But I can't hold a straight face, especially when Keats finally has a healthy color returning to his face. "Fine, he didn't." I wink at Keats. "I can still nail the comedy, though."

"You can, and it doesn't hurt as much when I laugh." Reaching over the small divide, he rubs my knee. "This is Sosie. I told you she's quite something."

I'm fascinated that they were talking about me. Wonder what the two of them had to say about me?

Michael says, "I can see the resemblance."

The remark has me raising a brow as I look at him. "Resemblance to what?" I ask, not liking the idea of being compared to another woman.

"Scarlet," replies Michael.

I dart my eyes to Keats, who pushes up to readjust on the couch. The hardening jaw and the tick of the muscle beneath reveal an underlying annoyance. When he doesn't offer any more information, I ask, "Who's Scarlet, Keats?"

He rubs his temple, but it seems more of a distraction

than something that needs to be taken care of. Shooting his friend a glare, he slides his gaze back to me and says, “She’s a character in my book.” He holds my chin between his fingers, and his touch reassures me. Our souls bond so clearly through the connection of our eyes. The love I see in his gaze helps ease the shame and makes everything feel better. “We should talk about it sometime in private.”

He doesn’t have to go into detail. But despite the curiosity that’s spinning faster than a busy hamster wheel, I nod. “I want to hear about your book.” I look at Michael with the joy that bubbles over for my incredible Poet. “He told you about the deal?”

“I’m trying not to be jealous.” He laughs. “I got low five figures on my recent work. This kid goes to auction for his debut novel.” Reaching forward, he taps the arm of the couch. “I may be jealous, but I’m also proud of you, Keats. It’s a brilliant story and deserves the attention it’s getting.” When he rests back again, he says, “Seeing a student succeed feels like a success of my own.”

Keats turns his way with a big grin on his face. It’s nice to see him interact with someone else, to see how he moves and talks with his friends. It’s similar to how he is with me but different at the same time. Everything with us feels so intimate that it’s easy to forget the rest of the world exists outside us. He laughs, and teases, “Is that what you have to tell yourself to justify the low pay?”

“Pretty much.” Michael stands, adjusting his pants by the belt. “I should go. This guy needs to rest.” He walks over to me to shake hands. While holding it, he adds, “It was nice to finally meet you, Sosie.”

“You, too.” I get up to walk him to the door as if this is my place. It’s not, but any place with Keats feels like home.

He shakes hands with Keats, wishing him a swift

recovery before I follow him to the door. As soon as I shut it, I come to the edge of the living room, and ask, "Tell me what you need."

"You. Naked. A blow job. Chocolate cake. Pasta. A glass of water—"

"Okay. Okay. You rattled that off a little fast." I laugh, returning to sit across from him again. "Are you hungry, thirsty, or want sex? Because truthfully, I'm up for any or all three."

His hand rubs along the top of my thigh. "I knew I fell in love with you for a reason."

Love? He fell in love and says it so casually now that it's like it's been expressed before. Sure, I feel it, and he's made me feel no less than welcome and loved in his arms. But are we just saying it now with no buildup? No easing into a relationship? Jumping feet first and dealing with the consequences later? I don't know what to think. I love him, but it's too big an emotion to regulate just yet. I tap his nose gently. "I'm not so sure you should be partaking in some of those things."

"It's the pasta and cake, right?" he asks, chuckling as he drops his hand to his stomach and rubs his belly. "Because I'm not running."

"Your workout routine isn't something I'm worried about. You have muscles for days, and they're not going away just because you're laid up for a week or two." I stand, but he catches my hand.

When I look back, the smile he wears that seems to come naturally falters. "How was the apartment?"

"Oh, um. Are you comfortable? Do you want to move back into bed?"

"Sosie? Look at me." When I do, he says, "What happened?"

My gaze is drawn to the outside while my thoughts scramble to figure out what I want to say or how I should respond so that I don't become a problem he has to solve. "We should talk about it." I glance back at him. "After I get you what you need." My fingers slip from his hand as I walk to the kitchen.

"That doesn't sound promising."

I stop, resting my weight on the palm of my hand that's anchored to the countertop. With my back to him, I say, "It was promising." The earlier situation comes back to haunt me by gripping my throat. I try to clear it before I turn back to look at him, but I fail. "My credit cards have been cut off." When I speak, the words are rough, leaving me raw and exposed to more embarrassment.

Anxiety builds in the silence as our eyes stay locked, and time extends between us.

Sitting more upright, he asks, "Is that why you brought your suitcases with you?"

My gulp is so loud that I worry all of New York state just heard it. "Yes." My voice doesn't reach the same volume and weakens as shame reenters the conversation. "I could have paid to go to another hotel, but I just needed to see you."

He gets up. It's slow but steady, his muscles working in waves to get him to his feet. Coming to me, he gets into my space and kisses my face. "I'm glad you came here."

"You say that now." My words rush carelessly out. "But I can't barge into your life like this. I'd only be taking from you with nothing offered in return."

That smile that was made for me settles into place where it belongs, and he says, "You give me everything, Spark. Life, a reason to breathe, you're my muse, and . . ." Taking my hand between the two of his, he looks at me as if too impassioned to speak. His breath stumbles as if the words come too quickly to get off his chest. And then he pauses like a second thought has ruined it. But the soulful browns never leave mine until he kisses my temple. "You're the one who got away and my biggest heartbreak." It's only whispered, but it's out there for me and the universe to know and deal with, and causes my own heart to break in the aftermath.

Cupping my cheek, he catches my eyes as they start to water. "You're not in this alone anymore. We're a team, you and me." When his hand grapples onto the side of the counter, he exhales slowly and closes his eyes. "I think I need to get in bed."

Panic kicks in, but I stifle it as I wrap my arm carefully around him. "Let me help you." As soon as I walk him to the bedroom and reach the bedside, he climbs in and gently lays his head down on the pillow.

"Stay with me, okay?" he asks, his eyes growing heavy like a storm just blew in.

"I'm not going anywhere." I climb in next to him and mold to his side. As much as I want to rest my arm over him or entangle my legs, I resist the urge for his benefit. We lie minutes together, but his breathing is still even as if he's still awake. "I failed," I whisper. "I don't care what my parents think of me, but I didn't want to let you down."

His hand finds mine and holds it. "You didn't fail." When he turns to face me, he cracks his lids open. "You're going to find your way out of this and be okay. It's a new experience, but that's how you grow and become independent." Giving my hand a squeeze, he adds, "It's not about having to figure out everything on your own. It's about no one ever being able to control your life again." Kissing my hand, he says, "You can stay here as long as you need, but if it's best for you to be somewhere else right now, I support your decision."

The disappointment I've felt, the shame and humiliation seem less potent when you discover you have someone in your corner fighting with you. It's not about money anymore. That comes and goes, so I'm learning, it's about cocooning into the next phase of life to become bigger and better than ever.

My parents won't win this battle.

They thought they could keep us apart. They were wrong. We're together and stronger than before. And I'm not alone in this fight. Not anymore. I just needed the reminder of what I'm really fighting for. *Us.*

Looking into his eyes, I caress his cheek, and whisper, "I love you, Poet."

A rogue grin cuddles his cheeks. "I love you, too, Spark."

CHAPTER 29

KEATS

Sosie's been staring at that paperwork for days. She seemed positive that getting the apartment was the right move when it arrived, but she can't bring herself to sign it to close the deal. So the rental agreement remains spread out on the countertop for her to peruse when she's in the mood to do such things.

It's been killing me not to say anything, but she must make this decision on her own, so I leave her to it. Looking over at me on the couch, she says, "I need to get out of the apartment. How are you feeling? Up to go out?"

"What are you thinking?"

"Fresh air and dinner. How do you feel?"

"Stir-crazy. It would be good to get out." It's been incredible to spend so much time together, cementing what we already knew. We're good together. Though we're in what some might call the newlywed stage of our relationship because it hasn't been tested. I know that's untrue because we fought to get where we are, even if it was years of being isolated from each other. She's given up her entire life to be here for herself and me.

Something deep inside had me sacrificing years of my life waiting for her. I could have been playing the field, and by most guys' opinions, I should have. But that wasn't me. Once I met Sosie, I was a goner for her. "Let's go out and be a couple," I say, hoping she understands what I mean. "I want the whole world to see us together."

She's in the shower not five minutes later. Frowning with a face covered in shaving cream, I analyze the bruising that remains. The swelling has gone down, though it's still tender around the one eye. Otherwise, it feels good to shave again now that most of the soreness has gone away. Looking worse for wear is apparently an aphrodisiac for my girl, so I'm not wasting any opportunities that present themselves.

She opens the door and peeks out. "I can't stop thinking about how you said you want the world to see us together."

I drag the blade through the soapy water in the sink, catching her eye in the reflection of the mirror, and grin—wild and goofy at the same time. I feel my age for the first time in years, rather than the old soul I'm always told I am. "What has you thinking about that?"

Her hair is wet and still cut crooked. If I had known she wasn't going to fix my sloppy haircut, I would have made a better effort to keep it straight. But like her, I like it. It's not perfect, just like we aren't. Water drips from the tips and off her chin, but she doesn't seem to mind getting the rug wet.

"Because Gregory, my mom, and even my father sometimes used to center everything on me. Gregory would say that other guys would be jealous when they see me, or he couldn't wait to show me off." I hate his fucking face and pretentious name. I hate that he paraded her on his arm like a trophy he'd won. I fucking hate that bastard. I grit my teeth when I turn around because she deserves more than my back. "My mom used to talk about guys wanting to talk to me because I would look particularly attractive one night or another, and my father . . . there always seemed to be a clause with the extortion regarding my appearance."

I'm not sure what I did that was so different, but I set the razor down on the counter and cross the bathroom. "Anyone is lucky to be with you, but it's not because of how gorgeous you are, *which you are*. It's because of who you are that has captivated my soul and made it yours for the taking."

Running her wet fingers across my chin, she eyes it before her gaze reaches mine. "That's just it. I'm not arm candy. I'm an equal in your eyes. You see me, and that's so incredibly sexy."

"Sexy, huh?" The towel wrapped around my middle never stood a chance against the vision of those full pink lips. My body's reaction is instant, and when the towel falls, I take it as the sign it is. Running my hand around the side of her slick neck, I kiss her and then deepen it as I walk her back into the shower stall and close the door behind me. The steam billows from the spray as I slide my hands down over her body.

I kiss my way across her jaw, then bend to tackle her neck with my lips, a carnal instinct kicking in to mark her as mine. I flatten my hand over her stomach and go lower, desperate to feel her pussy wrapped around me again. But no way am I passing up the opportunity to watch her come beforehand.

When I slide a finger through the silk of her slit, she moans before I swallow it whole, relishing the feel of her ecstasy against my lips. I pull back, realizing I not only want to feel her but I also want to hear everything she can't keep inside. My mouth waters for the taste of her euphoria, my name rolling off her tongue, and her body trembles as she loses herself in the love we make.

Water pools in the divots where her shoulders meet her neck, and I lower to lap it up as my hands knead the soft skin of her tits. Turning her head, her lips against my ear, she whispers, "I can't wait to feel you inside me again."

My dick twitches, my heart sent into overdrive to thunder in my chest. But it's my head, the thought of her wanting me inside her that stirs my core, already demanding an early release. Her hand comes around my cock as I slide my tongue across her collarbone while holding her against the wall of the shower. I lift to bring her higher, not sure I have the patience to wait to plow into her when she talks to me like that. The graze of her tongue across my shoulder pulls me back from the brink of existence to savor the here and now, her and the ecstasy of gratification ahead of us. I bite, igniting a gasp from the shallower parts of her chest. My cravings only harden my dick. "I've never wanted anything as much as I want you, Spark," I whisper in need to please her, and to get off again.

Her arms come around my neck, and she lifts onto her tiptoes. Swaying back as if in a trance, she tilts her head, allowing the water to wash over her. I stare in astonishment that this stunning woman is in my arms, that she wants me as much as I desire her. The graceful lines of her neck, the curve of her waist, the bow that caps her top lip, and the softness of her hips. "I was captivated by her beauty erupting all at once," I whisper, kissing the mounds of her chest and then nip her peaks to watch her react. "It wasn't one thing in particular that drew me to her. . ." I slide my hands between her thighs and kneel in front of her, quoting a line from my book. The hot water soothes the lingering pain in my muscles, but she makes me forget about it altogether. Looking up, I watch as she takes each breath like it can save her. She looks down at me, and I say, "But all of them that made her up."

Running her fingers underneath my jaw, she says, "Always my Poet." Her voice and the feel of her soft touch against the roughness of my scruff, the way her eyes shine like gold in the dimmer light of the shower, it all makes me feel like I've won the grand prize. But that exhilaration can't stick when her love shines down like a beacon in the night, guiding me home.

"Always yours."

My gaze journeys from that bottom lip being bitten to the awning of dark lashes that try to shadow the sparkle in her eyes and fails. With the weight of her breast in my hand, I massage and am rewarded with another plea for more. "I need you," she says in a voice already on the cusp of begging. I slide my hand down to her waist, digging my fingers in to hold her still as I find her entrance with my other hand and tease before dipping inside her.

Her breathing is lost to the sound of water raining down on us, her chest rising and falling while her hands are pinned to the cold tile until she drops them to my shoulders and follows through with pressure to keep me there. No way in hell am I going anywhere until she's coming on my tongue. I lean forward to kiss her before slipping my tongue between her luscious lips. "Oh God." She releases a jagged breath just as I peer up to catch how the color of her lips has already deepened as they round for me.

I lift her leg and tilt my head to go deeper, my tongue filling her and thrusting as she struggles to stand still. Gliding her back on the wall, she can't find the leverage she's seeking to sink down on me. I grab her hips with both hands and fuck her good and proper with my tongue, knowing this gets me closer to the heat of her body's embrace wrapped around me again.

Her fingers twist through my wet hair, and she tugs while her nails dig into my other shoulder. Anchoring her leg on my shoulder, I lift and lower her onto me several times before teasing her clit. It only takes a nip and flick of my tongue to send her over the finish line.

She pulls at my hair again, my shoulders taking the brunt of her fingertips as they grasp for something to hold on to. Her head falls forward under heaving breaths, and she opens her eyes. A smile, not showy or for display, glides into place. It's one I only see when we're in bed and falling asleep, happiness that can't be hidden inside even when she dreams.

Rolling her fingers around the hair behind my ears, she asks, "Want to get out?"

I hit the faucet and hand her a towel. I roughly dry myself off, appreciating every inch of her as she slides the towel over her body. Twisting it around her head, she takes my hand and leads me to the bedroom with confidence. The Sosie I met has made a full comeback.

She doesn't hide any part of her body when she climbs onto the bed and invites me to join her with a come-hither motion of her finger. I drop the towel and climb over her, licking the space between her breasts and wedging my knees between her legs. The scrape of her nails over my lower back encourages me to kiss a trail over her chest, along her neck, and higher to nip at her bottom lip before kissing it.

There's not an ounce of tension in her muscles or hesitation in her eyes. It's easy to forget that we haven't been able to do this as much as we'd like. It feels so effortless with her, like we'll never change or be apart. What plagues us isn't something to worry about as we find a new path forward. *Us against the world.*

I rest my elbows above her shoulders and kiss her once and then again, tasting her tongue as ours tangle together. The urgency to see her, to look into her eyes, penetrates my need to stay steady. I pull back and graze the back of my hand over the sweet pink of her cheeks. Desire becomes too much when a slip of a moan and, "Make love to me," follows as a plea from the tip of her tongue.

A hint of rapture has me pushing into her consuming heat. The release of a sigh relaxes her shoulders against the mattress as if this is what she needed as much as I did. Her arms tighten around me, and her kisses dot my neck. I tuck my arms under her to hold her just as tight, pulling my dick out and pushing with more power each time.

The slick of our bodies has us finding a rhythm together as the vibration between us overcomes all else. The spur of heels to my ass, the exhalations remind me of a symphony leading to the big finale, and the extraordinary sensation when I'm deep inside her. It's so good. "You feel incredible, babe." I kiss her head without missing a thrust or pull as I drive into her, seeking relief and pleasure.

But my mind plays tricks on me—the desire for her to reach her peak first, to fight the orgasm that races in my veins faster than it should. It's her. "I can't hold on."

"Don't," she whispers with the same burning desire coating her throat. "Please. Please. Please."

Meeting me thrust for thrust, the ache for more overtakes everything else, and we fuck and love and tangle together right to the cliff that leads to our salvation. The arch of her back leaves her wanton mouth unattended.

When I press my lips to hers, it's all it takes to have her cry my name in her angelic voice. The shift of her body is all it takes to send me over the edge with her.

A pledge.

A promise.

The pleasure.

The pain.

I crash into her as I push to completion, my body betraying me by not sparing a drop of energy when I come and land back in her arms. I can't move. I don't want to anyway. I feel too good. She feels even better beneath me.

"Keats," she says. "You trying to kill me?" She laughs as she pushes me off her.

"Sorry about that." I roll onto my back, letting my soul return to its rightful place.

With her head on my arm, she rolls toward me and drapes her arm and leg over me to get more comfortable. Kissing my chest, she asks, "Promise me it will always be this good."

Chuckling, I finally open my eyes and turn to kiss her forehead. "I'll do my best."

"I don't mean the sex." Propping herself up, she grins. "Well, I do, but I mean us. This. It feels like a dream, and I don't want to wake up from it."

"You're a dream come true. We don't have to sleep to find paradise. We found it in each other."

The response seems to satisfy her as she shifts her head back into place on my arm. Our breathing takes a while to even, but when it does, she whispers, "I wish I had my camera."

"What happened to it?" The aches from the week begin to sneak back in, but nothing an ibuprofen can't fix.

"I left it behind in my rush out the door." She snuggles,

shifting to close her eyes. "I thought I wanted to go out, but I'd rather stay home."

Whether she meant to say it or not, an uncontrollable smile instantly spreads across my face. Home. I've found a home in her as well. I don't call it out because it was said from the heart. She meant it, so I don't want to tempt her to take it back. "If you had it, what would you take pictures of?" I ask instead.

Her breath has leveled into a deeper stance as if sleep is dragging her under. "You. I don't have one photo of you."

Caressing her cheek, I whisper, "We should remedy that."

CHAPTER 30

SOSIE

Stansburys take what they want. We plunge forward no matter the cost.

That was how I was raised, so maybe that's why I hesitate to make a decision I know will hurt Keats. If I don't want to be like them, then he deserves to have a say in the next steps, even if he believes he doesn't. "What do you think?" I step just inside the doorway of the bedroom.

The room is too small for his large frame, but it's his presence that takes up most of the space. His expression contorts his handsome features as if a problem needs to be solved. Glancing at me, he says, "I don't fit on a queen-sized bed."

I want to laugh, but his concern is valid. I retrieve a measuring tape from my purse. "That's why I brought this." I hand him one end, and we walk to opposite sides of the room. Seeing the seventy-six-inch marker pressed against the wall, I ask, "Are we talking Eastern or California king?"

He chuckles. "I don't think we have a choice. A standard

will fit, but there's no room on the sides." He brings his end back to the tape holder and studies the space again with his lips twisting to the side. I want to kiss that perplexed expression right off his face. "It takes up most of the room, and there won't be space to walk around it since the mattress will be squeezed inside. We can just use the end to get in and out of it, I suppose, but making it up will be a bitch."

Waving my hand over the space, I can already imagine us here. "It can be like a bed cave. We can hibernate in here."

Scratching the back of his neck, he must still be fixated on the size of the room by how he's staring at the three walls in front of him. When he finally looks at me again, he says, "I'm confused. Do you want to live here, like full-time?"

"No." I laugh. "It's just sort of a retreat where I can do whatever I end up doing with my life."

"Why can't you do that at my place?"

Point proven with that one question. "Because it's yours, not mine."

"It's yours *as much* as mine, Sosie."

Who could have predicted my entire life would be changing in a single blink when it's taken years to get to this point? Not me. Obviously. But now that it feels like the sun is finally shining in my life, despite some of it being blocked by the brick building next door, I'm ready to embrace it.

I just hope it's with Keats since we've been living together unofficially, without discussing where it leads. He hasn't asked about my plans or made me feel like I had to be doing something to contribute. It's like we've been on an extended vacation. But soon we'll land back in reality. We already have in most ways. And aimlessly roaming around his apartment while he works doesn't sound appealing. I imagine he'd get sick of seeing me doing nothing with my days anyway.

"I need to figure out what's next, and having a witness to me failing—"

"Accomplishing your goals," he corrects without hesitation.

"I appreciate the vote of confidence, but you need to write or edit or do your finance stuff," I say, wafting my hand around. "You don't need me bugging you because I'm bored."

Car horns scream through the windows from the street below as I wait for him to respond. He licks his lips and is lost in thought for a moment too long, making me shift in discomfort. A man of fewer words than I'd like, but as always, they hold meaning, making them even more valuable to me. He runs his fingers through his hair, then follows me out of the room to look out the living room windows. "I hate talking about money on a personal level," he says, looking back at me, "but can you afford this place for the term of the contract?"

Going into the little kitchen area, I hop onto the counter and run my hands over the laminate like it's expensive marble countertops. "I have enough cash for one year."

"Then what happens?"

"By then, I'll have established a direction. I'll have a new job, and maybe I'll start taking photos again."

Though his eyes have wandered the apartment several times over, his gaze always returns to me. He grins as if he has no say in the matter. "It sounds like you have a plan. That's all you can do is get started."

I don't need his approval, but I desperately crave it, so

hearing him so amenable to the idea of me having this apartment means everything to me. I go to him, wrapping my arms around his neck and lifting on my toes to kiss him. He's swift with his hands, landing them flat on my backside. With a solid squeeze of my ass cheeks, he kisses me back.

I drop my heels to the floor again and do a spin. "I'm surprised no one else has snatched it up. I mean, I get that it's no bigger than a matchbox, but it's all I need."

"Is it *all* you need?" His tone shifts from joking to something unlike him, causing me to turn around.

Our gazes fasten as we stand next to each other. "You're not losing me, Keats."

"No?" he asks, angling to hold his arms out wide. "*We're* not gaining another apartment. *You are*. An apartment where you'll be sleeping away from me, starting your day without me, a place to be alone." He walks to the window that has more light streaming in than in the bedroom, and peers out like he'll discover something new each time. He suddenly turns back to face me. "It's all you ever wanted when all I ever wanted was you."

The punch to my gut is swift, defying any reasoning I thought I had anchored myself in to justify this apartment. But how could I miss what was happening right in front of me with him? I'm not on the same axis I once was, and I'm adapting to change as fast as I can. I've been reckless, even careless of how this might affect him. "Standing on my own feet doesn't mean standing without you, Poet."

I go to him, holding his face in my hands, and admire the man he's become since we met. Back then, he was a student working his ass off to make a future for himself. Now he's living the life he wanted.

He's so much stronger despite the path he was forced

down. His strength of character was always at the forefront. It's enviable. I had the dreams but not the power. But what upsets me most is that I let it happen. I can own my part and carry that shame, but I should use it to my advantage instead. I say, "I can never do enough to earn the love you've given me so freely, but I'll do my best to repay you in spades."

"I prefer kisses, and if we're really talking, spades pale in comparison to a blo—"

"Yeah. Yeah. I get it." I burst out laughing and kiss him. "Seems you get the point as well." Wrapping my arms around him, I rest my head on his chest because, other than how much I love being this close to him, I love hearing his heartbeat even more. "I love you." Looking up, I rest my chin on him, and add, "If you don't want the apartment, I don't want it either."

"That's not my decision to make, Spark." He strokes my hair back from my face. "But if you're asking me if I think you should get it." Sliding his hands down my body, he settles them on my hips. His touches always ignite a fire between us and trigger a chemical reaction in my body. I can't get enough of him, but I control myself since the apartment isn't mine just yet. "I'll be over anytime you'll have me."

He meant what he said.

After carrying this beast of a king-size mattress up all those flights of stairs, we discovered he does indeed have some spots he's still recovering from, although he insisted he didn't. Now we're both wiped, and I feel bad.

He crashes on top of the memory foam mattress in the

bedroom, his weight forcing it to tuck in nicely at the sides. Grumbling, he says, "The mattress stays with the apartment." His eyes are closed and feet hanging off with his arms spread wide. That's an invitation if I've ever seen one, and a sexy one at that. "I'm never moving it again."

I don't bother to remind him that he was moving it because he refused to pay movers when it would be, and I quote, "A piece of cake." I also won't laugh or rub it in his face. There won't be any I-told-you-so's because that's not part of the new life we're building. I kneel and crawl onto the bed cougar style, though I'm two and a half years younger than him, and lie beside him on my back. I'm giddy to have the first slice of a new life installed, and grin like a fool while staring up at the ceiling. I hadn't noticed the watermark before . . . I'm sure it's something that can be fixed or painted over. I prefer the view next to me anyway, and with a little nudge of my elbow, I suggest, "We could break it in?"

Clearly, he didn't miss the hope that rang through my tone because the most cunning smile I've ever seen him produce is elicited instantaneously. He rolls onto his side, reaching over to pull me close. I swear I'm the size of a doll compared to him. Our hips meet, and his erection is evident in the connection. Even denim can't repress how hard he is for me. Kissing my head, he whispers. "I like this idea."

I turn in his arms, quickly, and slide myself under him before our mouths collide. But this isn't what I want. I press my palms flat to his chest and pressure him to lie on his back again. As soon as he's flat, I toss my leg over and mount him, then lean forward to seduce him with my lips on his.

Sharp pieces of his new dusting of scruff scrape across my chin, but I'll wear the raw redness in the aftermath and soothe it later. I rock my hips over the seam of his jeans' zipper. The roughness feels so good through the thin material of my yoga pants, encouraging me to press harder. It wouldn't take me long to reach an orgasm, but I remind myself of my purpose. *To thank him for all he's done for me.* And I know exactly how to do it.

I slip down lower on his legs, fumbling to get the button undone, but when I do, a song I haven't heard in weeks violates our good time. I still my fingers and look up at him, my heart already dropping to the pit of my stomach. "That's my phone," I say as if I need to explain.

His fingers slip through my hair, tucking hair behind my ear. "Don't worry about it. If it's important, they'll leave a message."

I don't get many calls these days. It's either Marcy or Keats, and both tend to text me if they need me. My phone pings, alerting me to a message that's been left. I look from one of his eyes to the other, hoping this doesn't get ruined. But then it goes off again, causing me to sit back on my heels.

He lifts to his elbows and says, "That's a ringtone you've assigned to somebody?"

"Yes." I sound as meek as I feel. It's incredible how fast I can return to the person I always hated being. A generic ringtone, chosen from the phone's available options, works like Pavlov's dog to pull me right back into the life I thought I had escaped.

Sitting up, he slides down the mattress and takes hold of my hands. "Whose?"

My mind wanders to the repercussions of not answering. I tick through boxes of punishment and threats, what I want and what I'll have to give up. I keep my eyes locked on his, even when another pinging voicemail intrudes this small space of peace I thought I'd found, and when I'm startled and shaken to the core when the ringtone goes off again. Security is found in the comfort of his brown eyes. "Sosie? Who's calling?"

"My mother."

CHAPTER 31

KEATS

"What are you going to do?" Fear arises, followed by a boiling rage as I watch uncertainty fall across my girl's features. They did this to her.

"What should I do?" She voices the question so quietly I'm unsure if I've heard her right. The soft sound disarms me, the rage falling away.

She's shrinking before my eyes. The life that shone in her hazel eyes dims at the mere intrusion of a phone call, as if her mother were standing here in person. "I don't know, Sosie. What do you think is best?" I struggle with my own familial issues, so I'm not one to lecture on how somebody handles their situation.

"I don't know." Her voice is strained as her gaze treks through the windows. The irony of her paying extra to move in this week to start feeling truly herself, only to have it ruined by the ringing of her phone. Fuck them for doing this to her.

She needs support, not another obstacle. So I do what I think she needs to be able to put this behind her. I dig the phone from her purse and kneel beside her. Holding it out, I say, "She's left several messages. You don't have to answer her call, but you can still see what she wants, if you want."

She takes the phone from me and looks at the screen. Although I saw the voicemail transcribed into text, I didn't read it. Her gaze rolls over the words and then dart to mine.

"At a party . . ."

She rolls her eyes as she slides her phone open to hear the full message.

". . . dropped."

I quietly mouth, "What dropped?"

Tapping a finger against her lips, she shakes her head and looks down as if it helps her hear better. I only catch bits before her grip tightens on the phone, and she leans her head against it. Now I can't tell if they're threatening her or trying to reconnect, so I grow increasingly frustrated as the message drags on.

When tears wobble in the corners of her eyes, her hand trembles as she begins to fall apart. I rub her thigh to comfort her, though I'm not sure what she's dealing with to know what she needs. She pulls the phone down and hits the speaker button, and I hear her mom say, "Call me." The phone goes silent as we stare at each other.

I'm not sure what to say, but I can already see a myriad of emotions playing out across her face. *Shock. Guilt. Sadness. Pain.* But what I don't see is happiness from hearing from her or the tenacity she's shown since leaving.

Suppression only works to hide the trauma temporarily. Every kid wants to please their parents. Sosie is no different. Pain doesn't change that need. It reshapes it.

"I . . ." She stands with the phone at her side, her fingers whitening at the tips as if she needs something tangible to hold on to. One call is all it took to shake the foundation she built without them and rock my world in the aftershocks.

"What do you need, Sosie?"

When she wanders into the living room, her gaze is vacant as if the woman who was just tugging at the button of my jeans, the one that had her confidence highlighted in the light she carried in her eyes moments prior, is gone. Without warning, she was ripped from her new life and from me, from the happiness she had found on her own and dragged back into the hell of the past with one fucking phone call. Why are they so hell-bent on ruining her life?

The timing sends her into a tailspin. She hates silence, but it's too loud to ignore as it rushes my ears. She's too quiet as she searches for something that doesn't seem to be there.

When I enter the room, she plants her hands on the counter and levels her eyes on me as if finding the horizon to steady herself, and replies, "I need to see him."

My knee-jerk reaction is to question what she'll get from this visit other than more heartache. I don't voice that concern because it won't help the situation. But standing here, I fist my hands, struggling to cope with how helpless I feel as she processes what this means to her. Yet somehow, I'm supposed to let her find her own way of dealing with it when all I want to do is hold her until it goes away. "What happened?"

"My father had a heart attack."

Oh shit. Her turmoil is understandable under these

circumstances. But is it justified after the pain he's caused her? I can't stop from putting myself in her shoes and know I'd see my mom if she were in the hospital. But my mom wasn't good at the job. Her father used his role in her life to manipulate her into certain outcomes, which excluded me. *They're not the same.*

"I'm sorry," I say about the man who threatened me with harm if I ever contacted his daughter again. That's the difference between him and me. I'd be fine never seeing him again, but despite what he's done, he matters to her, so his life matters to me.

"No, I'm sorry," she says as if she's betraying me. "I can't explain it. I just . . ." She drops her gaze to the phone on the counter, her eyes rolling over the message again. They've caused her so much damage that I start to wonder if this is a ploy of some sort to bring her back into their fold. "I need your support."

"You have it. Do what you need to do to bring yourself peace. If that means visiting him, then so be it, but don't let your guard down."

"My father is dying," she snaps.

"That doesn't erase how he's hurt you. That ring on your finger was a trade he made—your peace for his gain." Her head jolts on her neck, the words smacking her in the face. Flames flicker in her eyes before her gaze drops to her finger that carried that diamond. Regret settles into my chest because he's still her father, no matter what he's done. But reasoning might not be something we can get to right now. "I don't want to fight with you."

"Then don't." Pushing flyaway strands back from her face, she raises her chin just enough for me to see it—resolve has set in. It doesn't matter what I say, she's going to see him. She's just missing the part that I'm not stopping her. But she needs someone to blame, and those misplaced emotions are falling on my shoulders instead of his.

It's not her reaction that concerns me. It's the lack of concern for her own safety. So I won't stop wanting to protect her since she won't.

She takes her phone from the counter and returns to the bedroom to grab her coat and purse she left on the floor. When she reaches the doorway, she stops to slip her arms into the sleeves and looks back at me. "I know you're worried, but you don't need to be. I need you to trust me, Keats."

"It's not about trusting you, Sosie. It's them." *How can she not see that?* Going blindly into the lion's den is never a good idea. "They cut you off, threatened you, morphed you into someone you're not to expand their own agenda."

"This isn't me choosing them over you."

Fear of losing her punctures the argument, leaving only holes behind. I have every right to worry about what they might do to her. What they do to her affects us. It's a chain reaction. "Then why does it feel like we're finally together and they're tempting you toward the door to the Vitrine you always dreaded? You said it was what you feared most when I met you." Her lips part and her eyes avert as if she'd forgotten her own worst nightmare. I take a breath and calm my voice. "We've been here before, Sosie. What if they try to make that choice for you again?"

I'm hit with ice this time when she says, "I got away once. I can do it again."

"But I wouldn't have caged you in the first place."

The resolve she's garnered to see her father isn't granted to me. She tightens the belt around her waist, and her shoulders fall as her interest in finishing this conversation wanes. She finally looks at me, and I wish she hadn't.

Disappointment colors the greens as she stares, and says, "Hides behind words and masks behind ideas instead of truths. Wasn't that what the email said?"

It's been years since I heard those words from her the first time as she read that email. They're words that stuck with me and shaped me as an author. Now used to strike their intended target, effectively hitting my ego where it hurts most. My purpose. My savior from a life I didn't want. *My writing.* "I'm impressed how you've saved that in your back pocket to use without discretion."

"I haven't been saving it. I've had my own shit to deal with, but you still haven't taken your professor's advice."

Crossing my arms over my chest, I ask, "And what's that?"

"You can say whatever you want, phrase it however you best see fit, but that doesn't make it an eternal truth. That's just your side of it." I lose our connection when she pulls her gaze away from me.

"Sosie, I—"

"It's a medical situation," she says, taking a sobering breath. "Not a trap I'm falling into."

I'm not near the door, but give her a bigger berth by moving closer to the window. "I'm not stopping you from going. I know it's something you need to do."

She walks out without another word, not even giving me the courtesy of a backward glance before I lose her presence entirely. I stand there, staring, as she disappears down the stairwell, the rush of her footsteps slowly fading as the distance grows between us. And silence. What feels like minutes passing, I'm still staring through the open door like she's going to magically reappear when I know she won't.

I fucked up.

My gut twists at the realization that the hollow in my chest means I might lose her anyway. I should run after her and catch her before she slips into a cab. Even go with her to the hospital. But I don't move, giving her time to get away, not because of what I said, though I'm already drowning in regret. I don't go because she needs to do this on her own. She needs to be the one not only to fight for us but, more importantly, for herself. We can't be together with this hanging around in the background, looking to attack us when we let our guard down. In the long term, we'll never be free until she finds that peace that any kid would want with their parents and living on her own terms again.

Although too brief, a weight had lifted since we left that pub together. I could see it in how she started moving through life with less tension in her shoulders, even daring to dream and talk about the future like she used to do. I finally got my muse. I don't want to lose her again.

"Fuck," I sigh, unsure what I'm supposed to do next. The urge to fix this is stronger than the logic of her doing what needs to be done to fix herself. Doesn't make it easier. I swear it makes it worse, even if it is the right thing to do.

Walking out of her apartment, I latch the lock on the inside and shut the door to secure it because this is the place where my soul will exist. It just won't exist as a part of me any longer. I'm really starting to wonder if we're cursed.

My phone vibrates in my pocket when I land back out in front of the building. A spot of good news would have been welcome at any other point in the day before my girlfriend ran back to a life that excludes me. But sure, I'll go identify the culprits who attacked me. *The fuckers.*

I head to the police precinct, where it takes less than twenty minutes to point them out and sign the prepared statement. I collect my stolen wallet, which is missing all the money and the credit cards, but they were kind enough to leave my old NYU ID and my New York City library card.

I take the two cards out and toss the wallet into the trash on my way out.

The detour was a temporary distraction from the situation with Sosie and the fears I have if she's not given a choice to return. I catch a cab and head home, hoping to see her belongings still around the apartment—her makeup bag open with products spilling across the counter and her seven hair products littering the ledge of the shower. But it's Winifred the Wallaby I hope to see still napping in the middle of the bed. As long as she's there, I know Sosie will return. If not for me, for her.

Rushing inside, I go straight to the bedroom to find her stuffed animal taking up space like she still lives here. If I can't have her, I'll take the wallaby. Who knew a stuffed wallaby would provide me with the relief I needed most right now? *Second to Sosie, of course.*

I make a cup of coffee, predicting a long night ahead, and pull out my laptop to work in the living room. I'll do anything to keep my mind from running wild with the fuckery she's facing on her own. Should I have gone?

She'd hate that. Not because of me, but it would make her feel bad. She's stronger than she knows. I know that. I just hope she remembers.

When I look up, the sun has set, and darkness rolls in like a fog around me. My eyes don't adjust quick enough after staring at the glowing screen for the past few hours. I caught up on some emails, but when I blink and rub my eyes, the burn only reminds me of other aching body parts.

I tap the phone next to me only to find it blank of texts or calls. Catching the time, I'm heading into three hours since I came home to an apartment without her or word of her return. Is she alright? Fuck.

I close the laptop and walk to the window to stare in the direction of the nearest hospital. I know her father won't be taken there, but it does have me thinking. I overreacted. Like she said, it was an emergency, not some ploy to steal her back. Right? Her absence is felt along with concerns still raising my hackles.

I walk down the hall, needing to keep my body moving, then turn around and walk in the other direction to repeat the pattern. It's not until I see the little tree on the nightstand that it finally makes sense to me.

It's not them or me. I know she'll choose me. But that doesn't mean she doesn't need to find peace with her parents and put that part of her life to bed. I could have just supported her instead of opening my mouth and letting my fear drain out. Feeling shittier now than before won't fix this. I have to do the work, too.

But how?

I eye the stuffed animal as an idea takes form. Going into the closet, I grab her carry-on from the shelf and prop it open on the bed. I dig through the clothes hanging in the closet and grab a top and a pair of jeans. I have no idea what underwear she would choose for this kind of outfit, but I'm not going to overthink this. Let's hope none of these clothes are needed, and she comes back to me. But if she does get stuck, I want her to have some clean clothes and tell her what I should have said the first time before she left.

After writing a note and sticking it inside, along with a few of her bathroom toiletries, I close it, but something across the room catches my eye, and I get it. I turn it over in my hands because it meant everything to me at one time.

She means more. I tuck it inside the suitcase and latch it tight.

Downstairs, I catch a cab, and since there's only one hospital where the Stansburys would go, that's where I head. With my phone resting on my leg so I don't miss a text from her, I stare out the window thinking about how an emergency has triggered all this. It only took Sosie seconds to feel the need to visit, her heart way more open than mine. If they hurt it, I'll take matters into my own hands.

No lessons need to be learned. She knows who they are and how they operate. So why go? The one piece I didn't put together before. Closure.

And here I was, warning her because of my own insecurities about losing her again. I'm not losing her, though. I know that. What we share is too strong to be deterred by threats anymore. We'll fight against anything thrown our way. *Together.* Sosie knows that.

I just wish I had realized it earlier. She didn't go for her father. She went for herself. I drop my head forward as the shame of my wrong assumptions might have fucked things up. It did for her, and I let her walk out feeling that way. Who's the asshole now? I am.

I get out of the cab and look up at the sign for the visitor's entrance. Holding the handle to her carry-on, I'm about to go in when someone calls, "What are you doing here?"

"I should have known," I grumble under my breath. I glare at Gregory with no patience for his shit. "I should ask you the same."

Carrying a tray of coffees, he stops just out of reach of me. Probably wise if he's going to get mouthy. "I'm a friend of the family," he spits like he's some tough guy when he's just a prick whose family has bought his way into the little respect he's given. "You're . . ." He looks up and down without shame in the weak act of sizing me up. I'm not the least bit intimidated by this jackass, but it bothers me that he's here like he's part of the family. "Nothing to the Stansbury family."

"That's where you're wrong." Am I really stooping to his level? *Yep.* I'll go to the gutter with this one-upping fuck. "I got Sosie when you never had her." My gaze hits the name on one of the cups. Sosie is scribbled in black marker. It's been hours at most with her, and he's already back in the fold and getting her coffee like the old days?

"We'll see how this plays out."

"No, we won't. You won't, especially. I don't have to force her to pick me. I don't have to lay threats at her feet. You do. Her father does. Me? I don't. We'll always find our way back together. You can fight fate, but you can't fight destiny."

"I don't believe in that woo-woo soulmate shit."

"We do, so you don't need to because she'll never choose you, Greg." I walk toward the sliding glass doors of the hospital, then stop and turn back. "I'm heading that way. You want me to take that coffee to her?"

He walks to the nearest trash can and dumps the entire tray in it. Such a spoiled fucking baby.

A guard stands at the entrance but doesn't look up from his phone. The walls are bleak in beige that's aged over time, and the railings are stained from all the hands that have held it. A TV blares, so I turn to see a room full of people waiting under a small screen airing *Jeopardy*, and my life standing before me. "Keats?" Sosie comes closer as if I might not be real. Each of her tentative steps is too slow, so I set the small suitcase down and close the gap.

Wrapping my arms around her and kissing the top of her head. "I'm sorry."

When her arms come around me, and she sinks against my chest, she whispers, "Me, too."

"No. You don't have to be sorry for anything. I would have done the same."

"I'm not sorry for coming to the hospital." She steps back, looking up at me. "I'm sorry for saying you use words as weapons when I realize now you use them as a protective shield. We all have our pasts to deal with. You overcame difficult circumstances, which is amazing. I'm trying to do the same, just not the same as how you handled it."

"I had no one who cared."

"I've lived under a microscope." Reaching forward, she tugs me closer by the front of my coat. "You're not losing me. Not again. Not ever. But I do have to see this through. It might be my only chance."

"Now I understand." I lean down to kiss her, and she meets me halfway. "I brought you some supplies just in case you end up staying overnight. I can bring anything else you need."

"No, this is more than I need." Slipping her hand in mine, she says, "Thank you, but keep my side of the bed warm, okay?"

"Winifred is already doing the job."

She laughs, and seeing her smile gives me the peace I needed. I just hope she finds what will give her the same peace. And if she doesn't, I'll be there to give her what she's missing. "Thank you."

"You're welcome." He's my least favorite subject, but I still ask, "How's your dad?"

A pop of her shoulders leads to her looking down the corridor and back at me again. "No news so far."

"He'll be okay." When I see her looking at me like I did something special, I give her hand a squeeze, and add, "I should go."

She'll devastate my heart if I'm not careful. One day, she'll realize she's way out of my league. I'll do everything I can to make up for it. Brushing her fingers over my cheek, she says, "I love you, Poet."

"I love you with everything I am."

Her smile brightens the dull space and my heart along with it. But this is her battle, and she'll fight it like the warrior she is.

As for me, I walk out of the hospital and pull my phone from my pocket. It only takes me searching three letters to pull up the contact I'm looking for. Maybe this is something I should have taken care of long ago, but life and work got in the way. I also pushed it to the back as something to deal with another day.

Sosie has inspired me in more ways than she realizes. I press call, and when the other party answers, I say, "Hi, Mom."

CHAPTER 32

SOSIE

I don't think I've laughed this hard since . . . well, since Keats made me last laugh. But this was unexpected and so endearing that I hold the note to my chest.

"It was the simplest task." My mom sits in the chair next to mine. I hadn't noticed she'd been gone. "And Gregory couldn't manage it." She hands me a coffee. "I had to go get them myself." The hospital has been a bit cold since I got here, but the chill of her presence has me tightening my coat. When she hands me a coffee, I'm still grateful. "Thank you." I take a sip and swallow, keeping my hand huddled around the warm cup. "I thought you were out of town?"

"We were, but he was transported here for better care in the city." Her gaze pivots to the entrance when a woman walks in. "I didn't want to take any chances."

"Understood."

When the distraction disappears and it's just the two of us sitting here in this section of the waiting room, she smiles as if it's the polite thing to do. I shift to hide the note, but her eyes home in on the small action, and she asks, "What is that?" There's nothing personal or private I want to share with her, especially when it comes to Keats. Everything will be held and used against me how they see fit. I start to tuck the note in my pocket, but she asks, "Why are you hiding that paper from me, Sosie?"

"Because it's mine and none of your business." I kind of hate myself for snapping at her, though I believe some of my animosity is where it should be. She's been tolerable since I arrived at the hospital and nice otherwise. A part of growing past the damage is changing my behavior if they don't change theirs. I can only control myself, and I don't want to be a miserable person. The note feels personal because Keats took the time to create it, but there's nothing I should feel so protective that I can't share a little joy in hopes of building a bridge for our relationship. Is that what I want with her? I can't help myself, but I do. I hand her the note, and say, "It made me smile, is all."

She takes the note and starts to read, giving me the opportunity to study her. It has been so long since I looked at her, much less this deeply beneath the surface, that I've failed to see how she's aged. Kelly Stansbury is still stunning. She may no longer wear tiaras, but she could still win a beauty contest. It's so hard to grow up the daughter of a beauty queen when you take after the paternal side. At least that's what I think. Everyone else says I'm my mom's twin. I could only be so lucky.

A sadness has settled in her eyes that didn't used to be there. I wonder when that tragedy occurred. She flips the note around, and a smile tugs on the corners of her mouth. "Is this from Winifred the Wallaby?"

I scan the note again, just as tickled reading it as I was the first time.

Dear Mom,

I'm being well taken care of. I miss you. Can't wait for you to come home.

Love,
Winifred

"It is." I giggle.

"That's darling." She sits back, folding her hands together. "How did you get this? Do we have another case of Paddington Bear syndrome with Winifred?"

My smile comes easier the more time we spend together. "I loved Paddington."

"I know." Her laughter isn't something I hear much of, especially in the past few years. "We had reservations for high tea in London when you were eight. We had just watched the movie on the plane ride over, and you had your mind set that he was going to be our guest at the tea."

Seeing my mom act like the one I craved so desperately when I was young has my heart aching for the time we lost when it could have been like this. Genuine. "I don't remember the tea."

"Mmm." She closes her eyes just long enough to recall a memory. "You were young. I should send you the photos we took."

"I have that bear in my closet. He still has a Harrod's tag on his coat."

A smile is evoked, and then she says, "Hold on to him."

Such a random request when she already knows I've moved out of the house. Our conversation drops off, so I check the time on my watch. "Any updates?"

"No." A thread of concern runs through her tone that doesn't suit her. "The nurse told me it shouldn't be long now."

"That's good." We sit in these chairs that lost their cushioning a long time ago. Silence is something I'm used to unless I'm in trouble. But it feels different between us this time. Anger is absent on my part, and she's showing genuine interest on her side. Different, but I don't let my guard down. Not fully anyway. But I am curious, and I really don't feel like I have much to lose anymore. "Can I ask you something?"

She looks at me with stoicism. "You should just ask, not ask if you can ask. It wastes people's time by unnecessarily dragging it out."

The stroll down memory lane can't erase all the other stuff that stands out so prominently in my mind. "Why do you hate me so much?"

Her jaw drops, and she stares as if this question came out of left field, but that can't be true when hate is all I've ever felt from my parents. I just didn't have the nerve to ask before. "What do you mean, Sosie?"

"Let's not pretend, Mom." Letting my head roll around my neck, I groan, "You know what I mean." It's not a bad thing to allow her to sit in discomfort. It might be new, but it's needed for her to understand where I'm coming from.

"I don't hate you. You're my daughter."

"Then why would you not stand up for me? Why would

you not protect me? Why wouldn't you want me to be happy?"

A tsk snips at her tongue, and she feigns offense. "That's quite the barrage of unsubstantiated accusations. And it's alarming you feel this way."

"Look, I'm not trying to be mean, but I am a Stansbury after all, and sometimes I take after my father. So you can act like this is news to you, but you know how he treated me, took away things I loved, and manipulated me into conceding to his demands. I was a good girl, but you both made me hate myself, and for what? Access to more wealth. You don't even care about the Lafoons, just as I don't love Gregory. So why would you force my hand in marriage to that man?"

She tries to lift her gobsmacked mouth off the floor and anchor it back in place. But her lips are still parted as if the shock hasn't retreated yet.

The truth should come quickly, so her lack of response is an answer in and of itself. Whether I like it or not, I need to accept that. It was pointless to think I'd get actual answers anyway.

Just as I angle away from her, she says, "I never hated you. I'm sorry I made you feel that way." An apology is the last thing I expected. An argument, a tit for tat, even a threat, but not an apology. I watch as she shifts in the chair as if this is a new situation for her. With me it is. There's no stiff upper lip or taking it on the chin. She looks me straight in the eyes with sincerity encircling the pupil, and adds, "I hope one day you can forgive me, but I also hope that you'll understand the circumstances I was under as well."

I don't owe her anything anymore, much less understanding, but she's been honest with me and sounds genuine. Instead of holding on to the pain, I release it and give her the grace I think we both need. "I hope so as well."

"Mrs. Stansbury?" A nurse approaches in lavender scrubs with an e-pad in her hand and wearing a smile that I take as a good sign. I have such a tangled mess of conflicted feelings regarding my father that I don't know how to individually compartmentalize them. It's not worth sorting through the past anymore for answers I'll probably never get when I have a present that matters more to me and a future to look forward to now.

My mom stands, looking at me. "I'll make sure you can see him as soon as possible."

"Thank you."

"And Sosie." She waits for my eyes to meet hers to say, "I like your hair. It always looked so cute short."

I automatically touch the back where I know it's uneven, which I thought she'd hate. "Then why were you always making me grow it out?" Although I asked, it doesn't matter anymore. I'm past caring what they think of me. I'll enjoy the highlights, like the story she shared, without needing anything from them. Because all I could want or need is waiting for me back at his apartment.

"I've made mistakes." The nurse pulls her gaze when she calls her name again, and then she follows her away from me. Just when we were getting somewhere, but an inkling of hope remains that maybe we're not so far gone that we can't find our way to neutral ground one day.

With too much time on my hands, I open the suitcase, thinking I'll be entertained by what Keats thought I would need for one night at the hospital. It's an interesting assortment of items, but the collated book tucked inside one of my shirts is what I reach for next.

"*Across the Bridge* by Keats Matthews." The heaviness of my heart doesn't sink but floats into my throat, where it's determined to stay lodged. The corners of the printed cardstock cover are bent, and chaotic creases run vertically from repeated use. It's thick and looks like it was printed at a printing center. How am I holding the original manuscript? Why would he give me something that means so much to him?

I glance up to make sure my mom or a nurse aren't coming to retrieve me before opening the well-worn bound pages and start reading.

To the muse that danced in the snow at Greene and Grant, who inspired me to write this book.

A tear falls on the bottom of the page. I'm quick to wipe it, but not quick enough before it crinkles and leaves a wet spot. It landed beside what looks like a Cheetos dust fingerprint, so I don't think Keats will be mad. But I retrieve a tissue from the nurses' station before I continue reading, just in case it happens again.

I find myself entranced by his prose. Hearing Keats's voice so vividly as the narrating main character has me turning the page for more. We never fully meet him from the outside although the other characters are so richly described that it's like I can see them before me.

Scarlet still exists. She just doesn't exist in my world anymore.

My breath ceases, and my heart aches. I've never been able

to describe the pain of losing him after that night, but he did so eloquently.

I'm only halfway when I read lines that I want to read again. Tapping my nail under the words, I whisper, "I was captivated by her beauty erupting all at once. It wasn't one thing in particular that drew me to her, but all of them that added up."

When tears spill down my waterline, I tilt my head back and dab with a tissue. I close the book, needing time to process the complicated relationships of family, friends, and loss, and the love and heartache he's written into every page. I don't know if I feel broken or healed. Maybe both.

I smile because this book is incredible either way and has me seeing Keats in a whole new light. He's not just talent. He's had his own demons to fight. But he's strong and steady, always supporting me the best he can be. I don't blame him for getting upset earlier. I understand his fear of losing us. But I'm never going to let that happen. I've never felt so loved and so connected to another person. Hugging his book to my chest, I'll always protect us.

"Ms. Stansbury?"

I look up to see the nurse in lavender coming to collect me. I quickly tuck the book back into the suitcase, making sure to wrap my shirt around it again to also protect this treasure he's shared with me. When I stand, I take a breath and exhale, needing all the strength Keats gives to carry in with me to see my father.

Carefully touching my arm with her other hand on the knob, she whispers, "He isn't awake, but your mother thought you should be in there."

"Thank you." I park my suitcase just inside the door of the darkened room. My eyes land on my father before I see my mother sitting at the far side of the room. "Hi," I say as if I'm disturbing her peace in the corner.

"He's going to be okay."

I'm not sure whether she's received official news or is manifesting good health, but it reminds me of Keats's earlier promise. "I'm glad." It's weird to have emotions roll in with the tide when tragedy strikes. But then roll back out when I remember all the heartache that could have been avoided if he'd let me love who I chose instead of trying to make the decision for me.

Standing bedside, I don't see my father. I see a man who wanted to control me. Does this man know how to love, or is that lack reserved for me alone? Maybe this was more of a business relationship, and I was just slow to realize it. Everything with him was transactional. I got a prize when I achieved his goals and was punished when I failed. So looking at him now, it's difficult to know what to feel. But I have a new perspective.

"He'll be okay," I say for my mom's sake and mine. He may not know how to love his own daughter, but thank God I haven't lost the trait.

I turn to sit by Mom, but my hand is covered before I leave. I look back to see my father's eyes open, the hazels that hold more brown than green, which is the opposite of mine. "Sosie," he says, then tries to clear his throat with a rough cough that only makes things worse.

My mom rushes to hold a cup of water with a straw for him. He drinks with the two of us staring at him. His hand vanishes from mine when he jerks his head to the side to signify that he's finished. Seeing disappointment crumple my mom's expression is painful to watch. The circumstances she mentioned earlier are now more obvious in this setting. How was I to see the strain she was under when I was just trying to survive?

As she retreats to the corner to take her seat and rearranges her expression, I'm starting to think I mistook fortitude for a stiff upper lip. My eyes have been opened, and there's no denying that it's not only grace I need to give her but also support. She's just trying to survive as well.

I can't stay here. The urge to leave is becoming too strong. "How are you feeling?"

"Terrible." His coloring is a lighter tan, his body holding on to a summer fling vacation he took in late August, while my mom is pale from the winter. "What brings you here?" His tone isn't as harsh as his mood, but it's not offered in warm fuzzies either. "Run out of money? That guy kick you out? Gregory would never—"

"I don't care about Gregory. I didn't run out of money, and nobody's kicked me out. I came because Mom called to tell me you had a heart attack."

He shoots her a glare that could stab through stainless steel. "She shouldn't have."

"Well, she did, and I'm here because I wanted to come by."

His efforts to rile me up aren't working. That's what happens when I reclaim my own power. "You're out of the will, Sosie, just in case that makes a difference if you stay or go away."

I laugh. It's not so loud that nurses will come running. It's more for me as I listen to him try so hard to hurt me. I guess not all of us evolve at the same pace. "I don't need your money."

"You sure about that?" he derides, wasting his energy to elicit a reaction. He won't win. Not this time. Not ever again.

"One hundred percent." I release a sigh, watching him on what could have been his deathbed, spending the time he just got back in such a hateful place.

"It makes no sense that you're here."

"I have to agree." I release the bedrail and take a step back. When I glance at my mom, a look is shared that reveals the pain I overlooked when I saw her. Maybe I never saw the real her at all. Until now.

Crossing the room, I bend down to hug her. It takes a second before she scoots to the edge of the chair to fully embrace me. "I love you, Mom."

"I love you, too," she whispers, almost as if she doesn't want my father to overhear.

I return to the door and grab my suitcase. "Dad?" I'm only given his eyes in my direction. "I hope you have a quick recovery. Goodbye."

Nothing is exchanged in return, and his silence is preferred to what he could have said next. I thought I felt it when I escaped the house, but as I wheeled my case onto the sidewalk, it wasn't then, it was now that I knew I was finally free.

My hot boyfriend is waiting for me when I step off the elevator. I run to him with my carry-on dragging behind me, dump it, and jump into his arms.

He kisses me like his life depends on it, my back against the wall, and his hand coddling my ass. When our lips part, I lean my head back to look into his eyes. "That's a welcome I could come home to every day."

"I'm hoping you do." He sets my feet on the ground and

retrieves the suitcase before following me inside the apartment.

I left the hospital just before midnight, so it's been nighttime for hours, but it's really dark in here. "I know you like to save money by turning out lights, but it's a little dark in here. Were you sleeping?"

"No. I've been waiting for you." I hear the bolts fasten into place before I'm scooped up into his arms and kissed while being carried into the living room. As soon as we part again, I rest my head on his shoulder. "I'm so tired. Are you ready for bed?"

"Not quite yet." He turns me so I'm facing the kitchen.

"Uh!" The gasp came fast. I'm a little slower processing the rest of what I'm seeing. "What is that?"

"A cake. Candles. Birthday presents—"

"Balloons." Carrying me closer, he sets me on the wide countertop.

He caresses my face before he lets me go. "Happy birthday, Sosie." He kisses my lips with tenderness before he releases me, then says, "You should probably blow out your candles before we set off the alarms."

He's whacked for that one, but I still laugh. "I'm not that old."

"You're not. I was kidding." He chuckles, but eyes the candles. That's when I notice there's a strain of stress he's failing to repress.

I cross my legs on the counter and lean forward. Closing my eyes, my head goes blank, so I reopen them again to find his. "Everything I always wished for has already come true."

Grinning like he relates, he says, "Guess you need to find new dreams to pursue."

"New dreams, huh?" Nothing new comes to mind, but I

realize I can still pull from an old compartment hidden in my heart of discarded things I used to dream about. One comes to mind, and I lean forward and blow out the candles.

He turns on a lamp nearby, and asks, "What did you wish for?"

Generally, I'm not one to share such things, but nothing feels off-limits with him. And maybe my mom is onto something with manifestation, and I should put my wish into the universe. "To be able to follow my passion again."

"I like that." He reaches for a present and sets it on my lap. "Let's open gifts."

I'm about to rip it open, but then it dawns on me. Holding the gift, which has some weight to it, I stop and dip my head to tap away the little tears threatening my good time. When Keats's arms come around me, he says, "We don't have to do this now if you're too tired."

I rest my hand on his arm and reply, "No, it's okay. I want to. I just realized this is the first time I've ever celebrated my birthday on the day I was born." It comes out heavier than intended, but I'm not upset. I'm so happy that everything feels like it's finally fallen into place.

Rubbing my back, he gives me a smile that he feels the same. "I wouldn't have it any other way." I rip the gift wrap, then pause to stare at the box. He says, "You can exchange for any camera you like. The guy said this was a good—"

"It's great, so much nicer than my other one, and that one was super advanced. I just can't believe you got me a camera." It's like he knew I'd be making that wish to get back into photography. We're so in tune with each other. I reach up and hug him. "Thank you."

"You're welcome. But there's one more."

Considering I know how much that camera set him

back, another present is the last thing I expect. I lift the lid on the box to see a key card and a metal one hanging from a ribbon. Being here was accepted like we'd had the conversation about moving in together. We haven't. I look at him with more love than my heart can hold and lift the ribbon between us. "Is this a hint?"

"No, it's a full out ask. Will you live with me, Spark?"

On a warm spring day in April, I use my keys to get into the apartment and call for him, "Keats?"

"Back here."

I run down the hall to the bedroom and dive into bed next to him. "What are you doing naked in bed in the middle of the day?"

He flips me under him, and the pressure of his erection prods between my legs. "Waiting for you." He attacks my lips with kisses and nips while his hands are busy getting me naked.

"I have good news." I wrap my arms around his neck and lift my ass so he can pull my pants down.

Tugging the collar of my shirt to expose my collarbone, he stops licking to ask, "What is that?"

"I got a new job."

CHAPTER 33

KEATS

Shutters snap in a barrage of swift clicks. The sound comes so fast that it used to freak me out when I'd be startled awake, but I've come to identify the rapid firing of Sosie's camera. Especially when the season changes or a storm rolls in, and the light is "just right" as she claims. I just wish I wasn't her favorite subject.

"Are you taking photos of me again?" I peek out from under my arm I've draped across my forehead to block out the light.

"I am." She doesn't even try to hide it, which makes me chuckle.

The blinds should be down, but Sosie loves this early hour, the one after night has gone and morning hasn't arisen. She calls it the magic hour. The evening has the golden hour, so it only makes sense, I suppose. The light is transformed for such a short time that she tries to take full advantage of the fleeting change. "Truthfully, how many photos does one person need of another?"

Another round of lightning-fast clicks sounds before I feel the dip of the mattress. She rolls to her back and lies next to me, making this my favorite time of day as well. She's naked beside me. Reaching over, I run my hand over her bare breast before encountering cold metal and hard plastic. She's fallen asleep with it looped around her neck before, spent hours at her apartment developing photos late into the night, and taken thousands of photos of me for practice. Though I suspect there were nefarious intentions all along when she started creating a wallpaper from the photos of me in the bedroom of the other apartment. Sometimes I really regret buying that camera. But for her, I'll continue endure this form of torture because it makes her happy.

I roll to my side and kiss her temple. "How long have you been awake?"

"A few hours." Her eyes close, the lack of sleep catching up with her just as I'm waking. Timing hasn't always been our friend. I complain, but I love that she's so passionate about what she does. And her talent blows me away on the regular.

The entry is now a gallery of her photos, and the hallway is lined with framed artwork. I hadn't realized how bland this apartment was until her vivid personality filled it with color and made it a home. I've never been one for clutter, but I come to enjoy finding random items appear here or there, then they're gone, replaced by another, or the surface is left bare.

Sosie can hardly keep her eyes open, so this erection will get attention tonight when she gets home from work. I take the wide fabric strap from around her neck and slip it off to set her camera on the nightstand. She moves into position, snuggling against me as if seeking warmth, her breathing deepening already a sign of her sweet slumber.

How did I get this life?

I hustled to get out of the neighborhood I grew up in. Right time, right place to meet the professor to get a shot at university, then spent years pouring my emotions, that had nowhere else to go, into the pages of a book releasing in a few months. *But this* . . . Her. I hold her closer wanting to feel her heat, her heartbeats, and hear the rhythm of her breathing. In a city of eight million people, how was I fortunate enough to find my soulmate?

That's the only thing I couldn't control or create my way into, but damn, did I luck out.

She shifts, and the sheet slips off her hip, revealing that freckle I'll never get enough of. I thought about it more times than would be considered healthy. Maybe it's because the only way to see it is when she's naked. Win-win.

I reach for the camera and take a couple of photos of my favorite thing—Sosie and that freckle. I set it back down, wanting to sleep some more with her, but I need to get a run in before I start work. And since she tried running with me twice and told me she's sticking to yoga, I'm on my own.

Despite the claims, the summer wool isn't thick enough to wick the moisture from my sweating palms, so I shove my hands in my pockets instead. Not sure why I'm nervous. It's my mom, not a stranger. This shouldn't be a big deal. But we both know it is. So when I'm led to the table where she's been seated, I catch a glimpse of her fidgeting with the napkin right before she sees me.

I move to her side of the table. "Hi, Mom," I say, giving her a quick hug, easygoing but not over the top. We're not there yet. But I hold out hope.

"Keats, you look so handsome."

"Thanks." I sit across from her and drag my napkin into my lap. "You look nice. I like that hairstyle on you."

"Oh, this." Her eyes dart to the table as she maintains a softer smile. We don't really look much alike, except in the obvious traits like hair and skin tone. We're similar in other ways like stocking pasta and turning off unnecessary lights. But that's more from lifestyle than anything else. After taking a sip of water, she says, "I just celebrated one year at the distribution center. I got a nice bonus and raise."

I knew she was working steadily for the first time in a long time. But I also see it in the clarity of her eyes. She looks healthy and not too thin like she used to be.

The server stops by to take drink orders, but she orders an iced tea, so I do the same. As soon as we're alone, she says, "I don't drink anymore."

"Oh. Was that your choice?"

"It was something I decided was needed. So I gave it up, and within two weeks, Miller did the same." There's a wistfulness to her gaze when she looks around the restaurant. "It wasn't doing me any favors but it's also been easier with a partner who supports you." It is. I know firsthand. I couldn't ask for someone to believe in me more than Sosie does. She laughs like she's remembering an inside joke. I never cared much for him, but I didn't give myself a chance to get to know him either. I probably should if he's giving up drinking to be with my mom. "We even started walking after dinner and bought some hand weights we use at the apartment."

"I can see the change. It sounds weird, but there's more light to you, brighter eyes and a glow. I'm proud of you."

The words cause her chin to tremble, and she grasps her clasped hands to her chest. "You don't know what it means to hear you say that, Keats." She reaches across the table and covers my hand with hers. "I failed you as a mother. You practically raised yourself, but it's hard to look at all your success and wish to change anything. But selfishly, I would if I could. I'd snap myself out of the daze I was living in sooner, go back to school, and even learn to cook a proper meal for my kid."

If she had said these things to me when I was a teen or even in my early twenties, I would have given her a chance. It's been years since then, since I spared my own feelings by isolating myself. But when I sit across from her like I am now, I can feel the need that little boy in me still has. Fuck my dad, but I miss my mom. "It was hard back then. I don't hold a grudge. We can't change it anyhow, only how we move forward."

"Can we move forward?"

"I'd like that, and to see you more often." I grin involuntarily because Spark is my heart and soul. "And introduce you to Sosie."

Sitting back, there's an easiness that shapes her body language. I feel it too. She asks, "Is she a special someone in your life?"

"She's my everything."

The smile rolls in gradually, but happiness is exuded in her eyes. "I can't wait to meet her. She's lucky to have you."

"Trust me, I'm the lucky one." I reach for my phone. "Want to see a picture?"

After dinner, we go for one of those walks she likes until we reach her subway station. I didn't dread seeing her. I've wanted her in my life, but I had concerns of being disappointed, of feeling like I might not matter. Still. This meal changed everything for the better. I think for her as well. There's a road back that's unexpected. I want her to be a part of my life, and Sosie's. "Hey Mom?"

We stop out of the path to the steps. She's still smiling like she can't believe she's seeing me. I recognize it because I feel the same. I say, "I have a signing in a few months at the Barnes & Noble in Union Square. If you have time to stop by—"

"I'll be there." Like me, she's not one to talk someone's ear off, but what she says, she means. Tonight, the difference in her, and how our relationship has grown, is noticeable, so I know she won't let me down. "I'll put you on the guest list."

I give her the type of hug I wanted growing up. The best part is that she returns it. "I love you, Keats. And I'm so proud of the man you've become." When we release the embrace, she laughs as she starts down the steps. "Heaven knows I get no credit for it."

"Sure you do. I wouldn't be here without you." When she glances back, the changes she's made shine in her eyes, but it's the joy she carries that reassures me she's finally in a good place.

The sun hasn't set since it's the summer solstice, so it's time to enact part two of my plan for the night. I would have thought I'd be more nervous. I'm not. This is right. The timing and the night.

Through the large panes of glass, paintings are mixed with photos hung on the gallery walls. From the street view, it doesn't take more than a glance to catch sight of my Sosie fluttering from one group of potential buyers to the next. Champagne in hand, she laughs like she was never locked in a life she didn't love.

Breezy happiness is what I sometimes call it. She makes everything better. Even molecules caught in her spotlight reorganize to stay there. I feel special by association, but that she chose me to love makes me a fucking hero.

Her lips twist, though it doesn't hide her smile when she sees me. A hand goes to her jeans-clad hip, and the cream-colored diamond-shaped fabric clings to her tits while showing off her arms and her stunning back. Should I be jealous of the other men who get to take her in as well? Nah, I'm the one who gets to unwrap that package later. She holds up a finger and tells me to stay where I am.

I don't mind being a voyeur as she zips across the room and whispers something in her coworker's ear. They both glance my way before giggling, making me chuckle under my breath. The little top knot on her head reveals the cotton candy pink streaks she recently added to her hair, and bounces when she rushes out the door. After a quick twirl, she lands right in my arms.

Her legs grip my center, her arms wrap around my neck, but it's her lips that kiss me like she hasn't seen me in a month when it's only been a few hours that confirms this is right. We are, together. Not that I needed reassurance. I knew she was the one when we met and she asked me for my cigarette like she already owned it. She did, and me, from that moment on.

With a smile shining brighter than the North Star, she asks, "Do you know how much I missed you, Poet?"

"Since two this afternoon?" I deadpan.

She nods, tossing her head back freely in laughter. "It could have been thirty minutes ago, and I'd miss you the same."

I study the sweet expression—the smile, those eyes that light up when I'm near, and the way she licks her lips after we kiss like she didn't get enough the first time. Her fascination with taking photos of me is quite the ego trip, but it's her love for me that is always coming through. "I missed you, too."

"Is that why you came to see me?"

Holding her up is easy, but I was built for loving her. "One of the reasons."

A mischievous smirk slips into her fine features. "What's another reason?"

"Do you remember I asked for a sign?" I set her down and caress her cheek. "One sign was all I needed."

The memories steal her smile and drain the happiness from her eyes. "I remember." She bites her bottom lip, but then says, "I cried for days, maybe months after you left. The tears just wouldn't stop. I knew in my soul that we were supposed to be together." And she calls me the romantic one.

"We're together now, but you were with me all along. A beacon for me to rely on. Every time we saw each other, every time we talked gave me the sign I needed to hold on, even when fate tried to keep us apart." I take her hand and twirl her out before bringing her back to me just to see her smile again and lead her into the empty cobblestone street to look up at the moon.

Her eyes glisten under clouds streaking across the deep blue skies as night bellows to greet us above the treetops of the West Village. I hold her hands in mine and do what I've always done—pour my heart into her.

"I was so fucking lonely, angry at the world for having to fight for everything I got. And then there was you, Sosie. A shining star. A muse in need of an artist to inspire. The most beautiful girl I'd ever laid eyes on in a Jackson Pollock shirt, dark eyeliner, and combat boots, bumming a smoke from a server ducking out on his break."

"Sounds like kismet, Poet."

"It sure was, and it changed my life for the better. You inspire me every day with the way you hold strength and still manage to stay soft at heart. I've said it before. I don't know what I did to deserve you, but I must have been one helluva guy in a past life to get the reward in this one."

Her bubbling laughter makes me think she's onto me. I'm not the best with secrets, always wearing my heart on my sleeve like she does. Reaching up to run the tips of her fingers over my jaw, she says, "Oh, I definitely earned you in this life. So I'm not going to take one day for granted. I love you too much for that."

"I love—"

A car horn blasts, sending my heart into orbit, just as the taxi's headlights shine so bright that we run for the curb to avoid being blinded. Laughing takes some of the heat off the situation and gives my chest time to retrieve my heart from outer space and calm down again. As soon as I do, I reach into my pocket and drop to one knee before her because I just want to be married to this woman. "Will you marry me, Spark? I promise to be the husband you deserve."

She kisses me before the words leave my mouth, sealing the deal like our destiny always was. "Yes, Poet. I'll marry you. You've always had my heart, so we might as well make it official."

CHAPTER 34

SOSIE

I couldn't wait to get my hands on it, and now I can't stop staring. It's so big and thick. GAH, holding it in my hands is incredible. I'm so glad I bought a copy of Keats's book as soon as the bookstore opened even though I preordered a copy for delivery at home. That copy didn't arrive until after lunch, so no regrets on the early morning trek. And now this evening, the line for the signing wraps around the block, confirming it's sold out.

I can only imagine how proud Keats must be feeling. I can't even contain myself around him and have had a blast celebrating this huge achievement. The cake decorated with the cover for hitting the bestsellers' lists last week made him laugh, but he didn't hesitate to scoop a bite right out of it. He devoured the miniature novel cookies I had customized for signing another book deal a few weeks back. And this morning, the English muffins were toasted and buttered before I branded them with a personalized novel just for him. He smiled just before I found out he doesn't even like English muffins. He was only eating them because I do. *He prefers bagels.*

That's important information to know, especially about the man I intend to marry and have a brood of children with. Okay, maybe not a brood, but a couple of little poets running around would be nice.

The line shifts forward several feet, flowing between stanchions before we enter the store. Did I have to stand in line to have my Poet sign my book? No, but it's fun to be a part of the excitement.

The woman in front of me is flipping through her copy when I lean over her shoulder, eyeing the dedication she's reading. "I read an early copy," I whisper as his biggest hype-woman. "It's as good as you've heard. He's an incredible storyteller."

Angling to include me in her circle of one, her smile is so welcoming that I just want to hug her. But my fear of being considered obnoxious keeps me firmly in place. Some people just aren't huggers. Those people don't include me, but I can respect boundaries. Closing the book, she tucks it behind her arms, leans in, and whispers, "He's my son."

"Keats?" I sound like a dummy, but I add, "Keats Matthews?" She's younger than I would have imagined, but so little has been shared, mainly highlights from the past few months of them having dinner here and there. The line moves forward toward the door, taking us with it.

My instincts tell me she really is his mom by the pride I find reflected in her eyes. "I'm Sosie—"

"Keats's fiancée." Marvel highlights the golden centers around the pupils, which is a direct match to Keats's coloring. She doesn't seem shy about how her gaze bounces so unabashedly from my face to my hair to the book I'm cuddling in my arms. "He's told me about you. I should have recognized you from the photos, but I must admit you're even more beautiful in person. You make a beautiful couple."

My heart feels tight from her sweet compliment. But it's the other part she mentions that most interests me. "He's shown you photos of me?"

Her laughter is so genuine, with a little bellow from her throat as she taps her chest. "Don't get me wrong. I love seeing all of them, but Keats is enamored and over the moon in love with you. So I've seen lots of pictures of the two of you and the ones he has of you on his phone." Touching my arm, she says, "I've also seen some of the photos you've taken. You have such an artistic eye for capturing the world."

"I think you're my favorite person right after your son." Seems my Romeo is off telling the world about me, as if he could be anymore charming. I wish I knew more about her, though. Keats treats their relationship as new and developing. It's become something he's enjoying, and he looks forward to their get-togethers. "He's going to be so happy you're here."

The doors are open before us, and when we're ushered to the first employee, our books are marked as paid as we're shifted inside the store. I can't see him until I stand on my tiptoes, and then just barely because someone decided to wear a giant sun hat indoors. Patience may be a virtue, but it's not one of mine.

With the line flowing, I spy Professor Johns already seated toward the front with his copy of the book on his lap. He waves, making me roll my eyes at myself. Here I thought I was more covert. Apparently, I'm not at all.

I wanted to sneak up on Keats. I was evasive today and have tried to be the perfect ninja for this surprise. But as soon as I pass a bookcase taming the line, the intensity of his eyes reaches mine. And then every other part of my body is enticed by his attention as if he verbally commanded it.

All while standing with his mother. So naughty it almost makes me feel guilty. *Almost.*

And then his eyes land on the woman next to me. The swift close of his lids isn't lost. Neither is the smile that follows. When we're finally standing in front of his table, I let his mom go first. I'm excited to see him, but I get him to myself later.

Their sweet interaction has me missing my own mom. The last time I saw her felt like an olive branch, the Paddington story something that bound us together. She even remembered who Winifred was after reading the note. I was given a glimpse into who she might be underneath the Stansbury title and the mother I always wanted. Neither has contacted the other. Did I let the circumstances make me think there was an opportunity? I don't know, and it's easier to get caught up in the life I'm living and the wedding we're planning.

One of the pieces that ties us together is something I can't wait to get rid of. Sosie Matthews has a much better ring to it.

I'm brought back to Keats's big moment by a kiss to the head, and him murmuring that I didn't have to wait in line to see him. As much as a part of me feels empty without my mom, I'm glad he has his again, so he doesn't have to live with that void any longer. I reply, "I wouldn't have met your mother if I hadn't."

It's two worlds colliding when he looks between us, and the grin displayed on his face only confirms my theory. He deserves to feel whole. So do I, but hopefully that will come in time. "I'm glad you've met," he says. "The three of us should have dinner next time."

Giving my wrist a gentle squeeze, his mom says, "That's a great idea."

I won't argue with having more family. If he's happy, I am. "I'd like that, Ms. Matthews."

"Call me Lori."

Life is busy. Too busy, but the final wedding to-dos on my list are being checked off with the help of Marcy. Keats finished his list last week. *It wasn't a competition . . .*

Being in a headspace I wanted to protect, I didn't ask my mom to come dress shopping. I kept that for Marcy and me. But I was missing her leading up to the final fitting. I just didn't know how to break the ice since months have passed since we saw each other. A text out of the blue seemed impersonal, and an email would be even more so. A call felt too in her face like I was putting her on the spot and guilting her into it. *Ugh.*

This should be fun, and the added pressure would ruin it. Keats is right. I'll know when it feels right. If I've learned anything, timing is everything.

So I asked Lori to join us. She's been a dream to spend time with, although not at all helpful with choosing which dress to wear for the ceremony and which for the small reception we're hosting at one of our favorite places. She loves them all. I swear I could say I'm wearing my Doc Martens, and she'd tell me to go for it. She loves anything I toss out there. I even tested her by throwing a curveball and saying I could dye one of the dresses dark purple. Without missing a beat and failing the test entirely, she suggested purple stripes in my hair to match. I couldn't even be mad at her. We've bonded like we're related. *And soon we will be.*

But Marcy's been my saving grace, my calm through the storm of this wedding chaos who pulls me back from monster bride behavior when Keats couldn't be there for me. Like now, helping me with the dresses. Our friendship has only grown, and although she once asked if I knew any guys for her, there's none I would set her up with. She deserves someone special and her very own poet.

With my dresses bagged and draped over my arms, I walk out of the bridal salon on cloud nine. "The combat boots would be a fun toss back, but I was thinking shoes that are pretty, sparkly, even sex—"

My mom looks as shocked as I am. Both of us stopped on a dime and stood frozen to the spot. The encounter brings a wave of guilt and shame as I stand in front of the woman who should have been here with me.

She spots Marcy and Lori and then tracks to the diamond sparkling on my finger before I can hide it. But I can't hide the dresses hanging neatly in the black bags that clash against the white dress I chose to wear for the occasion despite it being after Labor Day. When words evade me, she says, "Sosie, it's good to see you again."

I'm too quiet, making myself uncomfortable. I straighten my spine and steady my voice. This shouldn't be that difficult. We're not starting from scratch. The conversation at the hospital was nice, but do we start over like it never happened? "Hi. It's good to see you, too. I've been thinking about you."

Her expression eases into a smile as if that was something she needed to hear. "I've thought about you so much, sweetie." It's been so long since I've heard that nickname. I don't know if it's wise, but hope fills my chest. "How are you doing?"

"I'm good," I reply, tightening my arms under the dresses. "You?"

"You know me." I do know her, but I'm not sure what she means. She's good at obscuring her real feelings behind a smile. "You look happy, Sosie."

I close some of the space when a guy walks between us. "I am happy, Mom."

"I'm glad to hear that." Glancing at the bags, she adds, "Things are moving quickly."

"We're making up for the years we lost by not wasting anymore time."

She nods, but her expression doesn't match the sentiment that she understands. The response has me wondering whether she really was in on it, as my father claimed that day when he forced me to walk away from Keats. Maybe he lied. It's not a far-fetched idea. "Young love is always rushing like there's some kind of guarantee if it gets there faster."

"It's not a big wedding," I blurt as if she's made an accusation and I need an alibi.

"I'm sure it will be beautiful, just like you."

Healing takes time, but how long does a grudge take to get over? I've punished her enough, and now I'm thinking it was all in vain. *What would Keats do?* I glance over my shoulder at Lori, who's giving us space as if she knows who this is to me. Lori's only here because he gave her a second chance. *Can I forgive my mom to give us the same?*

A black car pulls up nearby, stealing the time I thought we had. We both look at it, knowing who it is, and then at each other, as if a timer has been started. I say, "You should come to the wedding, Mom."

Water glistens in her eyes. "Really?"

"Yes." I glance once more at the vehicle waiting at the curb. "He's not welcome and can't know anything about it. We want to celebrate our love and union, not battle it out with him."

She's a pro at controlling her expression. I suspect years of practice have honed her skills. But studied carefully, one might catch a streak of rebellion in the lifted corner on the right side. Maybe that's where I got it. "I'm incredibly good at keeping secrets." I'm starting to believe her.

I look back at my friends waiting for me, then turn back to Mom. "I'll text you the details."

As if cued, the window rolls down at a snail's pace. I already know the anticipation is easily bigger than what's behind it. My father's eyes go back and forth between my mom and me several times before he asks her, "You ready, dear?" No further acknowledgment of me standing here, still existing, thriving, in spite of his best efforts to destroy my independence.

But I feel nothing for him, so I smile in return because he can no longer hurt me.

She touches the back of her French twist, checking for loose strands. One last glance at her husband leads her to say, "Maybe one day I'll be brave like you."

There's no hugging her with him around, though the urge is strong. It will only cause her more strife, and I think she's had enough in her life. "You're already brave enough, Mom. You've just forgotten."

Giving my arm a little squeeze, she whispers, "It was great to see you." She starts for the car, but turns back to say, "I love you."

I want to say the words, but our time has run out when my father steps out. Giving me one last look of indifference as if I'm a stranger on the street, he slips into the car after my mom and slams the door shut.

Not lingering, I return to Marcy and Lori, where they hook an arm on either side of me. Carrying on like we just left the store, Lori says, "I still think the purple would be unexpected."

"Hear me out," Marcy interjects, lifting her eyebrows in mock surprise. "Purple is a lot, but adding something blue fits the occasion."

I cackle, needing levity. Though, admittedly, seeing my mom filled a little of that void today. When the three of us start in the opposite direction from where the car was headed, I ask, "What do you think about classic chocolate for the wedding cake?"

"Keats loves chocolate."

Grinning, I reply, "I know."

CHAPTER 35

SOSIE

I got the high heels—sparkling like diamonds.

The dress that hits just above the knees reminds me of classic photos from the fifties and sixties in New York City. I topped it off with a simple tennis necklace I stole from the tree just for the night. It will be returned to its proper place by morning.

And I got the husband, one who loves me more than anything. He even puts up with my early morning photo shenanigans. With our arms around each other and our lips pressed together, our tongues tempt the other into a slow dance.

A cleared throat disturbs the path we were headed down, which would have led us to bed instead of the reception. My eyes flutter open to find my dream come true already smiling at me. "We're married."

The man was enough, but that phrase alone sends my heart soaring. "We are."

Another clearing of the throat pulls us from our

daydream to the judge standing before us. "You don't have to stop, but you need to move it outside. I have another ceremony to perform."

Taking my hand, Keats leads me through the small group of friends and family who were here to witness the legal declaration of our love. Now, the only two who can tear us apart just willingly signed their names to a legally binding certificate.

The guests follow us into the large lobby, where voices echo if they don't keep it down. We could have gotten married anywhere, but a small ceremony at the courthouse was all we wanted. In the excitement, we're surrounded by our loved ones, but I sneak through to hug my mom first. The embrace is comforting, and the hold tight enough for us to silently say what we haven't been able to.

I'm sorry.

I forgive you.

I want you in my life.

I'm not sure we have to, judging by the steps we've made. She's here with a clean slate as far as I'm concerned.

"Congratulations. What a beautiful thing to witness." Her hand is over her heart while tears tease her lower lids. "I brought you these." She reaches down to grab a large tote that sat at her feet. "One's a wedding gift. The others are things I thought you should have, like your Paddington bear."

"That's so thoughtful. I'd love to have that." I glance as she hands the bag to me and do a double take. "Is that my photography portfolio?"

"You always took beautiful photos. I thought you might like to have them back." Her hands grip around mine holding the tote. "We can arrange for you to come get anything else you'd like. I know . . ." She looks down and takes a breath. "You left in such a hurry, so if there's anything you want."

"I'll let you know." Just before I hug her, Marcy swings by to sweep the bag from my hands. I say what I wish I would have said the other day, "I love you, Mom."

Keats captures my hand, and I slide against him, tucked under his arm. "This is my husband." I glance up at Keats. "This is my mom."

"Kelly," she says, holding out her hand. I don't think I've ever heard her referred to by only her first name. Kelly and Stansbury are always used together, or Mrs. Stansbury for those less acquainted. Stansbury is a name to drop for entrance into society. It has a standing invitation to every party of note and charity event. It's a mover and shaker in Manhattan and is used to get what they want.

Shaking her hand, Keats says, "It's nice to meet you, Kelly."

"Congratulations." Her eyes pivot to mine before returning to his. "My daughter is an incredible person. The best I know." Her words might be curated, but the true meaning is heard.

Keats holds me a little tighter. "Me too."

I could be embarrassed, but having her here and seeing them interact brings a fullness to my chest like the void is gone altogether.

Marcy's voice catches our attention. "We need to start toward the doors. There's a car waiting for the newlyweds after they take photos, and one for everyone else to take us to the reception." Pointing toward the exit, she says, "Let's move it on out." I can't help but laugh. You'd think there was a massive crowd and not just six of us in total.

Lori comes around to hug us, and I take a quick moment to hug Michael and Marcy before we leave. The four of them make their way down the steps, but we stay, the photographer already taking photos as the pigeons fly up in annoyance. That will make for a great photo. I'm sure the one of me screaming when a bird gets too close will as well.

Keats and I kiss, and when he pulls me up from a dip, he caresses my cheek and says, "I know what our book should be called."

"What's that?"

"Spark and Poet, a love story."

Wrapping my arms around his neck, I lift onto the toe of my shoes, which still doesn't make me tall enough to reach him, and sigh in swoony bliss. "Sounds like a blockbuster, but stories are for the world to enjoy. Our story is only for us."

He kisses me with the same tenderness as the caress, then whispers against my lips. "I couldn't agree more. You ready to go?"

"Are you sick of taking photos?"

"You know me so well." I do, like we're two beings sharing the same soul. We were just meant for each other.

When my heels touch down again, I catch my mom hugging Lori. She turns, and when our eyes meet, she waves and blows a kiss. I wave, knowing the risk she took to be here for me on my special day.

Putting on a smile and letting it grow into a full bloom for him, I reply, "I'm ready now."

I'll give credit where it's due. Lori was right. The purple dress is perfect for the reception. I went back at the last minute and bought it, and I have no regrets. Though I didn't have time to add purple to my hair. It's perfect for getting ramen at our favorite restaurant. We had a reservation, but we didn't close it to Joy's regular customers. We figure the more, the merrier. But we did pay for everyone's meals. It was fun to create so much joy from something so little.

But sitting at the platformed center table for two just like on our first date is a highlight. Our small party of guests sat at the table next to us, and Joy assigned someone else to work for her so she could join us. She even decorated our tables with a tablecloth and cloth napkins. Keats and I don't care about finery, but this was the perfect touch to make our evening extra special.

I capture moments of magic on my camera, taking photos of Joy laughing and the joy from others engaged in conversation. We cut the chocolate cake and feed each other the first bite before sealing it with a kiss. We're surrounded by love and by the people who support us, root for us, and make our lives better by knowing them. We save the first dance for later, but I'm swept into his arms before we leave for our own private reception at the small apartment.

"Out of billions of souls in this universe, how lucky are we to have found our other half?" He kisses my cheek and then my neck, eliciting goose bumps up and down my arms.

Cupping the back of his neck, I wait to catch his eyes. When they're locked together, I smile. "The luckiest of them all." Our lips come together in a collision of soft and sweet and the need for something stronger. We resist, both of us losing our breath when we pull our mouths apart. "Let's get out of here, Poet."

I flip off my shoes as soon as I'm carried over the threshold. As much as I love that he wanted to do that, I wanted these toe pinchers off more. I should have chosen comfort and worn my combat boots.

I'm tugging at the zipper on the back of my dress, thinking we both had the same thing in mind—consummating this marriage. But I still my hand when I see Keats dimming the lights and then scrolling on his phone to start a playlist. It's sweet that he wants to set the mood, but it could be noon on Broadway, and I'd want him just the same.

Opening the fridge, he pulls out a bottle of champagne. He can afford anything, but I'm glad he didn't buy the Bollinger Special Cuvee. My dad is the last thing I want to be reminded of with him. *Ugh.* I scrub my brain and admire how sexy my husband is instead.

We pop the champagne, and he fills our glasses. Our gazes never lose sight of each other as we take a sip and fall into a kiss that feels like I've waited my whole life for. Our hands don't grapple, and there's no frenzy to remove clothes anymore. Just us, the two of us, swaying to the music playing in the background. And as we dance, he says, "I used to think that John Keats had it right about the unheard melodies being sweeter." The man never misses a chance to make me fall in love all over again.

"The line we quoted when we met?"

He brushes the pad of his thumb over my bottom lip, then kisses me again. "He was wrong. We lived it, and life is definitely sweeter when we hear the music. I'd rather have you in my arms than live the rest of my life imagining what could have been."

I couldn't have said it better, so I leave that to the expert, and say, "You know who else got it wrong?"

"Who?"

"Professor Johns." We call him Michael these days, but the formal name feels right if we're traveling back to that time and place.

"How so?"

"You were never lacking authenticity. You've always been exactly who you are, and that's the man I fell in love with."

He sways me in his arms, then sends me out to twirl before pulling me back to where I want to be most. With him. "I was thinking about quitting my job and becoming a full-time author."

"I think you should. You've made plenty of money—"

"We've made plenty of money. It's all yours too, you know?" I'm dipped, and my neck is nipped, making me giggle. "More money than we have time to sin with."

When we swing back up, I take his hand and lead him into the bedroom. "Oh, we have plenty of time for that."

"Sounds like a good plan if I've ever heard one." He cups my face and smiles just looking at me. "I can't believe I get to spend the rest of my life with you, Spark."

"You say that like you had a choice." I smirk, thinking about how we were star-crossed lovers, but not anymore. "We were never going to beat fate. The moment you went on break, we were destined for each other, Poet."

EPILOGUE

KEATS

Sosie's gotten back into her photography, and the gallery takes up most of her time these days. She says she loves finding undiscovered talent, but she's overlooking herself. "Have you shown this portfolio to anyone at the gallery?" I flip the page, mesmerized by how she sees things in such a unique way and can capture them.

She comes into the living room and sets down two shoeboxes, which make my heart palpitate. "I haven't been brave enough."

"You should." My throat goes dry. "Why do you have those?"

Sitting on the floor in front of the coffee table, she crosses her legs like she intends to be there a while. "I've always wondered what was in them."

"Damn, I'm starving. Do you want to go tonight?"

"We already ordered food." Checking her watch, she says, "It should be here any minute." But then her eyes latch onto mine and narrow. "Are you trying to distract me?" She angles toward me, resting her arm on the cushion next to me. "If you don't want me to open the boxes, I won't."

"I don't want you to open the boxes. I'm sorry."

"You don't have to be sorry." She slips onto the couch next to me, cuddling up to my side. I can see her gaze still fixed on the boxes, her curiosity probably piqued more than it was before.

I'd love to find a way to wipe the curiosity from her face, but I know that's unfair. Clearing my throat, I choke out the words I don't really want to say. I do it for her. "We can open the boxes."

Perking up, she turns to me. "Are you sure?"

"No." I chuckle humorlessly. Running my fingers through my hair, I add, "It's stuff from my childhood."

"Would you rather I put the boxes up? I don't want you to be upset."

I sit forward, pulling one of the battered boxes onto my lap. Running my finger along the disintegrating edge of the lid, I warm to the idea of facing that time in my life again. "They were my mom's boxes. She was tossing them out, so I took them and shoved stuff I wanted to keep into them when I was little."

Sosie rubs my arm and kisses my shoulder. "Do you want privacy?"

I rest my hand on her leg and take a deep breath. "No. I want you here with me." I lift the lid and grin when I see the Pokémon cards I used to collect. They have no value, most just being trainer cards, but I liked to pretend I got a coveted one. I shift them to the side to pull out an old photo of my mom.

"Is that Lori?"

"Yeah, she had me right after high school. I don't think she even attended her graduation because of me."

Sosie laughs. "You didn't have a say in that decision." She takes the photo. "She's so pretty."

I dig out another with a bent corner. I remember this one too well. "This is one of the few photos I have of my dad." Cigarette hanging from the side of his mouth, a smirk that drove the ladies wild, from what I heard, and a great head of hair.

"I think you have Lori's eyes, but I recognize that expression."

"Hmm." I'm not sure what to think. I thought I'd feel more. Or something at all. "It's like looking at someone you pass on the street who looks familiar, but you don't know how you would know them. And then one day, you realize it's just because you've passed them before." I look at her, breathing heavily, needing to release it. "I don't even know if he's alive and . . ." I shake my head. "I don't need to know."

She runs the back of her fingers along my neck and says, "I stopped calling my father "Dad" soon after he broke us up." I swing my arm around her shoulders to hold her. "It didn't feel like he had the right to that title anymore, but I realize he never did. I like the progress my mom and I are making, but I don't know if I will ever make up with my father."

"Time heals old wounds."

She nods and kisses my cheek. "That goes for you, too."

We finish going through the boxes. There's a small ribbon from winning a race during field day, and a bouncy ball that I spent more than five dollars on a quarter machine to win. Most of the stuff is junk with a few photos mixed in. "I'm glad you brought these out. I'd built them up in my head, and I didn't need to."

She's holding a stack of photos of me as a kid and the ones of my mom that she particularly liked. "I'm going to put these in an album. One day, your kids will want to see them."

"My kids?" I scoff. She doesn't. Sosie's just staring at me like I'm acting ridiculous. "What?"

"We never did exchange wedding presents."

Out of left field. "We've been busy the past week. But I got you something good."

That brings a smile to her face. "What is it?"

I grab my phone and pull up the email I meant to print out. Handing it to her, I wait to watch her reaction.

Her eyes widen, and she shoots me a look. "You bought the building?"

"Rent is a waste. You love the apartment, and it works perfectly as your photography space."

"And a love nest for us."

Chuckling, I say, "And love nest."

"You shouldn't have but it's an amazing gift. Thank you." Moving the box, she slips onto my lap to replace it and straddles me. "What am I going to do with you?"

"You're doing it." She gets me hard so easily. She's hot, has a great ass, and fantastic tits. What's not to love and enjoy about that?

"Do you want your present now or later?"

Sliding my hands up the side of her shirt, I tease, "Oh baby, give it to me."

She laughs and then pulls something from her back pocket. "You got that right."

"Got what right?"

Holding a stick in front of my face, she says, "Oh baby is right."

Want more?

I'm so excited to offer a FREE Bonus Chapter. More Sosie and Keats? *Yes please.* Ever wondered what happened with that trust fund that was casually mentioned? Find out. What about that Paddington bear? All the details come out. Turn the page to read the bonus chapter.

BONUS CHAPTER

SOSIE

"Ugh." I almost have the bear, but he's frustratingly just out of reach. Who put Paddington on the high shelf anyway? That would be me when I was allowed to climb ladders. Since I'm not seven months pregnant, the challenges of being short strike again. "Keats?" I walk out of the closet in the baby's room and down the hall to the top of the stairs, and call again, "Keats?"

The framed photos of us, our honeymoon in the Hawaii, a photo of the apartment building where he lived when we met, and the front of the house where I grew up all hang together with the one of our home together. A lot has changed in our lives and seeing it hung on the wall in various stages of our lives reminds me of the life we're creating together.

The bad is behind us, no cages to fly in and out of, no dark clouds controlling my days and nights. Only good. Only Keats loving me to the fullest. I didn't believe love existed like this. I mean, I loved him. He was not just the one who got away, for a short time, but the love of my life. But this love, the one we share now, the one that bonds us together more than a piece of paper or legalities ever could runs deeper than the ocean and vaster than the universe. It's too big most days to hold inside so I shower him with all I have that I can't contain inside.

"Yeah?" he asks, peering from around the corner at the base of the stairs.

"Can you help me reach something?"

He's already walking up, that smile that still only reveals itself to me, the one that could get me into bed without a word said or ready to offer me ice cream. It always comes with something good attached. Stopping two steps lower, he leans forward, and says, "Kiss me."

As if that would ever be considered a burden. Never.

I wrap my arms around his neck and kiss him and then deepen it because I can never get enough of this man. Our lips part, and our tongues touch, tempting the other into seduction. Reaching around me, he lifts me off the floor. Realizing it's not quite the same as it typically is since my body is ever changing, I giggle. He sets me down and opens his eyes. "I can carry you."

"I know you can." I rub his bicep, partly for me, some for him as if he needs the reassurance because I didn't mean to insinuate the man couldn't lift me. Tilting my head, I caress his cheek. "It's not why I called you up here."

"Oh?"

Another bubble of laughter escapes my throat. How did I get so lucky? I was never the white picket fence kind of girl. I may have been raised in Manhattan society, but this city, the vibe, and all that it holds, tunnels through my veins like a subway. But Keats Matthews is my soul. Life with him is better than I could have dreamed. Marriage. A baby on the way. Moving from his high-rise in Tribeca to a Brownstone in Brooklyn. We crossed the universe to create our own little world just for me and him. I rub my bulging belly, and this little guy who will be joining us soon. I say, "'m flattered you came so quickly just from me saying your name."

"Well, *came* is subjective," he says, rubbing his hands together. "How can I help you?"

I start down the hall back into the baby's room with him following closely. "Can you reach my Paddington bear on the top shelf for me? I want to set it on the shelf near the crib."

He doesn't even have to lift to get the stuffed bear down. He squeezes its belly. "Why is it so hard?"

"It's old." I shrug.

Flipping it over, he lifts the little coat in the back. "You know there's a zipper?"

I take the bear from him and return to the room next to the crib, looking it over. "It's just for the stuffing, right?"

"Aren't most stuffed animals sewn closed?" Keats takes Winifred from dresser and points to her butt. "See?"

I grin. Lifting the coat on my bear, I pull down the zipper. "You act like I'm going to find hidden treas—What is this?" I pull out a spikey piece of metal. "A key? What would this go to?" I hand it to him.

He analyzes it for a few seconds. "Two. Four. One. Two forty-one is on one side." His eyes meet mine, and he says, "My guess is it goes to a safe deposit box."

"I don't have a box."

Holding up the key, the light catches the surface of the shiny silver metal. "Looks like do now."

I'd been planning a nap after organizing the last of the

items I wanted to display in the baby's room, but finding this key sent a thrill of excitement zipping up my spine. It was a mystery waiting to be unraveled and I knew a nap wasn't going to happen until I solved it.

Standing at the entrance of the bank, I've used my entire life because my parents did, keeping their money here as well, I wait for the guard to return. I shift, and then whisper to Keats, "Why am I nervous?"

His grin is soft as his eyes return from scanning the inside of the bank to mine. He rubs my lower back and then the warmth of his hand rests on my shoulder. "No need to be nervous. Maybe it's just a box you had when you were young, and you forgot about it."

"I didn't have a box. I had a safe built into my closet." Just hearing me say that brings up so many weird feelings for me. The amount of privilege, the access to wealth was natural to me. Now, I see how I took most of it for granted, but Keats never judges even when he has a right to. But there was a tradeoff. Nothing comes for free, and I paid a high price for everything I had. I gave up hell and everything that came with it for a chance at being happy and landed in heaven with my soul mate.

Sometimes I wish I would have done it the first time but testing my father's reach and power isn't something I was willing to risk Keats' future on. As he says, our timing worked out exactly how it was supposed to. So wasting another minute on the past isn't something I typically do, but this box has me curious.

He slips his hand in mine just as the guard returns. "Follow me." Leading us down a short corridor, he says, "The manager will help you from here."

"Thank you," I say, dragging my free hand down the side of my dress.

We enter the private room to find a small metal box on the table. "Here's your key," the manager says, handing it back to me. "When you're done, the box goes there. Lock it, and I'll lock the door behind you."

My heart is beating too hard, my nerves bunching in my throat. I clear it but I'm not ready to speak so I nod.

When we're alone, Keats and I sit the same side of the table. I drag my palms over the skirt of my dress once more and then lift the hinged lid back. I glance to Keats. "I don't know what I was expecting, but it was a letter." I take the cream-colored envelop out of the box and flip it over to see my mother's monogram embossed on it.

Keats comfort extends beyond how he rubs my back as if he knows I need his touch. His other hand rests on my leg, and he asks, "Are you okay?"

"I'm okay. I just . . ." I take a breath, not sure why tears are welling in my eyes. "It's a lot."

"Your relationship with her has grown in positive ways."

"It has. I enjoy my time with her. It's just hitting me that she gave this bear to me at our wedding. She mentioned it at the hospital and that was when we weren't speaking at all. I don't think this is a new box or letter. That's what makes me nervous. What if it says something hateful?" I look into his eyes hoping to find the assurance I need.

"You were already on a path of healing. She wouldn't have given it to you at the wedding and ruin everything."

I lick my lips, scrapping my teeth over the lower one. "You're right. I'm not going to overthink this. I'm just opening it." I rip open the envelope and pull out a letter. Unfolding it, I read:

Dear Sosie,

Your light has always shined brighter than this world could handle. But I finally realized it wasn't the world dimming your light. It was us. I stood by feeling helpless until I realized I'd enabled him to turn into the person he became. Maybe I caused it.

A tear slides down my cheek and lands on the wooden table. I wipe it away before taking a breath and glancing to my husband, who so patiently waits for my emotions to run the gamut. "She blames herself for the person my father became." It's not a question so I'm expecting some great revelation of an answer. That part just hit me differently. "She's not responsible for him."

"I have a feeling she had no choice. Sometimes we end up locked in a life of our own choosing. Maybe she was scared to leave or maybe she stayed to protect you. You could ask her." *I could ask her.* He says, "Life is complicated. Sometimes we believe we're doing what's right only to find out in hindsight that we hurt the ones we were trying to protect."

"I hate that for me." Leaning over, his holds me to him as I rest my head on his arm. Like everything else with my parents, my feelings are complicated. But if I can step back and give grace, I realize that things weren't as black and white as I once thought. There's a lot of gray between us. "But I got out of that situation. She didn't. Who knows what she's had to endure." I start reading again:

I'd like to tell you how your father was once a different person, but does it matter now? We can talk about it if it helps you. Otherwise, I'm so glad to be in your life. I love you. I always loved you, Josie. I'm sorry that I wasn't a good mother. I'm sorry for not being the one you needed. I regret every day I chose silence to keep the anger at bay instead of fighting for you.

The second tear falls, this time splattering across the letter and causing the ink to bleed. I rush to read the rest before the words disappear.

Nothing can make up for what you've been through but to see you with a husband who utterly adores you, a sweet baby on the way, and to know you fought for your happiness has hope blooming inside of myself. You're so brave, dear daughter.

I have something that I've been working on since you were little, a secret I've never told anyone. There's an account fully in your name. The number is on a slip of paper in the envelope. It was a little here and chunk from there.

Some for your account and some for mine. I predict big changes ahead in my life as well. It can't make up for anything, but I hope it helps in creating the life you love.

Love,
Your Mom

My heart clenches. "She's given me money."

"Why would she do that?"

I shake my head. I could jump to conclusions that it's to make up for not protecting me like she should have. But I think it's deeper than that. "I think she was helping me escape."

He releases a long breath, his hand rubbing my thigh. "You did it before she could give it to you."

Sitting back, the tears dry under the realization that she was looking out for me the best she could. "It makes me feel that I wasn't so alone after all." I sigh, the breath heavy as it leaves my chest. "I wish I would have known then."

I stand, closing the box, taking the letter and tucking it back into the envelope before pulling out the piece of paper with the bank account number on it. "As much as I love a mystery, I think my mom loves it more. She's been stashing cash for me."

"Unexpected." He chuckles as we walk to the door. "So what are you thinking? Twenty K? Fifty?"

Now he has me laughing. "Hrm. I'm thinking . . ." We walk to an available teller. I ask, "Will you please print a balance for me?"

She starts typing while turn to Keats and hook my finger around his belt loop to tug him closer. "What do I win if I get closer?"

Bending down, he whispers in my ear, "I'll make sure you see stars later when I eat your sweet—"

"Here you go," the teller says, handing me a printed balance receipt. for dessert."

My face is on fire from blushing so much. "Thank you." I rush take his hand and rush for the exit. I need fresh air outside, hoping it cools me off.

"Your naughty."

Dragging the tips of two fingers along my jaw, he says, "You love it."

"You're not wrong." With the paper crumpled in my hand, I say, "I'm thinking a million."

"A million? You said this is cash she was stashing?"

I shrug. "It was." As disbelief morphs his eyes to understanding, he chuckles again. "She handled the house finances while my father ran his business. That gave her access to a lot of money flowing through there. So I'm sticking with a million." I flatten the sheet to read the balance, and smile. This wasn't a short-term thing for her. The only way to skim this much money and to create an account of her own, she had to be doing it most of my life.

"What is it?" he asks.

I'm not sure he's ready though. He may not judge me for my family's extraordinary wealth, but this isn't theirs. This is now ours. I hand him the paper and then take his free hand between both of mine. And wait because I know a reaction is coming.

His eyes dart to mine and then bounce right back to the slip of paper. The pull of his brows is followed by bewilderment as he stares into the distance.

"Are you okay, Poet?"

It's not immediate but when his gaze finally returns to mine, he swallows hard enough for me to hear. "I've made millions in finance over the years, enough for us to retire and never work again." Holding up the paper, he says, "This is what she skimmed without your father noticing?" He rolls his eyes along with his head on his neck, making me smirk. "Fuck me." When he chuckles without an ounce of humor, his smirk matches mine. "So the Stansbury women are the craftier ones by far. Eight million, Spark?"

"Seems so." My grin blooms into a full-grown smile. "We have enough money, as you said, I think I'll put this in a trust fund for our kids." We start walking down the street, holding hands. We reach the corner, and I stop. Looking up at my gorgeous husband, I add, "Two things. One, since I won, I look forward to some action when we get home."

"My pleasure." He leans to kiss me. "And two?"

"Did I ever tell you about the trust fund I get when I hit thirty?"

Keats tries so hard for indifference, but shock wins out widening his eyes and parting those lips that I want to kiss so badly again. "I think you failed to mention it."

The crosswalk starts beeping but we remain standing at the corner. "Well, if you thought eight million was a lot, you haven't seen anything yet." I lift on my toes to kiss him and then turn to cross the street. But my husband is an immovable boulder. My body is jerked back when he doesn't walk with me. I turn back and laugh. "It's going to be okay."

"Sounds like more than okay."

"Yeah, we're going to be more than okay. Together." We start walking again. "What do you think about the name Austen with an e?"

I feel the gentle squeeze of his hand wrapped around mine. "As in Jane Austen?"

"You're named after John Keats. You never told me why by the way."

"It's a conversation for my mother. I like Austen."

"Me too." My hunger kicks in the moment I spy a bagel shop across the street. I start pulling him in that direction. "If I loved you less . . ." I wait to hear my poet recite sweet lines back to me. I haven't stumped him yet, but I still try.

"I might be able to talk about it more," he replies with ease as if it wasn't recall at all but slid straight from his heart off his tongue.

"Emma is one of my favorite novels. Bagel?"

I'm captured in his embrace and kissed like we're alone at home, the electricity between us reaching my toes. When I'm breathless and just a noodle of swooniness in his arms, he leans back, and says, "Yes, on the bagel and on the name. Austen Matthews has a great ring to it."

"It sure does."

The End.

YOU MIGHT ALSO ENJOY

Recommendations - These are books you'll enjoy reading after *Then There Was You.* These books will have you fall hard and love harder in these emotional romances.

READ IN KINDLE UNLIMITED AND LISTEN IN AUDIO

Best I Ever Had - This second chance epic and emotional, second chance, standalone romance that a has a surprise pregnancy, family drama, and readers raving "breathtaking and brilliant!" Free in Kindle Unlimited.

READ IN KINDLE UNLIMITED AND LISTEN IN AUDIO

Swear on My Life - We were lightning in a bottle, and everything felt possible when we were together. Life was perfect. *Or so I thought*... Years later, I'm no more prepared for him than I was the first time. He swears on his life that we are meant to be forever, but I know I can't survive this man twice.Free in Kindle Unlimited.

READ IN KINDLE UNLIMITED AND LISTEN IN AUDIO

We Were Once - We were never supposed to fall in love. ***We did it anyway.*** Together, we had it all. Desperately. Madly. In love. ***Until we didn't.*** One tragic night changed everything. Free in Kindle Unlimited.

ACKNOWLEDGMENTS

Thank you so much to this incredible team:

Kenna Rey, Content Editor
Jenny Sims, Copy Editing, Editing4Indies
Kristen Johnson, Proofreader
Andrea Johnston, Beta Reading
Cover Design: RBA Designs
Cover Photographer: Maxim Bobrov
Audio Producer: Erin Spencer, One Night Stand Studios.
Narrators: Tor Thom & Erin Mallon
Thank you for taking this journey with me. It's never easy pouring my heart into the words and pages but I'm so grateful to have the opportunity.

My husband, sons, and doggo Ollie, are my entire world. I love you more than the universe! Thank you for your endless support and love. Love you always. XOXOX

ABOUT THE AUTHOR

Suzie loves a great view of the ocean, spicy margaritas, and spending her free time with her family and sweet dog, Ollie.

New York Times and *USA Today* Bestselling Author, S.L. Scott, writes character driven, heart-racing, and swoony romances that will leave you glued to the page. With stories ranging from witty beach reads to heart wrenching and heart healing, her stories are highly regarded as emotional, relatable, and captivating.

Her books are more than escapes for the voracious readers of today. They are journeys of the heart that always come with a happily ever after reward at the end.

Find her at: www.slscottauthor.com

www.ingramcontent.com/pod-product-compliance
Lightning Source LLC
La Vergne TN
LVHW041103080826
845145LV00007B/1683

* 9 7 8 1 9 6 2 6 2 6 5 7 6 *